DEVILS
DANCE
A RATIONAL MAN

BOOK THREE

ERIK HENRY VICK

RATATOSKR PUBLISHING

NEW YORK

RATATOSKR PUBLISHING
769 BROADWAY #1060
MANHATTAN, NY 10003

PUBLISHER'S NOTE: THIS IS A WORK OF FICTION. NAMES, CHARACTERS, PLACES, AND INCIDENTS ARE A PRODUCT OF THE AUTHOR'S IMAGINATION. LOCALES AND PUBLIC NAMES ARE SOMETIMES USED FOR ATMOSPHERIC PURPOSES. ANY RESEMBLANCE TO ACTUAL PEOPLE, LIVING OR DEAD, OR TO BUSINESSES, COMPANIES, EVENTS, INSTITUTIONS, OR LOCALES IS COMPLETELY COINCIDENTAL.

DEVILS DANCE/ ERIK HENRY VICK. -- 1ST ED.
ISBN 978-1-951509-17-0

Table of Contents

For our new friend, Ryan Mahan, who has enriched our lives with his energy, positivity, and inventiveness.

The mother of all that is evil
Her lips are poisonous venom
Wicked temptress knows how to please
The priestess roars, "Get down on your knees"
The rite of the praying mantis
Kiss the bones of the enchantress
Spellbound searching through the night
A howling man surrenders the fight
One look in her lusting eyes
Savage fear in you will rise
Teeth of terror sinking in

—Dave Mustaine

I hope you enjoy *Devils Dance*. If so, please consider joining my Readers Group—details can be found at the end of the last chapter.

Chapter 1
Whispering
Winds

Publisher's Note: If you haven't read *The Bloodletter Chronicles* by Erik Henry Vick, now would be an exceptional time to do so. You can find it here: https://ehv4.us/4tbc.

I

The temple, Southwestern TX
Saturday, 2:43 am CST

The room smelled of the heat and burning frankincense and myrrh and the woman's fear and the hot blood of the goat draining from the long gash he'd slashed in the beast's throat. The air was dry, flinty, and hot against his skin, a lover's caress, even at almost three in the morning, and his nostrils flared to drink it in, to suck it through his nose and down his throat. The raging fire cast flickering black demons on the walls, jigging and jerking, flittering and flying, darting and dancing, and he could almost hear their cackling, braying laughter.

Outside the glassless window of the sanctuary, heat lightning lit up the far reaches of the desert, stabbing at his eyes, and the silence that followed spoke to him in ways no mere person ever could. The man in the coarse black robe with its shiny white fascia tilted his head back and smiled, his gaze following the serpentine coil of grayish-black smoke until it disappeared in the greater darkness above the roofless building. He drew in a deep breath, sucking scalding air through his nose and down his throat, smiling at the burn of it much the same way as he smiled when drinking a fine single malt.

He closed his eyes and willed himself to focus on the task at hand, on the demands of his position as First of the Brethren. With glacial slowness, he lifted his arms in a wide arc from his sides, a bloody Bowie knife in his coal-black right fist, the goat's heart in his left, luxuriating in the warm blood that ran down his arms in rivulets.

Tied to the altar before him, the young woman started to babble—to beg, to plead, to pray, to demand—but he paid her no mind. All of it summed to exactly nothing. She'd been selected, and that was the simple end of it.

The simple end of her, one way or another.

A soft grin, completely at odds with his costume, his knife, the blood, and the organ in his hand, stretched across his lips, and the woman whimpered, then fell silent as if the dark lord had reached out and taken her tongue. He nodded once, still smiling in that warm, fatherly way he'd cultivated over the years, and the believers who made up the core of his congregation stilled, ceasing their whispered conversations, their excited burble. An air of expectation built and built and built, and still, he stood, arms outstretched above his head, knife and organ dripping the goat's blood onto the rough concrete floor.

The wind seemed to pay homage to the dark lord, dying to a silent whisper, though the heat lightning continued to dance along the horizon, and the flames continued to leap and dance and cavort like so many devils dancing on the head of a pin. He let the atmosphere take care of itself, building and building the way pressure in his lungs had built in the vague, childhood memory he had—hands holding him down, under the surface of the clean, clear water, the face of his would-be murderer fuzzy and blurred, the dark brown face that seemed to match his own soot-black skin despite the difference in hue. For a moment, he lived that memory again, feeling the fear course through him, growing stronger and stronger with each passing moment, the demands of his body that he open his mouth and *breathe* despite the water that buried him, the strange, almost-calm curiosity that slowly overcame his fear, edging it out the way dawn closed out the night.

His reminiscence served a purpose—he imagined the young brunette on the altar before him felt something similar—the fear, at least, then the sense of calm that came with knowing her begging, her pleading, her praying, all would come to naught. Behind and around him, the elite members of his flock stood swaying, hands joined, rough-spun black robes hanging, their worn work boots peeking out from beneath the hems, red cotton sashes hanging from their waists. None of them spoke, not now, not at the cusp of it all.

He opened his eyes, his head still tilted back, and his eyes alighted on the bloody Damascus blade, its fine edge showing proud, telltale signs of other forays into other bodies. He drew in another deep breath, then loosed his booming, orator's voice into the depths of the night.

"Brother, hear me!" His voice rolled around them as if amplified, as if cast from the speakers of a giant public address system suitable for a stadium. He spun in place, turning to his right, now facing north. "Mother, hear me!" he shrieked, pouring all his dredged-up fear from the memory—the memory of when she'd tried to drown him—all his rage at the stupid cow, and before the echoes settled, he spun another ninety degrees so that he faced east. "Father, hear me! Father, *see me*!" he boomed, and to his joy, thunder answered him, rolling toward him from the far-away Gulf, buffeting their ears, and he imagined he could feel the awe of the worshippers behind him. He stood for an extra moment, his head thrown back, arms dropping, luxuriating in his father's acknowledgment. But after a few heartbeats, he sobered and spun once more, this time, to the south. "Great One! Hear us! Come! Partake in our ritual, the sacrifice we perform in your honor!"

"No! *No-no-no-no*!" cried the woman.

This time, he couldn't ignore her senseless noise. His eyes snapped down to her face, and he lifted the knife. "Your part in this comes later," he grated, his tone full of menace, full of the promise of things to come. "There are worse things than death, woman, and if you disrupt this ritual, you'll learn that out firsthand."

She whimpered and closed her eyes tight. "Don't hurt me!" she whispered.

"I won't," he said. "I promise I won't…not more than I have to. Not unless you make me." He tossed a grin at his followers, then lifted his gaze to the south once more. "Great One! Drink this blood, eat this flesh!"

"Come and feast!" intoned the group—ten men and a woman—surrounding him.

"Great One! Consume this girl's pain, partake in her suffering!"

"Come and feast!"

The woman's tears rolled down her cheeks in fat drops, splattering the blade-scarred surface of the ironwood altar.

"Great One! We seek you out, Scaled One. We call upon your holy name, O Snake of the Desert! We invoke the ancient rites, the old covenant, Sea Dweller! Walk among us! Lend us your power! Come, Walker on the Wind!"

"Come, Shadow!" cried his chorus.

"Come, Darkest Night!" cried the coal-black man, and his nostrils flared at the scent of alkali and flint, of heat and desolation, of desert, of brimstone, of plague and disease. "Come, Bringer of Chaos!" he screeched.

"Come!"

Eyes too-wide, too intense, the man dropped his gaze to the brunette on the altar. She took one look at his face and squeezed her eyes shut, her lips moving in silent prayer. He lifted his chin, and his eyes grew wider still. He lifted his hands, shaking, flinging dripping blood hither and yon, and screamed at the night sky—a sound of inchoate insanity, of incipient murder, of inarticulate rage against everything that was. He brought his hands down, slicing the air with the Bowie, flinging the goat's heart onto the ironwood with the other. His burning gaze settled on the girl tied to the altar, no pity it in, nothing but lust and avarice, and she recoiled, pulling against the rough ropes that bound her, stretching herself out in a vain effort to get away from him. There was nothing intelligent in her eyes—no plan of action, no pleas for mercy—just blind panic, wide-eyed terror, just the emptiness of the void, and the man smiled the way a cat smiles upon a mouse. "She's ready," he whispered, and his disciples fell into an expectant silence. "She's ready," he repeated, louder this time.

He lifted his gaze to the Stygian night, to the pall of the moonless night, eyes dancing, and drew the Bowie high above his head in a slow arc, playing the flickering light of the fire along its fine edge. Somewhere in the world, one of the Brethren held its mate. Somewhere, men sworn to the dark lord's service wetted that other blade in blood. Somewhere, another woman screamed in terror—or died in silence, the man hardly cared which, so long as she died, so long as her sacrifice powered his incantations.

"*Veni, tenebris noctis! Veni, lator chaos! Veni, tempestatum lator! Age, amator noctis! Veni, ambulator cum vento! Age, serpens magne de eremo!*" The man's rolling shout echoed across the desert plain that surrounded the compound, reflecting back at him from the night sky, filling the roofless room, rattling the glassless window frames. A small smile quirked the corners of his mouth—he knew the Latin was nothing more than an affectation. His father had told him so time and time again, and if anyone would know, it would be his father. Neither his father nor the Great One he called cared a whit about Latin—or any other language he knew of—but he found he couldn't resist the drama of it. "*Age, draco magne! Age, bellua profundi! Veni ad nos desolationis, pestilentiae et morbi baiulus!*"

Silence wrapped him in its sweet embrace, not even the woman tied to the ironwood plank dared break it. "*Veni, vocator chaos, bibe hunc sanguinem quem in tuo nomine effundo!*" Behind him, his disciples drew in a collective breath and held it. His eyes rolled down to the altar, and a moment later, the Bowie came whistling down, and the woman screamed, long and loud, a cut, long and shallow, traversed her upper arm from shoulder to elbow. "Oh, come now," he said to her, "that's barely a scratch." He leaned forward, his gaze locked on hers, until their noses almost touched. "And if you are rejected because you're a sniveling bitch, there'll be much, much more to come." He straightened, giving her a stern look.

The man watched as the blood mingled with the tears already on the altar, watched as the red swirled in a macabre dance, diluted by the water. He stood loosely, his hands at his sides, the wide Damascus blade tapping against his right thigh, leaving a smudge of blood on his dark habit. He waited a moment longer, not looking at her, not listening to anything but his own inner voice, then he lashed out, lightning-quick and another gaping wound appeared—in the woman's thigh this time—and another ringing scream echoed into the night.

Again, he shushed the woman, waving her pain away, and again, he adopted his frozen-limbed aspect of patience, of listening to the still, sweet voice within him. He glanced up at the smoke curling into the sky, watching for signs, for portents, for messages, for a reflective swirl in the smoke, then his gaze swept from horizon to horizon, searching for omens, for harbingers, for heralds. He heaved a sigh and closed his eyes a moment, then bent down to put his face in his victim's once again. "Don't ruin this," he grated. "We don't have much time left, and if you're rejected, you'll rue the day you were born!" Her only reply was a whimper, but he nodded as if she'd acquiesced.

He straightened, cast a glance at Marcus, the best of the best, his second-in-command while his brother was elsewhere, his mouth a grim line slashed through his face. Marcus nodded once, then gestured at the woman on the altar. The matte black man closed his eyes a moment, returning the nod, but not willing to give up so quickly. Without looking, he slashed across the brunette's torso, the razor-sharp Bowie leaving a long, red gash in its wake. "Is she not suitable, Great One?" he murmured as the woman shrieked and cried. "Does she not please you? Is her pain not to your taste?" He waited, listening with every fiber of his being, listening within himself, not without, as his frustration mounted.

He knew the Great One he sought was willing to make the journey if only he could find a suitable vessel. Hadn't his father told him so? But he'd never heard the Great One's voice, never experienced a vision, felt the tug of a great intelligence pulling at his own. His father said he had to have faith, he had to bide his time, to perform his rituals often, to attract the Great One's attention, to call out into the void, to provide a beacon, a signal, for the

Great One to follow. He knew his father spoke the truth. He knew it.

Again, he cast his gaze to the heavens, and again, it fell back to earth, unsatisfied, frustrated. He shook his head sadly, then motioned his disciples forward with each hand. As they approached, each of them withdrew a smaller Damascus knife from sheathes tucked into the bloodred fascia they wore, and each muttered words of thanks to the dark lord, his father. They ringed the altar and turned their expectant gazes on him.

He nodded, and they threw back their cowls, letting the dancing light from the fire wash the shadows from their faces. He met each person's gaze with a solemn glance, seeing lust in the eyes of the men, and seeing great hunger in all of them. He bowed his head. "Dear Father," he intoned, "thank you for this bounty we are about to receive. Thank you for your guidance, your protection, your blessings. Tonight, we failed yet again to summon the Great One. Forgive us for what we lack, Father. Forgive us for our failures in this and in our daily lives. We consecrate the flesh of the woman in your name, Father. We sanctify her blood to your will, your purposes. Bless us with divine nourishment that we may better serve you. Help us—*help me*—find the way to complete the ritual in a way that pleases both you and the Great One. Guide us, Father." He paused a moment to see if his father might speak, as he sometimes did, but the only answer to his prayer was the whistling of the wind in the keyhole of the time-grayed wooden door behind him. He shrugged—he had the vague sense that his father was busy, that his attention was somewhere to the east. "Amen," he said simply, and his followers echoed the word.

The Primo turned his gaze on the pig strapped to the altar and grimaced as he bent down to put his face inches from hers. "You've failed us, bitch," he whispered. "The Great One has rejected you." When she sighed with relief, he laughed. "Don't worry. We've still got a use for you." He raised the Bowie and let it fall like a butcher's cleaver, its heavy blade slamming through her flesh and clunking into the scarred ironwood altar. Her eyes widened with the shock of it, and he chuckled as he picked up his pound of flesh and turned to impale it on a spit and set it over the fire.

The woman screamed and screamed and screamed as the men and the woman went to work on her, their blades thirsty for her blood. The leader held out his hand, and someone—most likely Marcus—put a warm cup of blood into it. Smiling, he sipped, watching the dancing flames darken the hunk of the woman he'd selected for his dinner.

Chapter 2
Single Serving
Friends

I

Gavin Gregory sighed and opened his eyes. His body still felt wrung out, but his mind was starting to feel normal again—no more dreams of Fry or Glacadairanam or general craziness. He'd been allowed to leave Jackson Memorial Hospital, and the heat and bustle of Miami, Florida, two days prior, though he'd had strict instructions to take it easy and to rehydrate using the prescription electrolyte powder that the hospital doctor had given him—Hydrolite by any other name.

He glanced at the night table and grinned a little. Maddie had left him a big Yeti bottle that was no doubt full of cold water, with a packet of the junk lying next to it. He sat up, grabbed the little envelope, and tore it open, grimacing all the while. It tasted like kitty litter, though it claimed to be orange flavored. He uncapped the Yeti and dumped the powder into the water, then spun the lid back on and shook the stainless-steel bottle. He sighed and put his hand on the cap, then decided to shake the bottle a little more.

Anything to avoid drinking the foul mixture.

"Shake it more than a few seconds and you're playing with it," said Maddie from the door, a sly grin on her face.

"Yeah? And what if I play with you, instead?"

"Not until you've had your drink." She came into their bedroom, unable to resist a glance into the depths of the closet and the dark door of the ensuite. When her gaze came back to his, he smiled.

"I'm going to hold you to that," he said as he spun the lid off the Yeti. "But you're a girl. You shouldn't know the shaking rule."

"Drink," she ordered. "We'll see if you have time to hold anything." She came across the bedroom to stand in front of him, one hand on her hip, one eyebrow arched. "Or are you all talk this morning?"

He lifted the bottle to his lips, but that didn't hide his grin. He drank half the contents of the Yeti in one long pull, then set it on the bedside table. "Good?"

"Not from the way you describe it. And you're not finished, mister. All of it."

"I thought I'd save some of it for later." He flashed a saucy little grin at her. "You know...*after.*"

"Who said there's going to be an after?"

"Well, I guess there is the off chance of Armageddon arriving during our love-making, but—"

"Love-making? *Love-making*? Gavin Gregory, what have I told you about reading those twinkly vampire novels?"

"The only vampire books I'm interested in are yours."

"And besides, all those books are YA. You hardly count as a young adult."

He cocked his head to the side and gave her a shrewd look. "It seems to me *you* are the one who's all talk this morning."

Maddie sniffed, and her gaze wandered toward the Yeti on the nightstand.

"I'm *okay*, Mads," he said in a voice just above that of a whisper.

"Sure, you are. You're FBI. An invincible man in a boring blue suit."

"Right, but I'm also fine, Maddie. Yes, I got dehydrated down in Miami, and I—"

"Had a monster walking around in your head?"

"—suffered a few seizures as a result." He shook his head. "Fry is—"

"No, Gavin. No names. Not for him, and not for his bastard son."

"Honey, it's—"

"Names have power, Gav. I believe that. Before Glac…" She chopped her hand through the air. "Last year, I didn't believe in magic or the supernatural, but I still believed names were important. Now…" She shrugged as Gavin got up and came over to her. "Now, who knows? There has to be a reason for the myth that names have power. Why else would the concept exist in every culture? Why would we have true name myths? Why would—"

Gavin stepped close and took her in his arms. "It's okay, Mads. *We're* okay. Whether names have power or not, we survived a run-in with both of those monsters. They aren't omnipotent. They aren't omniscient. Hell, Fr—the father couldn't even keep me trapped in my dreams."

"Still." Maddie's voice was firm, but she melted into his embrace. "Still, he almost…"

"He didn't," said Gavin softly. "He didn't, hon. Besides, Kai is shielding us."

"From Adeline and her goons. Not from two demons."

"Demons?"

Maddie shrugged, an uncomfortable expression on her face. "Whatever. Do you have a better name for them?"

Gavin heaved a sigh. "No, I don't, but calling them demons makes me think of the *Exorcism of Emily Rose,* and I don't want to believe Fry has that much power."

"He makes me think of *The Stand*." Maddie frowned. "Of Randall Flagg and Walter O'Grim. The man in black."

"At least Flagg could be beaten. The demon in—"

"Enough, Gav," Maddie whispered. "This isn't helping."

"Okay. Okay, Mads. What should we call them? Randy and Walt? I don't want to keep calling them 'the father' and 'the son.'"

"Bastard one and bastard two," Maddie said with a hint of amusement in her voice.

"B1 and B2? And we could call them 'The vitamins' when we want to talk about both at the same time." He leaned his head back so he could watch her expression. "Or we could go with the tried and true: 'jerkface' and 'butthole.' But, hey, you're better at this whole naming business. If I were the writer, the characters would all be named Bob Smith and Judy Brown."

"Nah, you'd name them all Jerkface Butthole."

He chuckled at the impish expression that covered her face and the merry mischief that danced in her eyes. "Yeah, you're probably right." He leaned into the embrace, inhaling the slightly sweet aroma of her shampoo, luxuriating in the feeling of her body pressing against his. "It's nice to be home," he murmured.

"Yes, it's nice to have you home." She sighed and lay her hands on his shoulders. "But I do have a book to finish, and I'm already four days behind schedule."

"Yeah, I get it. Go play with your glitter and sparklers. And think up culturally acceptable names for those yahoos—and remember, there are three of them."

She frowned a little at that. "Right. The other son."

Gavin nodded. "Yes, the other son." He released her and crossed back to the nightstand to retrieve the Yeti. He took a big swig of the muddy-tasting solution and grimaced. "I don't know which is worse…seizures or this shit."

"Well, I know which is worse, so you can just ask me when you get confused."

"Yeah, but you don't have to drink it."

"No, but I do have to hear you whine about drinking it."

"Whine?" asked Gavin, crooking an eyebrow at her. "Nah, this ain't whining, Mads. This is—"

"*Whining*," she said and flashed a one-sided grin at him. "Keep it up, buster, and you'll be drinking *all* your meals because your jaw will be wired shut."

He looked at her for a moment, fighting a grin, then chuckled. "I've got to hide that Tae Bo DVD again, don't I?"

"Try it and see what it gets you."

"Let me see if I understand your position here. Sex is strenuous exertion, but you kicking my ass is okay?"

"Sure. *You* don't have to do anything but stand there and get punched." Her grin widened.

"I'd think the falling down part would count, at least."

"We'll call your doctor and ask…but later."

"Right, get back to your vampires. I'll find something to keep me busy."

"Something that involves resting and drinking water and more resting." She leaned her head forward and gave him a stern look. "You hearing me, Gav?"

"Yes, ma'am," he said as he gave her a quick salute. "I suppose I can find something to stream. Or one of my DVDs. Maybe a movie."

"*Dirty Harry*, again?"

"Hey, it's a classic."

"Opinions are like assholes—"

"Everyone's got one," he finished for her. "You're not making a strong case by quoting the movie in question, dear."

"It's a question of methods. Everybody wants results…"

Gavin sighed and shook his head. "Well, a man's got to know his limitations. Get to work, chickadee."

2

1289 Welcrest Drive, Minnieville, VA
Thursday, 1:39 pm EST

Gavin paused the *Dirty Harry* disc and grimaced at the horrifying collection of chimes his phone now played instead of the PTSD-inducing Glacadairanam-like chirp he'd used before. He glanced at the screen, and his grimace deepened a little. He thumbed the accept button and put the phone to his ear. "Hey, Pete. How's business?"

"Well, in our line of work, no business is good business."

"And business is good?"

"How are you feeling, Gavin? Getting rehydrated?"

"Uh, yeah. I drink three pounds of kitty litter a day, and somehow, that helps."

"Well…as long as it's working, I guess."

Maddie stuck her head in from the kitchen. "That better not be who I think it is."

"Don't worry," said Gavin. "Pete knows better than to try to pull me in. My wife is fierce."

"She is," said Pete.

"But…" added Gavin.

"Tell him we don't care about the case," said Maddie. "Tell him you're closed for business for at least two weeks."

"Don't worry," said Pete. "I have no plans of asking you to go anywhere. Tell her that so I don't get a call from Gloria in the middle of our chat."

"Tell him I'll—"

"Maybe you two should just talk to each other and then loop me in after you're done telling each other things." Pete chuckled, and Maddie stuck out her tongue.

"Tell me what's going on, Pete. Maddie promises not to call Gloria."

"Yet," called Maddie.

"There's something going on west of San Antonio."

"Nah, Pete. There's nothing west of San Antonio but desert and tiny little towns."

"Well, there's Chihuahua City."

"That's Mexico, Pete. No jurisdiction."

"True, Gavin, true. And our problem is on the US side anyway."

Gavin drew a deep breath in through his nose. "Problem?"

"Bodies, Gavin. Young women."

"What, dumped in the desert?"

"Yes."

"Forensics?"

"Well, as you probably guessed, the bodies lie out there for a bit before anyone stumbles across them—"

"And I bet there are more than have been found."

"—so the forensics are questionable at best, but on top of that, the arroyos flood at the slightest provocation. So we're not even sure the bodies are found at the place they were dumped."

"Sounds like you're in quite a pickle."

"We are, it's true. It isn't made easier by my top agent being out on medical leave."

"Who's on it?"

"Reynold Hall."

"He's good, Pete. Young but good. He'll do fine."

"He is good, but he's not you."

"Pete—"

"And he's stuck. Oh, he won't say so, but I can hear it in his voice."

"He'll get past it. He'll find his way."

"Sure, Gav, sure. I know he will, but he'll get there faster with someone to talk to."

"Someone like me?"

"See what I mean? You're good at this stuff."

"You can stop with the butter, Pete. I'll talk to him, but I'm not leaving Minnieville. After Miami—"

"I'm not asking you to, Gav. No, I don't even want you thinking about this one much. Just give Reynold a few minutes a day and let him bounce ideas off you. Let him do the work, you just point him in the right direction."

Gavin took a moment, staring at Clint Eastwood's snarl on the screen while he ran through it all in his mind. "Yeah, I think I can do that."

"I'm serious about the time constraints, Gavin. Even without the backchannel between Maddie and Gloria. Your health is—"

"I said yes, Pete," Gavin said gently.

"Well…I appreciate it." Pete cleared his throat and punctuated it with a sniff, then fell silent for a few moments. "Are you…"

"Dreaming? Of course, I am, but they're just regular dreams, Pete. Stupid little things like being in a speeding car while elephants chase us. Like that."

Pete chucked a little, but when he spoke next, his voice was solemn. "You'll keep me apprised if that changes."

There was no question in Pete's tone, but Gavin said, "Yeah, sure. Tell Reynold to call me."

"Will do. I'll have him call you right away."

3

1289 Welcrest Drive, Minnieville, VA
Thursday, 4:28 pm EST

Despite Pete's promise, Reynold didn't call until a quarter of *The Enforcer* had rolled by on the television—and before that, all of *Magnum Force*. The caller ID read "Reynold Hall." Gavin paused the DVD and thumbed the accept button on his phone. "Gregory."

"How you doing, Gavin?"

"Getting there, Reynold. I'm getting there. Drinking toxic sludge eighty-seven times a day, but the doctors say it's good for me. How are you?"

"Fine, fine," said Hall, but he sounded as though his mind were elsewhere. "Eating lots of dust, and no one says it's good for me."

"Yeah, Pete told me a little about the case, but it was broad-brush—bodies out in the desert."

"Yeah. That's it in a nutshell."

Gavin pursed his lips. "He said you need a sounding board?"

"It's…" The other agent fell silent, then heaved a sigh. "You know how some cases get…I don't know…weird?"

Gavin smiled a little at that. "You wouldn't believe me if I told you how weird they get for me, Ren."

"This case…" He sniffed, and something rustled on his end of the call. "I've got…"

"Look, Reynold, there's not much you can say here that I haven't thought in the last six months. Nothing you say is going to make you sound nuts. Not to me. It's the nature of the job."

The silence stretched for a few moments, and Gavin let it run. Finally, Reynold sighed. "Yeah, okay. Pete told you about the vics?"

"A little," said Gavin with a short nod.

"They've been butchered."

"You've seen that before, Ren."

"Yeah, I have, but…this looks different."

"Different how?"

"Some of the cuts are…*purposeful.*"

"I don't understand."

"It's… They're different from incised wounds I've seen in other serial cases. It's as if these cuts were necessary but follow-ups. The fourth act in a three-act play."

"What, like the killer did them post-mortem?"

"No, the vics were all alive when the cuts were inflicted."

"Then?"

"They seem…perfunctory, purposeful. Like something performed without… Okay, this is going to sound weird, but I think you'll understand."

"Go ahead."

"Like the unsub cut them without joy. Like he made the cuts because the skin was in the way. Like a surgeon made them. But I don't mean it like the killer is a doctor…just that the cuts are…"

"Surgical. Got it. Cannibalism?"

"No bite marks, no signs of cannibalism, but each woman is missing muscle and organs. And maybe surgical is the wrong word. Maybe cuts made by a butcher is a better description."

"The same organs or different ones each time?"

"Some are different, but each woman lost a kidney and part of her liver."

"I see. What are the different ones?"

"One woman lost her stomach; another had her tongue excised. The heart of another is missing."

"Pancreas? Thymus?"

"Not so far, but we don't have all the autopsy reports. This is a small county; they're swamped by all this."

"Sure. What county?"

"Kelly County. Listen, I saw *Red Dragon*, too. You're thinking we've got a real-life Hannibal Lector running around down here?"

"Could be, Ren. Offal is still consumed regularly in Mexico and countless other countries. And you know as well as I do that serial cannibals are a breed apart. They aren't true psychopaths—most do develop emotional attachments, and that's what leads them to cannibalism—their victims can't leave them. Not ever."

"Yes, I'd considered that, but—"

"The MO seems to fit. A quick death, then harvesting offal for dinner."

"But they're not. Quick deaths, I mean. These women *are* tortured, but the ME thinks that happens first, then the butchery while they are still alive."

"Well, that just makes our unsub even more of a rarity. A true psychopath who likes long pork."

"I guess," said Reynold.

"Hey, I'm not trying to dictate to you, Ren. I'm here to help. To listen to your theory of the crime and give you the benefit of my experience."

Again, the silence stretched between them, then Reynold sighed. "Yeah. I'm not sure I have one."

"Okay, we can deal with that, too. Tell me what's going on."

"The victims are between twenty-two and twenty-nine, all of a type—thin or athletic, no children—all unidentified at this point. None of the local officers recognize them, and with a county of only a few thousand souls…"

"How many vics?"

"Seven."

Gavin sighed and closed his eyes, suddenly exhausted. "Yeah, I'd think at least some of the victims would at least look familiar to local law enforcement. Are they cooperating?"

"The deputies? They seem to be."

"Okay, what else?"

"There's evidence the vics were restrained for a while, then tortured, then killed and butchered. The unsub uses a sharp non-serrated heavy blade to inflict long, shallow cuts in the victim's upper body. I think the point of those cuts are to hurt her, to make her scream."

"Sounds reasonable." Gavin shook his head. "Well, not *reasonable*, but—"

"I know what you meant. After she's bled a bit, someone goes to work on her. The ME thinks at least two blades are used to butcher her—the big, sharp one and one or more smaller blades. And that's the other thing? Why switch knives?"

"Maybe it's easier."

"Maybe…"

"You think there is more than one killer?"

"No," said Reynold. "You know how rare *that* is."

"Yes," said Gavin, thinking of the same conversation he'd had in Miami, "but it's not unheard of."

"All of the shallow cuts are inflicted by the heavy blade."

"A teacher-student relationship? Watch what I do, then you try?"

"No, I don't think so," said Hall. "It's like those two sets of cuts serve different purposes. Like the first ones are to *hurt* her but preserve her life."

"And by the time he gets to the second set, he no longer cares if she lives or dies?"

"Maybe," said Hall, but his tone said, "yes."

"What aren't you saying, Ren? What are you holding back?"

"Nothing. At least, it's not anything yet."

"Come on. Give." He waited the space of three breaths, then said, "Look, I can't help you sort through all this if you don't tell me everything."

"I'm not sure. It's not even a theory, like I said. More of a gut feeling. An idea."

"Fine, I won't hold you to it, and I won't charge you for the advice. Tell me."

"What if it's a Satanic ritual? Black magic?"

"A sacrifice?" asked Gavin. He thought about it a moment, and Ren gave the space to do it. "Yeah, that seems to fit what you've described, but—"

"You're not going to tell me how there's no documented case of Satanic rituals—"

"*But* it doesn't have to be an *actual* ritual. Ramirez wasn't part of any cult, but he thought he was doing Satan's bidding—or at least he claimed he did."

"He was mentally ill, though—"

"Does that matter? He was together enough to pull off eighteen home invasions and avoid capture for over a year. What if your unsub also thinks he's doing Satan's bidding?"

"El Paso," murmured Reynold.

"What?"

"Ramirez was from El Paso. That's just a few hours northwest of here."

"Maybe there's something in the water. Let's not get too fixated on the Night Stalker. I'm just saying it's possible for a fuck-up to think he's invoking Satan and not be doing anything more than committing murder."

"Okay. I'm not sure it matters, though."

Gavin shrugged despite Reynold having no way to see the gesture. "Only in how you present it to the bosses. If you say it's a Satanic cult, chances are you'll get laughed into a teaching gig at the academy."

"Ah."

"Either way, you'll be investigating the same way, right? You're still looking for the guy with the knife. If it turns out he really is in a cult, and you can find evidence to prove that, so be it, but if there's no evidence that will stand up to scrutiny, you're still covered."

"How do I investigate it?"

"The same way you'd investigate anything else, Ren. Basics. Evidence, profile, footwork."

"Yeah, okay. Okay," said Reynold.

To Gavin, he sounded relieved. "And, Ren?"

"Yeah?"

"Relax. All these cases are hard to carry. Hard enough without you adding a pallet of bricks to your shoulders. You'll solve it when it's possible, and no amount of self-flagellation will change that."

"But…" Ren sighed.

"Yes, Ren," said Gavin in a soft voice. "More bodies will drop before you get him—unless you are incredibly lucky. The sad fact is, we need more bodies to drop. We need evidence to refine the profile. We need behavior to analyze. In this job, that means victims…bodies. It's part of every investigation."

"I guess so," said the younger agent in a morose tone.

"Listen, Ren, there's no shame in deciding Behavioral Science isn't for you. It's brutal work—as you know—and any position in the Bureau contributes to the well-being of the country."

Ren was silent for almost a minute before he said, "I get that, but I'm good at this. Aren't I?"

"You are," Gavin said in a firm voice. "You'll be just as good in counter-terrorism or kidnappings or on one of the response teams. You're a good agent, Ren. You'll be a good match for any unit in the Bureau, and they'll be damn glad to have you."

"Well…thanks."

"It ain't flattery. You have options is all I'm saying. You don't have to stick with the BSU just because you're good at the work, okay? Keep that in mind."

Ren thought about it for another lengthy pause, then said, "I will, Gavin."

"Good." Gavin took a breath. "Is there any evidence that points at the supernatural angle?" He felt proud that he kept his voice even as if he were asking no more than how Ren liked his hotel.

"No, nothing concrete. The bodies are washed post-mortem, so no fluids or fiber evidence, and there are no marks or words inscribed in the flesh. But there's something about the case…an undercurrent, maybe." He chuckled. "Hell, maybe it's just my imagination."

"Maybe so," said Gavin, "but that doesn't mean your gut isn't right. Keep your eyes open. Look at the evidence with an open mind and let it guide you. Don't let your imagination pigeonhole you into one-track thinking."

"I won't," said Ren.

"Anything else?"

"Not at the moment. Thanks, Gavin."

"Any time, Ren. And feel free to call back. Don't worry about the clock, just call when you need to talk."

4

1289 Welcrest Drive, Minnieville, VA
Thursday, 11:08 pm EST

Maddie murmured in her sleep when Gavin's phone vibrated on its charging pad. He fumbled the phone, making it clatter on the nightstand. "Who's'at?" she asked.

"Shh, Maddie's sleeping," he whispered. "Go back to sleep."

"Then stop playing the drums."

"Sorry."

She grunted and rolled to her side as Gavin swung out from under the covers and stepped into the hall, closing the door as quietly as he knew how. Only then did he glance down at the screen, then lift the phone to his ear. "What's up, Renfield?"

"Reynold."

"Yeah, I know. Weak Dracula joke. Chalk it up to the middle-of-the-night stupor."

"Um, okay. Listen, I think I'm onto something, Gavin. I was thinking about the knives—the two different blades, you know? Anyway, like I said it's a small county, and—"

"Whoa. Slow down, Ren."

"Sorry. Metallurgy. I had the ME look for metal fragments. The steel in both knives is almost two percent carbon and has high nickel content."

"If that county is so small, how in the world do they have a spectrometer?"

"They don't, but the ME's sister teaches Materials Science at UT San Antonio."

"That's lucky. I'm guessing both blades are Damascus? Both from a similar formula?"

"That's right! Dr. Zimmerman—the PhD, not the MD—says the fragments are consistent with pattern-welded Damascus. They are so close chemically, she thinks both blades may have come from the same batch of billets. It's a small county, like I said, so I got to thinking about who might make Damascus blades in the area. I found a local knifesmith who Google says is a Damascus specialist."

"What a coincidence," said Gavin with a chuckle. "Have you called him?"

"Yeah, a minute ago. Got his voicemail, of course, since it's after hours. It probably won't lead anywhere— I mean what serial killer in his right mind would buy such easily identifiable blades from a local source?"

"No, that's a good lead, Ren. Don't sell yourself short. Good work."

"Well…thanks. I—" A thrum sounded on Reynold's end of the call. "Hold on, Gav. That's him on the other line."

"Conference me in."

"One sec," said Reynold, and the phone first beeped then fell silent in Gavin's hand.

He walked toward the kitchen, thinking about sneaking a cup of coffee while Maddie slept. Technically, he was supposed to be avoiding caffeine, but after three days of kitty litter-infused beverages, he thought he deserved a reward.

In the kitchen, he set his phone down next to the coffeemaker and pulled the giant can of coffee out of the cabinet over it. He glanced at the phone, wondering what was taking so long to connect the two calls, then fetched the machine's carafe, added enough water for three cups of coffee, then dumped it into the machine's reservoir.

He spooned in three heaping measures of coffee and set the coffeemaker to brew.

He frowned at his phone, then swept it up from the counter to check the connection. It had been almost five minutes, and though the call was still connected, he thumbed the disconnect, then dialed Hall's number in his recent calls list and lifted his mobile to his ear.

The phone rang four times and went to voicemail. Gavin shook his head, frowning, and redialed. On the third ring, the call connected. "Hey, Ren, don't leave me hanging here." On the other end of the call, someone grunted, and Reynold's phone clattered across a hard surface, then thumped into something hard. "Reynold!" Gavin shouted. Loud, confused noise hammered across the line, punctuated by grunts and the bruit of a street fight.

"Dammit!" Gavin muttered and sprinted for the countertop pad where Maddie charged her cellphone at night. He hit the speakerphone on his cell and dropped it to the countertop with a clatter, then swept Maddie's lock screen away, found Gloria Fielding's contact, and pressed the call button, pressing Maddie's phone to his ear and staring at the screen of his own.

"Maddie? What's wrong?" asked Gloria in a sleep-blurred voice. "Is Gav—"

"This is Gavin, Gloria. I need Pete right now," he said, using his command voice.

Gloria recognized the tone, of course, and knew what it meant. "Pete," she said. "Pete! Wake up, it's Gavin. Something's wrong."

"What? Gavin's at home, Glo—"

"Shut up, Pete. Take the phone and talk to him."

"There's no reason to be rude," mumbled Pete as he put the phone to his ear. "Gavin?"

"Reynold's in trouble. I've got him on the other phone—no, that's not accurate. I'm *connected* to his cell with mine, but he's not talking. Sounds like he's *fighting*."

"Right," said Pete, all hints of sleepiness gone. "Gloria, get my phone." The bedclothes rustled, and feet pounded against Fielding's hardwood floors. "He's in Kelly County, right?"

"Yes, I think that's what he said." Gavin kept his gaze riveted to the screen of his phone. In Texas, something shattered, followed by more thuds, more bangs, and a significant crash. "Sounds like he's fighting for his life, Pete."

"Firearms?"

"Not that I've heard, but there were about five minutes where I—"

"Here's Gloria. Stay on the line. With Hall and us."

"Right."

"Gavin, it's Gloria. I'll relay to Pete."

"Check," said Gavin. Reynold shouted something unintelligible, then came the sound of glass shattering. "Help's on the way, Ren! You hear me? Help's coming!"

"Gav? What's going on?" asked Maddie from the hallway.

He ignored the question. "How many, Ren?" he shouted. "Describe them if you can!"

"Five!" shouted Reynold. "Dressed in black. One fem—" A tremendous crash obliterated whatever Hall said next, followed by the sound of a chair smashing against something or someone.

"Five of them," Gavin said to Gloria. "All dressed in black."

She relayed the message to her husband, then said, "HRT scrambled, but they're out of Dallas. Kelly Sheriff's Office sending their version of SWAT—which amounts to two patrolmen armed with shotguns. Pete says to tell Hall to hang on."

"Ren! HRT is rolling, local SWAT, too. Hold on! Hear me, Reynold? Help's coming!"

"Gavin?" asked Maddie as she came into the kitchen. She took one look at his face, then nodded. The coffeepot beeped, and she moved to pour two cups of coffee, rubbing the sleep from her eyes as she did so.

In Kelly County, the sounds of the tumult faded after the horrendous sound of an aluminum bat bouncing off a skull. *Off Reynold's skull*, thought Gavin and grimaced.

"Find it," said a deep bass voice that rolled from the speaker like a wave of zombies. "Quickly."

"I think Ren's down, Gloria."

"He said 'man down,'" Gavin heard a woman say. "A second ago he said SWAT was on the way."

"No matter," said the bass voice. "Just find the damn phone."

"Leave it," urged the woman. "Let's get out of here."

"*Find it*, Cece," said the bass.

"Yes, Primo."

"Listen to me, Cece," said Gavin in his command voice. "Texas has the death penalty. Murdering an FBI agent is a sure-fire way to see an execution firsthand."

The bass voice laughed.

"Assault, on the other hand, buys you your life. Battery might get you twenty-five years, but that's a hell of a lot better than the death penalty."

"Primo…"

"*FIND IT*, Cece! Don't listen to the man trying to lead you out of my father's warm regard."

My father's warm regard… My father's warm regard… The phrase echoed inside Gavin's head, and his heartbeat accelerated. "Listen to me, Cece—" Gavin snapped his mouth shut at the sound of someone picking up Reynold's phone.

"Here it is! Here, Primo!"

"Very good, Cece. You men take him out to the van."

"Van," Gavin whispered to Gloria.

"Got it," she said.

Into his own phone, Gavin said, "Listen, whoever you are. You wouldn't be there if you didn't want something. Leave the agent there, and I can get it for you. Don't compound your troubles by abducting a federal officer."

"You can't get me what I want, so your promises are meaningless," said the man in his deep voice. "Your threats mean even less. This man…he *might* help me get what I want, though, so I think I'll stick to my original plan. Still, thank you for your concern."

Gavin grimaced and closed his eyes. "His name is Reynold. Reynold Hall. He's a father—two boys. His parents are both still alive, they live near him in Virginia. His boys are named—"

The man laughed, a high cackle at odds with his deep, rich voice. "It won't work, FBI-man."

"What won't work?"

"Trying to humanize this slug. It won't work because I abandoned my humanity a long time ago…if I ever had any."

"Listen—"

"No, you listen to me, FBI-man." The phone rattled a moment. "Listen to me, Gregory." The man's voice gained a mocking lilt as he said Gavin's name. "None of what you were trained to say to me has any relevance in my world. *You* have no relevance in my world…" The man hummed for a few seconds, a vaguely Arabic-sounding melody, then he laughed. "*Gavin* Gregory? Is that your name, Agent?"

Gavin shot a glance at Maddie, and she shook her head. Despite that, he opened his mouth to acknowledge the question, but before he could, the man cackled again.

"I think it is. I *feel* it is." The man chuckled. "That was quite a show you put on in Miami last week. Quite the show, indeed. Tell me something, Agent Gregory?"

"Leave Reynold there, and I'll tell you anything you want to know."

The man laughed. "Even the name of your pretty wife? Even your address?"

Gavin snapped his gaze around to meet Maddie's once again, and he mouthed, "Gun safe." He jerked his chin toward their bedroom, and unbidden, the image of a knot of black-robed figures standing around her as she lay sleeping sprang to his mind, tying his guts in knots, Fry's voice ringing in his ears: *I could take her, spark. Any time I want.*

As she turned and sprinted down the hall, Gavin said, "Tell me your name, and I'll consider it."

"No, not yet. You haven't earned that knowledge yet, Gregory. Are you at home or are you still recovering in Jackson Memorial Hospital?"

"Still in the hospital, Glacadairanam."

Once again, the man lost his peculiar cackle into the night, and Gavin cringed. "No, I don't think so. And who or what is Glaca-shama-langa-ding-dong?"

"Are we playing it that way? I suppose you've never heard of Fry, either?"

"Fry? Like in Futurama?"

"Right. Okay, you're just some random psycho who happens to know who I am? A regular Joe Citizen who knows what happened to me last week?"

"Our relationship is destined for failure if we begin by calling names. I do try to keep up with the news reports, though, and you've featured in them recently. A lot. I suppose congratulations are in order."

But the man's voice was anything but congratulatory. "Uh-huh," said Gavin. "Leave Reynold there... What should I call you?"

The line hummed a moment, then the man said, "Sure. Why not? You've probably already heard one of my disc— *Friends*, that is... You've probably already heard one of my friends call me 'Primo.' That will do."

"Primo? As in, look at that primo car?"

"Sure."

"At least you don't have an inflated sense of self-worth," Gavin grumbled. Maddie came back into the kitchen, his service weapon in her hand and the Mossberg 500 ATI Tactical 12 gauge tucked under her arm. He'd picked up the shotgun after their abduction in

Manhattan—not that it would've helped against Glacadairanam, and not that it would help against Fry, but it did make Maddie feel better. She handed over the pistol, then switched to the scattergun. "You started to say disciples a minute ago. What's the name of your group?" Reynold's voice rattled through his mind: *What if it's a Satanic ritual? Black magic?* He held out Maddie's phone, and she took it, then put it to her ear and murmured something to Gloria.

Primo laughed. "My *group?* How enlightened of you, Agent Gregory."

"I don't follow."

"Well, clearly you mean my *cult.*"

"Group, cult, whatever. What's its name?"

Primo chuckled again. "No, we ain't organized. We're not a religion, not an official group. We're just a bunch of friends who have the same ideals, the same viewpoint."

Gavin heard someone in the background say the van was loaded and ready. "Primo, don't do this. Leave Reynold there. We can roll medical if he's hurt. We can—"

"Well, this has been fun, but like all good things, it must end. See you in the funny papers, Agent Gregory."

"No, wait a—" Gavin sighed and closed his mouth as the call went dead. He looked at Maddie and shook his head.

"Glo, here's Gavin again."

Gavin took the phone when she offered it and switched it to speakerphone. "Gloria? I couldn't talk him out of taking Reynold. At least, that's what he said. Better have Pete roll medical, too."

"He already did," she said. "They left? They're already gone?"

"I don't know. The guy said they were leaving, but he hung up before I heard any engines."

Gloria's phone rustled, and then the quality of sound changed. "You're on speaker, Gavin," she said. "Pete's on hold—"

"The SD is a minute out," called Pete.

"Maybe a minute too late. What about the hostage rescue guys?"

"HRT's scrambled out of Love Field in one of their jets, but travel time alone—"

"Yeah," said Gavin with a sigh. "We need trap and trace on his phone. We need to know who he called."

"Right," grunted Pete. "I'll get it started after we hear something."

Gavin checked the clock over the stove, then his gaze jumped to Maddie's. "Listen, Pete—"

"No, you don't," said Maddie. "You're not well, Gav."

"It doesn't matter if I drink the kitty litter here or in Texas, hon."

"Listen to your wife, Gavin," said Pete.

"Reynold is one of our own," said Gavin. "There's no way we're leaving his abduction in the hands of a sheriff's department that thinks two guys with shotguns are an adequate response—"

"It's what they have."

"—to the in-progress abduction of a federal officer." He shook his head. "No, we need boots on the ground, Pete. We need—"

"Someone else," said Maddie. "Someone else can go, Gavin Gregory."

He heard the note of exasperation, of anger, of warning in his wife's voice, and Gavin shook his head. "This isn't a normal situation, Mads."

"No, it isn't," she said with a shake of her head. "You almost…" She shook her head and swallowed hard. "You almost checked out for good less than a week ago. You almost—"

"I *didn't*, though," he said. "I—"

"Gavin," said Pete in an iron voice.

"No, hold on," said Gavin. "Everyone just hold on a second. Listen, I got dehydrated and…and I was worn out, but I've done nothing for these past six days but rest. I feel fine. I'm rehydrated, I haven't had any dreams, any—" He snapped his mouth shut. He'd almost said "visitors" but remembered at the last second that Gloria was on the call, too. "I haven't had any threats, any calls."

"What did he say when you called him Glacadairanam?" demanded Maddie.

"Who? What was that name?"

"Never mind, dear," said Pete.

Gloria sucked her teeth. "I think I can be trusted, Pete Fielding, after all these years."

"She's right," said Gavin. "It's okay to tell her, Pete, but later." He dropped his gaze away from the burning coals of ire in Maddie's eyes. "Honey, I'm—"

"I'm not raising this child alone, Gav," said Maddie in a cold, flat voice.

For a moment, no one spoke, then Gloria broke the silence by shouting, "Yes!" Gavin grinned at Maddie, but though her lips twitched once, the cold anger burning in her eyes didn't fade one iota, and his smile faded.

"No, honey," he said. "You're not. I promised you that. I'm done taking foolish risks. I promised you that, too, back in Miami."

"You did!" she snapped, rage pouring forth, reservoir water sluicing past the broken dam that had once retained it. "You did, and now you're talking about flying to Texas where one FBI agent was just abducted! About heading into the lion's den as if you were Daniel himself and putting your damn head right in the beast's gaping maw! Not even one week after the last goddamn psychopath almost killed you! Not even one week after something that might as well be Satan himself went on walkabout inside that thick skull of yours! *Goddammit, Gav! You promised!*" She stood there as her shout rang in his ears, tears sluicing down her cheeks as though the thing damming them up had broken, hands shaking on the forgotten shotgun, blazing gaze boring into his own, lips trembling.

"Hey, Mads, I—"

"Don't you dare say you're okay. Don't you dare say you'll be fine. *Don't you dare!*"

As if from a great distance, Gavin heard Pete clear his throat. "We'll call you back in a few minutes," he said.

"Call if you hear back from the SD before we call back."

"Uh, sure," said Pete.

Gavin disconnected the call, set the Glock on the island behind him, and took a step toward her. Maddie raised her hands, bringing the shotgun between them at port arms, then looked down at it, disgusted, and shoved it on the counter.

"And since when do we need guns in our own home? Tell me again how safe you are, Gavin, and I might scratch your eyes out!"

"I won't, Madeline," he said in a dead calm voice. "I won't tell you that. Never again if you don't want me to. I'm sorry I've been saying it too much."

Maddie slumped, leaning against the counter. "It's not… That's not…"

"I know," he said in a quiet voice. "Can I say I'll be careful?"

She looked up at him, brows furrowed, eyes snapping. "*Will* you be? Do you even know how?"

"That's not fair, Mads."

"Neither is running off into the night and fighting devils and gargoyles and psychic assassins and whatever else you can think up."

"I didn't ask for any of this, Mads. A year ago, I'd have expected you to have me committed for talking the way we do now."

She closed her eyes, squeezed them shut, then scrubbed away the tears furiously. "But you can't resist the call, can you? Can't resist running off into the darkness, alone and unprepared."

"I won't be alone this time." He shrugged. "I haven't been alone either time, if we're going to be honest about this."

"Yeah, some new Podunk hick from the sheriff's department you've already said is a joke!"

"That's not what I mean."

Maddie sighed. "Then who is going to—"

"I mean Kai."

She snapped her gaze up to his.

He nodded. "That's right. For the first time since all this started, there will be someone watching over me. Someone who won't get distracted, who won't lose contact when I get out of radio range." He stepped forward, and this time, she let him gather her into his arms. "*And*," he whispered in her ear, "this is the first time I'll have someone watching over you every minute of the day. Someone who doesn't need to sit outside in a Crown Vic to ensure you're safe."

"Kai," she whispered.

"That's right."

"And he can do both at the same time?"

"I think he can do both, the New York Times crossword, knit a sweater, and bake bread and not drop a stitch. I think the man has reserves even he doesn't know about."

"And...*him*? Fry?"

"Not for nothing, Mads, but Fry can get to me here or in Timbuktu or Paris or on the moon. These walls, that expensive security system, that Glock on the island, none of that matters if Fry decides he's coming for me."

She shuddered in his arms, then leaned into him and wrapped her arms around his waist. "Are you sure you don't want a teaching career?"

He grinned into her hair. "You want me to single-handedly ruin the Bureau?"

"I want you to single-handedly stay alive, you jerk."

"I'm okay with that," he said. "In fact, I'm kind of partial to breathing, myself. I'll make you a deal. I won't get killed very often, and in return, you won't kill me more than is required."

She sighed without even a hint of laughter. "Do you have to go?"

Gavin drew in a lungful of air. "Mads, you know I do," he said softly. "It's how I'm wired. I'm not the type of guy who can sit at a desk—not if I know an investigation in the field can benefit from my skills."

"Your insanity, you mean."

"That, too."

"There's nothing I can say to keep you here, is there?"

"Of course there is, Mads," he said in the same soft voice. "You can tell me not to go. You can tell me to take that teaching job. You can tell me to quit the Bureau and become a…a…"

"Pshh. You can't even think of something else you can do. You can't think of *anything* else you can do, can you?"

Gavin shrugged, and Maddie pulled him closer. "I…"

"Yeah, I know," she whispered, "but I'm allowed to freak out from time to time."

"You are. And you're allowed to tell me not to go."

"Don't go."

Gavin nodded against the side of her head and inhaled the scent of her. "Okay. I'll call Pete and help him coordinate from here. I'll ask him to move me to a desk in the morning. I can't dump all that on him right now, though, it wouldn't be fair."

Maddie pulled back a little and locked her eyes on him. She watched him for a few moments, her focus jumping back and forth between his two eyes. "I think you mean it."

"I do, Mads. Of course, I do."

"But you'd be miserable."

Gavin lifted a shoulder and looked away. "I'll be fine."

Maddie's brows bunched. "No, you won't." Her voice was low but firm. "You know that."

"Take 'yes' for an answer, Mads."

She reached up and turned his face back toward her. She stared into his eyes, brows still bunched, a moue of concern on her lips. "And the two creeps?"

"They'll be out there, waiting, doing whatever they want to do."

"And Reynold?"

"Pete can send someone else."

"Someone? Who?"

"Aaron Meyer. Jeremy Freshcorn." He shrugged. "Someone."

"And I'm supposed to believe you're okay with that."

"I have to be, don't I?" He smiled at her to take away any sting that might come with the words. "You're more important to me, Mads. Our little one is more important than the Bureau."

"But…"

"Madeline, I'm giving you what you want."

She shook her head slowly, her gaze never leaving his. "You're sacrificing what *you* want to do it. You're giving up your dream—"

"I can have other dreams. *Safer* dreams. We can move, keep our heads down. We can hide."

"Gavin, you've never hid from anything in your life."

He treated her to a one-shouldered shrug. "I never met Fry before."

She nodded once.

"So, you're doing this because you're scared of Fry?"

He shook his head. "No, I'm doing it because I love you, and you need me to."

Again, Maddie's head shook slowly back and forth, her gaze locked on his. "I…" Her eyes slid shut. "I can't, Gavin. It would be like you telling me to stop writing, to…I don't know…become a bank teller or something. I can't do that to you."

"Hey, Mads, if you need this, then—"

"I *want* it, Gavin." Again, the slow shake of her head, her gaze stuck on his. "Because I'm feeling weak and scared. But I'm stronger than that, and I don't *need* it." She straightened and stepped back, though she kept her hands resting lightly on his shoulders. She lifted her chin. "Call Pete back. I'll go pack a bag for you. We never repacked your go-bag after Miami."

"Mads, I…"

"Call Pete," she said and dropped her hands to her sides. She picked up the shotgun, then pointed at the phone.

"I don't have to—"

"Yes, you do, Gavin," she said in an almost whisper. "We both know that." She dropped her gaze to the floor. "But, thank you. Thanks for being willing to give it all up. For me."

"I mean it, Mads. If it makes it easier for you—"

"We can talk about it later. *After* you've sorted Texas out. We'll both think about it."

"Okay," he said, but his expression was one of worry.

"I mean it, Gavin. I'm okay."

"Do I get to say I'll scratch your eyes out if you say that again?"

"Not if you want to walk without limping," she said as she strode toward the hall leading to the bedroom. "Call Pete. I'll be fine."

He stared after her, frowning, his hands itching to pick up the phone.

5

Somewhere above eastern Texas
Friday, 12:07 pm CST

Gavin moved in his seat, trying to get comfortable. His throat was dry, and that gave him a moment's panic, though Dr. Tremaine had said his electrolytes were good. He had a bunch of the Hydrolite packets in his bag, but so far, turbulence had prevented an inflight service. He glanced forward, then up at the call button.

"First-time flyer?" asked the guy across the aisle—a man in his late forties or early fifties but still fit as a fiddle.

"Hardly," grunted Gavin, sparing the guy another glance. "I'm just thirsty."

"Ah," said the man. "I've got a bottle of water that I picked up in that little shop near the gate. It's a little warm, but the seal's still unbroken. It's yours if you want it."

Gavin turned his head and looked the man up and down. He seemed average in every way: average height, dark hair, dark eyes, medium build. He shook his head. "No, I can't accept it, but thank you."

"I'm a doctor," said the man, "and if you don't mind me saying so, you look dehydrated. Almost to the point of being unwell." He held out the bottle of water. "Take it. Doctor's orders."

Gavin stared at him a moment, then nodded. "To tell you the truth, I am recovering from a bad spell of dehydration. Seizures, the whole thing."

The doctor frowned. "Water's not enough, then. Have you been treated somewhere or are you—"

"I was in the hospital. I have these packets of kitty litter to add to my water."

The man flashed a lopsided smile at him. "Kitty litter?"

Gavin grinned. "Yeah. It's supposed to taste like orange, and I guess it might if you've never tasted an orange before. It's called Hydrolyte."

The doctor grimaced. "You piss-off your attending or something? That's about the worst tasting formulation I can think of." He wagged his head side-to-side. "But still, better than nothing." He gestured with the bottle of water. "Take it."

With a grin, Gavin took the proffered water bottle. "Thanks, Doctor…" He quirked an eyebrow as he unbuckled his seatbelt and stood.

"Withers," said the man.

"You're not 'posed to get up," said the boy sitting by the window. "Turbulence."

"Mitch, leave the man alone," said his mother with an apologetic smile at Gavin.

"It's okay," Gavin said. "I'm FBI, Mitch. I'm one of the few people who don't have to follow the seatbelt rule." He opened the overhead compartment, unzipped his carry-on bag, and found a packet of Hydrolyte, then closed everything up and regained his seat. He showed the packet to Dr. Withers and grinned. "See? Says right here it's orange-flavored, but it should say it's kitty litter flavored. The name's Gavin Gregory, by the way."

Withers nodded, then waved at the bottle. "Drink up, Mr. Gregory."

With a nod, Gavin set to the task of getting most of the disgusting powder into the tiny opening of the too-thin plastic bottle, then replacing the too-small cap and giving the bottle a vigorous shake. As the water changed from crystal clear to muddy brown, he shook his head. "It's not even orange." He opened the bottle and took a mouthful, fighting the urge to spit it out—as he had for the first mouthful of every serving he'd consumed in the past week. He forced the foul liquid down his throat instead, then smiled at Dr. Withers. "Thanks. I really appreciate the water."

"No problem." The doctor's brown-eyed gaze rested on him lightly. "Were you telling the truth?"

Gavin cocked his head to the side. "About the flavor?"

Withers shook his head. "About the FBI-thing."

"Oh, that." Gavin shot a wink at the kid near the window, then nodded. "Honest."

Withers nodded. "I used to be a forensic pathologist in Western New York, but now…" His eyes grew unfocused for a moment, then he shook his head. "Now, I focus on my company. My *community*." The doctor's lips twisted into a half-smile as he said the last word.

"Company? Community?" asked Gavin.

"I provided backing to a couple of friends who had a good idea for an online community and an infrastructure for crowd-sourcing research." Dr. Withers shrugged modestly.

Gavin lifted his eyebrows. "That sounds expensive. You got rich as a pathologist? That must be a first?"

Withers chuckled. "No, and to make matters worse, I was a *teaching* pathologist. Back in medical school I wrote some software, and it provided extra income."

"What kind of software?"

"A…game," said Withers.

As the doctor spoke, alarm bells rang in Gavin's mind, and he was suddenly sure the man had just lied to him. "Anything I might've played?"

Withers shook his head. "No. It was a small FPS. It never got much traction, but it made enough that good investments could turn a little into a lot."

"Ah," said Gavin. "And this new venture? How's that doing?"

The man grinned a little. "~~It's~~ doing a lot better."

Gavin nodded, drank more Hydrolyte, and turned toward the front. There were many reasons rich strangers might lie to someone who just said he was an FBI agent: fear of an IRS audit ranking toward the top.

"What do you do for the Bureau?" asked Withers.

"BAU," said Gavin.

"Ah! Behavioral Analysis Unit. You're a profiler?"

Taking another sip, Gavin nodded.

"Then we have interests in common. Have you worked any big cases?"

Gavin threw a glance across the aisle. "Some."

"Come on, Agent Gregory," said Withers with a laugh. "You can't stop there!"

"The Smith, The Saint Mary Psycho—though that was after he'd turned himself in—Richie Arbarth, The Mauler…and most recently, The Bogeyman in Miami."

"Men, not man," said Withers. "There were two of them, right?"

With a nod, Gavin shifted in his seat. "Yes. The Bogeymen, then."

Dr. Withers leaned back in his seat, a faint smile on his face. "That was *you*."

"Yeah," said Gavin with a modest lift of his shoulders. "It's what I do."

"The news said you were injured. Was the dehydration a result of that?"

Again, Gavin only nodded, not wanting a conversation about the case in public. "More like the other way around," he muttered.

Withers seemed to sense the emotion behind his words and nodded as if he understood. "I have some experience in profiling—not in Miami, but in Western New York. I worked a few cases up there."

"Ah," said Gavin.

"You're like Fox Mulder?" said Mitch.

Gavin chuckled and nodded. "Sort of, though more like Clarise Starling than Mulder and Scully." It was something he'd said numerous times before at writer's conferences or publishing parties, but this time, it rang false to his ears. He felt a helluva lot more like Fox Mulder than a straight FBI man. He glanced across the aisle at Dr. Withers and caught the man giving him an unfathomable look. He lifted his eyebrows, and Withers shook his head smiling.

"Off woolgathering. Sorry."

"Who's Clara Scarthing," the kid mumbled.

"Uh-huh," said Gavin with a brisk nod. He didn't believe it, though. Not even a little. "You an X-Files fan?"

Withers shook his head—a little too violently. "No. There's too much ugliness in the world already. Too much of the unknown."

Gavin cocked his head and lifted an eyebrow. "That's true, but entertainment is just entertainment."

"Sure," said the doctor, "and I'd never try to talk someone out of enjoying what they find entertaining. But for me? No, I prefer to listen to music. Or read nonfiction. And these days, I keep myself busy enough I hardly have time for entertainment at all."

"Ah." Gavin turned his gaze to the front and leaned his head back against the headrest.

"Have you ever experienced something you couldn't explain? At least not in a way that didn't make people look at you like you're insane?" asked Withers.

Gavin shrugged, suddenly interested in how the Hyrdolyte was settling toward the bottom of the plastic container.

"I see you have," said Withers with a knowing grin. "I have, too, and unfortunately, it's ruined things like The X-Files and horror movies for me. Well, to be honest, I've never liked horror movies. Not since I was eleven."

"Yeah?" asked Gavin, casting a glance the other man's way and noting his intense grimace.

Withers nodded. "What's that Shakespeare quote?"

Gavin's face twitched in a one-sided grin. "'There are more things in Heaven and Earth, Horatio, than are dreamed of in your philosophy.' That the one?"

With a chuckle, the doctor nodded. "English major?"

"Nah," said Gavin. "Married to a writer. I hear shit like that all the time. You married?"

The doctor's face contorted—almost crumpling inward on itself—and he sighed. "No."

"Ever come close?"

Withers opened his mouth but said nothing for the space of a few breaths, then finally said, "After a fashion, but in the end, I had to break it off."

"Sorry to hear that," said Gavin. "Marrying my wife is the best thing I've ever done."

"My…marriage…wouldn't have been like that," mused the doctor. "But still, I find I regret having walked away from her from time to time." He seemed to gather his wits about him and gave Gavin a wan smile. "She was one of the things that make watching The X-Files no fun."

"Trouble, huh?"

Withers shrugged. "With a capital T." He gazed into the distance wistfully. "But her…family…is what made it impossible."

"Ah," said Gavin with a nod. "Yeah, families can be tough."

"Hers was… Well, I found myself constantly coming up against her daughter and her…sisters."

"That makes it hard."

Withers leaned his head back and turned his gaze on Gavin. "Yeah. And there were…elements…facts…about her family that if I spoke about them, people would look at *me* like I'm insane."

"Yeah?"

The doctor nodded. "Supernatural things."

"Ah," said Gavin again and looked away.

"You don't believe in the supernatural?"

"I wish I didn't," muttered Gavin. "I wish I could go back to not believing in them."

"You've experienced…something?"

Lips pressed together, Gavin cast a probing glance at the doctor but said nothing.

"That's answer enough," said the doctor. "It's okay, though, Agent Gregory. I doubt you've experienced anything I would think was beyond belief."

Gavin made a sound that was half-chuckle, half-scoff. "I'm not so sure. Hell, I'm not sure *I* don't think my experiences are beyond belief."

Withers arched an eyebrow. "That sounds serious."

Gavin lifted one shoulder and grimaced.

"But you *do* believe it, Agent Gregory." The doctor leaned forward and gazed into Gavin's face, an intent, probing expression on his face. "I can see that."

"And schizophrenic patients believe in their hallucinations, psychotics believe in their delusions."

Withers shook his head. "You're not delusional. You didn't hallucinate whatever you experienced." He relaxed back into his seat, a gentle smile on his face. "But you know that. You know that whatever it is that has you spooked really happened."

Gavin squirmed uncomfortably, then took a sip of Hydrolite. "You don't know me, Doctor."

Ben Withers chuckled and steepled his fingers in front of him. "Maybe not, Agent Gregory, but I do know people. My childhood required that I build an understanding of how people work, how their minds work. I've been doing it all my life, profiling. I just never knew it."

Gavin took another sip of the foul concoction. "That must've made your professional life easier."

"As a forensic pathologist?" Withers asked with one eyebrow cocked. "Most of my patients didn't have much going on up here." He tapped his temple with his index finger.

Gavin found a grin on his lips and nodded. "Yeah, I would guess profiling the dead is easier than one would think."

Withers nodded, but his grin seemed forced.

"I bet it helps in your high-powered business life."

As his grin faded, the doctor shrugged. "To be honest, I've never found it much of a challenge. People are people, and when it comes to business negotiations, motivations are easy to guess. But that's not something I need to tell you, is it?"

Gavin nodded. "I suppose you're right."

As the pilot came on the intercom to announce their impending arrival at the San Antonio International

Airport, Doctor Withers fished a business card out of his pocket and leaned across the aisle with it. "It was nice to meet you, Agent Gregory. I hope to run into you again sometime."

"You too, Doctor." He pulled out his own business card and handed it to Doctor Withers as he took the man's card.

Withers held up Gavin's card for a moment, then slipped it into his pocket. "My personal contact information is on that card. Feel free to contact me if you ever want to discuss what happened to you. You'll find me a sympathetic ear."

"I…" Gavin glanced down at the man's card. "Thanks, I'll keep it in mind."

Then Withers leaned back in his chair and tightened his seatbelt. "It helps, Agent Gregory. Talking about it. That's something I've learned."

6

Between San Antonio and Odolavesta, TX
Friday, 1:18 pm CST

The tires hummed on U.S. Route 90's hot asphalt, thumping over the rough bits. Gavin drove with single-minded concentration, but he was still aware of the two SUVs and the pickup stalking him. He'd picked them up as he drove away from San Antonio International Airport, two black-on-black SUVs dodging in and out of the surrounding traffic as though they were invisible. They had an "official" air about them, but they didn't appear to be government issue—too fancy, the wrong brand, and too much bling.

Kai, do you have a line on these jokers tailing me? he thought, hoping the man was listening. He didn't know how all this psychic chit-chat worked, didn't know if he had to "establish contact" first, or if he could just think at the fixer. He waited a few minutes, driving with a slight frown of concentration on his face, peering in his mirrors, watching the two SUVs, who, for their part, clearly didn't care if he spotted them or not.

Even with all those distractions to think about, Gavin's gaze was drawn to the well-worn pickup truck behind them all. He supposed it could be an innocent motorist, but his gut said differently.

Kai? He sent the thought with as much oomph as he could muster—though he also had no idea if oomph was required. *Are you out there?*

He eyed the vehicles tailing him—shifting his attention constantly between the three—occasionally thinking at Kai, wondering all the while what good it was to have a psychic over-watch if he couldn't talk to the man without mundane comms. Finally, he tore his gaze away from his mirrors long enough to fish his phone from his jacket pocket and hit the fixer's contact.

As he lifted the phone to his ear, the old pickup accelerated with a cloud of blue smoke and overtook the first of the SUVs. It continued accelerating in the fast lane, its decrepit engine clanging and banging, spitting smoke like a crop-duster, passing the second SUV and closing in on Gavin at a good clip.

It roar-clatter-sputtered by on the left, then swerved in front of him. Tightening his grip on the steering wheel with one hand, Gavin pitched his phone onto the passenger seat, muscles across his upper back and shoulders rippling as he tensed for evasive maneuvers or impact.

Then the righthand blinker on the old pickup flicker-flashed the way old cars did when the electrical system was on its last legs and pulled onto the shoulder, slowing at a sedate pace. As he zipped past, Gavin leaned toward the passenger window, peering at the vehicle's driver. His speed was too great to allow for a good look, but he had the impression of a woman—brown curly hair, a floral print on a black shirt—and then he was past her. He flicked his gaze to the mirrors, hoping for more, just in time to see her crank the wheel to the right and slew the old truck off the blacktop and onto a dirt road heading north.

He flicked his gaze toward the SUVs and arched his eyebrows in surprise. One of them was already braking hard, and the other was slowing as if its driver didn't know whether to continue following Gavin or follow the pickup. After a moment, it, too, went nose-down in a hard brake, then turned aggressively to follow the other SUV through the column of dust raised by the pickup.

Lifting his foot off the accelerator, Gavin dithered a moment, intrigued. He'd assumed he'd been the focus of the two SUVs, but it seemed he might have been a curiosity rather than their focus.

Or maybe he was camouflage. Maybe they wanted the pickup's driver to think they were following Gavin in order to put her at ease until she led them to a point where they had to reveal their true intentions.

He flicked his gaze back over his shoulder, half-turning in the seat, but all he could see was dust hanging in the air. With a shrug, he put his foot on the accelerator pedal again. He had places to go, crime scenes to investigate. Reynold Hall was more important than the strange tails.

7

Gavin sucked his teeth and cocked his head at the deputy. "Deputy Lister, you've seen my credentials."

"I have, sir, but golly gosh, I've got my orders from the sheriff, himself, don't I?" The deputy towered over Gavin—closer to seven feet tall than six and looking as if he'd never passed up a second biscuit at breakfast in his life.

"Do you think my badge is fake? Do you think I made my ID and printed it off at a local office supply? That I laminated it myself with an iron?"

"No, sir, I don't think none of that. It's just the sheriff said no one gets in. I've got to live here, Agent Greg. I've got to—"

"*Gregory*," said Gavin. "Agent Gavin Gregory. You realize the guy abducted from this shithole—"

"Agent Gregory, there ain't no call for language like that."

"—was another FBI agent, right? He and I worked—*work*—together. He's got kids, a family. Why in the hell would you obstruct my investigation?"

Deputy Lister shook his head once, cocked his hip, and spit into the dusty parking lot. "I don't much care for y'all city cops coming down here, spewing swears, talking like y'all ain't never set foot in church. *And*, like I said, the sheriff said *no one* gets in. He didn't say, 'no one but Agent Gregory from the Eff Bee Eye.' Nawsir, he said *no one*. Capiche?"

Gavin froze for a moment, spittle drying in his mouth and throat, and stared at the man. "Why'd you say that?" he demanded.

Lister cocked his head to match his hip. "Ain't I explained it well enough to you, yet?"

"Not that! I mean, why'd you say, 'Capiche?'"

The deputy paused, looking at him like he'd grown a scaly arm out the side of his neck, "Because it means, 'do you understand,' in Italian. Ain't you never seen *The Godfather*?"

Gavin took a half-step closer to the man, staring into his face, switching his hot glare from one eye to the other, then back again. "And there's no other reason?"

"Like *what*?"

"Like someone you talk to a lot uses it?"

The giant man shook his head. "I got to say, Agent Gregory, you ain't makin' a heck of a lot of sense. You—"

"Yeah? I don't much care, Deputy Lister. Answer me!"

"*Dang*, hoss. Settle down a mite."

"And that!" Gavin jabbed his finger at the man's barrel chest. "Why'd you call me 'hoss?'"

Deputy Lister muttered something under his breath, something that sounded a lot like, "head-shrinker," then shook his head. "It's an expression, Agent. Ever hear of 'em? Expressions?"

"But why those particular expressions? Why—"

"It's just how I talk. And if you got a problem with that, I'd sure tell you to keep it to yourself in Odolavesta. More people 'round here talk like I do than like you." He tilted his head to the other side, then gave Gavin a slow blink. "Now, if it's just the same to you, while we're waiting for the sheriff, you can wait in your car. I think you done wore your welcome right out as far as I'm concerned." Lister crossed his thick arms across his chest and set his mouth, staring down at Gavin as if he were nothing more than an unsavory perp.

Gavin stood there a moment, grim-faced, and simmered. He thought of a lot of things to say, a lot of comebacks to hurl at the man, but none of that would help. Judging by the man's expression, *nothing* Gavin said would help. He sighed, giving the deputy one last probing look, then turned and strode back to his car, shaking his head.

He slid behind the wheel, loosening his collar, then started the car and cranked up the air conditioning. In addition to the dust and desert-dry air, Odolavesta was hot, hot, hot. He wished he'd stopped for another bottle of water so he could drink another Hydrolyte, but he'd been in a hurry. Gavin considered a short trip to whatever served the little shit-berg for a convenience store to pick up a bottle or ten, but he discarded the idea half-thought. He didn't want to risk missing his eminence the sheriff and delaying gaining access to Ren's room by another hour or two.

Lister glanced his way, contempt plain on his sunbaked slab of a face. Moving deliberately, he hawked and spat into the parking lot again.

Gavin took a deep breath, closed his eyes, and tried for a Zen-like calm, though he hadn't felt very close to Zen since before his trip to Miami. "Got to stop this," he muttered.

His phone jangled Maddie's ringtone, and he swiped it open and thumbed accept before the second ring sounded. "Hey, Maddie," he said with a sigh.

"What's wrong?" she said. "Did you…"

"No, I haven't found Reynold. I haven't found *anything*, and that's what's wrong."

"I'm no cop, but it's unreasonable to expect every crime scene to yield fruit, isn't it?"

He grimaced, looking at Lister from the corner of his eye. The deputy's gaze was on a loop—looking at the road, scanning to the hotel's small office, then across the road to the desert vista, then at Gavin, then back at the road. "That's just it. I haven't even *seen* the crime scene. I've been denied access until the sheriff gets here." He told her about the confrontation with Lister, then sighed. "I've got to—"

"—get a lock on your Post-Traumatic Fry Disorder? Yeah, you do, but you've already used up your Superman credit this month by surviving Miami. Cut yourself some slack, cowboy."

"I guess."

"And lay off the Fry-isms. Fry uses those phrases because they're a part of our popular culture. People are going to say those things to you from time to time. It doesn't always have to mean something."

"I suppose you're right."

"Could you say that again? But give me a moment, I'd like to record it."

"Smartass."

"You bet. Does that mean you won't repeat it for the recording?"

Gavin chuckled.

"So.…nothing you can do to salvage the deputy's opinion of you?"

He watched Lister's gaze make its ponderous circuit again from the corner of his eye. "I don't think so."

"Then put the big dufus out of your mind. Focus on winning over the sheriff. Screw the deputy."

"Nah. The person I want to screw is farther east."

"Promises, promises, Agent Gregory."

The smile in Maddie's voice was evident to Gavin, and he couldn't stop himself from smiling in return despite the negative emotions generated by his run-in with Deputy Lister. "That's a promise I intend to keep, hon."

"I'm going to hold you to it."

"I was more thinking about holding it to—" Deputy Lister's gaze snapped to the road at Gavin's back, and his own gaze snapped up to his rearview mirror as his mouth snapped shut. A large, emerald-green Cadillac had pulled to a stop on the two-lane blacktop. Its windows were blacked out with a heavy-duty limousine tint that Gavin's vision couldn't penetrate despite the bright afternoon glare.

"Gavin?"

He darted a look at Lister and noted the quirky little grin on the deputy's face. The deep bass throb of the Cadillac's exhaust rumbled in the pit of Gavin's stomach. The car just sat there, oblivious to the milieu developing, the driver not seeming to care he was blocking a state road with his dinosaur of a car—though to be fair, since Gavin had pulled into the lot not a single car *except the Cadillac* had used the road.

"Earth to Agent Gregory? Are you still there, Gavin?"

Gavin heard the note of exasperation in her voice, but most of his attention was devoted to that throbbing, monstrous, ancient vehicle growling away behind them.

His next glance at Deputy Lister informed him that the man's little grin had blossomed into a one-sided grin that bordered on a sneer. The Cadillac's horn blew—three short, sharp blasts—and Gavin twisted his head to stare at the car directly.

"Gavin? Are you there?"

Narrowing his eyes in a vain attempt to penetrate the car's dark tint, Gavin said, "Who the hell are you?"

"If you've forgotten already…" Maddie's exasperation had blossomed into something very close to outright irritation. "What's going on?"

The driver of the emerald-green vehicle revved the engine once, twice, and again, for all the world like some teenage would-be drag racer, torque from the 505 cubic inch big block making the car lunge and buck like a sled dog in the traces. Gavin's free hand left his own steering wheel to flutter down toward his service weapon. "Maddie…"

"What is it?"

The dark green Caddy rolled forward, and the driver cranked the wheel, bumping the big car off the asphalt, through the dusty median, and into the hotel's parking lot, eschewing the paved entrance fifty yards ahead of him. The tires crunched and popped through the gravel and loose dirt at the edge of the lot, and the nose of the car came around to point at Gavin's passenger door.

"Dammit, Gav! Talk to me!"

"I've got… I've got a situation here, Maddie." Gavin turned, watching the Cadillac's ponderous advance across the asphalt. "*Maybe*," he added at a volume just above that of a whisper.

"What do you mean 'maybe?'" Stress sang in Maddie's voice.

"He's just sitting there…" Despite having a clear view of the car's windshield, he couldn't make out the driver.

"Who, Gavin? Who's sitting there?"

"Maddie, I just don't know. There's—" Gavin gave a little cry and jumped at the tap of something metal on the driver-side window. He whirled around, his hand landing on the butt of his Glock, throwing himself a little to the side.

"What is it?" Maddie demanded in a harsh, insistent voice.

Deputy Lister rolled his eyes, shaking his head a little, then showed Gavin the key to the hotel room he'd used to knock on the window. With his other hand, he made that canonical roll-down-your-window gesture.

With a slow blink and a deep breath to both slow his racing heartbeat and shove down the surge of anger that raced through him, Gavin lifted his hand and straightened up in the seat. He twisted his head to look at the green Cadillac, which had come to a rest five feet from his passenger door. The door of the car popped open, and a short, skinny man with a full black beard climbed out, then settled a big gray Stetson over his unruly black hair. His gaze swam toward Gavin's, a creepy little grin surfacing on his face.

"I've got to go, Mads," said Gavin. "The asshole sheriff is here."

"Gavin, remember to play nice."

"Yeah, I know, but these hicks aren't making it easy." His hand went to the door handle. "I'll call you after."

"Okay, Gav. Be *nice*."

Gavin thumbed the disconnect as he opened the door. The guy in the gray Stetson stepped up and held the door open, grinning all the while and stealing surreptitious glances at Deputy Lister. Taking deep breaths and fighting for calm, Gavin stepped out of the rental car and plastered a grin on his face. "You must be the sheriff."

With a widening smile—or maybe a sneer—the man nodded and stuck out his hand. "Red Westral."

Gavin squinted at him, peeking under the brim of his hat.

Westral chuckled. "No, you didn't see it wrong the first time. It ain't red. Red's short for Eldred."

"Agent Gregory, Behavioral Analysis Unit, Federal Bureau of Investigation." He flipped open his badge carrier and handed it over. "I explained all this to your deputy, here."

Sheriff Westral nodded and accepted Gavin's ID, giving it barely a glance and then passing it onto Deputy Lister. He sniffed and lifted his chin.

"I tried to tell him, but he didn't want to listen to the explanation," the deputy drawled.

Red glanced at Lister, who nodded, then turned his gaze back on Gavin, his eyes hardening a little. "And Jonas did exactly as I ordered him to. This ain't Washington DC, Agent Gregory. This here's Odolavesta. And in Odolavesta, the buck stops with me, not with the FBI."

Suppressing a sigh, Gavin cut his gaze back and forth between Westral and Lister, then gave a curt nod. "I get that, Sheriff Westral. It's your court, it's your ball."

Red peered at him from under the wide brim of his Stetson, his expression inscrutable, then nodded once. "Seems like we might just get along then." The sheriff hooked his thumbs into his wide leather belt on either side of his shiny belt buckle, cocked one hip to the side, then froze, staring into Gavin's eyes.

"I hope so," said Gavin. "It's just that we have a missing agent. As I'm sure you can understand, there's a sense of urgency, a sense of exigency."

"Sure, sure," said Westral. "We ain't never lost one of our officers before, but I can imagine how it must make y'all feel."

Gavin couldn't be sure, but he thought he detected a hint of judgment in the man's tone. He sniffed, glanced at Lister, then pointed at Reynold's door. "Then you can imagine how important it is that I examine the scene. I'm sure you understand the motivation to see something with your own eyes, to get a feel for what happened, to *see* it, not have to read about it." He cocked his head to the side. "It's no reflection on you or your department."

Westral threw his head back and laughed at the sky. When he settled a little, he nudged Lister with his elbow. "Hear that, Jonas? It ain't us, it's him."

Jonas cracked a smile that never reached his eyes, then held out the hotel key, letting the dark green diamond dangle from the worn brass ring. He held it for a moment after Gavin grasped the keychain, the smile fading from his lips. "It ain't you, Gregory. It's *him*." He jerked his chin toward Westral, flicking his thumb in that direction as well. "*He* decides."

"I get it, I get it."

With a grunt and a glance at the sheriff, Lister let go of the key, turning his gaze away as if Gavin had disappeared from his mind. "If it's all the same to you, Red, I'll go on down to Millie's and eat my dinner."

Nodding, the sheriff tracked Gavin's progress as he turned and walked toward the hotel room door. Behind him, his dark green Cadillac rumbled and spit stinking exhaust into the evening air. Gavin had the idea the man intended to stand there, staring at the hotel room, keeping Gavin in his sight.

8

Room 19, Odolavesta Resta, Odolavesta, TX
Friday, 7:26 pm CST

Gavin grimaced, almost snarling as he cast his gaze around Reynold's room one more time. It was a wreck—the bedding heaped and torn, the bedside lamps smashed to splinters and shards of glass. The furniture that hadn't been destroyed lay topsy-turvy and helter-skelter, drawers cockeyed in their holes, chair legs pointed at the ceiling. Reynold's belongings were gone, including his Bureau laptop and bag, his clothing—in fact, any sign that Agent Hall had ever been in that room had gone missing.

He couldn't contain a sigh of frustration. There was no sign that anyone had investigated the abduction—none of the telltale marks that a crime scene investigation team had processed the scene, no fingerprint powder smeared on surfaces, no smell of Luminol, nothing. It appeared that the only thing Sheriff Westral had done was locked the door and ordered Deputy Lister to keep everyone out.

Gavin pulled on a pair of nitrile gloves and sifted through the wreckage.

9

Odolavesta Resta parking lot, Odolavesta, TX
Friday, 8:34 pm CST

"Was it everything you hoped it would be?" asked Westral with a sly grin.

"Did you have *anyone* check out the scene?" Gavin demanded in a venomous tone.

The sheriff took a long, slow sniff, treating Gavin to a narrow-eyed cold stare all the while. It was a look Gavin imagined worked well on his deputies, one designed and practiced, a *cultivated* glare. When Gavin didn't react, Red Westral hawked and spat onto the still-hot asphalt—which seemed to be his department's default expression—then looked at the open hotel room door sidelong. "I don't imagine in your fancy training out in Virginia that you teach people to leave a crime scene open to the elements. *Unsecured.*"

Gavin threw up his hands. "What does it matter? You haven't investigated that scene and you seem to have no intention of doing so!" He chopped his hand through the air, ending up pointing at the open hotel room door. "I get that you've got a small department, Westral. I get that you have limited resources, but you haven't had anyone in there. Anyone at *all*! And you kept me out here, cooling my heels for *hours*. I could've called in Bureau crime scene techs from San Antonio or El Paso! I could've called in the Rangers!"

"Hell, Gregory," drawled Westral, "I could've done all them things, too." He glanced at the open door once again. "Simple fact of the matter is, ain't no evidence anyone was abducted in that room. Simple fact is, it looks more like this man *you say* is a federal agent destroyed poor John Hooker's hotel room, then cut out."

"Westral, I *heard* the abduction! I *talked* to one of the—"

"Right, right," said Red. "The mysterious 'Primer' and his—"

"*Primo*," hissed Gavin. "Primo as in number one."

Red hitched his shoulders as though he didn't care a whit. "Like I was saying, ain't no evidence of none of that."

"What about the testimony of an FBI agent? What about the word of the supervisor of the Behavioral Analysis—"

"Ain't know either one of you," said the sheriff.

"You can't be serious!" snapped Gavin.

Westral turned a slow gaze on him, his eyes devoid of any human emotion, his lips pressed into a thin, straight line. "Out here, we rely on what—and *who*—we know. Jonas's word means more to me than yours. Now," he said, holding up his hand in the classic stop pose, "I ain't calling you a liar. All I'm saying is, I *know* Jonas. Known him almost his whole life. I know when he's fibbing to make hisself look better. I know when he's—"

"This is ridiculous," muttered Gavin. "I'm calling the Rangers." He turned and stomped toward the car, feeling the sheriff's gaze on his back the whole time.

"You do that, Agent Gregory," said the sheriff in a bland tone. "See how far you get, then come on back. I'll be here."

Without turning, Gavin said, "Maybe the Rangers *know* the FBI better than you do, Westral."

"*Sheriff* Westral, if you please."

Gavin scoffed and slid into the car, slamming the door behind him. He got out his phone and hit Pete's contact.

"Gavin," said Pete by way of a greeting. "What have you got?"

Gavin chuckled sourly. "What I've got here, Pete, is an asshole of a sheriff and at least one deputy who would rather obstruct me in my duty than help me. We're going to need to get the Rangers involved."

He paused a moment, then said, "It's a rare thing, Gav, for you to find someone you can't work with."

"Yeah, but I found two of them right here." Gavin glanced out the window and found Westral standing where he had been, staring at Gavin from under furrowed brows. "Assholes, the pair of them," Gavin muttered.

"I can call the Rangers, Gavin," said Pete. "And I know you, I know you work hard to get along with people, so please don't take this the wrong way. Are you sure you're ready to be back out there?"

Gavin suppressed a sigh. "Yes, Pete, I am. I'm sure, and I *am* ready to be out here. Besides, Reynold is one of our own, Pete. I can't sit at home while someone else looks for him."

"I understand that, and I appreciate that. And as much as I'm worried about Reynold, I'm also worried about *you*, Gavin."

"Yeah, I know, Pete. I'm drinking my kitty litter and taking care of myself. I promise."

"I know that, Gav. Just the same, I'm going to send you some help from the San Antonio office. A new agent, yes, but someone to watch your back, someone—"

"Pete, this is hardly a time for me to start training an agent. You know new agents are—"

"Michaels is a new agent, Gavin, but with years of law enforcement experience. He was a police chief, even. He knows what to do. Besides, you need the help. Someone to run interference; someone to watch your back."

Gavin sighed and scrubbed his hand through his hair. "This sounds suspiciously like something my wife might have put you up to, Pete."

"It might sound that way, but it isn't."

"Yeah, okay. We're going to need a Bureau CSI team to go through this mess. Can you smooth that over with the Rangers and get them on their way? This asshole sheriff didn't do anything but lock the door. He even said he doesn't believe Reynold was kidnapped, said it seemed more like destruction of private property than an abduction."

"You're kidding?"

"I wish I was, Pete. I wish I was."

Pete's sigh rumbled across the line. "I should've known your assessment of the man would be spot on. All right, let me get started. Anything else?"

"There was… Nah, never mind."

"What is it, Gavin?"

"I would say that it's probably unrelated," said Gavin with a sigh. "But the way things have been going…"

"Sure, sure. Tell me."

"When I left San Antonio, I didn't go alone."

"Kai?"

Gavin shook his head and said, "No, I haven't heard anything from Kai. This was something else. Two black

SUVs—fancy foreign jobs with dark tint and lots of bling—seemed to be following me."

"Seemed?"

"Yeah. There was this other vehicle…a beat-to-shit old pickup truck, a woman driving. It seemed like the SUVs were following me and she was too. She peeled off, though, onto an old dirt road in the middle of nowhere. The SUVs followed her, not even trying to appear inconspicuous, but one seemed unsure whether to follow me or not."

"That may be innocent citizens going about their business."

"Maybe…but it didn't feel that way. I mean, those SUVs braked *hard*, Pete."

"Well, then perhaps it was a private matter. Private investigators harassing someone for a disability insurance company, bounty hunters tracking someone who skipped bail, something like that."

"I guess it could be something like that," said Gavin.

"If Kai had been paying attention, we wouldn't have to guess. I should have insisted that he went with you."

"No, Pete, he was right. He doesn't have to be here."

"Perhaps not, Gavin. But he *does* have to be watching out for you. I've had a mind to give him a tongue lashing."

"I'll call him."

"Well, one of us should. What good does it do to have him on overwatch if he's not watching over you?" Pete's voice had taken on a strident quality that Gavin hadn't heard before. "If he hadn't spoken directly in my mind…"

"Yeah, I know."

"You'll call him, though?"

"I said I would, Pete."

"I know. Forgive an old man his worries."

"You're not that old, boss."

"No? It sure seems that way to me. Especially on days like this."

"We'll find him, Pete." Gavin tried to force as much confidence into his voice as he could. "I will find him."

"Oh, I know that, Gavin. The question is whether you will find him alive."

10

Millie's Table, Odolavesta, TX
Friday, 9:28 pm CST

After hanging up with Pete, Gavin ignored Sheriff Westral's glower as he started the car, put it reverse, and backed out onto the road. As he pulled away, the sheriff was stomping toward him, holding up his hand. Gavin pretended not to see him.

His tires hummed on the reddish asphalt, and he grimaced at the arid scenery on either side of the road. Day-Glo orange barrels and cones were set up along the left side of the road as he passed both the Texas State Parks and Wildlife installation and the US Border Patrol Station on the right.

As he approached the street his GPS told him was named West Waco, he saw a strange combination of rundown prefab buildings, decaying wooden fences, and patio umbrellas. A string of eight pickup trucks and one Jeep were parked along the grass strip between the road and one of the fences. A Pepsi machine was visible above the front fence, standing underneath a crudely made sign that looked hand-painted—red text reading, "Millie's Table" on a yellowing white background atop a resting pole.

Gavin slowed, watching the GPS to see if another restaurant might pop up—something that seemed a little less greasy spoon—but Odolavesta seemed to boast only one hotel and one restaurant. With a sigh, he turned off the road and pulled in next to the Jeep. He killed the engine, then sat staring down at his phone a moment, wondering if he should try to call Kai or leave the man be until he really needed something.

He owed Maddie a call, as well, and he chose her contact instead of Kai's, then got out and walked toward the closest prefab building. He eyed the half-painted building—half tan with orange trim and half white with flaking white trim—and shook his head, wondering how long he'd be up dealing with the aftermath of eating in a place like Millie's Table.

Maddie answered on the second ring. "Gav?"

"Hi, Mads."

"Did you find anything?"

Gavin grimaced and shook his head. It didn't seem to be a door, so he circled around, eyeing the Pepsi machine as he walked by it. "In Reynold's room? Just a mess. The locals don't seem to have much on offer." The patio area was empty—round concrete tables and their umbrellas that would have seemed more at home around the pool, which had a slightly Tiki-bar feel, but no people.

"Besides being hicks and assholes, you mean?"

Gavin chuckled and stopped, turning a half-circle, and trying to spot a way inside. "Yeah, besides that. It seems like the only thing they did was secure the scene. The damn sheriff went so far as to say he didn't believe Reynold was abducted, that the evidence pointed at misdemeanor destruction of private property and cutting out before paying the bill. Can you believe it?"

"In this day and age? Sure. Look at it this way, at least neither the sheriff nor that deputy dude are ghost-demon-vampires."

Behind the half-painted prefab building near the road, another building sat—this one made of steel and painted adobe-tan. A red arrow had been hand-painted with a three-inch brush pointing toward the rear of the property. "And no chirps. Also, no dreams." He began to walk toward the rear of the property, following the red arrow, his shoes scuffing through gravel, the odor of sage and dust and creosote filling his nose. "Although I haven't slept yet, so maybe I better shut up about that last one, or I might jinx myself."

"Yeah, shut up."

Gavin could hear the smile in her voice and grinned in answer. "You like that a little too much, hon."

"Hey, I was just agreeing with you. I can't help it you had a poor choice of words. And…shut up."

"Oh, boy."

"You better believe it. I just opened a can of shut up, and it's too much for me to eat by myself. Sharing is caring, Gav."

Chuckling, Gavin circled around the rear of the large steel building and stood facing someone's backyard. He shook his head, turned, and retraced his steps back to the front prefab building. "This is a one-horse town, Mads, and it seems like it's run by crazy people."

"What now?"

"I'm at this little greasy spoon called Millie's Table, and I can't find a way inside."

"Most people would just use the door," Maddie said.

"You're such a smartass."

"You don't know the half of it, mister."

"After all these years? I think I do." He circled around the back of the prefab building and finally found the door on the narrow side facing the backyard he'd seen before. "Crazy little place," he muttered.

"Trust me, Gav…and trust Frank, who says to tell you, 'you don't know the half of it, buddy.'"

"Frank? Again with the plumber? I haven't even been out of town for a whole day yet, Mads."

"Yeah, I know, but I spent almost an entire week with you. A girl needs a break."

Gavin chuckled and pulled open the door, pausing a moment as the scent of grease and raw meat and Tex-Mex spices assaulted him. "Yeah, but a break with the plumber?"

"Hey, who lays pipe better?"

"Boo! Hiss!"

Millie turned out to be an enormous woman wearing a wraparound apron and standing in front of a commercial cooktop that was separated from the dining by only an old register counter. She gave him a strange look, then motioned at one of the worn tables with a greasy spatula. "Seat yourself."

Gavin surveyed the room, noting the hodge-podge of mismatched tables and the exhausted-looking people who sat around some of them. No one met his eye, though he noted a few glances in his direction. Gavin moved to the table next to the window and sat in an unbalanced chair. "Found my way inside, Maddie. You'd *love* this place."

"Oh, yeah? Fancy French place, is it?"

"Well, I haven't seen the menu yet, so I don't know if the food is French, but it *is* fancy."

"White linen tablecloths?"

Gavin grunted a laugh, looking down at the scarred tabletop. "Maybe once. Thirty or forty years ago. There might even have been red gingham at some point, but right now, the table covers seem to be limited to grime and a little more grime."

"Jenny!" yelled Millie. She darted a glance at Gavin over her shoulder and grimaced. "Damn girl's hardly worth keeping on the payroll."

Nodding to show he heard her, Gavin lifted his empty hand. "Maybe I'll even get a meal at some point tonight," he murmured into the phone.

"Well," said Maddie, "don't order anything that'll make you sick."

A twenty-something woman came bustling in the same door Gavin had used and glanced around, her eyes dull with fatigue or drugs or something else. Her hair was disheveled, and acne dotted her chin and cheeks. She ran her tongue over her dry-looking lips, then fished in the short black apron she wore and pulled out one of those small spiral-bound pads, flipping the bright green cover over toward the back and then going fishing for her pen. When she had it, she glanced at Millie, then approached Gavin's table. "Get you something, mister?"

Gavin moved the phone away from his mouth and smiled at her. "A menu would be nice."

She froze for a moment, her pen held half an inch over the first page in her pad, her eyes going vacant. "Menu?" she repeated in a voice that sounded confused. Her gaze drifted a little aimlessly toward Millie, never quite reaching her.

"For God's sake, girl!" snapped Millie. "Tell him what we serve!"

The woman's cheeks reddened, and she dropped her gaze to the floor. The hand holding the pen drifted, then dropped to her side.

"Mads, my waitress is here, so I'm going to let you go."

"Oh, so she's *cute*?"

"Yeah, Frank's daughter, maybe."

Laughing, Maddie said, "Then I'd better hang up so you can chat her up."

"Love you, Mads."

"Always and forever, you lecherous old jerk."

With a grin on his face, Gavin disconnected the call and slid his phone into his pocket. He half-turned in his seat, giving the waitress his full attention in a wide, sunny smile. "I'm easy," he said. "Give me a cheeseburger, fries, and a Coke Zero, and I'll be a happy camper."

Her gaze drifted to his face and seemed to sharpen a little. "Oh, we got cheeseburgers. Fries are from a bag, not fresh-cut or nothing—we ain't fancy or nothing."

"Neither am I, Jenny," said Gavin.

As he said her name, her gaze locked on his, and she smiled a little. "What's a Coke Zero? Is that like, Diet?"

"It's a Coke with zero calories and zero sugar."

She tilted her head to the side a little, confusion swimming in her eyes. "What's the point of the Coke without no sugar, and how is it different from a Diet Coke?"

Gavin shrugged and lay his hand on the table. "It tastes better than a Diet Coke."

"As good as a regular Coke?"

"Girl! I don't pay you to flirt with my customers."

The girl's shoulders twitched at the sound of Millie's harsh voice, and she snapped her pen up to her pad. "Cheeseburger, fries, Diet Coke. We ain't got none of that Zero. Sorry."

"That's fine," said Gavin as she turned away. "Thanks."

Jenny twitched a look in his direction, punctuated with an unsure smile, then crossed the room and handed the slip of paper to Millie.

The big woman looked at her like she was the dumbest rock in the pile. "Well, I *heard* him, didn't I?" She turned her back on Jenny and reached into a cooler to fetch a premade hamburger patty that she slapped on the grill top. With the same hand that had just touched the raw meat, she reached into a bag to grab his bun, buttered it with a greasy-looking table knife, and slapped it face-down on the little shelf six inches above the cooktop.

Jenny stood frozen in place, her arm extended, the paper with Gavin's order on it held out and shaking a little. After a moment, she started, glanced around, and then shoved the pad, the pen, and the torn-off sheet of paper into the pocket of her apron. She whirled around and walked back outside, letting the door bang shut behind her.

11

Gavin choked down the last bite of his cheeseburger, trying not to grimace. It tasted more of grease than beef—despite the two slices of American cheese and the generous portions of ketchup, mustard, and mayo. In fact, there wasn't much difference in taste between the fries and the cheeseburger if he ignored the mustard and mayo. He swished a mouthful of his warm Diet Coke around his mouth, trying to clear away the taste of old fry oil, of the dirty cooktop, wishing he could wash away the memory of the meal.

As he pushed his plate away, Millie glanced at the door and frowned. "You done?" she asked over his shoulder.

"Yeah," he said. "What do I owe you?"

The door banged open, and a middle-aged couple came inside. Millie glanced their way, nodded, and said, "Evening, Jon. Cecelia."

The man—Jon, Gavin assumed—was average height, carrying an extra pound or two, and had long blond hair. The woman was standing with her back to Gavin but had shoulder-length curly brown hair and wore a black shirt with red flowers emblazoned on it.

"How's business, Millie?" asked Jon.

Millie turned back to her griddle and waved her greasy spatula vaguely at the room behind her. "As you see. The Friday night usual?"

"Yes, please, Ms. Millie," said the woman in a pleasant contralto. She turned, then, to survey the room. Her gaze flicked over most of the tables, and she nodded to a few women, but when she came to Gavin, she froze, and her face drew into an angry moue, recognition dancing in her eyes.

Gavin cocked his head to the side and returned her gaze. He hadn't gotten a good look at her face back on Route 90, but he'd recognize that shirt anywhere. She was the driver of the beat-up old pickup truck.

She narrowed her eyes a moment but then treated him to a slow nod. Her husband came to stand by her side and glanced at her. "He the one?" When Cecelia nodded, Jon gave her a single nod in return, then walked over to Gavin's table and looked down at him, arms akimbo. "Call 'em off. She ain't done nothing."

Gavin leaned back in his chair and cocked his head, flicking his gaze at Cecelia and then returning it to Jon. "I believe I saw your wife driving into town, but I assure you that I have no idea what you're talking about."

Jon rolled his eyes. "We're simple folk, poor folk, but we have a lawyer. Keep harassing her and you'll meet him."

Gavin spread his hands. "I'm not harassing anyone. I'm just here to eat dinner, and I'm done with it, so I guess I'll be on my way."

"The black SUVs!" snapped Jon. "Your hound-dogs! Call them off."

Gavin nodded slowly. "Back on Route 90—where I first saw your wife—there were two black SUVs that followed us out of San Antonio, but I have nothing to do with either of them."

"But you're that Fed… Jonas told me about you. You're in from Washington DC." Cecelia's soft voice floated across the otherwise silent room.

Gavin stole a glance around and found all eyes on him. "Yes, I'm an FBI agent, and yes, I'm the one Jonas Lister must have told you about. But I'm not here about you"—his gaze rested on Cecelia's face for a moment—"and I'm not here about you, either." He flicked his gaze back to Jon's. "Until Millie spoke to you, I didn't even know your names."

Jon arched one eyebrow, his face a study in suspicion.

With a slow nod, Gavin fished out his ID case and presented it to Jon. "Gavin Gregory, Federal Bureau of Investigation. I'm here about the abduction of one of our agents from Odolavesta Resta. Happened just last night. Maybe Jonas mentioned that, too."

Hooking his thumb toward the door, Jon's lips twisted in a half-sneer. "If that's true, then who are them people out in SUVs?"

Gavin glanced at the door, eyebrows arched. "They're outside? Here, I mean?"

Jon nodded. "They was when we came in, anyway. They pulled into the lot next door."

With a quick nod at Jon, Gavin took back his ID case and stood up. "Wait here."

As Gavin strode toward the door, Jon turned to look at his wife, one eyebrow arched.

Gavin pushed out into the warm night air, then navigated through the weird patio area and back out to the street. He turned to the south and walked the fifty yards to the squat concrete building with a reddish asphalt parking lot in front of it and a fenced lot behind. The building was unmarked, but Gavin didn't really care what it was.

His attention was focused on the two black SUVs.

He approached the closest of the two, his ID case in his left hand, already open. As he drew near, the driver of the SUV rolled down the window and grinned at him.

"Well, hello, Agent Gregory," said Ben Withers.

Gavin stopped and narrowed his eyes at the man from the airplane. "What are you doing here? Why are you following the woman in the pickup truck? Or are you following me?"

Ben's grin grew wider for a moment, but the bearded man in the passenger seat leaned forward to stare at Gavin, and Withers nodded, his smile fading as if the man had said something to him. He took a deep breath. "Agent Gregory, I've been dishonest with you."

Here it comes, thought Gavin. *This is where he says he works for the Enquirer or some other rag.* He waited, one eyebrow arched. "Go on, Doctor Withers."

The man lifted his hand from the steering wheel and flapped it back and forth. "Our meeting on the plane wasn't coincidental. The rest is true." He grinned a little. "Mostly."

"Who's that with you?"

"We need to find a place to talk—"

"That will have to wait," said Gavin. "Like I said on the plane, I'm here on official business. I have to get back to work."

"But there are things—"

"Listen, Withers, there's an agent's life at stake here. A guy in my unit."

"We can help—"

"I'm sorry, but you can't. This is an official investigation."

"That's part of what we need to talk about. Remember that company I mentioned on the plane? The name of it is International Datawerkz. It's the software company behind SEMPRe."

Gavin frowned and his eyebrows shot up. "SEMPRe?"

"The Society for Extrasensory, Metaphysical, and Paranormal Research," said the man in the passenger seat.

"The guys with the app? With the what-do-you-call-it…"

Withers smiled. "We call it a human search engine. Yeah, that's us."

Moving slowly, Gavin closed his ID case and slipped it inside his pocket. His gaze snapped back and forth between the two men in the SUV, and he opened his mouth several times, but in the end, he shook his head and closed it without speaking.

"See?" said the man in the passenger seat.

"We *can* help you, Agent Gregory." An expression of earnestness rested on Wither's face.

"What's your name?"

"Ben," said the doctor, while at the same time the passenger said, "Benny."

Gavin cocked his head to the side, an unbelieving smile dancing on his lips. "I'm supposed to believe you're both named Benjamin?"

"My friend…misspoke."

There it is again…that hesitation, that little pause, his tell that he's about to lie, thought Gavin. He leaned his head farther to the side in order to get a better look at the passenger. He was thin with a beard and dark shoulder-length hair, though gray was making its appearance amidst all the brown. The man met his gaze with something that seemed like amusement to Gavin. His eyes were…*strange*…too intense, too *knowing*. "Did he, now?"

Withers nodded once. "He did. He…does that from time to time. It's an artifact of the childhood trauma."

"I see," said Gavin. "The same trauma you experienced?"

It was Wither's turn to take a protracted moment to stare at Gavin, then he gestured toward his friend. "This is Tobias Benjamin. And that's why he sometimes tells people to call him Benny—the last name, see? He's one of those friends I mentioned back on the plane."

"Ah, one of the brain trust. One of the men behind the SEMPRe idea."

Tobias issued a slow nod, his gaze flickering to Ben Withers.

Gavin glanced at the dark sky and squinted. "SEMPRe…International Datawerkz…what is it that I can't quite remember about your company, your…community?"

Ben Withers turned his attention back to Gavin, his gaze intense. "We really can help you, Agent Gregory.

And not just with processing whatever it was that happened to you."

Gavin snapped his fingers, grinning, and dropped his gaze to meet Ben's. "I've got it! There was trouble a few years back? Something with Abaddon and one of your executives? Joe Steves? Something like that anyway."

Ben nodded and looked down at the asphalt between them. "Joe Stephens. Abaddon and an accomplice kidnapped him." Withers shrugged without raising his gaze. "We managed to save Greg that day, but it led to…"

"Something with your chief of security?" The memory of the incident, and the violence that followed it, came flooding back, but Gavin didn't let on.

Withers frowned and slouched back into his seat. "Scott Lew—er, Louis Scott. Yes. We…" He pursed his lips. "That night…when we saved Joe, I… We…" He shook his head. "Someone gave us the key to a mystery we'd been working on. Intel on a…woman…named Brigitta. She had a cabal of…serial killers…in a town called Oneka Falls. We went to…confront…her and her goons." He closed his eyes, and his voice dropped to a whisper. "That decision cost Scott his life."

Each hesitation, each deliberate pause, set Gavin's internal lie detector to squalling. Each phrase that came after one of those pauses seemed like a Halloween mask—something held together with cheap elastic, that looked good from a distance, but was cheap and shoddy up close—and the flip-flopping on Louis Scott's name felt…important, though he couldn't say why. And when he first spoke of the kidnapping, he'd said, "*We managed to save Greg that day.*" He narrowed his eyes. "A town full of serial killers? I would have heard something about that."

The doctor shook his head. "They had…accomplices…that helped keep things quiet. One of them was the Oneka Falls town manager." He lifted his gaze to stare out the windshield, and his eyes took on that unfocused, thousand-yard stare typical of woolgathering. "That's where most of us grew up. My friends, I mean. The board of SEMPRe. We…our childhood was…" He shook his head again and sighed. "Listen, this is a long story, and not one I can tell you here."

"You know I'm FBI," said Gavin in a quiet voice. "Why would you tell me *any* of this? It sounds like you and your friends went to war on this Brigitta woman and her crew, and vigilantism is against the law."

Ben chuckled at that and turned his gaze to meet Gavin's. "Why tell you?" A one-sided grin twisted his lips. "You need help. You need our help."

The hair stood up on the back of Gavin's neck, and he shook his head a little. "Why is it everyone thinks I need their help?"

"I can't speak for everyone, but SEMPRe wants to help you, Agent Gregory, because you have a"—Ben Withers glanced around the empty parking lot, then leaned out the window of the SUV and dropped his voice to a stage-whisper—"demon problem. You've had it since that run-in with The Smith in Manhattan, haven't you?" He leaned back and cast an assessing look at Gavin's face.

Gavin knew he should scoff or deny it or do anything but sit there dumbfounded, but his brain wouldn't engage. He couldn't think up a single protest.

"Have some more water," said Withers, grabbing a bottle and holding it out the window toward Gavin. "You look pale." He held the water out the window with one hand and mimed taking a drink with the other. After Gavin had taken a swallow, Ben leaned close once more. "And you've attracted the attention of something called the Program. Psychic assassins," he whispered.

"How do you know all that?" asked Gavin.

"Human search engine, remember? SEMPRe monitors the news, the Internet, certain organizations, the dark net... We look for specific keywords, specific data, and extrapolate from them. And some of my friends are gifted...researchers. Your face just now tells me we guessed right on both counts."

"Guessed..." muttered Gavin.

"They are informed guesses, to be sure," said Ben, "but still guesses."

"And they sent you out alone—your friends, the board of SEMPRe—to feel me out, to see if I'm open to…what? Joining you?"

Withers grinned and shook his head. "First of all, I'm here to make sure *you* weren't possessed by the thing you ran into in Manhattan. Good news, you aren't. Number two, obviously I'm not alone." He hooked his thumb toward Tobias Benjamin, then he waved his hand wider to encompass the second SUV. "Most of them are here with me."

Gavin took a step to the side and peered at the other SUV. An extremely tall man sat wedged behind the wheel of the second black vehicle. He lifted a hand and gave Gavin a little wave.

"That's Joe Stephens, the man Abaddon kidnapped," said Ben. He turned and pointed at a beautiful woman sitting in the passenger seat. "That's Sh—Bertie Benjamin."

Gavin nodded at her, and she smiled in a way that made him think of Maddie and treated him to a slow nod. "This is the whole crew? The four of you are the board of SEMPRe?"

"No," said Tobias with a shake of his head. "There are others, but they're busy."

Gavin turned and pinned Withers to his seat with his best FBI agent stare. "What makes you an expert at determining if I'm a demon or possessed by one? Are you supposed to be a priest?"

Ben chuckled at that and shook his head. "That's another long explanation that requires more privacy than we have in Odolavesta, but I'll say this: we were all exposed to something as children that left most of us with unique gifts. Mine is sensing demons, possessions." He chuckled. "Actually, I can see them, if they've woven an illusion around their true form or if they've simply possessed a person."

Gavin lifted his eyebrows and gave his head a little shake. "Six months ago, I'd have called the men in white coats if anyone said something like that to me."

"But not now."

Wither's tone made it clear that it wasn't a question, but Gavin nodded anyway. "Not now, no." He looked Withers in the eye. "Tell me something, though. If you can…*see* past the illusions, can see a demon in possession of someone, why are there four of you? Why not just drive by and look at me while I'm mowing the lawn? Or—"

"We did try. You haven't left the house since you got back from Miami."

Gavin wagged his head from side to side. "Fair enough. But why not just you?"

Ben nodded as if he'd expected the question at some point. "We've learned never to do things alone. Not since Greg got himself kidnapped."

"Greg?" Gavin asked, quirking his eyebrow. "That's the second time you called the man you said was Joe Stephens by that name."

Withers ducked his head, but not before Gavin saw him frown. He gestured at the other SUV. "We call him Greg sometimes. Inside joke."

"Uh-huh," said Gavin in a tone that said, "tell me another one, why don't you?"

"You said on the plane that you wished you could deny the supernatural existed. What changed?" Ben asked without looking up.

"That's a story that requires more privacy than this parking lot affords us," said Gavin, grinning slightly at turning the tables on the enigmatic doctor.

"Your own abduction. In Manhattan."

Gavin hesitated, treating the man to a narrow-eyed stare. "It wasn't so much an abduction as a surrender. She had my wife."

"The Smith was a woman? I missed that fact in the news coverage. That's rare, a wom—"

Gavin shook his head. "I misspoke. *He* had my wife. He'd kidnapped her from—"

"Your home at 1289 Welcrest Drive in Minnieville, Virginia." Withers face twisted with a small smile.

Stiffening, Gavin glared at the man.

"We can teach you how to hide your address better," said Withers in a mild voice. "Among other things." After a staring contest that lasted almost a minute, Withers nodded. "Go on with your story."

Gavin stood for a moment longer, staring at the man through narrowed eyelids. He sensed deception from Withers but not about the offer to help. "He took her to use as bait, and to motivate me to kill for him."

"And what about that changed your mind about the supernatural?"

"Let's just say I saw through The Smith."

"Ah, you saw the demon, then," said Withers with a nod. "And have you seen others since?"

Gavin lifted the water bottle to his lips, to give himself a moment. He took a mouthful and swallowed hard, then looked Withers in the eye and nodded.

"We thought as much. Something to do with The Bogeymen?"

Gavin treated the man to another narrow-eyed stare.

"What?" His expression slackened a moment, then he nodded. "Adeline d'Clara. I get it."

"How do you know that? *How do you know her*?" demanded Gavin.

"Benny told him," said a voice from the cover of darkness around the side of the building.

Gavin frowned at the dark-skinned man who came around the corner, his gaze locked on Tobias Benjamin's. He waved at the SUV. "I let them scan you a little, but I was here, I would have cut either of them to pieces if they'd tried anything more invasive." The man flashed a smile at Gavin.

Withers looked shocked, his gaze darting first to Tobias, then to the dark-skinned newcomer, but Gavin's frown turned into a wide smile.

"You're not the only one with friends," said Kai Washington, turning to look at Ben. "It's okay, Gav. These people are on the up and up—*mostly*. And better yet, the Program doesn't even know they exist—which is a feat unto itself." He cocked his head to the side. "But Toby's doing it again. They didn't fight a town of serial killers, they fought a town full of things like Glacadairanam. Parasites that—"

"Toby? Who's Toby?" asked Gavin.

Kai pointed at the man who'd identified himself as Ben Withers, and said, "His name is Toby Burton." He pointed at the bearded man. "Benny Cartwright." He flicked his finger at the extremely tall man driving the other SUV. "Greg Canton." He twisted his head and smiled at the beauty in the passenger seat. "That's Shannon Cartwright née Bertram. If you didn't catch the name, she's Benny's wife." He bunched his brows. "That's interesting," he murmured, then a spasm of concentration flicked across his face as Kai stared at Shannon Bertram. "That's a neat trick. She can make you see what she wants you to see. I've never seen that before." He frowned with concentration, and the physical characteristics of the four SEMPRe board members changed. The woman was still a knockout, but her hair was a different color, and her husband had far more gray in his hair than he'd appeared to have before, and his hair was neater, more clean-cut. The man who'd introduced himself as Ben Withers now appeared older, with dark hair parted on the side and dark, penetrating eyes. Greg was still way too tall for the size of the SUV but was now blond and blue-eyed.

Gavin turned his gaze on the doctor and gave him a single shake of his head.

"Sorry," said Toby Burton. "Old habits die hard. And if your nightmare is anything like what we experienced, you'd be careful who you shared your real identity with, too."

"Then it's Burton? For real this time?"

Toby nodded. "For real. Toby Burton, at your service."

"And the other stuff? The pathologist thing? The software company? SEMPRe?"

"All that's on the level," said Kai. He cocked his head at Toby, then frowned. "If anything, he minimized the trauma these people have experienced."

Toby gave him a wary glance, then flicked his gaze toward Benny.

"I can help them—him and Greg—to develop their power, but right now, neither one stands a chance against me," said Kai. He glanced back at Shannon. "I can probably help her, too, but I have to understand what she's doing first."

"Benny can help you there," said Toby. He shook his head and narrowed his eyes at Kai. "What are you?"

Kai nodded once. "I understand what you're thinking, given your experience with Herlequin, LaBouche, and Brigitta, but I'm just a human. A man who escaped from the Program. I escaped both the physical constraints and the psychic ones. I'm a teletechnitic—a fixer. That means I can see into people's minds, both the physical brain and the consciousness. I can sense other psychics, and to this point, I can sense what they are doing." He stared at Toby a moment, then shook his head. "I have no idea what to call what you can do. The Program has no analog."

Toby nodded as if strangers said things like that to him every day. "Does it work with demons? Your fixer-thing?"

Kai's lips stretched in a lop-sided smile. "I'll tell you after I meet one."

Burton's gaze flicked toward the other SUV. "Greg says to stop being disingenuous. He says you've met Fry, and that guy has to be a demon."

Kai's eyebrows arched, and he flicked his gaze toward the tall man, then nodded. "Interesting," he murmured. "He shouldn't be able to read past my shields—his psi's too low."

With a chuckle, Toby leaned back and lay his head against the headrest. "I think you'll find a lot about Greg is surprising."

Kai gave the tall man a long look. "Yes, I think you're right. When does Mike arrive?"

"Mike?" asked Gavin.

"Greg's husband," said Toby. He cocked his head a little and arched one eyebrow at Gavin.

Gavin shrugged while meeting the man's stare dead-on. "If you're waiting for me to get all squeamish or something, you might as well stop. People are people, and they love who they love." He glanced at Greg, and the tall man smiled and gave him a small nod.

"He's a cop," said Kai.

Toby chuckled. "He's not a cop—at least, not anymore. He just graduated from Quantico." He turned an amused gaze on Gavin. "He used to be the police chief in Oneka Falls."

Gavin grinned a little, though he felt a little queasy. "Let me guess. He had himself transferred to the San Antonio office."

Toby made a gun of his fingers and shot Gavin with it. "In the Bureau, he is known as Richard Michaels. His real name is Mike Richards, and I've known him all my life." He nodded his head toward Benny. "And so have Benny and Shannon."

"How did you arrange it? How did you get him assigned to me?"

We have our ways, said a voice in his head. A voice that didn't belong to Kai.

Gavin couldn't stop the shocked expression from exploding across his face, but he managed not to gasp or anything melodramatic. His gaze found Kai, his brows furrowed, but the fixer only nodded. "Someone said 'we have our ways' in my head." Again, Gavin cut his eyes to Kai's, but the fixer only shrugged.

"You should be used to it."

"I'm used to *you* doing it," murmured Gavin.

Toby grinned but seemed a little exasperated as he nudged Benny's bicep. "He does that. I told him it's rude, but he forgets. He doesn't mean anything by it. It's just 'efficient' to his way of thinking." He dropped his gaze away from Gavin's. "He spent a lot longer inside than I did. He spent a long time pretending to be me, pretending to be crazy, and from a very early age— eleven, that's when we…" A shudder rattled through him, and he shook his head in its wake. "He was sort of my cover, so I could go out into the world, under the radar, so to speak. He never really learned social graces, and he's had to cram it all in in the last few years."

"Yeah, I get that, but having people rummage around in my *cabeza* is a bit of a sore subject."

"Sure, because of Adeline d'Clara. I get it." Toby nodded and cut his gaze toward Benny. "He'll tone it down. I'd tell him to cut the shit out, but...." He shrugged, wearing a wry grin. "I haven't been able to make an impression so far, and I've known him since we were in grade school."

"You said he spent longer inside." Gavin shifted his gaze from Benny to Kai and then to Toby. "Juvie? Prison?"

"No, he spent a lot of time in a mental hospital. *We*. We both spent time in the nuthatch. It's not something I ever want to repeat."

"Because of the childhood trauma you talked about?" Gavin treated him to another probing glance, and Burton smiled sadly.

"What?"

"You sort of remind me of Scott. That was his real name, our head of security. Scott Lewis. He was a state trooper." Toby dropped his gaze. "He had that same kind of no-nonsense stare like he could look right through you."

"Oh. Sorry."

Burton waved it away. "It's not your fault."

"Necessary evil in my line of work," said Gavin.

Benny shrugged. "It's a tool. You use it to get what you need. No one begrudges you that, Gav." Gavin flashed a look at him, and Benny pulled his head back. "It's what Maddie calls you, right? Maddie and Pete?" When Gavin frowned, Benny winced. "Too much? I always do that. Toby tells me I have to learn to stop, but I spent so much of my life *hiding*—hiding what I could do, hiding who I was…" He shrugged once more. "It's all…*right there*. It's like a neon sign. I can't help but read it."

Waving his hand at Kai, Gavin flashed a smile at the man. He didn't know why, but he couldn't help but like him. "It's nothing. Well, I mean it's *something*. Something I'm not used to." It was Gavin's turn to shrug. "And to be honest, every time someone besides Kai has done something like that to me, it hasn't been a good thing." He glanced at Kai and offered him a quick grin.

Benny followed his gaze and frowned. "He's not really there, you know."

"What do you mean? He's right there." Laughing, Gavin pointed at Kai, who only smiled like the Sphinx.

Benny shook his head. "No, Kai's in Ohio. That's an astral projection. He's only making us think he's here in person, that he's solid."

"Astral projection?"

"Yeah," said Benny with a nod. "The image you see is something Kai manufactured. Like an illusion, but that's really him. I mean, that's what he really looks like."

Gavin glanced at Kai and raised his eyebrows. "Yeah, I've seen him…in person, I guess." He frowned and bunched his eyebrows. "At least, I *think* I have."

You have, sent Kai. *In Miami. That was my corporeal form.* As the man's voice sounded in his mind, what appeared to be a solid human body became translucent, ghostly.

"He said—"

"I know." Benny waved at Toby, then at the other vehicle. "He's broadcasting so we can all hear."

"Oh, I see." Gavin couldn't recall a simple phrase ever being so far from the truth. "But I do want an answer to my question."

Toby arched one eyebrow at him.

"How did you get Richards assigned to this case? Assigned to me?"

"Ah, that," said Toby. "SEMPRe has…friends. People in—"

"You're a terrible liar, Toby," said Gavin. "You do this pause, this hesitation, every time you're about to lie. Do you know that?"

Toby pursed his lips, looking for all the world like he was trying to suppress a smile. "Do I?"

Gavin gave him a firm nod. "You do. It sets off my alarm bells."

Losing his fight to suppress his grin, Toby nodded. "I'll keep that in mind." Beside him, Benny's grin stretched from ear to ear.

Feeling as though he were the butt of some joke, Gavin frowned.

"SEMPRe has supporters in our government," said Toby. "People that we've *helped* in the past few years. People we've left with a good impression of us, of our skills."

"People you saved from the supernatural? From ghosts?" asked Gavin with a sour smile.

"Some of them," said Benny without a hint of a smile. "Others…" He shrugged.

"What else does SEMPRe do besides watch for ghosts and demons?" Gavin scoffed and rolled his eyes. "I can't believe I just said that."

Toby chuckled, then shrugged. "It's just like anything else, Gavin—can I call you Gavin?"

"Why not?" said Gavin.

"It's just like anything else—the novelty of the jargon will wear off. It will start to feel more natural."

Gavin lifted one shoulder in an uncomfortable shrug. "You said you took my flight to check me out, that you have friends that got Mike assigned to this investigation. But…"

"But Hall was just abducted last night," said Toby, lifting one hand to tick points off on his fingers, "and we followed the woman inside instead of you earlier today."

Gavin nodded.

"Besides your experience with your personal demon, do you—"

"Demons. Plural. The one in Manhattan and Fry."

Toby nodded slowly. "Besides your experience with your personal demons, are you aware of any other paranormal activity?"

Gavin shrugged and waved a hand at Kai's ethereal form.

Chuckling, Toby said, "See what I mean about the jargon?" When Gavin didn't join his laughter, the man sobered. "I'm so used to this…psychic thing, but it doesn't even seem paranormal to me anymore. It just seems…*normal*."

"What other kinds of activity are…"

"Real?" asked Benny, and Gavin nodded. "Most of the monster-myths we looked into trace back to the demons we fought in Oneka Falls, but not all."

"And then there are the human activities," said Toby with a grim frown.

"Human activities?" Gavin thought about it a moment. "SEMPRe tracks cults?"

"Yes, some of them," said Toby. "The ones that aren't just scams, that aren't just teenagers trying to get laid.

That's why we're here." He arched an eyebrow at Gavin. "Have you ever thought about the name of this town?"

"Odolavesta? What about it?"

"A strange name, don't you think? It sounds Spanish, which makes sense for a small town near the Mexican border. *La vesta* means 'the dress' I think, but '*odo*' means ear, so that doesn't make a lot of sense."

Benny pulled out his cell phone and tapped on it for a few seconds. "Ah! It means 'I heard her.'"

Gavin quirked a grin at him.

"What? I translated it. I was curious."

"'I heard her,' though?'" said Gavin dubiously. "That doesn't make much sense for the name of a town."

"Google Translate," said Benny, lifting his phone and giving it a shake. "Though I'm not sure since if I reverse the look up, I get a different translation. *La escuché*," he said. He frowned down at his phone a moment, then tapped a little more. "Maybe it's not *odo la vesta*," mumbled Benny, slashing his hand through the air after each Spanish word. "Maybe it's *o de la vesta*?"

Gavin shrugged with one shoulder and quirked an eyebrow at Toby, who only smiled.

"That means 'or from the dress,' right? Or maybe it's not *la vesta*. Maybe it's from *la vestía*."

"*Anyway*," said Toby. "This town is the focal point for a wide swath of cult-like activity, though it could be attributed to criminal activity, I suppose." He gazed up at Gavin. "Oneka Falls shared the same distinction."

"The murders Reynold was here to investigate," said Gavin.

"The *sacrifices*," said Benny dropping the hand holding his phone to his lap and gazing at Gavin with an uncomfortable intensity.

"Well, I don't—"

Benny hitched his shoulders up and down, rapid-fire. "I do." He turned his gaze down to his lap and tapped at his phone screen again. "*Odo la bestia*?" he murmured, clicking away.

"I don't really care what it means," said Gavin. "Know anything about someone called 'Primo?'"

"That means 'first' in Latin?" grunted Benny.

Gavin shrugged. "I guess. It's used like a name or a title."

Burton frowned. "Nothing off hand, but I can have Benny start a couple of researchers on it right away."

"On it," said Cartwright, though he didn't stop his fiddling with the phone.

Gavin watched him a moment, then quirked his eyebrows at Toby.

"He's already started his two best researchers," said Toby. "He doesn't need a phone to communicate, remember?"

Gavin nodded.

"Does this Primo have something to do with your missing agent?"

"Ren—Reynold—was closing in on the unsub responsible for all those bodies dumped in the desert. In fact, he'd found a good lead and was trying to follow it up. This Primo and four of his friends abducted him while he was on the phone with me."

Toby gave a low whistle. "Did they know he was a Fed?"

Gavin nodded. "Took him right out of his hotel room."

"In San Antonio?"

"No," said Gavin with a shake of his head. "He was staying at the Odolavesta Resta."

"Mike is on his way," said Toby with a brisk nod, "but he's not the only one who can help you. We all have our gifts, and my gut says that before all this is over for you, you'll need help from each one of us."

"I appreciate that, but I'm an FBI agent. Mike is too, so I can accept his help, but…" He hitched his shoulders up and down. "You can help with the information, you do the research, what your company is set up to do, but you're not trained, not equipped to—"

"Let me explain our *other* capabilities, the full extent of what we can offer you, Gavin," said Toby. "We have experience fighting these…entities. Fighting them and *beating* them. We have techniques that—"

"All this goes back to your…*interaction* with this Brigitta woman?"

And more, said Benny in his mind. *Toby took care of a lot of demons* all by himself. *Law enforcement officer or not, he can help you, Gav.*

I agree, sent Kai. *The guy figured out how to take on the things they called demons one-on-one and how to take them out. Over sixty of them.*

Gavin sent a probing gaze at Toby. "Kai just told me you…uh…took on over sixty…uh—"

"Demons," said Toby with a firm nod. "I fought sixty-one of them before I remembered Oneka Falls."

After a slow nod, Gavin said, "Fought…and took them out."

Toby shrugged. "Well, that was kind of the point."

"You killed them."

A lopsided grin emerged on Toby's face. "The FBI agent in you is showing, Gavin. Besides, I didn't kill them. Not really. I sent them home."

"Home? To Hell?"

"I asked Lily—" He snapped his teeth together and squeezed his eyes shut, an expression of misery dancing across his features.

Gavin gave him an assessing glance. "That's your ex-fiancé?"

Benny frowned and turned his gaze on Toby. "She was the demon behind it all," he murmured. "Without her, none of it would've happened. She wasn't his fiancée."

Toby sucked in a deep breath and let it sigh out. He lifted both hands and scrubbed his face. "She was both."

"But she—"

"Benny, she was *both*! She was the first of them, the best of them. Her passage to our realm allowed the others to come, to follow behind her, but she didn't have that much to do with them. She lived her life, they lived theirs."

"But fiancé? You barely—"

"You weren't there, Benny. You don't know everything. Lily took me… When she teleported me away… We lived in the desert for…" Toby covered his eyes with his hand. "I can't explain it to you. It was something you'd have to experience, something you'd have to *live*."

Benny stared at his friend for the space of a few breaths, then nodded. "I didn't know you considered her…" He shrugged.

Toby slashed his hand through the air in front of him. "It doesn't matter. She's gone. I-I-I had to…*choose*. She's not coming back."

Gavin couldn't be sure, but based on the man's tone, he thought he might choose differently if he had the opportunity to do it over again. "I need to know your story—all of your stories—but I don't have time for that right now. I'm on the clock, here." He shook his head and shrugged. "Hell, it's probably too late, Ren is probably dead, but I have to *try*. I've got to do everything in my power to find him, to *save* him."

Eyes still closed, hand still covering his face, Toby took a shuddering breath. "Yeah. To all of that. But, Gavin, *let us help*." He dropped his hand and turned his red-eyed gaze on Gavin. "It's what we do. It's all we do. Fight…evil, I guess." He dropped his gaze to his lap and took another shuddering breath. "It's all I have left."

In the passenger seat, Benny's face crumpled a little, and he shook his head, resting his hand on Toby's shoulder. "No, it's not, Toby. You have us."

"I know you have…these experiences," said Gavin slowly. "I believe you, but—"

"I thought you didn't know them? I thought you didn't know nothing about all this?" Jon's voice grated from behind the fence surrounding the patio belonging to Millie's Table. "You almost had me, lawman. You almost got me believing you, but I knew right off there was something about you I couldn't trust."

Gavin turned toward the fence. "I didn't lie to you, Jon. I met these people today. They aren't FBI."

"Sure thing, lawman. I suppose I'll just have to take you at your word."

Gavin glanced at Toby and lifted his eyebrows. *Why were you following them*? he asked silently.

They are part of it, Benny sent. *The cult.*

"Jon—"

"Save it, lawman. Y'all just stay away from me and Cece! You hear me?"

Cece… Gavin tensed. Part of the last call Reynold had made replayed in his mind at hyperspeed. "*Find it, Cece,*" Primo had said multiple times. Even Gavin had used her name. "Cece? You were there, right? At the Odolavesta Resta?"

"Stay away or you'll get what's coming to you all the faster. Hear me, now, lawman! All y'all will get it soon enough."

With a grave nod, Gavin pulled his Glock and walked toward the fence. "I hear you, Jon, but why put it off. Start with me. Start now." His voice crackled with authority, with his ire.

Behind him, Benny gasped. *Don't say that*!

Gavin reached the fence, Glock held at the ready, and peered over its top, but Jon was already gone.

12

Gavin followed the two black Mercedes north on US Highway 385, then turned west and continued down First Street. The town of Aeonia, Texas wasn't much bigger than Odolavesta, and by the look of it, the amenities wouldn't be much better, but Benny had insisted that Gavin stay somewhere outside Odolavesta's town limits—*anywhere* outside the town limits. Since the crew from SEMPRe already had reservations at the Aeonia Motel & RV Park, and Aeonia being a small town out in the middle of nowhere, it made sense to check if they had vacant rooms. It turned out they did.

For his part, Gavin thought it nice to be in a big group of people instead of the lone FBI agent in the hotel for a change. He pulled his crappy rental into a space between their vehicles and got out, nodding at Benny and Toby and continuing around to the rear of his own car to get his suitcase. Though the two towns were geographically close, Gavin thought the air in Aeonia seemed cleaner. Fresher, maybe, and at nearly midnight, the oppressive heat had faded away, and he found it…pleasant.

The tall man from the other SUV walked over to him and held out his hand. "Greg Canton," he said. After nodding toward Benny, the beautiful woman ambled over. "And this is Shannon Cartwright, Benny's wife."

Taking the man's hand and nodding at Shannon, Gavin introduced himself.

"We have something in common," said Shannon. She nodded at Greg. "All three of us."

"Oh yeah?" asked Gavin. "What's that?"

Greg nodded, a grave smile and solemn expression on his face. "The three of us have all been kidnapped by human demons. Serial killers." He tapped his chest with his thumb "Abaddon." He jerked his chin at Shannon. "Owen Gray." He looked at Gavin. "The Smith."

Gavin frowned but nodded. "In my case, that human designation may not apply. The Smith was possessed. In all the various iterations."

"That's okay," said Shannon. "I was kidnapped by Owen Gray *and* Brigitta, and she's anything but human."

"And whether or not The Smith can be called human or demon or…what is it? A wraith child? *Wrath child*?"

"Yeah—wrath child, that's what it called itself, a wrath child. If you want to know what that is, though, you're out of luck because I have no idea."

Shannon shrugged, grinning. "It's a good thing you just made friends with the people that run the most powerful paranormal research organization in the world."

Gavin smiled, liking her already. "I think I like you, Mrs. Cartwright."

"Right back at you, Mr. Gregory." Then she smiled, and it was as if she were the sun itself.

Maddie's going to love her, Gavin thought.

Greg bounced his gaze back and forth between them for a moment, grinning. "Oh! Mike said to tell you that he'll be here bright and early tomorrow morning. There's a knot of red tape in San Antonio, evidently, but he said he'll get it sorted out."

"That's your husband, right? Mike Richards?"

Canton colored and looked a little uncomfortable. "Yeah, though his FBI ID will show a different name. Richard Michaels," he said and chuckled. "And we…" His blush deepened a little.

"I already told your two friends, Greg, who you marry, and who you love, isn't my business. You don't have to hide anything from me."

Greg nodded but still ducked his head. Shannon slid her cool hand into the crook of his elbow. "Come on, Greg, honey. We'll let Gavin get settled."

"It was nice to meet both of you," said Gavin. He bent to pull his suitcase out of the cheap little car's trunk, and when he straightened, he found Greg's gaze on his own.

"You're right," said Greg as he turned his gaze on Shannon. "I think Maddie will love her, too."

"Um…"

"You'll get used to it," said Shannon. "They all say it's more efficient, we don't even think about it, force of habit, blah, blah, blah." She flapped her hand, first at Greg, then at Benny. "But they can't fool me. They just like to show off." She grinned up at Greg, and the tall man chuckled as they walked away.

Toby came striding out of the Aeonian Motel & RV Park's office and headed straight for Gavin, holding out a room key card. "We're in 1402, 1403, 1405, and 1406. They gave you 1408 so we can be close together since 1404 and 1407 are taken for the weekend."

Gavin glanced down at the key card. "Thanks, but I'll need to check-in for myself. FBI regs."

With a devil-may-care grin, Toby shrugged. "SEMPRe's treat, no FBI regs to deal with."

"Again, thank you, but I can't accept that."

"Loosen up, Gav," said Toby. "You are among friends. The FBI won't care that we paid for your room." He pushed the card into Gavin's hand.

"Well…" Gavin looked down at the rectangle of plastic. "I really should—"

Good grief. He's not going to let you say no, so you might as well come to grips with it, Benny said in his mind, and Toby chuckled.

He couldn't really say why he was objecting, so Gavin shrugged and grinned at Toby. "Well, thanks. I guess I'll be having thirteen filet mignons for a midnight snack."

Laughing, Toby slapped him on the back. "We all have our vices, Gavin, and if you can eat six and a half pounds of beef, more power to you. Personally, I'd rather have a beer or two."

"Me, too, to tell the truth. Did they say if the rooms have refrigerators?"

Toby nodded. "Water."

"Kitty litter," said Gavin with a laugh.

"Right," said Toby with an answering grin. "But yes, there are in-room refrigerators. You go get settled in, I'll run down to the—"

"Nope," said Gavin shaking his head. "I can get it—"

"Christ! Both of you go, so Benny will shut up!" yelled Shannon from the door of room 1405.

"Say, why do the rooms all start with fourteen? This joint doesn't even have a second floor, let alone a fourteen."

Toby shrugged and gestured at the door to Gavin's room. "I didn't ask. But it's probably some obscure movie reference. Put your stuff up, and let's go get that water. I'll drive."

13

Kwik Mart, Aeonia, TX
Friday, 11:53 pm CST

Toby wheeled the SUV into a space in front of the convenience store's double glass doors, then opened his door and got out. "So how did you end up so dehydrated?"

Gavin felt his cheeks go hot. "I…" He glanced at Toby, then sighed. "This is part of what might cause people to look at me like I'm insane."

Toby nodded, then looked at the night sky. "It's okay. I won't think that."

Gavin swallowed and dropped his gaze. "On my last two cases"No judgments here, Gavin."

"They *were* dreams. I mean I was asleep when they happened, but…"

"But they were also true." Toby kept his gaze on the stars above their heads.

Gavin winced but nodded.

"Tell me about your true dreams. Tell me how dreams led you to dehydration."

Gavin pursed his lips and shook his head once. "That's a story for another time." He looked around the dark town, seeing no one but unable to dispel the feeling of being observed. "Another place."

"Fair enough," Toby said with a nod. "Come on, let's get you some water." He gestured toward the twin glass doors of the old convenience store. The sign above them read "Kwik Mart," but the age-grayed paint behind the sign read "Magic Market."

Gavin nodded and stepped up on a curb worn shiny and smooth by thousands of footsteps and the harsh desert clime. He strode to the door, letting his eyes wander across the store's interior as was his habit— locating doors, noting the locations of the other customers and the employees, making a threat assessment, plain and simple.

The store was well-stocked for such a small town, with three rows of shelves stuffed to overflowing, each shelf filling the thirty paces between the cash register and the coolers in the back. Two men stood back near the coolers, their backs to the door, their heads close as though they might be whispering to each other. Both wore cowboy hats, dark T-shirts, dusty jeans, and heavy work boots. Not cowboy boots, as Gavin had expected, but well-worn linesman's boots with scuffed toes, dusty black uppers, and bright orange laces.

Something about the boots bothered Gavin, but it was nothing he could put his finger on. He opened one of the doors, taking a step back to allow Toby to enter first, and as he did so, one of the men glanced toward them over his shoulder and then tapped his friend's arm with the back of his hand. Both men turned, fixing them with expressionless gazes, and fell silent.

"Well, now I feel all welcome," said Toby in a jocular tone. "All small towns are essentially the same, aren't they?"

"I don't know," said Gavin. "Most of them seem to have a character all their own."

"Maybe," said Toby, "but they're all 'us versus them.' If you're not from there, you're an outsider and therefore suspect."

Gavin nodded, a solemn expression on his face. "I don't think that's unique to small towns, though. It's the same in neighborhoods, apartment buildings, wherever. It's that whole stranger thing."

Toby shrugged with one eyebrow. "Maybe you're right. I've lived in big cities, but at heart, I guess I'm a small-town boy. I can't help but see things through that lens."

"We are about to close," said a tall woman from behind the counter. Her voice was cold, flat, and her copper-colored hair looked slightly out of place in the harsh lights of the convenience store's interior.

Turning on a thousand-watt smile, Toby glanced at her and nodded. "That's okay, we know just what we want."

"Then I suggest you go get it." The cashier's voice hardened as she spoke.

"No problem," said Gavin. They turned and walked down one of the aisles—as fate would have it, the one stocked with warm sports drinks, packs of trail mix, and stay-awake pills.

As they passed the drinks, Toby picked up a few in random flavors. "Mix your kitty litter and these. They won't add anything to what the Hydrolite gives you, but they might improve the flavor."

"I don't think anything can improve the flavor. Maybe motor oil."

"If you want, I can have something better shipped down here. I can't prescribe for you here, but I can back in New York. My PA can fill it and ship it overnight. It will be here the day after tomorrow."

Gavin nodded and took two of the random flavors from the collection in Toby's arms and put them back on the shelf, replacing them with ones he liked. "I'm only supposed to take them for a few more days, but two fewer days of torture would be welcome."

"That's where you're wrong," said Toby, shaking his head. "I'm not sure you noticed it, Gav, but we're in the middle of the desert. Your doctor's orders changed the moment you landed in this climate. You will have at least four doses of electrolyte replacement per day, and you are to drink at least sixty-four ounces of water in addition to that—every day you're here." The man gave him a stern glance.

"All that?" Gavin couldn't help but grin at Burton's demeanor.

"Well, I suppose you *could* go back to having seizures."

"I'm not really sure that was all from dehydration."

Toby lifted one eyebrow, his stern expression unchanged.

"The…dreams I told you about."

"Ah. Trust me, Agent Gregory, the dehydration played a part in those as well, most likely. But hear me: as long as you are under my care, you will not get dehydrated. If I have to, I'll get Shannon to distract you while Greg and I hold you down so Benny can shove a funnel down your stubborn throat and pour the liquid in." Even though his tone was firm, a smile blossomed on his face as though they were old friends giving each other a hard time. After a moment, though, his grin faded a notch, and he looked down.

"Scott?"

Toby nodded without looking up. "I can't help it. You two would've been peas in a pod."

"I'll consider that a compliment."

Toby looked up, then, a sober expression dominating his face. "You should, Gavin. Sometimes I think he was the best of us."

Gavin nodded. "A high compliment, then, from what I've seen so far."

Without a word, Toby turned and walked toward the back of the store, toward the stacks of plastic-wrapped cases of bottled water. Gavin followed him and glanced at the two men in work boots who stood frozen, staring at them and tracking their every move. He halted, arched an eyebrow, and said, "Should I come closer so you can get a better look? You want to take a picture?"

The man who had noticed them first sneered but didn't turn his gaze away, though the second man dropped his gaze to Gavin's chest.

Shaking his head, Gavin joined Toby by the water. "So much for Southern hospitality."

Burton chuckled. "That's your first mistake. Texas isn't Southern. It isn't the west. Hell, it isn't even the southwest. Texas is Texas. "

Gavin shrugged, a small smile playing on his lips. "So much for Texan hospitality, then."

Toby stole a quick glance at the two men, then stepped closer to Gavin. "They're not... I mean, they're human. Weird, maybe, but flesh and blood just like you and me. No illusions."

"Okay, just assholes, then."

A small grin surfaced on Toby's face. "Small-town assholes."

"Who you callin' assholes?" The man's voice was high, almost squeaky.

"Mind your business," said Gavin in a hard voice without looking around.

"Maybe *you* are my business, boyo," said the first man Gavin had noticed in a deeper, more confident tone.

Toby stiffened on the last word and darted another glance at the two men. He seemed to relax once he laid eyes on them, and Gavin quirked an eyebrow at him. He shook his head, though, and Gavin let it drop.

Turning slowly, Gavin faced the two men, his expression bland, bored, even. "That would be a mistake."

The man with the high-pitched voice shook his head. "Nah, a good example of the mistake would be whatever brought you two fags here."

Gavin threw back his head and laughed. "Is that it? Is that what's got your panties in a bunch?"

"We're *closing*," said the woman by the cash register. "That means everyone."

Mr. Squeaky turned a flinty glare toward her, and with deliberate slowness, raised his hand and lay a finger across his lips.

"We've got what we came for," said Toby as he hefted one of the cases of water. "Let's go, Gavin."

The first man, the confident one, shook his head again and strode toward them. "Maybe it's too late to go."

The cashier sighed.

"Mary Beth, shh!" hissed the second man, his finger still laid across his lips. "You know better, girl."

"Look, fellas," said Gavin holding his hands up and turning his palms toward them. "Don't you think this is getting a little out of hand? I'm—"

"Shut your mouth, rabbit!" squeaked the first man.

"Rabbit?" said Toby with a derisive laugh. "What's that about? Did you forget your dictionary of derisive terms?"

Gavin pinched the bridge of his nose. "Gentlemen, I'm an FBI agent, and I'm armed. I really think you should find someone else to pick a fight with. Now, we're going to take our drinks, pay for them, and leave. I'd suggest you two go home and sober up before you get into more trouble than you're bargaining for."

"Is that so?" said the squeaky-voiced man. As he took a step forward, his friend stuck his arm out and halted him.

The confident one glowered at Gavin, his lips pressed into a thin, cruel line. After a moment, he gave a terse nod and pointed at the cashier, though he never took his eyes off Gavin.

Gavin nodded back and nudged Toby. They turned and approached the cash register, and Toby dropped the case of water onto the counter. Gavin put the sports drinks down next to him and looked the cashier in the eye. "We're sorry about the trouble. What do we owe you?"

Mary Beth glanced down at the counter, and then raised her gaze to meet his. "Twenty. Even."

Toby nodded and slipped a wad of cash out of his pocket. He flipped through until he found a twenty-dollar bill and lay it on the counter. He glanced at the woman, then flipped a ten down next to the twenty. "For all the excitement," he said.

"She don't need your charity, asshole," said the shrilled-voiced man.

"Shut up," said the other.

"But, Marcus, I—"

"Thanks for telling them my name, *Roger*."

"I—"

"*I said shut up!*" hissed Marcus.

The woman glanced past Toby and Gavin, then, quick as a snake, she snatched up the two bills and shoved them in her front pocket. She turned her gaze back on Toby and nodded, then jerked her head toward the door. "You better go," she whispered.

"Do you need my help?" asked Gavin in a very low voice. "I wasn't lying about the FBI thing."

"I've known them since the second grade. I'll be okay."

"Why, Mary Beth! What's all the chit-chat about?" asked Marcus.

She flicked her gaze over Gavin's shoulder. "Nothing, Mark. Just—"

"*Marcus!*"

"—giving them directions."

"I can—"

Mary Beth's gaze snapped back to Gavin's, and she shook her head, then jerked her head toward the door again. "Thanks," she whispered and then went on in a louder, colder voice. "Get out. I gotta close."

Gavin nodded once, then picked up the case of water, and he and Toby walked out to the car.

"Do you think she's okay?" asked Toby, his gaze slipping back toward the store.

Following his look, Gavin nodded. "She knows them better than we do." The two men had left the coolers in the back of the store and were slowly walking toward Mary Beth. Roger's face bore a nasty expression, but Marcus showed a slick, car-salesman smile. "Besides, I think she can handle the likes of them."

Still watching the tableau inside the Kwik Mart, Toby shrugged. "Still…"

"We can stay. Watch for a few minutes." Gavin turned his gaze on Toby. "But if anything pops off, you've got a stay out of it. Let me—"

"I can handle myself, Gavin."

"—handle it. And it's not about whether you can handle yourself or not. I'm law enforcement, and you are a civilian." When he turned back to the scene inside the Kwik Mart, Marcus stood at the doors, staring out at them, his lips twisted into the bastard-child of a smile and a snarl. Moving with deliberate slowness, he lifted his hand and pointed down the road. Behind him, Mary Beth nodded her head once, and Roger leaned across the counter to grab her bicep. Gavin moved, taking three long strides from the side of the SUV toward the door, and then Marcus glanced over his shoulder, snapped around, and slapped Roger on the back of the head.

"He's *FBI*, you dumbass!" His shout carried to the parking lot. "Do you know what that means? Use your head!" Marcus grated. When he turned back to look at Gavin, his hand darted up to the deadbolt and snicked it closed. "She's safe, FBI-man. Roger, on the other hand…" They stood there, neither one of them moving, staring at each other for half a minute. Marcus gave him another slow nod, then lifted his hand, three fingers extended, his pinky tucked under his thumb. "Scout's honor."

Gavin stared at him a few moments longer, his expression hard, set. He tapped the deadbolt with his left index finger.

Without hesitation, Marcus snapped the lock open and stepped back, sweeping his hand past him as if inviting Gavin in.

Instead of going inside, Gavin lifted his gaze to meet Mary Beth's and quirked one eyebrow. Her gaze flicked to Marcus, then back to Gavin, and once more she nodded, then jerked her head. Gavin met Marcus's gaze one last time and lifted his finger to point at the man. Marcus narrowed his eyes but nodded once more, and Gavin turned to retrace his steps to the car.

Toby stood just behind him, wearing an expression as cold, as *empty*, as that of any serial killer Gavin had had the displeasure of coming into contact with. His gaze shifted from Marcus's to Gavin's, and his face relaxed into an easy smile. "All good?"

"Toby, I meant it when I said you had to stay out of it. I can't have you—"

"Oh, I heard you, Gavin. I chose to ignore your suggestion."

Gavin shook his head once. "It wasn't a suggestion."

Toby's grin stretched wider, as did his eyes, giving him a slightly crazy aspect. "I know that, but I'm not in the FBI. I don't have to play by your rules."

Gavin tilted his head back. "And what would Scott have said to something like that?"

Laughing, Toby nodded, then spun on his heels to go back to the car. "He would've told me to kiss his ass."

After climbing into the SUVs passenger seat, Gavin took one last look at the Kwik Mart and found all three of them staring out at Toby and him. "Toby?"

Toby twisted the key, and the engine growled to life. "Yeah?"

"Kiss my ass." He tried not to, but he couldn't help but grin.

Roaring laughter, Toby put the car in reverse and backed them out onto the street.

14

Room 1408, Aeonian Motel & RV Park, Aeonia, TX
Saturday, 12:39 am CST

Gavin closed the door on the crisp night air that smelled of desert and asphalt and wormwood, and sniffed the hot, stale air inside his room. He shook his head at how much he liked Toby—how much he *wanted* to like the man—given the short time he'd known him. But then again, he liked all these strange people, these refugees from a town infested by demons. He froze halfway to the bed and made a sound that was half-chuckle, half-scoff, half-derision. *A town infested by demons*, he thought. *Last year, I'd have—*

Yes, Gavin, said Kai. *Last year you didn't know any better. And remember that people—especially children—*

create superstitions to fill in when shit happens that they can't understand.

You mean to say they didn't get abducted? That these demons are just...delusions? Do you know how rare shared psychosis is? And—

Woah, woah, woah, Gavin, sent Kai, amusement coloring his mental tone. *I'm not saying any of that. Did they get abducted? Without question. Was their mutual abductor a demon?* An image of Kai shrugging filled Gavin's mind. *I can't say, but their memories feel real to me. This trauma happened, and what they remember does not feel like fiction—either intentional or otherwise.*

I'm sure there are plenty of patients in mental hospitals that can say the same thing. Where does the line between what's real and what's in their heads lie? Gavin waited, standing stock-still, his head cocked to the side as if they were having an auditory conversation and Kai was hard to hear, but if Kai replied, he didn't catch it. *Kai?* Again, he waited, and again, he received no response. "That's a little rude, yeah?" he murmured as he walked to the front window and checked to see if it could be opened, if he could let in some of the wonderful desert night air. "What's the etiquette for hanging up on an ESP call?" He clicked his tongue. "ESP call," he murmured with a little scorn in his voice. "Get a grip, Gav." The window wasn't meant to open, and with a sigh, he set the inadequate air conditioner to its coldest setting.

He continued to the room's tiny refrigerator and deposited his stash of water, putting his packets of Hyrdolite on the desk next to it, then he went into the bathroom and got ready for bed. Moments later, he slipped the comforter off the bed and heaped it next to the room's little round table that was shoved into the only possible space—the corner between the window and the other wall of the room.

He slid between the sheets, marveling that even in southwest Texas, even in a small, stuffy motel room, the bedclothes felt cool and crisp. He sat with his back against the headboard and scanned his domain for a moment, grimacing as his gaze tracked across the darkened bathroom door. "I need to remember to turn that on after I call Mads," he told himself, then he grabbed his phone and dialed Maddie. She picked up almost before it rang.

"You do remember I'm on the east coast, right?" she said in a voice clear of any sign she'd been asleep.

"You were reading about your sparkly vampires. Admit it."

"No. No, I was reading about a guy with leprosy whose wife left him and he's stuck in this little town where they townsfolk pay his bills so he won't come into town anymore."

"Sounds kind of grim, Mads. Even for you."

"'Even for me?' What's that supposed to mean?"

"I mean, pages and pages of a guy moping around his house, depressed and—"

"Like you've ever read a word Stephen R. Donaldson wrote. Anyway, it's almost two in the morning here in the real world, Gavin McSmartasspants."

"Yeah…you've made better efforts. You are an author, right?"

"Shut up, smarty-pants. I'm tired."

"And reading the most depressing book in the world."

"No. No, it's about to turn all freaky. It's one of those world-hopping books. You know, one of those stories where it seems like the protagonist is always the last to know that something weird is about to happen." The line hissed with silence for a moment. "Sound familiar?"

"Yeah," he said with a gusty sigh. "Is there somewhere I can tender my resignation as the protagonist in this creepy tale?"

"You're not allowed to do that, Gavin, because then you wouldn't be my leading man in the movie."

Gavin scrunched down the headboard until he lay flat, his head nestled on the pillow, and he stared at the standard hotel-room-white ceiling. He drew in a deep breath and let it hiss out between his teeth.

"Rough day?"

"For Ren, I'm sure."

"For you, too, Gavin Gregory. Despite your protestations, everyone and his cousin knows you're not at one hundred percent."

Something rustled in Minnieville, and Gavin guessed that was Maddie scrunching down under the covers. "Done with Mr. Covenant?" he asked.

Maddie chuckled. "You like to play unread neandertal, Gavin Gregory, but you always slip up. Have you read the whole series?"

"No, just that first one."

"You should. Read all of it, I mean."

"I'll take it under advisement." He let his eyes drift shut. "I… Have I told you about the man on the plane?"

"The man on the plane? No."

"Doctor," he said. "Well, a pathologist, really, and not anymore."

"Oh?"

"Yeah. He's… He backed the people who set up that app. SEMPRe."

"Oh." Her tone was a mix of raw surprise and trepidation. "Those people can be a little nutty. The people who use the app, I mean."

"It's a human search engine, he said. I'm not quite sure I get what that is."

"It's like crowd-sourcing for information. You ask a question of the group, and they run around and find the answers."

"Run around?"

"Metaphors, Gavin. Look the word up after we're done. They do almost everything via the Internet."

"Why's that better than Google, then?"

"Because there are tens or hundreds of them doing the same thing. It's like when you ask the wonks at Quantico for help but on a massive scale."

"Oh."

The line hummed in his ear for a few seconds. "What aren't you telling me, Gav?"

"I, uh, ran into him again. Down here in Odolavesta."

"He's following you? They're probably on the scent of the cult activity."

Gavin grinned at his wife's streak of genius. "You're pretty smart, you know that?"

"Hold on a second. I didn't hear you, but before you repeat that, I want to get my recorder running."

"Never happen, Mads."

"Tell me about him. Did you warn him off?"

"Not precisely. He, uh… *They*—the founders of SEMPRe—all had experiences with…"

"With Fry?" she asked, her tone sharp.

"No. They have their own brand of crazy."

"Um…"

"Yeah. It seems they were all tortured as kids by a thing like Glacadairanam in the '70s. They have… Some of them have a lot in common with Kai."

"But they're not…"

"No. They know about Adeline's group, but they managed to avoid detection. It seems that…" He shook his head, then began speaking in an excited tone. "They surprised Kai a few times. He thinks he's got the button on them, but I wonder. This woman, Shannon, she can—"

"Is she a plumber?"

"What? No," he said with a chuckle. "And she's married to Benny. Anyway, she can—"

"Wait, Benny?"

"—create illusions and make you see what she wants. Kai can, too, I guess. He made me think—"

"Illusions? Like what?"

"—he was here—in Odolavesta, rather—but Benny said—"

"There's that name again. I think I need a program."

"—he was in Ohio, and Kai confirmed that." He paused, then chuckled. "Geesh, hon, let a guy finish a sentence."

"Names, Gav. Give me all the names and tell me who they are."

"Right. Toby Burton is the pathologist. He can pierce the illusions cast by the 'demons' in their town. Benny Cartwright—"

"Woah. Wait a minute. There's a whole town full of things like Fry?"

"Yeah. Their hometown was overrun by the things, I guess. They cleared them out. Banished them."

"A roving pack of exorcists, then?"

Gavin's shoulders twinged against the pillow in an aborted shrug. "I guess."

"Go on with the naming of names."

"Benny Cartwright has telepathy. Shannon Cartwright, *his wife*, the illusionist. Then there's Greg Canton, who's like Benny, but it seems like a little less powerful. Or maybe more…" He squinted at the ceiling. "I think he did something Kai said shouldn't be possible at his psi rating. He's married to Mike Richards, who happens to be the new agent the San Antonio office assigned me, but so far, he's just normal. Like me."

"Husband of your new partner? Small world, huh? But you're hardly normal, Gavin."

"Yeah, yeah."

"Does Pete know all this?"

"No. Not yet."

"Think you should bring him into the inner sanctum and update his decoder ring. Or are you going to let him twist in the wind?"

"No, I'll tell him, but…"

"But it still seems too crazy?"

"That's it," he said with a smile. "Kind of like you."

"Crazy? I'll show you crazy!"

"Greg was kidnapped by Abaddon in Western New York. Toby said they rescued him and then went to war with the demons in their hometown. SEMPRe has resources, evidently."

"Yes, they do. According to Mr. Google, SEMPRe has quite the balance sheet. I wonder how they make their money."

"Toby backed them. He said he made most of his money through investments, starting from a big wad he made on a video game."

"Hmm."

"What?"

"Doctor. Pathologist. Video game developer. Software magnate. Leader of a cult-like organization that seems to hunt cults."

"It sounds strange when you say it like that."

"Right?"

He could hear the annoying click-click-clickety-click of her phone's keyboard as she ran searches. "Think I should sic the wonks at Quantico on them? He alluded to having ways of hiding everything they do."

"Which is what?"

"Investigate stuff."

"By stuff, you mean cults?"

"And demons. Ghosts. Whatever."

Maddie said nothing, but her thumbs were still dancing across the phone's keyboard. "And…they seem…trustworthy to you?"

"Not at first, but Kai says they're okay."

"And you're sure it's Kai and not this plumber woman?"

"Yeah, of course…" His voice trailed away. "Okay, that's a fair point. How can I ever be sure of anything with an illusionist nearby?"

"That's the question, isn't it?"

"Maybe I can ask Kai something only he would know."

"You said the illusionist's—"

"Shannon."

"—husband is—"

"Benny."

"—a telepath?"

"Oh, right. Then that's out. He could just lift it from my brain and send it to her so she could answer."

"Maybe."

Gavin? Kai asked in his head.

"Kai's calling," Gavin said. *Kai?*

Maddie sighed. "Go ahead, put me on hold. Frank's going to…entertain me."

"Plumbers charge extra after hours. I hope you've got your checkbook. And never mind about the hold. Kai's *calling.*"

"Oh. Right."

Maddie and I were just discussing a problem—

Yes, it's really me. No, I'm not an illusion. Shannon's asleep, and I already told you those people are on the up-and-up.

"Kai says he's really himself. Says that Shannon is asleep." *Yeah, but you see the problem with that, right?*

"Yeah, but you see the problem with that, don't you? We just went through all that."

"That's what I just said to…*thought* to Kai."

"And?" There was a moment's hesitation, then she said, "Oh! Kai says he's the real thing. Does this Shannon woman know about me?"

"Toby does, and they knew our address, though I don't know if they know your name."

For fuck's sake, Gavin… Across the room, the table rattled in place. *There. Believe me or not. I don't have time for more of this nonsense.* For a moment, Kai's mental voice sounded so much like the real Adeline d'Clara that Gavin winced. *I'm about to go on an expedition down there. I'll see what I can find out by casting a wide net.*

"Kai moved the table in my room. He's going on—"

"The illusionist could—"

"We can go on like this forever, hon. Hell, from my point of view, all this could be a psychotic dream, and I'm really still in New York under the influence of the chirply little bastard or his father."

"But I'm not."

"Yeah? Prove you're real. Prove you're not dreaming." Gavin scratched behind his ear.

"I…" She fell silent, and he could almost hear the gears spinning in her head. "Yeah, I see what you mean."

"Kai's going to go rooting through people's heads down here. Hopefully, he can find Ren, the killer, and we can do the busts tomorrow."

"In fiction, we'd call that a bit of *deus ex machina*."

"Yeah. In the FBI, we call that a pipe dream."

"Speaking of pipe…I wish you were home."

Grinning a little, Gavin said, "Me, too."

"I'll see what I can find out about SEMPRe, Gav. In the meantime, don't trust them too much."

"It might seem strange, but I do trust Toby. Kai's scanned them, too."

"Well, just be careful."

Gavin chuckled. "Aren't I always?"

"If you were here—no, not even here, but just within driving distance—I'd pop you right in the chops so hard you'd think your name was Sally."

"How is letting you punch me in the mouth being careful?"

"Who said you'd have to let me?"

"I'm going to stop, now. I don't want this to develop into an Inspector Clouseau-Kato type of thing."

"God, you're really old, aren't you?"

"We're virtually the same age, dear."

"No, we're not."

"Five years, Mads."

"Might as well be a lifetime." She sounded smug.

"Are all authors as weird as you?"

"Weird *awesome*."

"You know that doesn't help, right?"

Maddie yawned. "This bores me, this verbal grinding your bits to dust thing. There's no challenge in it."

"When I get home, there will be a challenge all right."

"Promises, promises." She yawned again. "But I'm sleepy, so I'm going to sleep. You can keep talking if you want. It might help you feel like you've won."

"Love you, sleepyhead."

"Yeah, I love you, too, Frank."

Chuckling, Gavin hung up. He glanced at the dark bathroom door, started to pull back the sheets, but he stayed his hand with a soft groan. He glanced at the clock—it read eleven minutes to one in the morning—then lay back and closed his eyes.

Chapter 3
The Temple of Doom

I

Kai Washington grinned a little at Maddie's wit, and for a moment, he indulged the part of him that felt a pang of loneliness evoked by Gavin and Maddie's relationship. He'd had relationships in the past—intense relationships that burnt to cinders in short order—but they'd always failed to satisfy him, even before they self-destructed.

He felt his lip curl in a one-sided sneer.

The relationships didn't self-destruct. *He* burned them down. Part of him ripped them apart—the side of him that rejected intimacy, trust, made sure they failed and that they failed early. It was as though he were two separate individuals at times: one who longed for commitment, for tenderness, for *love*, and another who looked at everyone and everything with an aloof detachment, with distrust. From time to time, he'd give in to the former and have a few days or a week of pleasure, then the latter would take control and it would all be over. At first, he'd thought he just needed to find the right partner, but he'd eventually come to terms with the fact that the "right partner" simply didn't exist. He'd briefly considered fixing someone to be his match, to put up with his self-destructive quirks, to love him no matter what, but that level of manipulation of another mind—an *innocent* mind—smacked too much of the Program and everything it stood for.

Besides, it would be cheating. That part of him that demanded intimacy also demanded his mate accept him as he was, without contingency, knowing who and *what* he was and loving him anyway. Unconditional love, that's what he longed for, what he hadn't experienced since his mother sacrificed herself to allow him time to get away from the Program, from Adeline d'Clara, from *Fry*.

His skills as a fixer left him fully cognizant of these two distinct and opposing forces within him. He could go in and snip out those needs—either the ones that drove him toward people or the ones that drove him away—or perhaps both. He had the skill to do that kind of self-surgery, he had the power to fix himself and make it stick, but so many hands had shaped his mind—through direct psychic means, through manipulations of the Program, and by example such as his mother had—that he felt uncomfortable with editing who he'd become.

He'd resigned himself to settling for eavesdropping and pretending. For longing.

With a sigh, he settled back in his La-Z-Boy and let his eyes droop to half-mast. He flung himself outward, leaving his mortal coil behind, and zipped south at the speed of thought.

As always, he gave no thought to the slim possibility he wouldn't make his way back to his body. He just left it and didn't look back.

2

Marcus lifted his hand to knock on Primo's door, but then he let it fall back to his side. He dithered, straining his ears for any telltale sound from within the man's quarters. In the years they'd known each other—at least those years in which Marcus had borne the man's trust— he'd never woken Primo up, no matter the hour, no matter the previous day's activities. He'd never had to. Every time he brought an emergency to the leader of their group, Primo was already awake—no dregs of sleep, no drowsiness, no confusion, ever. The man just sat there in his bed, back against the headboard, thick legs splayed almost across the entirety of the bed. It was as if there was a sensor somewhere that could turn him on or off like a robot. Sound asleep one second, fully awake the next.

Marcus lifted his hand, but once more, he didn't knock. He was struck by indecision in moments where he found himself thinking too hard about what made Primo tick, about what made him the first among the Brethren. He often wondered if the man avoided sleep, knowing there was a problem coming somehow, or if Marcus broadcasted his need like sonar ping, and that need was what woke the First Son from his slumber.

Or maybe he didn't need sleep. *If his father is who he says it is…* Marcus shrugged and shook his head. Questioning Primo's nature was an exercise in futility. *He's Primo*, he told himself. *That's enough, ain't it? Ain't it?* He shook his head and tried to marshal his thoughts down more proper, decorous avenues of consideration. He lifted his hand, but again, he didn't knock. *Does he know I'm here?*

The door opened, and Primo stood there, wearing a surprised look. "Oh! Marcus, you gave me a fright, brother."

"Sorry, Primo."

Primo's gaze flicked to Marcus' upraised fist, and he quirked his eyebrow.

"Uh. I was just about to knock."

"Indeed?" Primo dropped his gaze, but not before Marcus caught something in his expression that might have been amusement.

"Sorry about the late hour… Something… Something happened over in Aeonia, and it's still with me. It…" He shook his head and pumped his shoulders up and down.

Primo's gaze flicked over his shoulder.

Looking down the hall? Was he waiting for someone, or does he have something he wants to do? Marcus stepped back. "It's probably nothin' worth worryin' over. We can talk about it mañana."

Primo's smile widened, showing all his teeth—teeth that appeared too white in contrast to his flat midnight skin. "Don't be silly. I always have time for you, Marcus. Isn't it so?" He arched one eyebrow.

"Yeah, you do at that. And I hope I always come across as appreciative, 'cause I am."

With a chuckle, Primo clapped him on the shoulder. "Oh, you do, Marcus. You do."

The big man stepped back without turning, his grin frozen on his face, and again, Marcus found himself thinking about robots and who the man claimed as his father and found himself wanting to shudder a bit. "Well, I do 'preciate you, Primo. Every hour of every day."

"Come now, let's not get maudlin, Marcus."

"No. 'Course not."

"Come in, brother, and be welcome." Still wearing that strange expression that might be barely contained mirth, Primo backed farther from the door. Staring Marcus in the eye, he swept a big arm behind him. "Have a seat. Make yourself comfortable." The corners of his mouth twitched at that, as though he were fighting to keep from laughing outright.

"Well…sure," said Marcus. He crossed the room, doing his best to ignore the gooseflesh creeping up his back as he passed Primo. "I'm sorry about the hour, is all."

"Put it out of your thoughts," said Primo. "Tell me what's wrong."

"Well, nothing's wrong." He pursed his lips. "It's just…"

"Out with it."

There was an edge to Primo's voice that Marcus didn't much like, and he nodded. "Roger and me was down to the Kwik Mart in Aeonia. He wanted a beer, and—"

"Yes, yes," murmured Primo, and Marcus swallowed hard and sat on the couch.

"I took him, see? Drove him, I mean. We was standing in back while he had to read every damn label in the cooler—like there's ever anything different, you know how he does—and these two *strangers* came rolling in. Drove one of them fancy German SUVs. A Mercedes-Benz—"

"Tell me about the men," said Primo in a sharp tone. He moved to an armchair that he sent crab-walking over to face Marcus with an almost absent-minded flick of his wrist. When he sank into the chair, it was more like watching a helicopter come in to hover, and he perched on the edge of the seat as if giants did things like that every day.

"We figured they was faggots," said Marcus. "Two men, out late at night, going into the Kwikie for some beers or soft drinks."

Primo lifted his eyebrow, and the serious, thunderous demeanor that had been growing on his face shattered. He shifted his bulk back into the chair and flopped his hands on the armrests.

Marcus furrowed his brow a moment, then relaxed and chuckled. "Yeah. Okay, I get it. That's what me and Roger was doing, and we ain't gay."

"Doesn't matter if you are," murmured Primo.

"Right, but we *ain't*. That's my point."

"The men," said Primo, and Marcus could almost hear him snap his fingers, though the man didn't so much as twitch.

"One of them was a bit…" Marcus frowned, then shook his head. "He seemed like any other fella, but there was something…*wrong* feeling about him. Like looking in a gator's eyes, I expect. All smiles, all nods, all the while planning to eat my guts like sausage." Again, Primo's lips twitched, and Marcus nodded, swallowing hard again. "The other man, well, he was FBI."

Primo rocked forward, sliding to the edge of the cushion once more. "*What*?" he thundered. "You didn't start with the FBI agent in our midst? I'd have thought you'd view that fact with more alarm, given our…"

Marcus swallowed and closed his eyes. "Stupid of me. My brain's all…" He flopped his hand in the air beside him. "The guy—the FBI-man—freaked me out a bit."

Narrowing his gaze, Primo pulled back a little. "Freaked you out?"

"Yes," said Marcus as he ducked his head to break eye contact with Primo. "I… He wasn't…" He shook his head and fell silent.

"He wasn't scared of you."

With another shake of his head, Marcus glanced at Primo. "Neither was the gator."

Primo inclined his head, faintly humming a tune that made the hair on Marcus's arms stand on end. The melody sounded wrong, jangly, like they lived in a haunted house or maybe the deepest desert ergs where no man thrived, but sand demons moved to the music of the wind. The big man's index fingers tapped an arrhythmic beat on his knees that seemed out of time with what he hummed but complimentary at the same time.

Marcus's mouth itched with the need to hum along, though he didn't know the tune, and his feet wanted to move, to run, to kick sand skyward in a frenetic dance, a desert dust devil made flesh. He gritted his teeth and squeezed his eyes shut as a terrible thirst assaulted him, drying him out in an instant. Despite the sunbaked feel in the tissues of his throat, he wanted something…*salty*. Salty and warm…like blood. "What's…" he croaked.

"Speak up, boy," said Primo in a harsh voice. "If you're going to interrupt my thoughts, the least you could do is speak audibly." As always, his pronunciation was careful, almost clipped, and he enunciated every consonant, every vowel, with precision.

"What's that song?"

"Song?" Primo shook his head once. "Oh, was I humming aloud?"

Marcus nodded, though he doubted Primo had been absent-mindedly humming. In all the years they'd known each other, he couldn't recall a single instance in which Primo had acted on impulse, let alone thoughtlessly. He tried to speak, but with his throat as dry as dust, he managed no more than a croak. He swallowed, then tried again. "Sorry, I'm spittin' cotton all of a sudden. That song…"

"Never mind that, Marcus. Just an old lay from my childhood." His intense gaze lingered on Marcus's face. "Did it…upset you?"

Marcus shook his head, trying to give his lie credence by meeting Primo's probing stare head-on. "Made me want to dance, is all. Dance and…" His attention drifted back to those haunting tones, and he shook his head.

"And what, Marcus?"

Hitching his shoulders up and down, Marcus shook his head. "Dance and drink blood. Maybe coat myself in it." The admission felt shameful, like something he should've kept to himself.

Primo chuckled. "Yes." He widened his eyes. "Is that all?"

"Ain't it enough?" growled Marcus, sudden fury rattling his veins like air in a water pipe.

"Don't carry on so, Marcus," said Primo in that deadly calm way of his—a manner that said there was nothing Marcus could do to cause him discomfort, let alone cause injury. He leaned across the distance between them, bending at the waist and reaching over to pat Marcus's knee. "I didn't mean to upset you. What else about the two men?"

"Mary Beth acted up a little. You know her. Works over to the Kwikie most nights."

"I know of her," said Primo with a nod. "Perhaps we should speak with her?"

"Roger got his tail up and—"

"Yes. The man has a…what did you say that one time?" He held up his index finger and grinned. "Ah! The man has a ten-gallon hat."

Marcus grimaced. "*Mouth*. He's got a ten-gallon mouth."

"Oh, yes," said Primo in a flat tone. "Thank you for correcting me."

"I figured you'd want to know. You like to speak correctly."

With a ponderous nod, Primo said, "I do." His gaze never left Marcus's, and though his expression was empty bordering on pleasant, it left Marcus with the distinct impression that he'd overstepped—not by a yard, but maybe an inch or two. "Tell me what Roger did."

Marcus told him the tale, how the FBI-man and his alligator-friend left but then came back to make sure Mary Beth was all right. "I tried to shoo him on his way, but that only made him come closer. I told him Roger was acting wrongheaded, that she wouldn't come to no harm, but…"

"But he didn't believe you."

Marcus hitched his shoulders again.

"Of course, he didn't, Marcus, but that's nothing unexpected. What else?"

"I'd locked the door to keep him out. He tapped on the deadbolt, so I opened her up and invited him in like he was the pope hisself."

"And did that satisfy him? Did he come inside?"

Marcus shook his head. "He looked to Mary Beth again, and she must've nodded or something because the FBI-man relaxed a little bit."

"But…"

"But when he looked at me again, his eyes went flinty. He leveled a finger at me like it was a gun, like it was a promise of trouble to come…a threat."

Primo leaned back, rolling his gaze toward the ceiling, and again, he hummed a few notes that set Marcus's skin to crawling. "Do we need to deal with Mary Beth?"

"Naw. She's a good woman. She knows better than to talk to outsiders about us and our business. She'd've never said nothin' at all, and Roger should've followed my lead."

"Yes. That was clumsy of him."

Marcus nodded. "We had words."

Primo tilted his head. "And words will be enough to ensure proper behavior next time? He's been…clumsier of late."

"If they ain't, I'll tan the hide of him myself."

"Very good. Leave the rest with me."

"Yessir, Primo. But…"

"But?"

Marcus dropped his gaze to the big man's bare feet. "I'm just wondering if we should move him."

"Move who, Marcus?"

The room seemed very quiet all of a sudden, like a library or a church, and Marcus wished he hadn't said anything. "The man from the Resta."

"Ah," said Primo. He sniffed and rocked his head back, his gaze resting on Marcus's eyes. "Let me think on it. For now, Cece has him well in hand."

When he started to hum again, his gaze boring into Marcus like twin diamond-tipped drill bits, Marcus's skin started to itch and crawl. He thrust himself up, to his feet, and nodded, then almost ran to the door, feeling the big man's smile on his back like a bullseye.

3

The temple, Southwestern TX
Saturday, 1:27 am CST

Cece Clark opened the door a crack and peeked out. She shifted it a little wider to get a better view of Marcus' retreating back as he hustled past out in the hall. She glanced at Jon and lifted an eyebrow. Jon gave a faint grin as he picked out a few bizarre-sounding licks on his battered old acoustic. The corners of her mouth turned down a little, and a faint line appeared between her brows. The new music Jon had been working on was at once strange and familiar—sounding Middle Eastern to her ear—but definitely unnerving. Plus, he was so absorbed in its creation, he wasn't actually paying attention to her. "Jon?"

He nodded, but his gaze—though pointed at her—didn't focus on her. He sat there and played, his eyes dreamy, vacant, as though he wasn't even aware he was playing anymore.

Cece slid the door closed with a quick snick. "Jon? Are you listening to me?" Her gaze dropped to the hooded man sitting in the chair in the middle of the room as he shifted position as if to cock his ear toward the music, then looked at her husband once more. "Jon?"

A loose smile that would be at home on someone gorked to the gills on painkillers surfaced on Jon's face as his fingers danced across the fretboard, the sounds coming from the guitar growing stranger and stranger with each note. He nodded, as slow and aimless as a sun-drunk lizard, and she clicked her tongue against her teeth in exasperation.

"Jon! Earth to Jon Clark!" She waved her hands in the air as if signaling a search plane, then moved toward him.

"What... What is that?" murmured the hooded man as she passed him.

Without looking, she slapped the side of his head. "You shut up!" she snapped. When she reached her husband, she leaned forward at the waist and lay her hand across the strings. "Jon!"

The dreamy, "I'm-so-stoned" expression slid off his face in slow, distinct steps as if he were waking from a dream as he continued to pluck the muted strings. He shook his head a little and blinked his eyes, then lifted his hands from the strings. "What…" Reaching across his body, he scratched the side of his head, then shook it again, rubbing one of his eyes with his other hand. "I…"

"You were doing it again, Jon. The Arabic music, the lost-in-space routine."

"What? I was just noodling, Cece."

"No, Jon. It happened again. You got lost in one of those weird little songs you've been writing."

Jon scratched his head again. "I was just…" His eyes unfocused, and his voice drifted away. As if without his conscious control, his fingers returned to the fretboard and started dancing among the frets, his other hand twitched as if plucking notes.

Cece sighed and snapped her fingers in Jon's face. "Wake up! Don't go away again!"

"What? I…" Jon widened his eyes, a soft grin on his lips. "It's so…*wondrous*, Cece. I wish you could—"

"One of us has to keep her wits about herself." She waved her hand at the hooded figure behind her. "We've got a job to do, you know."

Jon's gaze flicked to the man. "He's not going anywhere."

"Wh… What was that music?" the man murmured.

"Shut up!" Cece snapped. "Mind your business!"

The hood rustled as the man shook his head. "You… *kidnapped me*, right? That's why you have this hood on me? Why'd you do that?"

"This again?" demanded Cece, furrowing her brows at Jon. "See? It's affecting him, too."

"It's just a song, Cece."

"I want you to stop playing it, Jon. That and anything like it. It's…it's *creepy*."

"Cece, I…" Jon locked his gaze on hers. "I *love* this new stuff, hon."

"It's creepy and…and…and *intense*, Jon!" She planted one hand on her hip and gave him "the look."

He ducked his gaze away, leaning the guitar on the wall behind him. "I…"

"Why did you kidnap me? What do you hope to…to…" Cece rolled her eyes and Jon scratched his head, but neither looked at their captive, neither spoke to him. "I know this sounds silly, but I don't remember." He inclined his head and sighed. "It's all hazy…who I am, why I'm here, who you all are…"

"Oh, shut up, Agent Hall!" Cecelia half-turned, glaring at the man.

"Is that… Is that my name?" croaked the man, sounding on the verge of tears.

"Oh, for Christ's bloody sake!"

"It's the…" The man shook his head. "I don't understand it, but I think that music is…is…" He paused long enough to suck in a deep breath. "I think it's stealing away parts of me," he said in a harsh whisper.

Cece turned back to Jon and gave a few more watts to "the look."

"Dear, I don't know if I *can* stop. I set out to play something…else, but then my fingers…" He glanced down at his right hand and stilled his fingers. "They just…" Shrugging, he shook his head. "I don't even know what I'm playing. It just… It sort of writes itself as I play." He frowned at the guitar. "It's a mode of harmonic minor, I think. Phrygian dominant, maybe."

"I don't care about the music theory lesson, Jon! Are you telling me you can't stop or that you *won't* stop?"

Jon lifted his shoulders and let them drop again. "I'm saying that maybe I *shouldn't* stop."

"Shouldn't? Why in the hell not?" demanded Cecelia.

He raised his gaze to hers. "Think about it. Think about what we're working toward here."

"But…" Cece glanced at the door, then in the direction of Primo's quarters, then shook her head and returned her gaze to her husband's. "*But it doesn't work*," she hissed.

"Maybe not," said Jon. "Maybe we haven't succeeded, not yet, but…" His gaze swam lazily to the guitar. "But maybe we just need something… Something like this music. And anyway, *something's* happening. I can feel it getting stronger each time we complete one of the rites." He looked at her askance. "Can't you?"

Cece turned away, fighting a grimace of sudden pain. Then, with a snarl and a savage swipe at the spray of diamond tears forming in her eyes, she took a step toward the hooded man and mashed her fist into his face.

4

Aeonian Motel & RV Park parking lot, Aeonia, TX
Saturday, 2:51 am CST

Benny and Shannon closed the doors of the Mercedes Benz GLS and grimaced at the sharp, flat sound that rolled around the parking lot. Both of them stared at the door to room 1408, faces tight. After a moment, though, Benny relaxed and smiled at his wife.

We didn't wake him?

Nope, sent Benny. *He's dreaming, but it's a good dream.* He started the car and reversed it out to the road. *We'll have to pick up the beater in San Antonio.*

Why didn't we just bring it with us when we came out here?

Benny grunted and slipped the vehicle into drive. *Because we couldn't risk it being seen.*

Shannon shrugged. "I could've made sure that didn't happen."

"We don't know what these people are capable of, yet, Shan. We can't take risks like that."

"Well, I think what we're about to do constitutes a much larger risk than driving an old beat-up Chevy pickup around, don't you?"

Benny nodded, a one-sided grin on his face. "Sure, but that risk grows larger if we don't take basic precautions."

"Maybe, but we'd actually get some sleep tonight. That has to count for something."

My poor baby, Benny sent with the mental equivalent of a sardonic smile.

"Do that again, and I'll 'poor baby' you all over the great state of Texas."

Still grinning, Benny pointed the nose of the Mercedes east and gave it the gas. "Sleep if you want. Lord knows you need your beauty rest."

Shannon said nothing, she just turned in her seat to stare at his profile while Benny studiously pretended not to notice.

5

Red Westral cleared his throat and sipped a little of his smokey three-hundred-dollar scotch, gazing into the amber depths of the full-sized glass his guest had insisted on—all to avoid meeting the man's too-intense gaze. Even with his gaze averted, even focusing on the liquid gold in his glass, he couldn't help but take notice of the man through his peripheral vision. It was as if the man were a magnet and Red's eyes were made from iron filings.

It wasn't that the man was pretty per se, Red had seen much more attractive men in Dallas nightclubs, but there was something about him…something about his snowy, almost lucent, skin…or maybe his washed-out eyes, his bright nigh-onto-colorless irises. Whatever the attractive thing was, it was fetching…bewitching…

Confusing.

Across the darkened room, the man chuckled, a sound with a qualmish, queerish quality that half made Red want to run and hide. "Don't carry on so, Eldred."

Red grimaced. His bastard of a father had called him Eldred, and he hated it. "I wish you'd call me Red. That or Westral. I don't much care for Eldred, Shay." The air grew chilly as the man narrowed his anemic azure eyes, and Red jumped as the windowpane beside him crackled as ice rimed its lower edge. Ice on the *inside* of the window.

"Think I give a fuck? Think I give a *solitary fuck*, old hoss?"

"I…" Red closed his mouth, then filled it with liquid fire that he could never have afforded on a sheriff's salary.

"You and your old man, Eldred. What a couple of fuck-ups."

"Yeah, well, he's dead now." Red sniffed and held the glass of scotch against his chest, grasping it loosely with one hand.

"More's the pity, son. More's the pity." Shay's chair creaked as he shifted position, but the sound of it was wrong, too heavy. The man didn't weigh more than a thirteen-year-old soaking wet, and his chair had no business creaking like he was Brahma bull. "Take my boy over there"—he hooked his thumb to the east—"in that old rundown crackhouse he calls a temple. We don't spend much time in palaver these days—too much to do, too many people to…well, never mind that. We don't spend much time together, no, but he don't hold it against me. He don't—"

"*My father* was an evil bastard, Shay—"

Shay threw back his head and shouted laughter at the ceiling, punctuating it with harsh, hacking coughs and paroxysmal pounding on the arm of his chair. "And I ain't? And I ain't?" he hissed between gales.

Glowering at the shadowy corner—anywhere but at Shay, there was no telling how the man would react to something like that, but Red guessed it wouldn't be nice—Red said, "If he were afire, I'd keep my piss to myself."

Sobering as abruptly as the storm of boffolas had come on, Shay turned his gaze on Red, his face gone slack, his liquid white eyes filling with ocherous clouds that seemed to pulse and glow. He stared at Red long enough that the sheriff wanted to squirm, to take it back, to give up on the happy horseshit that had taken over his life and tuck tail, then he said, "That ain't nice, Eldred. Your old man was a friend to me. He might not have been perfect, but he—"

"Perfect?" Red spat. He knew better, and he hadn't meant to say a word, but the very idea that his father had been anything other than an abusive, lubricious motherfucker had startled him out of his common sense.

Shay cocked an eyebrow at him, and the orange glow of his gaze grew more distinct. "Can't say I cotton to interruptions like that, Eldred Westral. Nawsir. Can't say I cotton to it, *a-tall.*"

"I apologize," Red said instantly. He might've been the sheriff of Kelly County, might've inherited the job like a noble title when his father "passed away," but he'd seen Shay literally skin a man alive for insulting the black woman he'd been spending time with. "It was the shock, Shay. You know how me and the old man got on."

Shay stared at him, utterly still, not even a flicker in his hot glare, for the space of ten heartbeats, then he gave a curt nod and took a swig of his own scotch. "Yeah. No need for things to get hot. We're still friends, right?"

"Absolutely," said Red instantly. "Friends forever, Shay. No matter what."

"Well, ain't that *sweet*?" said Shay with a hint of laughter in his voice. "You sweet on me, old hoss?"

Red got up and walked to the east-facing window, wanting to change the subject, to change the track the conversation had started down. Luckily, Shay seemed content to allow the flow to go where Red wanted. He raised his hand and pressed his fingers against the glass, marveling at the frost, the chill in the glass, then stood gazing out on the night. "Wouldn't you rather be over there? At the temple with your boy, I mean?"

Shay rose and came over to stand next to him, his shoulder almost touching Red's, almost an invitation, and Red fought the urge to shudder. "Nah," said Shay. "Too much hullabaloo over there. Too many rituals. Too many prayers. Too many *supplicants*. After eight thousand years of it, that shit don't interest me. None of them hangers-on interest me." He cocked his head to the side. "Though there is that fella with the guitar. Him and his mean wife. *They* might be interesting. *She* might be worth keeping around."

"You don't want to be there when…" His voice failed him, winding down to a soft asthmatic wheeze.

"God damn, son! Spit it out!" Shay's voice danced with amusement, with mockery.

Red shrugged, turning his face away to hide the blush. "Don't you want to be there when they bring 'em in? The new girls for the…ceremony, I mean? Don't you want to be there when—"

"*Fuck no*, Eldred. Ain't you never seen a woman right after she travels?" He shook his head, his shoulders quaking with restrained mirth. "Grumpy!" He stomped a booted foot, and it sounded like cannon fire to Red. "Cantankerous!"

"But if one of them's to be your mate—"

"Who said my mate was a she, boy? Who said it's a woman?"

"I assumed it was, what with Primo littering up the desert with all them dead girls and importing more from up to Dallas. Anyway, I thought—"

"Who cares, Eldred?" asked Shay in that deadly quiet way common to gunslingers and serial killers. "Who cares what sex the serpent chooses? I ain't above switch-hitting, son. You know that, and my kind ain't limited by biology. I mean, you met my other son, right? Hell, I made the boy over yonder"—he jerked his chin the direction of the old building Primo had taken over—"with a *human* like you. I make another kid whenever I've a mind."

Shay's voice was raw, almost sultry, and Red's skin prickled with goose-flesh. Heat and cold swept across him in waves, and though he didn't look, he felt sure Shay was staring at him, those cold, almost-white eyes unblinking, drinking him in, eating him up. He shuddered a little and closed his eyes. "I... I just thought..." he croaked.

"Because of that pig-headed squaw. Because of Primo's mama."

Red swallowed hard and nodded.

"She ain't a part of this no more. She had her time. She chose a different road, and I let her walk it for Primo's sake." A wet rustling sounded behind Red, almost as if Shay were disrobing, but his robes were made from skins that hadn't been de-fleshed. "Besides, I can choose, too, just like my friend." As he spoke, his voice first roughened to a growl, then rose in pitch to that of a pleasant contralto, smoothing as it rose, his usual sharp tone and country accent sliding into that of a glib seductress. "I'm not limited in such things, Eldred. Once

I have flesh to play with, I can do anything I want with it."

Shuddering, Red stepped quickly away. "I could use a refill. How 'bout you, Shay? Want s'more scotch?" He continued walking toward the kitchen, not waiting for an answer but fearing Shay would call him back, that if he did, Red would go.

"Sure, old hoss. Why not?" The contralto was gone, replaced by Shay's customary rough-hewn tone and accent, though salted with a liberal dose of amusement. "A bit more fire-water sounds good." Again, that soft, wet rustling filled the room.

"Lord knows I could use it after the day I had."

"Yeah?" asked Shay, his voice suddenly empty and flat.

"For sure. I met this asshole from the F-B-I." He said the initials with a distinct pause between each and with a sneer in his voice. He strode into the warm light of his kitchen, leaving the dark room behind and feeling all the better for it.

"You what?" asked Shay in a tone that could have dropped a flying bird right out of the air.

"Yeah. Gregory." Red flapped a hand in the air. "Real arrogant son-of-a-bitch."

"*Gavin Gregory?*"

Red hadn't heard Shay move, hadn't heard his footsteps, but the words had been uttered right into his left ear, the hissing shriek of molten rock dropped in cold water. He screamed and jumped, flinging the three-hundred-dollar bottle of scotch to the fieldstone floor. "Jesus, Shay, you—"

Blazing heat washed across him, and forge-hot fingers twined into his black hair, jerking his head back. "*I asked you a question, hoss, and I'll have an answer.*" Shay gave his head a savage jerk. "And quick-like if you want this hat rack to stay attached."

"Yuh-yes! I think that was it. Gavin Gregory! Yes, that sounds right!" Tears sprang into his eyes, and fire danced across the top of his head. It felt like Shay had started to scalp him with a rusty knife. "I can check! I can—"

"I'll be damned," muttered Shay, the fearsome edge gone from his voice. "I'll be *damned!*" he shouted with a cackle. The blazing pain in his scalp abated as Shay turned Red's hair loose and did a little jig. Red slumped, hunching forward over the counter. "I'll be motherfucking god-shitting-damned!" shouted Shay, glee and laughter descanting in his tone. "Can it be? Can it be true, then?"

"I wouldn't lie—"

"Do good things come to those who wait?" Shay threw his head back and cackled up at the ceiling joists. "I'm beshitted if they don't!" he cried. He slapped Red on the back. "That's great news, Eldred. Where are those drinks? We got some celebratin' to do, spark!"

"It's…" rasped Red. "It's a good thing, then?"

"Hell yeah, boy!" Shay clapped him on the back. "Fuck yeah! I got plans for that boy, Eldred. Plans upon plans upon plans!" He grabbed Red by the shoulders and whirled him in a circle. "Plans upon plans, Eldred! Plans upon plans!" He threw back his head and cackled at the ceiling. "And now he's here, right in my backyard! I don't even have to go lookin' for his contrary ass!"

Red staggered in the compulsory circle, feeling a little woozy—and not only from being spun around like a rag doll. Shay seemed oblivious to his nausea, or more likely didn't care, and he pulled him closer so that they whirled around, chest to chest, and the heat coming off him only added to Red's need to puke. It was like leaning against a blast furnace.

"Whoop!" cried Shay, stamping his booted feet, barely missing Red's toes. "Ain't we gonna have us some fun!" he shouted in Red's ear. "Fuck yeah, son! *Fuck yeah*!" He grabbed Red's chin and planted a kiss on his cheek, hot as live coals, and at the same time, cold as the grave. He froze, and they skidded to a halt on the blue linoleum that had been the favorite of Red's mother while she was alive.

Shay's muscles stood out against his hot skin, taut as metal cables drawn past their limits, and his jaw muscles bunched and released, bunched and released like some horrible engine of destruction idling along on the eve of

Armageddon. His pale, pale eyes seemed less and less blue with each clenching, more and more orange, and Red would've sworn they'd grown hot as well. The atmosphere in the kitchen changed, the temperature dropping like a stone from a ledge, and the pressure seemed to grow and grow and grow.

"Uh, Shay? What's—"

"Who you got in there, Eldred?" he asked in an almost conversational tone. The air between them crackled with potential energy, with charged ions, with unspent fury.

"What? Who do I—"

"*Don't play coy!*" Shay screamed. "You been cheatin' on me, old hoss, and I'll know the vulture's name!" The force of his fury beat against Red like the sea during a thunderstorm.

"Shay, I—"

He hurled Red to the ground with a strength that belied his thin-limbed form, and the sheriff struck the ground with the force of a man ejected from his car during a traffic accident.

"*WHO YOU GOT IN THERE, GODDAMMIT!*" Shay howled, spittle flying, his orange-eyed glare weighing on Red's face like fifty pounds of pig iron. He raged around the kitchen like a dust devil with nowhere to go, smashing dishes, sweeping things off the counter, kicking chairs and sending them spinning—all while Red lay in a semi-daze and tried to draw breath past the ragged pain in his side. "*WHO? WHO IS IT?*" Shay screamed again and again, not even pausing to give Red a chance to speak, and each time he did, the pressure mounted. His tornado of fury ended with him standing at Red's booted feet, glowering down at him, nostrils flaring and relaxing, flaring and relaxing, fists clenching and releasing, clenching and releasing, his burning orange glare never wavering from Red's face. "Better tell me, boy, before I lose my temper and do something I can't take back." He said the words in an almost conversational tone, and as he did so, wisps of blue flame danced from his nostrils.

"Shay…" Red wheezed, "I don'…know…what you're…talking about." Each utterance brought a fresh wave of agony from his chest and abdomen, but he imagined being skinned would hurt considerably more. "I don't!"

Fists still doing their dance, Shay walked around him slowly, eyes narrowing with each step. He squatted on his hunkers at Red's side for a heartbeat that seemed to last forever, then swung his leg across the sheriff's battered chest and sat on him, one knee on either side. He rocked forward, dropping his hands to either side of Red's face and dropped his own head down so they shared each other's breath, barely a finger's width between the tips of their noses. "I'll kill you, boy. You know that." Shay spoke as though he were saying nothing more dire than "please pass the butter" or "nice weather we've been having." He didn't blink, and he didn't switch his gaze back and forth between Red's eyes the way a human would, he only hunched there and pinned the sheriff to the blue linoleum as surely as if he'd skewered him with a fireplace poker.

"I know it, Shay," croaked Red. "I don't have no—"

Shay rocketed forward, dodging his head to one side at the very last moment, ending up with their cheeks pressed together so hard that it hurt, so close his skin seemed to burn Red as sure as Millie's griddle would have. They ended up eyeball-to-eyeball, Shay's eyelashes feathering against Red's. "I see you in there," he growled. "Who's that? Who is it?"

Red tried to move his head to the side, but even as he decided to pull his face away, Shay's hand slapped to the side of his face, and he couldn't move, couldn't budge that hand. "I—"

"Shut up, Eldred," murmured Shay. "The adults is talking, now."

Red quaked inside, sure that Shay had rounded that last bend on the track to the asylum—something Red had believed close at hand for almost a decade. He thought about struggling for half a heartbeat, but he wasn't a strong man, and even a strong man would lose a wrestling match against someone as crazy as Shay.

Shay grabbed his chin between two iron-like fingers and turned his head from side to side, never moving his own face, never withdrawing his hot gaze, tracking Red's eyes with his own. He drew in a long breath, then sniffed like a hound dog searching for a trail. "Is it... No, that couldn't be, could it? Is that..." He leaned closer and closer until their cornea almost touched, until each blink of Red's eye beat against Shay's orange eye like a moth's wing. "Adeline! Is that you? How'd you *find* me, woman? I thought I told you to leave me be?" He sniffed again, then shook his head. "Nah, not old-woman-ish." He muttered as he drew his head back and cocked it to the side at an extreme angle given the circumstance. "Is it..." He released Red and threw back his head to cackle at the ceiling. "Well, I'll be *damned*! I've got all the luck tonight, Eldred!" He snapped forward at the waist, gaze suddenly intense again. "Oh, no you don't, Kai Washington! No, *you ain't gettin' away this time, boy.*"

A vague pressure began behind Red's left eye, something that itched and burned and seemed to wriggle like a snake. "Shay, I—"

"Hush your mouth, Eldred!" snapped Shay. A look of intense concentration settled over the man's fish-belly-pale face, locking his expression in hard, cruel lines. "I'm busy a minute." His eyes glowed with orange light that seemed almost alive, that made Red want to run and hide and suck his thumb the way he had when his daddy was on a bender. He lay there, trying not to make a sound, not stilling his breath, hoping it would end, hoping Shay would go away again.

As the orange light filled the kitchen, the air quality of the air changed. It grew hot, heavy, and tasted vaguely of burnt onions. It was like breathing another man's foul breath, and Red detested it.

After an eternity and then some, Shay rocked back on his heels and grinned. "There, now," he said. "That one won't bother us again. I got him pinned down now." He looked to the left and frowned. "Wonder if I should tell his grandmother?" He hummed a little as if considering his options while Red drew himself toward the wall on his elbows. "Nah," he muttered. "She made her choice. Let her live with it." He sniffed and turned his gaze on Red.

"Shay, I didn't—"

"Oh, relax, Eldred. I know you didn't have no part in it."

"What... Who..."

Shay drew another deep breath in through his nose. "Damn, boy, it smells like old gym socks in here. You need to open up a winda or something." He rose smoothly to his feet, and then, stepping over Red's legs, he returned to the living room without a backward glance. "Where's that drink? The service in this place leaves some room for improvement."

Red pressed a shaking hand over his mouth to stifle his terrified sobs.

Chapter 4
To Live and Die
in Odolavesta

I

Gavin rolled out of the bed onto his hands and knees, disoriented, lost in the darkness, and didn't know why. *Kai*? He didn't think he'd been dreaming, but he no longer felt confident he would know for sure. Without knowing the reason, thinking about Kai filled him with trepidation. *Kai, are you there*? After an interminable wait, he sighed and shook his head, unable to shake the idea that Kai needed him. He knelt there for a moment, feeling the cheap carpet beneath his toes, knees, and knuckles, and sent quick, darting glances into the gloom around him. *Didn't I leave the bathroom light on*? he asked himself. His breath rasped in and out of him, and he still felt like he was holding his breath, like he couldn't catch it. *Why didn't I leave the bathroom light on*? A feeling of doom enveloped him, a feeling that Kai stood on death's door at the center of it, but he hadn't been able to raise Kai by psychic means the day before, so his failure to answer didn't mean anything.

That's what he told himself, anyway.

The Aeonian Motel & RV Park didn't offer many amenities—no coffee machine, no hairdryer, no iron—but there was an LED alarm clock with giant numbers. However, the one in Gavin's room was ancient, and the LEDs barely cast light past the edge of the nightstand anymore.

He opened his eyes as wide as he could, then closed them, and then repeated the process again, again, and a fourth time, taking deep breaths each time he did so. His vision adjusted to the gloom, but he didn't feel any calmer. He climbed to his feet, leaning heavily on the bed as he did so, then turned and sat, wondering what had woken him.

Then the knock sounded, and Gavin breathed a sigh of relief. *Nothing supernatural. Nothing hinky, just some drunk at the wrong room.* His pulse slowed, and a lopsided grin surfaced on his lips.

The knock came again, more insistent, louder this time.

"Coming." Gavin slid into a pair of jeans and a T-shirt, then went to the door barefoot. He peered through the peephole and saw a tall man, his features obscured by the early morning gloom. "Who's that?"

"It's Greg."

Gavin opened the door and held it open. "I'm going to guess that Mike called?" He gestured for Greg to come in, then stepped back.

"Yeah," Greg said with a sigh. He stepped through the door and closed it behind him.

"Another one? Already?" asked Gavin.

"Unfortunately, yes." His expression was grim, Greg's lips turned slightly downward at the corners of his mouth. "Mike said—"

"Male?" Gavin asked in a tight voice, feeling the muscles in his face tense all at once, and his hands curling into fists.

Greg's facial muscles tightened, drawing his normally buoyant face into a harsh grimace. "Oh, no! Sorry, I didn't think. Mike said it's a woman. He's already on the scene." Greg's expression soured." And he said to tell you that Sheriff Westral and Deputy Lister are out there, too."

Gavin closed his eyes in a long, slow blink, forcing himself to relax. "Did he say where?"

Greg nodded. "It would be easiest to text you the coordinates, but I realize none of us have your cell phone number."

"Ah. Let's correct that right now." Gavin went to the closet and pulled his suit coat off the hanger. He reached into the breast pocket and withdrew four business cards from a polished card case. He gave the cards to Greg. "My mobile number's on there. And you give everyone else a card?"

"Of course." Greg busied himself entering Gavin's contact into his phone.

Gavin went into the bathroom and filled the sink with hot water. He wetted one of the thin washcloths, then scrubbed his face with it, his brain already sweeping away the last vestiges of sleep. He turned and went back into the main room as his phone buzzed.

"That'll be me. Coordinates."

With a nod, Gavin walked to his suitcase and pulled out a pair of old, but well-cared-for combat boots and a pair of thick socks. He sat in the nearby chair to put them on. "Out in the middle of the desert, again?"

"According to Google maps, yes."

Gavin pulled on a long-sleeved work shirt and buttoned it up. "Did Mike say if I can get there in my rental car?"

Greg shook his head. "You'll never make it in that crate."

Gavin nodded but grimaced. "I doubt Westral will provide me with a vehicle. Can Mike come back for me?"

"That won't be necessary," said Toby as he stepped into the room. He tossed a key fob onto the bed. "You can take that."

Gavin eyed the Mercedes emblem on the fob and arched an eyebrow. "Not for nothing, but I'm not sure those little SUVs will make it either."

Toby glanced at Greg, and the two men shared a secret smile. "Trust me, Gav. SEMPRe never goes anywhere unprepared."

Opening the nightstand drawer, Gavin shrugged. He reached inside, withdrew his Glock, and slid it into his holster, which he slipped inside the waistband of his jeans. "All right, I'm ready." He opened Greg's text and tapped on the GPS coordinates. "I can use the app on my phone as a navigation system."

Toby chuckled again. "Use the one in the truck. Come on, I'll show you."

Gavin followed Toby out into the cool early-morning air, and he paused, flicking a finger toward the empty space between his rental and one of the black SUVs—the other was gone. "Did we lose a couple? Benny and Shannon? Did they get spooked already?"

"What?" Toby asked, turning. His gaze tracked to the empty space, and he grinned. "Don't worry, Gavin. Everything's under control."

Gavin shrugged. "If you say so."

Toby nodded, then turned and strode across the parking lot to an olive-green Mercedes G-class wagon. It sat on huge off-road tires and sported a mildly lifted suspension. Toby waved at the wagon. "That will take you anywhere you want to go."

"I want to go back to Minnieville."

With a smile and a nod, Toby waved at the Mercedes. "It can take you there, but a plane ride is quicker."

"Yeah," said Gavin with a sigh, "and I have a job to do." He looked the big boxy SUV over. "This beast must have cost you a hundred and twenty-five thousand dollars, Toby."

"More," said Toby. "But it's SEMPRe's money, so don't worry about it." He held up a hand like a traffic cop. "And don't start that 'I can't drive that, Toby' nonsense. This is why we formed SEMPRe in the first place." He offered a small shrug. "At least in part."

"But—"

"No buts, Gavin. You're a good man, fighting to make the world better. Your enemies are the opposite and are fighting to make the world worse. You're exactly the kind of man SEMPRe wants to help."

Gavin turned and looked at the big SUV, a small grin blossoming on his lips. "The matte black roof is a nice touch."

"Wait until you see the interior," said Toby with a smile.

2

Roys Peak Vista, Southwestern TX
Saturday, 5:08 am CST

Gavin allowed the G-series wagon to coast through the scattering of scrub trees at the end of Old Ore Road and into a wide-open space dressed in gravel. He parked between a late-model gray pickup and Sheriff Westral's Cadillac. A Kelly County Sheriff's Department car was parked on the other side of the green dinosaur, but there was no medical examiner's vehicle, no CSI truck. Gavin shook his head and got out.

Wearing the "uniform" typical FBI agents everywhere—a conservatively cut, dark-blue suit over a white button-down with a boring tie—the blond man walked toward him. His expression was grim. Behind the blond man stood Westral, Lister, and a grizzled man wearing a tan Stetson. The man was obviously a cop, and he turned a curious stare at Gavin.

Gavin stepped forward holding his hand up toward the blond man. "You must be Mike."

The blond man grimaced and shook his head, cutting his eyes toward the other officers behind him. "Actually, it's Rick. Richard Michael's out of the San Antonio office."

Gavin slapped his forehead. "God, I'm an idiot."

Mike shook his head and grinned. "That's all right. I get it all the time. It's par for the course for a man with a name like mine." He took Gavin's hand and gave it a shake. "You met Joe and the crew, then?" he said, jerking his head toward the Mercedes.

"I did."

Rick nodded, then turned back toward the other three men. "Have you met Deputy Lister, Sheriff Westral, and Lieutenant MacArthur?"

As they approached the other three men, Gavin said, "I've had the pleasure of meeting Lister and Westral, but I haven't met Lieutenant MacArthur." Lister looked at him as if he were a slug, but Westral merely looked at him, a half-smile on his lips and absolutely nothing in his eyes.

The grizzled cop stepped forward and held out his hand. "Bud MacArthur, Texas Rangers."

"Gavin Gregory, FBI."

They shook hands, then Bud turned to the side and waved at the darkness with his Maglite, a grimace settling over his features. "She's over here." He flicked the flashlight on, and its powerful white beam stabbed into the night.

"Bad one?" asked Gavin.

"Ain't they all? Come on, I'll take y'all back for a peek."

Gavin grunted and fell in with Bud as the ranger led them to the crime scene. Westral and Lister brought up the rear, whispering like a bunch of kids. Mike walked on the other side of Gavin, silent, his expression impassive.

"Have you been to the other scenes?" Gavin asked the Ranger.

MacArthur shook his head. "We just got the inter-agency request earlier this evening. Or I should say early yesterday evening."

"From Sheriff Westral?"

MacArthur looked at him sidelong, then gave a slight shake of his head. "From your boss. SSA Fielding, I think his name was."

Gavin nodded once. "Pete. Pete Fielding."

Bud grunted and nodded, his gaze on the ground before them. "That's him. I take it you had something to do with it?" He glanced back at Westral and Lister. "*After* you met the sheriff?" he murmured.

"I asked Pete to involve the Rangers on our missing agent. I found Kelly County's investigative techniques…" He shrugged his shoulders.

The Ranger grunted, again, casting another quick glance over his shoulder, then leaned closer. "You didn't hear it from me, but KCSD ain't known for law enforcement prowess."

"That was my experience. To be honest, they seemed more interested in obstructing."

Bud shrugged. "Think of 'em more as border agents for the sovereign nation of Kelly County. They're more interested in keeping everyone out."

Beside Gavin, Mike grunted.

"What are you girls talking about?" said Westral as the other two drew closer.

"Comparing notes about the case."

"Uh-huh." Westral's voice was laced with a heavy dose of suspicion.

"Maybe y'all should consider talking to the people who have investigated this case," added Lister.

Gavin scoffed. "Happy to, only I can't find any. I wasn't under the impression that you investigated much of anything."

"Now, Agent Gregory, that ain't very neighborly," said Westral. "I might get the impression that you don't think much of me and my men. I might get the impression that you think you're better than us."

Gavin bit back the comment that came to mind and instead said, "Sheriff Westral, I'm sorry if that's how you interpreted my comments."

"That ain't exactly an apology," said Lister.

"That's okay, Jonas. We can't all be fancy FBI agents."

"You could try being law enforcement officers," said Mike.

"Now, Agent Michaels, you don't know me. You don't know my men. You don't know how I run my department. Hell, man, you *just* got here!"

"Your reputation precedes you, sir."

"Well, ain't that just dandy. I guess you FBI ain't scared of pillow talk."

Gavin glanced at the sheriff, meeting his gaze for a fleeting instant and noting the amusement and the scorn there. He rolled his eyes at the man, then turned his gaze forward.

Bud MacArthur pointed his Maglite at a boulder off to their right, and the bright white light washed over the body of a young woman with red hair. He stopped and said, "The sheriff and Deputy Lister have already approached, so I'm going to ask them to stay here to limit any further degradation of evidence at the scene."

"You too, MacArthur? Can I expect the Rangers to be busting my balls from now on?"

McCarthy turned a slow, cold gaze on the sheriff. "Should you?"

"Well, if you believe these FBI wankers."

Bud scoffed, then danced his Maglite's beam over the footprints surrounding the body. "Maybe I can just believe my own eyes. You know the Rangers offer training on crime scene processing, right?"

Westral sneered at the lieutenant. "We know how to process the crime scene. After all we've been doing it all these months and ain't heard a peep from you Austin Johnny-come-lately's."

MacArthur turned his face away. "I'm from Uvalde, and you know it."

Red Westral shrugged his shoulders. "Wherever you're from, then. I couldn't care less. You don't want us in your little club, and it don't bother me none because I never wanted to be in it."

Mike turned and pinned the man with a freezing glare. "Then stand here and shut your goddamn mouth."

"My, my, lawman. Ain't you just a big deal."

Mike treated the man to a glance and then dismissed him by turning his head away and looking at the crime scene. "Do we have an ID?"

"Nothing was with the body," said Lister.

"Small town," said Mike. "Do you recognize her?"

"Well, we might," said Sheriff Westral, "but we hayseeds are just standing here shuttin' our goddamn mouths."

Mike cast a scathing glance the sheriff's way, then quirked his eyebrow at Lister.

"She ain't from Odolavesta, but I know her, just the same. That there is Bobbi Bradley. Her folks have a place halfway to Alpine. I believe she was living with them."

"Address?" asked MacArthur.

"I don't have that, right off, but I'll get it to you."

Westral scoffed and turned his back on them, walking away into the darkness. Lister blushed but didn't follow his boss into the gloaming.

"What do we need to know about Bobbi Bradley, Jonas?" asked Gavin.

Lister glanced at him and shrugged. "What do you mean?"

"Her habits, her routine. Did she work?"

"Did she hang around the local bars? Was she promiscuous?" asked Mike.

Lister's face clouded over. "Listen here—"

"They ain't digging for dirt on the girl, Lister," said Bud MacArthur. "They're looking for a place to start. They're looking for how this killer latched on to her, *where* he latched on to her."

The deputy closed his mouth, then nodded, but his expression didn't soften by much. "I've seen her out and about," he said. "She didn't have a regular job, at least not that I know of. I had heard she was lookin', but there ain't much around here. She took the fill-in occasional shift back to the hotel."

Gavin raised his eyebrows. "At the Odolavesta Resta?"

Lister's gaze flicked to his, and he nodded.

"Interesting." Gavin glanced at Mike. "Any of the other victims have a tie to the hotel?"

The deputy scratched his chin, then shook his head. "I just don't know, Agent Gregory. I'll have to check into it."

"We can help with that," said Gavin. "How soon can you get us a list of the particulars for all the victims?"

Lister glanced over his shoulder into the darkness, then shrugged. "An hour or so after we get back to town at best. Depending on…*resistance.*"

"We need to gather as much information as we can get. It's like food to us. Don't starve us, Deputy Lister." Mike gave the man a significant look.

The big man turned his gaze on Mike, then gave him a single, slow nod.

"Now that we got all that out of the way…" said Bud as he copped a squat next to Bobbi Bradley's remains. "To me, Agent Gregory, these cuts here"—he flicked the beam of his Maglite to several long, shallow cuts—"don't look serious. They look like a warm-up."

Gavin moved around the body, noting the positions of the long, shallow lacerations, and the relationship of those cuts to the gaping wounds in other areas of her body. "With as many bodies as we are talking about, I don't think our killer needs warm-up. These are for some other purpose."

"An appetizer," said Mike moving to stand at her feet. "Have any of the victims been sexually molested, Deputy Lister?"

The big deputy shook his head. "The medical examiner says no."

"Any mutilation?" asked Gavin, and then shook his head. "To genitalia, I mean."

Again, the big deputy shook his head. He cocked his head to the side, then took a few steps closer. "She almost looks…"

Gavin nodded his gaze directed at the large gaping wounds. "That's right, Deputy Lister. She was butchered, and I don't mean that in the colloquial sense."

Lister nodded. "Some of the others looked…almost like they was field dressed. You know, strung up and bled, like a deer."

"Souvenirs?" asked Bud. "A sadist?"

"Worse," said Mike, and Gavin nodded.

"Meat." Gavin nodded, a sour grimace on his face.

"My God," murmured the ranger.

"Someone's…" said Lister in a tremulous voice.

Mike lifted his gaze, a grim expression on his face. "Eating them, yes."

Lister paled, and again, he glanced into the darkness, then shook his head. "We ain't equipped for this."

"Duh," said Mike.

3

US Route 385, south of Aeonia, TX
Saturday, 7:39 am CST

Mike and Gavin traveled in an easy silence, perhaps lulled by the hypnotic hum of the off-road tires on the asphalt. Mike had refused the key fob, saying that Toby had loaned the G-class to Gavin, and that he should keep it for the balance of the investigation, that that's what Toby intended. They'd stayed just long enough for the sun to make an appearance and light the crime scene. Mike had watched Gavin go through his routine of walking through the crime scene alone and muttering to himself. They'd left after the ME gave his initial impressions, after making an appointment to meet Bud near the Odolavesta Resta at half-past ten.

"Sorry about the name thing," said Gavin.

"He should've given me a better alias," said Mike with a shrug. "It's confusing."

"It must be. Especially if all your closest friends—your husband, even—all have multiple identities. I don't know how you keep track of who's who and when."

"I treat it like being undercover. Rick has his own personality, though I admit it's a lot like my own." He shrugged. "Toby and Benny have done it their whole lives, so for them, it's second nature."

"You mean the whole switching names thing, Toby mentioned?"

"Yes. I don't know how much Toby told you, but he assumed Benny's identity and went out into the world, where he immediately developed another alias and began living as someone else entirely. Benny stayed in Millvale, pretending to be Toby."

"How in the world… Wait a minute…did you say Millvale? Millvale, Pennsylvania?"

Mike treated him to a confused look. "No. Millvale State Hospital"—he pumped his shoulders up and down—"in New York. I think it's closed, now, but it was one of the big ones back in the 70s and 80s. There's a Millvale in Pennsylvania?"

Gavin nodded. "I don't know why I'm surprised, but Millvale, Pennsylvania is the town where the Briar Ridge State Mental Hospital is located. *Another* former state facility where I've investigated a…serial killer."

"Part of The Smith investigation, right?" Mike lifted an eyebrow. "What a coincidence. Think it's significant?"

Gavin shifted in the driver's seat, switching which hand he held the wheel with, and sighed. "Who knows? Given the turn my life is taking into the twilight zone, I'm tempted to say everything is significant, that nothing happens by chance."

Mike lifted an eyebrow. "Greg shared your story—the parts you told them, *and* the parts you didn't tell them."

Gavin shrugged uncomfortably.

"Part of the fun when you hang out with psychics," said Mike. "No secrets."

Gavin cleared his throat. "You were involved in this vigilantism-thing that Toby mentioned? The fight against Brigitta?"

"It was a lot more than just a fight against Brigitta," said Mike in a grim, enervated voice. "It was a war. A war with…a certain unsavory element—"

"The demons, you mean. And Abaddon."

"—that inhabited our hometown."

"Oneka Falls, right? You were police chief there?"

Mike blushed a little. "Sort of. I split my time between being police chief and the town's worst drunk. I didn't know it, but my boss was one of the demons running everything."

"Then you can't…*see* them? Sense them?" He shot Mike a quick glance. "Or something else?"

"You mean, am I psychic?" Mike chuckled. "Benny always says he hasn't figured out what power to give me. I *think* he's joking, but with Benny, it's hard to tell."

"I'm not even sure what that means, Mike."

"If you ever figure it out, please let me know." Mike chuckled and shook his head. "I know what you mean, though, Gavin. All this"—he lifted both hands and waved them in small circles—"is crazy, even to me, and I've had years to get used to it."

"Tell me about the demons."

Mike's face fell into grim lines. "I'm not sure they are demons like from the Bible, exactly. They aren't from here, they're from…somewhere else. The main one, the one whose conjuring allowed all the others to come through… Jesus, I sound like a science fiction writer."

"No, go on. Like you said, all of this is crazy. How can you talk about it and sound sane?"

"Yeah." Mike heaved a sigh. "Before all this, I was intensely unhappy. Shannon was living in a made-up world, and Benny was locked up in Millvale. Toby had no memory of any of it, but he was out there killing demons with abandon. Even with all that, sometimes I wish I could go back in time, that I could go back to my blissful ignorance—working for demons, living with them, just *not knowing it.*"

Gavin nodded. "I understand that."

"Anyway. Some joker way back in history conjured a super-powerful demon named Lilitu, and the fact that he summoned her opened a path for the rest of them to follow her. We beat them by…I don't know…casting spells in Akkadian, then performing some ritual to banish Lilitu." He shrugged his shoulders. "Toby says she can't come back."

Gavin was silent for a moment, then asked, "Is this Lilitu the one he says was his fiancée?"

Mike grimaced and shook his head a little. "He hasn't said that to me. At the end of our war with the demons, she kidnapped Toby. She took him to the desert or to some other reality or something, made him see what life with her would be like. He's got…" Mike shrugged again. "It's like Stockholm Syndrome, I think."

"He seems…" Gavin shook his head.

Mike looked at him curiously. "Go on."

"No, I just met him a few hours ago. I don't know anything about him, not really."

"Tell me."

Gavin cleared his throat. "Last night, Toby and I went for water. We ran into these two shit kickers—you know the type. Local guys with chips on their shoulders. They called us names and wanted to fight. There was a woman there, the cashier, and one of them seemed to think it was his responsibility to keep her in line. I told Toby to stay in the car, and I went back to make sure she was okay. Instead of doing that, he followed right behind me." He heaved a sigh. "Anyway, he seems...*eager*. To fight, I mean. Disappointed when nothing pops off."

Mike nodded. "I think that's accurate, especially since his encounter with Lilitu. He's always been a man of action rather than a man happy to kick back and relax." He glanced at Gavin sidelong. "Did he..."

Gavin grinned a little. "Did he tell me about the sixty-one demons he killed before you all became a vigilante gang? Yeah, he did."

A wide grin surfaced on Mike's face. "And none of my friends are in jail. That's a good sign."

"Half-year ago, it probably would've been different. But in the last six months..." Gavin shrugged.

"In the last six months, you met someone—*something*—truly evil."

Thinking of Glacadairanam, Fry, *and* Adeline d'Clara, Gavin nodded. "More than one. I'm not sure they're the same kinds of things that you guys faced, but they're definitely evil."

Mike leaned his head back against the headrest and watched the empty countryside click by. "Lots of evil in the world, Gavin. Not all of it's supernatural, but some of it is."

Gavin let the conversation lie as the buildings that marked the edge of Aeonia became visible on the left. He lifted one hand from the steering wheel and gestured at them. "Civilization, such as it is."

Mike grunted.

Gavin turned left onto First Street, then continued west. As they passed the Kwik Mart, he pointed at the store and said, "That's where Toby and I went for water last night." Mike turned his head to look, and as he did so, the two men from the night before came around from the back of the building. They stopped and stared as the G-class rolled by. "That's them."

"Oh, *that* type," said Mike with laughter in his voice. "Yeah, I know that type."

Neither one of them saw one of the men pull out a cell phone and make a call.

4

The off-road tires of the Mercedes crunched through the gravel on the side of the road as Gavin turned into the parking lot of the Odolavesta Resta. Bud's pickup truck was already in the lot, and so was the patrol car from the Kelly County Sheriff's Department.

"More hassle?" asked Mike.

Gavin scanned the area, but nothing moved. "I have no idea, but I hope to God not. Yesterday, Westral had Lister posted up outside the door. But the sheriff drives the giant green Cadillac, and he's not here."

Mike scoffed. "Yeah, I know that type, too." He glanced at the black Mercedes with Toby at the wheel and Greg in the passenger seat as it pulled to the side of the road on the opposite side of the street. "Hopefully, the sheriff shows up while we are here."

"So Toby can see if he's a demon?" asked Gavin.

Mike nodded and pointed at an empty spot next to the ranger's pickup. "At least we can check out Lister."

Gavin put the G-class in park and glanced at Mike. "It must be tough living in a world where you can't trust your eyes."

Mike wagged his head to the side. "It's not so bad since we banished Lilitu. I mean, Toby's on guard—we are all on guard—but the demons from Oneka Falls are gone."

"Does Toby's trick work on other kinds of…" Gavin shrugged his shoulders.

Chuckling, Mike nodded. "We're not sure. My friends got their abilities through exposure to Lilitu and her kind. That's the running theory, anyway."

Gavin glanced at the black SUV. "But what about Greg? He's not from Oneka Falls, right?"

"No, he's from Florida, but his grandparents had a house on Genosgwa Lake. He had direct exposure to Herlequin and Brigitta as a child."

"What, like Toby, Benny, and Shannon?"

"The chase through the woods? No, he didn't have to play that game, but I think they were leading up to it. It was a time when Herlequin was in hiding, and he took his time grooming Greg, setting him up. He did the same kind of thing to Benny—the grooming, I mean—but on a much more accelerated basis. And Brigitta was hiding in the lake, pretending to be a lake hag. The locals had all kinds of legends about her. She must've been doing it for a long time, and she fed off the fear."

"They *fed* on fear?"

Mike gave him a solemn nod. "Negative emotions, according to Benny. He once asked Herlequin how anger tasted, and the demon king said it wasn't as good as fear, but it would do."

"And Toby, Benny, Shannon, and Greg all survived these vile creatures at the age of ten or eleven?"

"None of them escaped unscathed, but yes, they *did* escape."

"How did you guys figure it all out? The Akkadian stuff?"

"We have the help of thousands and thousands of people. That's how SEMPRe works. You post about something mysterious, something supernatural, and people jump on it. They use all kinds of tools to mine data from the Internet and then combine the results of all of their work into a big picture."

"Do you think…" Gavin dropped his gaze.

"It's already in the works, Gavin," Mike said softly. "Teams are already pursuing your…experiences."

When Gavin raised his head, he found Mike gazing at him with an expression of compassion. "Benny?"

"Benny and Greg. They don't have to wait for the story, you see."

"Yeah, I—" Gavin closed his mouth as Bud MacArthur stepped out of the door to Reynold's wrecked room and beckoned them. "We're on."

"Yeah." Mike glanced over his shoulder and nodded at the SUV. "Greg says he's human."

Gavin arched an eyebrow.

"Greg says *Toby* says he's human."

"Ah." He opened his door as Bud stepped off the stoop and came toward them. Both he and Mike got out and walked forward to meet the Texas Ranger.

"Lister is inside," said Bud. "He brought the case files and the evidence sheets"—his lips turned down in a fierce grimace—"what little they gathered, anyway."

"And the sheriff?"

"He ain't here, thank goodness."

"Have you known him long? Westral?" asked Mike.

Bud shook his head. "I haven't had the pleasure before this case. I've seen him, during training events and the like, but I've never spoken to the little cockroach before this morning."

Gavin grinned and nodded. "That was my initial impression of him, as well."

Mike chuckled. "He's not a very likable fellow."

MacArthur's gaze flicked behind them, and he narrowed his eyes. "Looks like the newsies are on to the story."

Gavin froze, but Mike only laughed. "No, we know them. I do, anyway. They're innocuous."

Bud gave him an odd look. "I don't consider anyone following federal law enforcement officers around innocuous."

"They are just a couple of crazies from that watchdog group."

Gavin arched an eyebrow at Mike, and Bud said, "Crazies? What watchdog group?"

"Yeah. There behind that group on the Internet. The people who chase ghosts and things like that. Simper, or something like that. We ran into them earlier this morning—they think there's a cult behind all these murders."

"SEMPRe—the Society for Extrasensory, Metaphysical, and Paranormal Research—I was just brought up to date on them. They must have followed us," said Gavin.

Bud arched his eyebrow at him. "And you didn't see them? It ain't like there's a bunch of traffic around here."

"I guess not."

"We got to talking," said Mike. "New partners, you know. Telling each other stories, like that." He glanced over his shoulder at the SUV. "They're harmless crazies."

MacArthur's gaze flicked back and forth between them for a moment, then he gave them a curt nod. "I could collar them, send them to Bexar County lockup, have their fancy SUV towed to El Paso County. That would slow them the hell down."

"Like Mike said—"

"It's Rick," said Mike.

"Dammit," said Gavin. "Sorry, Rick. How many times is that now?"

Mike flashed a wry smile at Bud. "Oh, I'd say about a hundred."

"I'll get it eventually," said Gavin with a chuckle as a blush crept up his cheeks. "But like *Rick* said, those jokers are just a distraction. Let them have their fun, let them play cloak and dagger."

Bud looked at Mike, then at Gavin, and finally, he shifted his gaze to Toby and Greg parked across the street. "Pretty dang irregular."

"Yeah," said Gavin. "It happens from time to time on cases, though usually only with cases where there's more media coverage. I found it's best to leave them alone. Not that they cause trouble if I run them off, but it's just not worth the time, not worth the distraction from the case."

Bud shrugged. "If you say so. But I'll tell you this, if they get in *my* way, they are going to the hoosegow."

"I don't have a problem with that," said Gavin. He glanced at Mike. "You got a problem with that, Michaels?"

Mike grinned and shrugged. "They're not my friends or anything."

Bud grunted and spun on his heels. "Come on, you got to see this."

They followed him inside and got to work sifting through the pile of case files.

5

Gavin stepped out into the warm Texas sun and blew out a sigh. His mind was awhirl with useless facts, relevant data, and what seemed like the ravings of a madman. Sheriff Westral had edited every single case file, scrawling his thoughts wherever there was space—seemingly without a filter. The case files themselves were a mess—reports filed in any convenient space, notes filed upside down or back to front. The sheriff had refused to treat them as a serial crime for months, and so the deputies hadn't looked for links between the early victims.

But like Reynold and Bobbi Bradley, a small number of them had either stayed at or worked at the Odolavesta Resta. A very small few appeared to be transients, or maybe hitchhikers, and some had yet to be identified, but for the most part, the victims had died within one hundred miles of where they lived—including four citizens of Mexico.

Gavin's head hurt from a combination of little sleep, Westral's horrible handwriting, and most likely the dregs of his dehydration. He went to the car for a bottle of water and found it disgustingly warm. Toby and Greg had changed positions in the SUV across the street, but both men sat there pretending not to know him when he glanced their way.

He leaned against the G-class, standing next to the open driver's side door, forcing himself to add a packet of Hyrdolite to the piss-warm water and drink it, despite the temperature, despite the stale, flinty taste of it. He wished he had Toby's alternative prescription but it hadn't arrived from New York yet.

Inside Reynold's hotel room, Mike had been a Chatty Cathy, conversing with Bud about Bexar County and the San Antonio area. Lister hadn't said much—he seemed embarrassed by the other three men's reaction to Kelly County's case files—and his hostile attitude toward Gavin had evaporated.

Pulling his cell phone out of his pocket, Gavin dialed Pete Fielding's number. It was Saturday, but when his agents were in the field on an important case, Pete worked when they did. It was one of his long-standing non-negotiables, and one of the reasons Gavin admired him so.

"Fielding."

"Pete, it's Gavin."

"Hello, Gavin. I understand there's another body."

Gavin took a swig of mud and nodded. "Yeah, unfortunately. It's—"

"It's not Reynold." Pete's voice had a strangled quality to it that Gavin didn't much like.

"No, it's a woman. One of the deputies recognized her. Her name is Bobbi Bradley, and she's local."

"Oh, that's…" Pete sucked his teeth.

"Yes, boss, it is good news—as weird as that is to say."

"Good news for us, anyway."

"Yeah," Gavin said with a sigh. "But our good news is almost never good news for the victims or their families. Only when we catch the bastards doing the killing."

"Tell me you're keeping up with your hydration, Gavin. I've got Gloria hounding me every fifteen minutes, and that's in addition to the three calls from your lovely wife this morning."

"I am, Pete. Scout's honor." Gavin turned his gaze to the too-bright sky and squinted against the glare, but he enjoyed the feel of the warm sun on his face too much to turn away. "How's that trace on Reynold's phone coming?"

"We should have—"

Gavin nodded, not really listening as he watched Sheriff Westral roar into the parking lot, tires squealing, one hubcap abandoning ship and racing into the ditch. The car fishtailed, right on the edge of control, but Westral held it. He slammed on the brakes, leaving ribbons of smoking rubber in his wake. As soon as the car came to a rest, he jammed the gear selector up and sprang out of the car, the image of wrath incarnate. "Where the hell are my files?" he shouted.

"What in the dickens—"

"Sheriff Westral," said Gavin. "He likes to make a flashy entrance."

"Have the Rangers put in an appearance?"

"They sent a Lieutenant. Lieutenant Bud MacArthur."

Westral glared at him. "Say, boy, I asked you a question!"

"Have MacArthur run interference," said Pete. "You can't afford to waste your time on a strutting cock like that."

"Sure," said Gavin. "He seems to hate him, too."

"Let Texas deal with Texas, Gavin."

"Right you are, Pete."

"Dang it, I'll have an answer from you, Mister FBI-man!"

"I'll let you go," said Pete. "I want to call the county supervisor down there."

"Good luck with that, Pete. So far, almost everyone I've met down here has either been suspicious of strangers, rude, or downright hostile."

"Noted. Call me back later, I'll have an update on those LUDs."

Westral strode toward him, a smoldering glare burning on Gavin's face. "Didn't you hear me?"

"I will, boss."

"And call your wife, Gavin, before she has a stroke."

Gavin chuckled. "I'm going to tell her you said that."

"Not if you like me and want me to continue drawing breath, you won't. Gloria will have my hide."

Westral reached Gavin then and stood glowering at him.

"Talk to you later, boss. The sheriff has a question." At that, Westral narrowed his eyes to mere slits. Gavin hung up, then took a long draw of his kitty litter before meeting the sheriff's gaze. "What?" Gavin asked in a sharp voice. "What do you want, Westral?"

"I'm the sheriff of Kelly County, Mister FBI-man, and if you'll look down, that ground you see between your expensive shoes is *mine*. In fact, all the land you see around here belongs to me. When you're standing on my land, you dadgum better answer me when I ask you a question!"

"Yeah? Is that how it is?"

"You better believe it, cowboy."

Gavin glanced around, then took another long drink of Hydrolite. He pushed away from the car and stood towering over the short sheriff. "Let me tell you something, Eldred—"

"Don't you call me that, and don't you tell me nothing, I'm—"

"—I don't work for you. You aren't in my chain of command. And, judging by your notes in these case files and your performance in all these murders, I seriously doubt you'll be in anyone's chain of command after the next election. But regardless of all that, you want to come strutting at me like a bantam cock, shouting your questions, making your demands, fine. I won't stop you. But, let me tell you this: I don't respond well to bully tactics."

"You done, hoss?" asked the sheriff in an utterly flat tone, his head tilted to the side like a bird.

After the initial plummet of his stomach at the word "hoss," Gavin took another pull from his water bottle, then turned a bored stare on Westral. "You know what, Westral? I think I am." Before the sheriff could say another word, Gavin turned and walked back to the hotel room. Behind him, he heard the man's boot heels rattling angrily on the asphalt, and he grinned. He stepped through the door, hooking his thumb back over his shoulder, and said, "Look who I found."

Lister frowned down at his lap as Westral slammed through the door. The sheriff glared at him, then flicked his hostile gaze to Bud. "What's going on here, Ranger? What gives you the right to come into my jurisdiction, co-opt one of my"—he flicked the fingers of his right hand toward Lister—"less-than-brilliant deputies, and then start going through my private records?"

With a faint smile on his face, Bud MacArthur returned the sheriff's glare. "First off, Westral, I don't work for you. Second, though this man *does* work for you, he's clearly not of your ilk—he seems to actually care about solving this case, about stopping this perp from killing every young woman within three hundred miles. Third, I am a lieutenant, not a sergeant, so don't go calling me "ranger," you call me 'Lieutenant MacArthur.' This is now my crime scene, and the whole damn state of Texas is *my* jurisdiction, so you can just shut your damn mouth."

Mike chuckled and rolled his jocund gaze on the sheriff. "Does that clear everything up for you?"

Westral's eyes flicked toward Mike but never made it to his face. "*Dang*! Ain't this just a kettle of stinky catfish? I wonder what Captain Jensen would say about this?"

MacArthur grinned out of one side of his mouth. "Why don't you go back to your office, give him a call, and ask him?"

"Whoop, there it is," said Mike with a chuckle. "I think you just lost your crime scene privileges."

"Not at all," said Bud, spreading his hands out to the side. "But as far as stomping in here, throwing your weight around, acting like a little prima donna? Eh, you never had that privilege to begin with."

Flicking his narrow-eyed gaze back and forth between Mike and Bud, color rose on Westral's face. Then he shot Gavin a murderous glance before shifting his gaze to Lister. "Why ain't you on patrol, Lister?"

"I—"

"If that sentence don't finish with, 'am on my way, Sheriff,' I suggest you reevaluate your priorities. That or go ahead and put your application in with the Texas Rangers and hope they'll accept a moron like you."

"That's enough, Westral!" snapped Gavin.

Lister didn't say a word, he only got to his feet and settled his hat on his head without meeting anyone's gaze. He sniffed once, then gave his head a single shake and walked out into the parking lot.

"Well, *now* you have lost your crime scene privileges, Westral," said Bud in a grim tone. "I'll let you get on back to…well, whatever it is you do." When Westral didn't move, only stood there staring daggers at him, Bud stood up and pointed at the door. "You don't want to test me, Westral."

With a sneering, lopsided smile, Westral met each of their gazes in turn, then pointed at the files. "Them there belong to Kelly County."

"Not anymore," said Mike.

"I can't stop you ducks from coming in here, waggin' your tail feathers in everyone's face, quackin' and quackin' like you's something special, but I do know my rights. Them files belong to the Kelly County Sheriff's Department"—he tapped the gold star on his chest with his thumb—"and this here tin says I'm the sheriff. That means they're *mine*."

"Yeah?" asked Bud. "Agent Gregory, as a lieutenant of the Texas State Rangers, I request you begin an investigation of the Kelly County series of homicides represented by these case files."

"Sheriff Westral, I'm officially notifying you that pursuant to US code title twenty-eight, part two, chapter thirty-three, section five-forty B, having heard the request for assistance by Lieutenant MacArthur of the Texas State Rangers, the FBI is asserting jurisdiction over these cases. We require your assistance in the form of all materials your office has generated pursuant to your earlier investigation of these cases."

Westral shook his head once, pretended to lunge toward the closest stack of case files, then chuckled as Mike lurched to protect them. "You want them? Take 'em. But don't come to my office looking for help." He spun on his heels and tromped out the door, slamming it behind him.

"I don't think his daddy raised him right after his momma met her end." Bud sank back into his chair and picked up the case file in front of them. "You ask my opinion, that boy needed a switch once or twice in his formative years."

"If you ask me, he might need it now," said Mike.

Gavin stood, head cocked to the side, staring at the door. "That guy…" He shook his head.

"Yeah," said Bud with a sigh.

"Does he give you a—"

"Headache? Yeah. Yeah, he does," said Mike.

"—hinky feeling?" Gavin grinned at Mike. "Headache and a bellyache." He turned his gaze back to Bud.

The ranger sat, his head tilted back, his gaze directed up at the corner. "I ain't going to argue that the man isn't a pill, but he's all hat and no cattle."

"No, I don't mean that," said Gavin. He quirked his head to the side and grinned at the ranger. "At least I think I don't…" His smile faded, and he shook his head. "He just…" He shrugged. "The way he acts…it's just…"

"Off," said Mike. "Like he's a skell."

Gavin nodded and opened his mouth to reply, but his phone jangled, and he glanced down at the screen instead. "Pete," he said, lifting the phone to his ear and accepting the call.

"We've got him," said Pete. "The knifemaker."

"You've got Reynold's phone records."

"Yessir, and it's right here in the LUDs. Desert Heat, Odolavesta, Texas."

"Text me the address. We are on our way," said Gavin, beckoning the other two men and heading for the door.

6

Gavin wheeled the G-class around the bend on Stone Circle Road, and grimaced. He gestured toward the landscape with an open hand. "This is ridiculous! How do we sneak up on anybody in this mess?"

In the backseat, MacArthur chuckled. "You mean this foreign monstrosity?"

"No, this landscape! I mean, there aren't even trees!"

"There ain't much sneaking up on people out here."

"At least there's not much traffic going out this way," said Mike.

"Well, there's only the half-assed golf course at the end of this road. Who the hell wants to play golf out in the middle of the desert?"

"Who the hell wants to play golf?" asked Gavin.

Bud grunted, then reached forward between the door and the seat and tapped Gavin on the left shoulder. "There's your turn-in."

"The two-rut track?"

"Yep. Right before those half-built eyesores." The eyesores in question seemed to be a failed attempt at building golf condos. The architecture stuck out like a wart on a pretty girl's cheek, and only a single building of three conjoined condominiums had been built, with an empty concrete pad next door and only cleared ground after that.

Gavin cranked the wheel, barely slowing, but the big G-class handled it with a little tire noise and a lot of body roll. A huge plume of dust leaped skyward in their wake.

"No movement," said Mike, squinting at the three buildings at the end of the little road. He pointed to the left. "Some kind of dirt bike track off through the desert pan."

Gavin glanced across the scrub at the snaking trail, but it was empty, and he gave his attention back to his driving. He slid to a stop in what amounted to the side yard of the long ranch-style house with two metal buildings behind it and hopped out. "Which one?"

"One of the metal ones," Bud said, gesturing at the closest one with the 1911 he carried. "His forge."

"Looks like a house," said Mike, pointing at the ranch with his chin.

"Dual-purpose properties aren't rare out here," said Bud. "That'll be where his family is."

"Or where he's got Reynold," Gavin said, peering at the house.

Bud only shrugged. "Your call. Or we can get back in your fancy car here and wait for backup."

"I'm not sure I want backup from Kelly County," muttered Mike.

"And your rangers are too far out."

Bud nodded, then gestured at the buildings with the muzzle of his .45 again. "Like I said, your call."

Gavin gathered, shifting his gaze back and forth between the three buildings. The metal buildings looked new, no more than three years old, and the sign hung from the one closest to them. The sign that read 'Desert Heat' with 'High-Quality Blades' under it. He flicked his index finger at the building with the sign. "Forge," Bud said. He flicked his finger at the other metal building. "Storage shed."

"Seems reasonable," said Mike.

Gavin gave a single nod and pointed at the forge. "We'll go in there. Mike, cover the house. Sing out if there's any movement."

"Right."

With Bud following close behind, Gavin ran toward the forge in a half-crouch, his Glock drawn and ready. He flattened himself against the wall of the building next to the door, and the ranger took up a position on the other side of the closed door. Gavin flicked his eyes toward the door, then nodded, and Bud jerked the door open so Gavin could charge through. "FBI!" Gavin shouted.

The showroom was empty, but a cup of coffee steamed on the counter next to the computer. Gavin jerked his chin at a hall that led down the side of the building, then moved toward it, covering the doorway. Footsteps sounded from deeper in the building, and Gavin moved to the right, taking cover behind the sales counter. At the same moment, Bud moved all the way to the end of the counter, circled around behind it, and stood close to the wall, his line of fire parallel to the wall.

"FBI!" shouted Gavin once more. The footsteps slowed, then stopped.

"Uh…" murmured a male voice.

"Identify yourself!"

"Come out of the hallway slowly, hands up!" shouted Bud.

"I'm coming out. Don't shoot me." A giant of a man with the barrel chest and cannonball-shoulders of a blacksmith came out of the dark hallway, his steps tentative, his eyes wide. He held the wide blade of a Bowie in his left hand.

"Knife!" shouted Bud. "Drop it!"

The knifesmith glanced down at his left hand as if he'd forgotten what he held there. "Oh," he muttered. He raised his gaze to Gavin's and shook his head a little. "I don't…"

"Put it on the ground and walk away from it," said Gavin. He still held his Glock in firing position, covering the man with it, but the tension drained out of him.

Metal clanged on the concrete floor as the man bent forward slightly and tossed the unfinished blade on the ground. "Okay... Okay, the blade is on the ground...I didn't..." his gaze swam toward Bud MacArthur, and he started a little when he saw the ranger covering him at an oblique angle.

"Turn around and put your hands on the counter," commanded Gavin. "Don't reach for anything, and once you get there, *do not move.*"

Moving with deliberate slowness, the knifesmith did as Gavin said, even though it meant hunching down at an uncomfortable-looking angle. "What's this all about?"

"It's about the kidnapping of an FBI agent," said Bud. "You know anything about all that?"

"FBI agent?" He started to turn toward Gavin but caught himself and froze in place. "Sorry!"

"Got him, Bud?"

"Bless your heart, Gregory, but this ain't my first rodeo. This corn-fed Brahma bull moves, I'll jump on him like a duck on a June bug." He fixed the weaponsmith with a cold stare. "Hear what I'm sayin', Brahma bull? If it ain't a fact, God's a possum."

"Yessir, I hear you loud and clear, but I don't know why…" He closed his eyes in a long, slow blink. "Oh. The man who called about that Damascus."

Gavin stepped forward, holstering his service weapon as he did so. He put his hand flat on the man's back, right between his shoulder blades. "Go easy. I'm going to pat you down."

"You go right on. I'm standing here grinning like a mule eating cockleburs, but I ain't fixin' to do *nada*."

"That's the right of it. You just take a tater and wait," said Bud.

Gavin shook his head, his lips hinting at a little grin. "Is there a translation app from Texan back to English?"

"That would be like putting socks on a rooster," said the blacksmith with a chuckle.

Beneath his palm, Gavin felt the man start to relax. He stepped forward, putting his left foot between the smith's, and frisked him quickly but thoroughly. When he was done, he stepped back and nodded at Bud.

The ranger gave him a curt nod and holstered his big Colt 1911. He stepped closer, walking down behind the counter, gazing at the man the whole time. "What's your name, big fella?"

"Is it okay to stand up straight?"

"Why not?" said Gavin.

Across from him, Bud rested his hand on his sidearm and tapped it twice with his index finger. "You just answer Agent Gregory's questions. Give us the bacon without all the sizzle."

"I'm Brad Masterton." He jerked his chin toward the back of the building. "This here is my forge. I'm a knifesmith."

"You reckon?" Bud asked in a wry tone.

"Tell me about the man who wanted to know about Damascus steel," said Gavin.

Masterton shrugged. "We howdied, but we ain't shook yet. He called a couple days back, but I've been panting like a lizard on a hot rock these past couple months, so I couldn't just drop everything and jaw with him. I called him "Is that a fact?" said Bud.

"If I say a hen dips snuff, you can look under her wing for the can."

"Then what happened?" asked Gavin.

"Nothing. Just the sounds of that tussle, and even that eventually wound down. I could hear some people talking in the background, a fellow with a deep voice, a woman..." He shrugged his big shoulders. "Couldn't say who for either of 'em."

Gavin glanced at Lieutenant MacArthur, who nodded. "Reynold—Agent Hall—was working on a case, Mister Masterton. He found evidence, metal shards to be specific."

Brad nodded. "The Damascus. I figured as much."

"It's important we find the owner of the knife the metal came from."

"Chances are that metal came from right here in this building. I'm the only knifesmith for miles in any direction."

Gavin gave him a single nod. "These knives…they were used to kill some people."

Though he grimaced, Brad nodded. "And you want to know who my customers are."

With a shrug, Gavin nodded. "It's important."

"You said." Brad glanced at MacArthur. "He's FBI, but you ain't."

Bud stuck out his hand. "No sir, I'm a ranger. Bud MacArthur, out of Uvalde."

The big smith shook Bud's hand.

"Now, if you could get us that list…" said Bud.

"I can do that," said Brad. "Only problem is I do a lot of cash business. Ain't no law says I have to keep records on people who pay me cash."

Bud glanced at the knife blade on the floor. "No, there ain't…as long as that blade ain't longer than five and a half inches."

Masterton followed his gaze. "It won't be once I get the hilt on there."

"The person we're looking for is probably a loner. You might have seen him around, but more than likely, he's a newcomer. An out-of-towner. He may be charming, just standoffish. He is probably very particular—demanding, even."

Brad chuckled a little. "Mister, on that last bit, you just described every one of my customers."

Gavin nodded and gave a little shrug. "This man might make you feel a little hinky."

"Hinky?"

"All cut up like a boardinghouse pit," said Bud.

"If that means nervous, he's right. Something—the way he reacts, the way he won't look you in the eye when he talks to you, maybe something he said—might have made your hair stand on end." Gavin shrugged again. "Then again, he might be the most charming bastard you've ever met, but there's probably still something…a small voice in the back of your mind, maybe…that says he's not right."

Brad lifted a massive hand and rubbed it across his bald scalp. "No, I don't recall anyone like that."

"Do you do Internet sales?"

Masterton nodded. "I do, but I only take plastic for them."

"They'll be in your records, then."

"Yessir."

Gavin's mind took him back to the confrontation in the Kwik Mart—miles away, but not that far. "What about people from the area but not from Odolavesta? Say Aeonia?"

"Well, there ain't much to Odolavesta or none of the other towns around here. We don't distinguish based on town limits much around here. I'm from Odolavesta, but folks up to Aeonia won't think of me as an out-of-towner. We know most everybody from the local area. Hell, not a single town in Kelly County that has its own schools. Kids from all over all go to the same ones. If you grew up here, you might've had friends who lived in Odolavesta and Aeonia and Sanderson and Dryden and Alpine and everywhere in between."

"I see," said Gavin. "I ran into two guys in Aeonia. Two malcontents, if you take my meaning."

Brad shrugged. "Stewed skunks come from all over."

"Yeah, for sure, but what I mean is, both these guys gave me that hinky feeling, even though I've never met them before. They acted funny—staring at us, calling us names, telling the cashier that she knew better than to serve us, like that."

"Yeah, people can be contrary with city folk."

Gavin grinned a little. "Yeah, I get that, but these two…they take it farther than that."

The big knifesmith grimaced. "Well, there're some who…" Masterton closed his mouth and dropped his gaze to the counter.

"Go on."

He looked at Gavin then, his eyes hooded. "These are my neighbors." He glanced at Bud, then dropped his gaze again. "I shouldn't say anything."

"One of your neighbors may be responsible for the deaths of eight women," said Gavin.

Brad's gaze leaped up to his. "You don't know that. It might be some out—" He snapped his teeth together.

"Some out-of-towner."

"Well…yes. Or a Mexican."

"Did any out-of-towners buy one of your pig-stickers?" drawled Bud. "Any Mexicans?"

Masterton frowned and narrowed his eyes. "You don't know it's one of mine. You can't know that."

"Logically it—"

"Logic be *damned!*" growled the knifesmith. "Logic don't sit next to me at socials down to the Baptist church in Aeonia. Logic don't buy me no beer at the brewery, no suppers at Millie's. Logic don't—"

"Murder no one," added Bud, and Masterton fell silent, his eyes squeezed shut.

Gavin opened his mouth, but Bud cut his hand through the air, so he let silence reign. Outside, a dog barked and barked, loud enough to raise the dead. Inside the building, the air conditioner cycled on, and slightly cooler air wafted down around them. Gavin glanced at Bud, but the ranger shook his head.

Eventually, Brad sighed and blinked. "Yeah," he murmured. "There's a rough element around here. A bunch of people with some weird ideas." His gaze came up to meet Gavin's. "But I came up with some of those folks. Known 'em all my life. Hell, I even got kin messin' around with 'em. They might act all uppity when they's all together, but get one of 'em alone and they act right. They ain't broke bad, they just got their heads full of weird ideas."

"Weird ideas like what?" asked Gavin.

"For one thing, they stop going to Sunday-meetings." The big man shrugged. "And they won't talk about it. It's like it's *Fight Club* or something. Hell, I tried asking my little cousin why she hangs out with all those old men— my age, you see? She's only nineteen."

"And what did she say?"

"She just laughed, told me to hush, to stop making a fuss. When I asked her again, she went and raised hell and stuck a chunk under it." Brad shook his head. "And that's cattywampus, if you ask me. She's always been as sweet as stolen honey." He shook his head again and sniffed. "I asked her mama, and she's usually willing to beat her own gums to death, but about this? She just shook her head. Wouldn't say a word."

"Is she involved, too? Your aunt?"

Masterton shook his head once. "Ain't my aunt. She's my cousin. Her daughter's my little cousin, like I said."

"Okay. Are they both involved?"

"Nah." He frowned. "At least I don't think Mary's in it. Never seen her out and about with the rest of them." He shook his head. "And she don't wear the uniform."

"Uniform?" asked Bud. Outside, a door banged shut prompting another barrage from the dog, and all three men glanced at shop's entrance. "That old mutt's tearin' a hole in the sky."

"He acts up," said Brad. "Thinks everything's out to get him."

"Tell us about the 'uniform,'" said Gavin.

"You'll know it when you see it. They dress kinda normal, except they all look alike. Pants, dark shirts. It's the boots that sets 'em off."

"Fancy? Ropers? Riding boots?" asked Bud. "What?"

"No, you got the wrong idea. They ain't cowboy boots at all."

"Linesman boots," said Gavin. "Orange laces."

Masterton nodded. "That what them fellas over to the Kwikie was wearing?"

"Yep," said Gavin. "Both of them. Marcus and Reggie, I think."

Brad grimaced. "That'll be Roger, most like."

"That's it."

Masterton turned a severe glare on the door as the dog outside began raising Cain again. "What's got into him?" he muttered, then he shook his head and his expression darkened. "Went to school—hell, played ball—with both of 'em, but we ain't spoke much since them days. Roger's as useless as two buggies in a one-horse town. Marcus, though…" He shook his head. "I always thought he'd go off and play ball for some big college—Austin or College Station or somewhere out of state. He was good enough, and he had the grades for it."

"But he didn't go?"

"Nah. He piddled around here for a year or two, drinking a lot and working construction But then, out of the blue, he took to wearin' them boots and actin' all persnickety."

"Last names?" asked Bud, taking out a leather covered pad and a stubby pencil.

Brad looked uncomfortable, but said, "Roger Martinez, Marcus Wallace."

"They live close?" asked the ranger.

Masterton shook his head. "I guess I don't know for either of them."

"Who else is in the crew?" asked Gavin.

"Jon and Cece Clark, Bobby—"

"*What* did you say?" asked Gavin.

"Jon and Cece Clark."

"Describe them."

Masterton frowned at Gavin and quirked one eyebrow. "Well, Jon's about average in most respects, except he wears his hair long like a rock star. Cece's on the tall side for a woman, brown curly hair." His frown deepened. "Why? Was they at the Kwik Mart too?"

Gavin gave his head a single shake. "Never mind. Clark is the last name? C-L-A-R-K?"

"Yeah. Listen here, Agent Gregory, the Clarks are all right. Not as friendly as they used to be, but a fella doesn't get the idea they're looking down their noses at him. Not like some of them others."

"Uh-huh," said Bud, glancing at the door as the dog began another auditory assault, then crooking an eyebrow at Gavin. "Besides looking down on folk, any of these jackholes in the linesman boots ever do anything?"

"Do anything?" asked Brad.

Without breaking his gaze at Gavin, Bud rolled his hand in the air. "Fighting. Thieving."

"I wouldn't know about that, would I?"

Tilting his head a little to the side, Bud rolled his gaze toward the knifesmith. "Don't start chewin' your bit now, hoss. You been going on like you was vaccinated with the Victorola needle for the past five minutes."

Brad shook his head and frowned down at the floor. "I ain't nervous, and there ain't no reason to go mean. All I mean is, there is real lawmen about." He waved a thick hand toward the door leading out into the yard. "Go on and ask one of them."

Bud grunted, but then gave a single nod and glanced back at the door as the next peel of thunderous barking began. "You need to go deal with that hound?"

"I might."

"Forget that mutt," said Gavin. "Tell me about the rest of these people who—" He left off as the weaponsmith's gaze snapped to the door. Just as he turned to look, Mike barged through the door.

"Cars," he said. "Three or four, coming up the road fast." He hooked his thumb over his shoulder. "That dog is going nuts about something out in the brush, too."

"Probably just some critter," said Brad.

Mike's gaze never left Gavin's as he shook his head. "I don't think so."

Gavin nodded, then jerked his chin toward the dooryard. Mike turned and retraced his steps outside.

Bud leveled a finger at Masterton and said, "We're fixin' to go outside now, Brahma bull, and you're a-goin' with us. When we get out there, you are gettin' in the back of the fancy German SUV standin' in your driveway. You're gonna sit on your hands, you hear?" The weaponsmith sighed but nodded, and Bud motioned him out the door with a snap of his head.

The three men walked outside, and Masterton got in the back of the G-class, while Mike, Gavin, and Bud stopped near the front of the vehicle—not quite taking cover.

Three cars jounced up the two-lane track and skidded to a halt just inside the drive, blocking the exit, where they sat, engines idling. The drivers stayed inside the cars, though each leaned far enough forward to film them with their cell phones.

Gavin arched an eyebrow at Bud, but the ranger only shook his head and shrugged. "Let 'em film us if that's what they want."

"Should I go over there?"

"You can if you want, but I'd bet you'd be whistling up the wind." He turned and glanced at the scrub as the dog began to bark yet again.

Gavin followed his gaze, scouring the scrub and squinting into the bright noon-time sunlight, grimacing at the decidedly hinky feeling that was growing inside him. "This doesn't feel right."

"No," agreed Mike.

Bud only grunted, his gaze scanning back and forth across the desert landscape.

Gavin walked around the vehicle, keeping the SUV's bulk between him and the cars at the end of the driveway, and opened the rear door. He ducked down to look Masterton in the eye and jerked his chin at the three cars. "You know any of those people?"

Masterton nodded. "I don't recognize the cars, but that woman driving the middle 'un is my little cousin."

Peering at the center vehicle, Gavin nodded. "Do you think she would listen to you? Are you willing to tell her to stand down?"

Brad tilted his head and gazed out at him a moment, then said, "I might could."

With a curt nod, Gavin waved him out of the vehicle. "Let's try it, then."

Masterton shrugged and slid across the backseat, then his gaze crawled over Gavin's shoulder, and the man froze. Gavin whirled around—ready for a fight, ready for anything—but the yard was empty and nothing in the side lot moved.

"You! In the scrub! Step out of there!" commanded Bud, his hand on his .45's wide grip as he spread his legs, bending a little at the knee and the hip.

Mike slid his service weapon out of its holster, squatting a little and trying to keep tabs on both the scrub and the line of cars at the same time.

Masterton's gaze jumped to Gavin's, then on to the Texas Ranger, before zipping back to a clump of creosote, yucca, and cholla squatting just across the line marking the end of his property and the beginning of wild desert. He shook his head once and grimaced.

"Why, Brad Masterton!" came a voice from a different clump of scrub behind and to the left of the one that had drawn the attention of the knifesmith. "What in the Sam Hill are you doing?"

Gavin's gaze crawled over the brush, but he couldn't see anything other the vegetation.

"They's law!" called Brad. Under his breath, he muttered, "Marcus."

Lifting his chin to indicate he'd heard, Gavin glanced over his shoulder at the line of vehicles boxing them in. "This thing will handle the desert, right?" he asked in a quiet voice, his gaze on Bud's.

"Might could," said the ranger, not taking his eyes off the scrub. "A Ford on big tires'd do her better."

"Law?" Marcus called, a sour laugh trailing behind. "I don't care if they's law, Brad. *We're* your neighbors. You and me is friends, have been since school."

"When you want something," Brad muttered.

"What's that? I didn't quite hear you, hoss." When Brad shook his head, the sour laugh rolled out of the desert, again. "If you lay yourself down with dogs, Brad, you're liable to get up with fleas in your fur."

"What choice is there? They's law, like I said."

"And we're your neighbors, like *I* said. These 'uns don't have no call to come into your place and truss you up, then put you in the back of that monstrosity. You don't owe them foreigners the spit under your tongue."

"Lick that calf again?" called Bud. "I'm from right over in Uvalde."

"You might live there, John Law, but you smell like you're a hundred percent Austin."

"Come out of there!" demanded Bud.

"Well, ain't that about as friendly as a bramble bush? This here's public land, John Law. I have every right to be out here. Look down at your own boots and see if you can say the same."

Bud cut his gaze toward Gavin for a fraction of a second. "Listen here. You come up out of there and we'll thrash her out. Keep to your skulking around, and I'll slap iron on your wrists."

"For what?"

MacArthur slid the 1911 out, holding it loose at his side. "Last warning."

"Wash off your war paint, porky. I'm coming out." The creosote rustled, and Marcus stepped out into view. He wore camo in desert colors, an empty holster on his hip, and, of course, linesman boots with orange laces.

"Where's the pistol?" Mike leveled his Glock on the man.

Marcus rolled his eyes skyward. "Over yonder." He flipped his hand back toward the brush. "I didn't want to give you all no cause to fill me up with lead. Rifle's back in there, too."

"Tell your friends to step into sight," said Gavin.

Marcus's gaze slid toward Gavin, and he sniffed. "We have every right to be here." He jerked his head toward the house. "Brad's pretty little missus called me. Said there was some strange foreigner sneaking around her property, acting suspicious. When we got out here, we saw him"—he jerked his chin at Mike—"doing just that. Watched him a bit, too."

"He's a federal law enforcement officer."

Marcus shrugged. "*She* didn't know that, and neither did we. Anyways, we have a right to be here. Ain't no laws against us monitorin' the situation."

"Watching is one thing," said Bud. "Interfering with public duties, however, will get your ass locked up."

Marcus sneered at that. "Don't dig up more snakes than you can kill, Wyatt Earp." Even so, he turned and waved, and men stood up in three separate thickets, each dressed in camouflage, and each holding up empty hands. "Now, *boss*, we ain't interferin' none, and you ain't got no call to arrest no one." He turned a narrow-eyed gaze on Brad. "Not even Brad."

Gavin shook his head. "You a lawyer, Mr. Wallace?"

Marcus's eyes blazed at Masterton a moment, but he shook his head. "No, I ain't."

"Huh," grunted Gavin. "You'd think a man who is so interested in dictating the law to law enforcement officers would be *educated* about the law, at least."

"There's more ways to learn than in a classroom, FBI-man. And there's more to lawin' than studyin' the letter of the law. Our Second Amendment grants—"

"Oh, here we go," said Mike, earning a glare from the man.

"—us the right to form militias." He glared at Mike. "Scoff all you want. It only shows your true colors. Meanwhile, we're here to ensure you don't slip your leash, to keep you from overstepping your bounds. The Constitution says militias are necessary, and we've sworn our oaths as Article VI demands."

Gavin lifted an eyebrow at the man and pointed at his boots. "And those?"

Marcus looked down at his boots, then lifted his gaze to meet Gavin's and smiled. "Good fashion sense."

"And what about religion?"

"What about it?" asked Marcus with a shrug.

"Does your…group espouse religious mandates?"

The man grinned. "Is we a cult? Is that what you're askin' me?" His chuckle was derisive.

"Are you?" asked Bud.

"The Constitution says I don't have to tell you if we was, but we ain't. We're Perry's Irregulars. We protect these parts from"—he turned a narrowed-eyed glare on first Mike, then Gavin—"*foreign* influences."

"I don't think you understand the intent of—"

"All our members got to *read* and *understand* the thing," said Marcus. "Can you say the same of the FBI?"

"Actually—"

"Ain't no use arguing with a wooden Indian," said Bud as he slipped his .45 back into its holster. "We're burin' daylight. Got anything else to ask Masterton?"

Gavin pulled out his pad and pointed at Marcus with his pen. "Marcus Wallace." He moved the pen to Roger. "Roger Martinez." He turned his gaze back to Marcus and lowered the pen to the pad. "Introduce your friends."

"Nope. Don't think so," said Wallace.

"Fine. I'll take some identification from each of you."

Marcus turned his gaze on MacArthur. "We under arrest?"

"Not worth the paperwork," grunted Bud.

"Then I don't have to give you my ID."

The ranger pointed at the holster on each man's belt. "If you're carryin' a firearm, you do."

Marcus grinned and gestured at his waist. "But we *ain't*. All I see is holsters. *Empty* holsters."

Bud nodded once, then walked toward the closest of the thickets. "That's fine, but if I find pistolas in this here creosote, I guess the paperwork will become necessary."

Though he narrowed his eyes at the ranger's back, Marcus said, "Fine. *Fine.*" He introduced the others, then, at Gavin's insistence, named the drivers of the cars. When that was finished, he turned a cold look on Brad Masterton. "Come on out of there, Brad. Your missus is worried on you. You don't have to say nothin' else to these men." He glanced at Gavin and gave him a wink. "Rumor has it, you have the right to remain silent. You also have a right to legal counsel, and I recommend you exercise that right, Bradley. *Strongly.*"

Masterton looked at Marcus for a long moment, and to Gavin, it seemed like something passed between the two men in that staring contest. Finally, Brad dropped his gaze to the ground. "I guess Marcus is right. If you want to ask me any more questions, Agent Gregory, you'll have to do it with my attorney present."

"My, my," said Bud MacArthur. "I guess we can arrange that, Masterton. Hell, for all y'all. What do you think, Gregory? Should I make that call and get some buses on the way down here?"

Gavin shifted his gaze back and forth between Marcus Wallace and Brad Masterton, trying to understand what hold the former had on the latter, trying to understand what had passed between them unsaid. He glanced down at the list of names Wallace had given them, then nodded. "We know where to find them," he said to Bud. "I think we're wasting our time here."

"Finally, the man sees sense," grunted Marcus. "I go so far as to say you're wasting your time *here*." He lifted his arms and waved them to his sides to encompass the entire state of Texas. "You should go back to wherever it is you're from, FBI-man. Just ride back to San Antonio and get on one of them big airplanes, leave us to wallow in our dusty desert, our *filth* as you, no doubt, see it."

Gavin pinned the man with the cold glare. "You don't know me, Wallace."

Marcus laughed, and it was far from an amused sound. "Maybe I don't, FBI-man, but I know your kind. You'll be much happier as far from this place is you can get."

"Healthier, too," murmured Roger, though he at least had the good grace to look at the ground while he said it.

Marcus sucked his teeth and rolled his eyes. "You need to learn when to shut up."

7

Odolavesta Resta parking lot, Odolavesta, TX
Saturday, 12:52 pm CST

Bud MacArthur shook his head, lifted his hat off his head, and scrubbed his hand through his hair. "I don't understand why we didn't drag them all in. Maybe them charges wouldn't have stuck, but we did have cause. We could have at least stuck them in boxes and hammered 'em with questions." They stood next to his truck at the Odolavesta Resta.

Mike shook his head once. "Their lawyers wouldn't have let them say anything."

MacArthur shrugged. "Only Masterton lawyered up."

"Yeah, but under Wallace's orders. He'd have told the rest of them to do the same. Hell, maybe this Perry's Irregulars thing is providing the lawyers," said Gavin.

"What is that, anyway? Militia?" asked Mike.

"I've never heard of it," said Bud as he reseated his hat on his head. "When I get back to the ranch, I will put a call into Austin. Talk to the ranger who keeps track of the unorganized militias down here near the border."

"Let us know what you find out."

"Yeah," said Gavin, holding out his hand. "And thanks for your help today. Can I call you to translate Texan into English if I need to?"

Bud took his hand, treating him to a grave stare. "You might could, but I don't hold out hope that you'd understand me any better."

Gavin grinned.

The ranger glanced at Mike and gave him a nod. "Can I give you a ride back to Bexar County?"

Mike shook his head. "Thanks, but my family is here on a vacation of sorts. I'm headed over to meet them as soon as we're done. I haven't seen them in a while— training with the Bureau."

"I bet you can't wait to see 'em, then. I'll get out of y'alls hair, but call me if anything develops."

Gavin nodded. "Will do, Bud. I hope you can salvage your weekend."

MacArthur nodded toward room number nineteen. "I expect I'll be thinking about your man, about all these women. I don't reckon I'll get much relaxin' in before all this gets resolved. "Well, I'll see y'all." He turned and climbed in his truck, cranked the engine over, then put the vehicle in reverse before rolling down his window. "Listen here, boys. These assholes we met today…they don't represent Southwest Texas. Them bad apples at the KCSD don't neither."

Gavin sobered and treated the ranger to a grave nod. "I imagine they are the minority. There are assholes in every geographic locale, Bud. Racists. Homophobes" he flapped his hand—"whatever."

MacArthur nodded once, then backed away. As he pulled out of the parking lot proper, he blipped the horn once and then was gone in a swirl of dust.

Mike sighed and pointed at the door to room number nineteen. "What now? More case files?"

Gavin shook his head, rubbing his temples with his thumb and forefinger. "I don't think I could stand much more of it today. No, let's pack those files up in the back of this behemoth and head back to Aeonia. I bet you can't wait to see Joe and the other three."

Mike chuckled, shaking his head. "Let me guess. Toby didn't mention the undercover mission?"

"Uh, what undercover mission?"

"Typical," Mike said. "Toby probably thought you'd tell him not to do it."

Gavin nodded once, his face hardening a little. "That would be a good guess." He unlocked the hotel room's door and stepped inside. "Let's grab these files and get a move on."

"Where to?"

"Aeonia," said Gavin as he picked up a banker's box full of case files. "Let's hurry. I want to stop this nonsense before it's too late."

8

Aeonian Motel & RV Park parking lot, Aeonia, TX
Saturday, 1:18 pm CST

Gravel crunched beneath the wide off-road tires as Gavin slid the G class into an empty space in front of room 1406. He popped the door open and hopped out, slamming it behind him, leaving Mike to follow at his own pace. He strode toward room 1402, his face settling into harsh, angry lines. As he passed 1404, the door opened, and Toby beckoned him inside. "Listen, Burton," said Gavin. "I meant what I said. You can't just—"

"Shhh!" Toby waved his hand toward the bed, where Greg lay, his eyes closed. Gavin frowned at him as Toby stepped closer and whispered, "He needs to concentrate."

Mike stepped through the door, and his gaze fell on his husband, a small smile tickling the edges of his mouth. He crossed the small hotel room and sank into the armchair closest to the bed, then leaned forward and took Greg's hand, giving it a squeeze.

"They're still hooded," Greg murmured, "but there's something going on in the other room. Hi, Mike. It sounds like a couple of people have shown up." His brow furrowed. "Maybe more."

"Toby, you can't risk—"

"We've done this before, Gavin. It's okay, we know what we're doing," Toby whispered. "We're *good* at this."

"You could say they are uniquely suited for this kind of undercover work, Gavin," said Mike in a quiet voice. He waved his hand toward Greg. "There are no technical glitches, no interference. Shannon is the perfect disguise, and Benny will know when it's time for them to run. And they're not helpless. They can defend themselves easily."

Gavin sucked his teeth and waved his hand to encompass Mike, Greg, and Toby. "No backup, either. No support. No *legal standing*."

Mike shook his head. "I thought you understood. The legal system is—"

"These things go beyond legalities, Gavin," whispered Toby. "This is more like hunting the bear that's marauding in your town. You have to kill that bear whether it's in season or not."

Gavin covered his eyes with a hand. "There are better ways—"

"Quiet!" snapped Greg. "People have come into the room with them. Benny says he can feel them, that it feels like he and Shannon have to be very careful. He said one of the men feels like a psychic…or something, anyway."

"Where are they?" demanded Gavin. "Come on, Mike. We can go get them out of there."

Gavin, said Greg in his mind. *I'm watching over them. It's too late to do anything else.*

"God dammit! It's *not* too late! Where are they?"

When he spoke next, Greg's voice seemed detached, far away. "They haven't spoken to Benny or Shannon, but Benny says one of the men is Marcus Wallace. The other, the psychic one, he'll take a little effort, but Benny's working on him… Wallace is coming toward Shannon. He looks suspicious. He wants to know—"

<u>Chapter 5</u>
<u>Midnight Sons</u>

I

"Who the hell are you two?" asked the shorter of the two men, the one wearing linesman's boots festooned with orange laces.

"I already told the others."

The man narrowed his eyes and glowered at her. "Well, sugar, tell *me*."

Shannon pretended to be cowed at the man's intense gaze, and she dropped her gaze away from his, letting it float toward the corner, to swim past the man's big companion, scrubbing along the time-grayed floorboards to the peeling, once-white baseboards, which looked for all the world like snakes shedding their skin.

"Look at me!"

She jerked her gaze back to the man in the linesman's boots and shrugged her shoulders, wincing as the ropes that bound her to the chair cut into her wrists. "No problem. I'm Bertie Stevens"—she jerked her chin toward Benny—"and this lunk is my husband, Andy. What are your names?"

The man in the linesman's boots frowned at her, narrowing his eyes even more. "You'll learn our names when you've *earned* the right to do so, little chickadee."

Again, Shannon shrugged her shoulders. "Whatever you say. I just thought it would be easier if we had something to call you."

Careful, Benny thought at her. *He's twitchy.*

The other man, the giant with coal-black skin, cocked his head to the side, a small half-grin blossoming on his lips.

Be careful yourself, thought Shannon, keeping her mental voice quiet, tightly focused on her husband. *The big one looks suspicious.*

"That makes sense. I'm Primo," said the giant man, tapping his chest with his thumb. "This is Marcus. He's my second." Marcus jerked his gaze toward Primo, a momentary flash of irritation appearing on his face.

"Primo? Is that Spanish?"

The large man smiled a little. "It's an older language than that," he said in a voice that smacked of pridefulness. "Latin. It simply means 'first.'" His pronunciation was crisp, perfect.

Shannon feigned confusion. "First? What kind of name is that?"

Primo boomed laughter at the ceiling. "It's not a name, dear. It's a title."

Glancing at Benny, whose actual face was a study in concentration, at odds with the smooth, calm façade she projected for him, Shannon murmured, "Title?"

"Chickadee, you're starting to annoy me," said Marcus. "We're the ones askin' the questions. Y'all are the ones who need to start answering questions."

Primo put a hand on Marcus's shoulder. "These are *friends*, Marcus." He turned his stare on Benny. "Isn't that right?"

Benny nodded, his face settling into stark lines that Shannon kept hidden. "That's right," said Benny. "We read a lot about this"—he cut his eyes from side to side—"*group.*"

"Yeah?" asked Marcus. "What have you read?"

"About Perry's Irregulars, for one," said Shannon. "We like how you contribute to the security of this—"

Marcus scoffed and shook his head.

Feigning hurt feelings, Shannon dropped her gaze. "Well, it's true, isn't it? You all help protect the borders?"

"No, that's correct," said Primo, tightening his grip on Marcus's shoulder. "And that's not all the Church of the Midnight Sons does to contribute to these so-called backwater communities."

Benny cocked his head to the side. "Like what?"

Primo chuckled. "We help those in need, brother. We protect those we care about from governmental overreach. We patrol our communities, helping to ensure the safety of our neighbors. And"—a large grin blossomed on his face, his very white teeth a stark contrast with his coal-black skin—"we bring those who are willing to listen into grace."

Shannon grimaced a little. "But it's not like all those other churches, right?"

Primo cocked his head to the side. "What does the Internet say, Bertie?"

"Oh!" Shannon loosed an uncomfortable-sounding chuckle. "Right. Well, we read that the community is more like a family than a church."

Primo nodded once. "That's true. What else?"

"That… The Internet beats around the bush, but…" A sigh gusted out of him. "It's more than just a church, isn't it?" Benny asked quietly.

"What does that mean, hoss?" asked Marcus.

Benny pumped his shoulders up and down. "Just what I said. Churches are"—he shrugged again—"empty shells. Well, most of them. We read on a private Discord that you do more than just go to Sunday-meetings. More than just pray and sing and read from some old book."

Primo's magnetic gaze settled on Benny, not quite boring into his own. "Not all old books are worthy of your disdain, Andy."

"No, I know that. Like the Sumerian books that are—for the most part—the mythological basis of a lot of the stories in the Christian Bible."

"Ah. And what makes those better?"

"They're…more true."

Without letting his gaze move an inch from Benny's, Primo nodded. "Have you read any?"

Shannon giggled, an intentionally flighty sound. "All that cutie-form?" She shook her head.

For the first time, the amusement left Primo's eyes. "Cuneiform," he said, enunciating each syllable with precision.

"Whatever," murmured Shannon, dropping her gaze to the floor once more.

"I've read some translations online," said Benny, "but I don't know what those are worth… If they're *true* or not."

Primo's gaze fell on his once more, and his lips settled into a flat line. "That depends on the source. Some are no more than butterfly wings in a hurricane."

"Of course," said Benny. "But still, without speaking Sumerian, I have no way to judge if what I'm reading is an accurate translation or not."

"Makes sense," said Marcus. "You need someone to guide you in your studies, someone to help you learn the right way of doing things." His gaze turned toward Primo, and his expression became one of awe. "Someone who understands things at a basic level."

The flat expression on Primo's face dissolved into a mildly pleased one. "We all need that, Marcus."

"Yeah, maybe you're right, but not so many of us find it." He nodded at Benny. "Maybe Mister and Missus Stevens have." His gaze flicked back and forth between them, and though his words and the sentiment behind them sounded warm, welcoming, his eyes remained cold, suspicious.

"Well, *gosh*," said Shannon. "I sure hope so. We came all this way."

"Indeed," said Primo with a slow nod of his head.

"What happens now?" asked Benny with an uneasy shrug.

Marcus cocked his head a little and narrowed his eyes. His not-quite distrusting gaze settled on Benny's. "Now," he said in a quiet, though algid voice, "you prove yourselves."

Shannon tittered in an empty-headed way. "Like loaves of bread?"

Primo's impenetrable, hypnotic gaze came to rest on hers. "Yes, in a way"—he glanced at Marcus—"and, like with bread, it can be slow and cool or hot and fast. Because of recent…uh…interference in our activities, we don't have time for slow."

"Uh…that sounds a little scary."

The giant ebony-skinned man nodded his head slowly, a solemn expression on his face. "It is." Then, without another word, he spun with the grace of a ballet dancer and walked out the door. "If you are disingenuous."

Marcus gave a grudging nod to Benny. "You'll do alright here, Stevens, provided you pass the test."

"What about me?" Shannon asked with another nervous titter.

Marcus gave her a wink that left Shannon feeling oily, soiled. "We'll see, sweetie-pie."

She opened her mouth but closed it without speaking, pretending to be cowed by his act. *This guy is as greasy as they come.*

Yes, said Benny, *but also extremely dangerous. Don't push it too far.*

Flicking his gaze back and forth between them as though they'd been whispering instead communicating telepathically, Marcus watched them a moment, devoid of expression but leaving them feeling as threatened as a dangerous snake would have. "How long y'all been hitched?" he asked at last.

"Is this part of the test?"

His gaze snapped to Shannon's. "Everything that happens between now and the end of your initiation, should you merit that, will be a test, sweetheart."

"Oh…"

Benny cleared his throat. "Since 2017." He held out his hand, gazing at Shannon warmly. She slipped her cool, dry hand into his, and he grinned as she squeezed it. "Best thing that ever happened to me."

"Me, too," she murmured.

"Well, ain't that as sweet as an old maid's dreams." He turned on his heel and closed the door with a bang.

Well…

Benny grunted. *Well, we've met them. Getting into this crew is going to be more difficult than we thought. Something's put them on guard.*

Agent Gregory?

With a shrug and a simultaneous shake of the head, Benny sent, *No. Maybe. It feels…bigger than that.* He frowned. *I couldn't get a good read on Primo, but Marcus is as nervous as a virgin on his wedding day. It's like they're the ones being tested. We're just an afterthought.* His gaze tracked to the wall behind her.

She frowned but then heard it—the subtle scraping of wood on wood—and felt someone watching them. "Well, now…" muttered Shannon. "What do we do now, Andy?"

"Whatever they ask us to, Bertie. I…" He shook his head. "I have a feeling about them. I don't want to screw this up." His gaze bored into hers. *Love you.*

Me, too.

"This is *important*, Bertie, and you playin' stupid isn't helping things."

"Me?" she asked with a grin in her voice.

"Yes, you."

She chuckled and flopped her hand over in the air. "But it's so easy. They're inclined to see me as a dullard. I might as well play the part."

"I know you like to do that, Bert, but…" Benny filled his voice with earnestness, filled his expression with entreaty. "All I'm saying is, let's not antagonize them. Let's try and make a home for ourselves here."

Shannon nodded. "*If* those stories on the Internet are true."

Benny grimaced. "We can't exactly come right out and ask them if they can really do magic."

"No. If they can do magic, they'd say no, of course, and if those stories are just lies, they'll think we're crazy." She pursed her lips. "Hey, you don't suppose they have us bugged, do you?"

Nice one, Benny said in her mind while fighting to contain a grin. "Nah, what would be the point. They're going to put us to the test, either way. They said as much."

"Well, if they *aren't* what those people on the Internet claim, then their tests are just psychology, right. They can't read our minds to see if we're fooling them."

"Bertie—"

"I mean, if they're just some *cult*, some crazies who like sex or something, then they have to rely on their own brains, their own suppositions and assumptions. So, they'd want to listen to us, to hear what we talk about when we don't think they're around."

"But their tests—"

"Oh, piss on their tests, Andy," she snapped. "If they're swindlers, their con relies on appearing omniscient. To do that, they have to get information about us that we don't know they have."

Benny dropped his gaze to his lap. "I don't think they are swindlers, Bertie," he murmured.

"They want us to 'prove ourselves honest,'" she said. "All I want is the same."

"But even if—"

"Andrew Stevens, you listen to me. We're not here looking for friends, for a crew to hang out with. We're here looking for *truth*. We agreed on that before we came down here. That hasn't changed, has it?"

"Well…"

"Andy…"

"I'm tired, Bertie. Tired of floating back and forth across the country, looking for something real and only finding con men and magic shows. Can't we just…"

Shannon nodded, squeezing his hand. "Go on," she said softly.

"Can't we just find a place here? Can't we just decide to believe and put our faith in Primo?"

"Of course, we can, Andy," said Shannon. "But we can do that at the Baptist church down the road, too."

Benny heaved a long sigh. "Yeah."

2

The temple, Southwestern TX
Saturday, 1:33 pm CST

Marcus stood pressed against the splintery wall, his eye pressed to the peephole, watching the newcomers the way a hunting cat watches prey. He had one of his feelings about the woman. Something seemed...put on about her...like those citified high-school friends who came back from Dallas in their shiny cars, wearing their slick clothes and flashing their cash around.

He hadn't trusted her, hadn't—*couldn't*—believed she was as dumb as she had pretended, and now he had the proof. She *was* running a game on them.

Well, that's fine, Marcus thought. *We have our own games to play. I've got to tell Primo about this.*

3

"It's the power, Andy, that we're interested in. Proof that these people actually know something everyone else has forgotten. Proof that—" She stopped speaking and turned to look at the door as a loud rustling punctuated by booming thuds sounded outside in the hall. "What's—"

"Sounds like a bruhaha," said Benny. "Someone getting kicked out?"

"Or someone being abducted," said Shannon in a hushed, scared sounding tone. "Maybe they're stopping someone from leaving."

Benny nodded once. "Should we…"

"Help? Leave? What?"

Shaking his head, Benny frowned. "No. I don't know." He got up and walked to the door, laying his palm flat against the rough wood. *They're dragging someone down the hall…a man…he's awfully beat up.*

"Come away, dear," said Shannon. "It's good you want to help, but they don't trust us. Yet." She took a step toward the door, a frown of concentration dancing across her face as she animated the expressions on both of their projected disguises to match the scene. *Part of their test*? *Is it real or fake*?

Is it live or is it Memorex? Benny sent with a mental chuckle.

4

The temple, Southwestern TX
Saturday, 1:35 pm CST

Cece grunted as the hooded man lurched toward her, but she'd learned the knack of rolling with mad lunges toward freedom, of hanging on and letting the moment dissipate before she righted the course. Over Agent Hall's hooded head, Jon grinned at her and shook his head before jerking the man back to true.

"Cut it out, sparky, or I'll get mean," Cecelia hissed. "You don't want that."

"Let me go," Reynold Hall said. "I haven't seen anyone's face. You won't gain anything by keeping—"

"Let us worry about that," said Jon.

"But—"

"Listen, Agent Hall. We take our orders from them that's above us, just like you do. We *follow* our orders, and by doing so, we earn our place in what's to come. Normally, I'd offer the Path to you, but—"

Hall planted his feet just long enough to pull her off balance, then sprinted forward, running blind, but *running*.

Until Jon swept his legs out from under him that is.

5

The temple, Southwestern TX
Saturday, 1:37 pm CST

Marcus glanced at the secret door hidden behind a bit of paneling in the hall as the Clarks dragged their charge toward a more secure room. From the sound of it, Agent Hall wasn't going along meekly, but that didn't bother Marcus much. Between the two of them, the Clarks could handle anything that city-slicker tried on for size.

He turned and pressed his eye to the peephole once more.

6

The three of them landed together in a heap, and Cece made sure she landed *on* Reynold Hall, making her knees and elbows count as she did. He grunted, and the air whooshed out of him. "Now, you *behave*, Agent Hall, and maybe we won't make it hurt so much."

Jon rolled off the dogpile, dusting off his knees, a little grin playing on the edges of his mouth. "Cece, you crack me up."

She grinned at him and got up, making her fists and feet count as she did so, and Hall grunted with each new blow. "Well, I'm a comedian at heart, Jon."

"You are…" Jon's gaze blanked.

Cece frowned at him as he cocked his head, a small smile playing on his lips. *It's that damn song again!* There was no transition, no gradual fading away of his consciousness, just zip, gone. "Jon! Not now, Jon, we have *responsibilities*!"

Hall rolled over and sat up. "What's wrong with him?"

"Never you—" Cece snapped off the words as Hall tried to surge upward, two legs pumping like a sprinter bolting from the blocks. She leveled him with a knee to the face and a kick from her booted foot as dessert. "Come on, Jon! I need your help here!"

7

The temple, Southwestern TX
Saturday, 1:37 pm CST

Benny stepped away from the door and turned to face his wife. *In any case, I think we know where the missing FBI agent has come to rest.*

Maybe. Unless it's like Oneka Falls, unless it's a trick, an illusion.

Shan, the demons from Oneka Falls are gone. I know it doesn't feel like it sometimes, but we banished them and severed their connection to this realm. Breaking that bowl revoked Lilitu's claim—

I know that, Benny. Shannon's mental tone was calm, patient. *But there's* something wrong *here. Can't you feel it?*

Benny frowned and dropped his gaze.

Keeping things from me, are you? Protecting your fragile little woman, again? She wore a grin, but her eyes cast sparks.

Lifting one shoulder and letting it drop, Benny hung his head. *Sorry. You're not supposed to know, right?*

Neither are you.

I know, but I'm used to pretending I don't know things.

Hello? Remember who you're talking to. I spent years pretending I didn't know Mike was gay, that I was a mousy little try-hard. She chuckled sourly. *That I enjoyed cleaning.*

I said I was sorry.

She crossed the room and put her hand on his shoulder. *I forgave you before you said it, Benny-bear. I'm getting good at doing that. Lots of practice.* She hit him with a saucy grin. *Did you ask Greg to pass the information on to Gavin?*

Chapter 6
Madness Season

I

Gavin lurched to his feet, sending his chair a-skitter behind him, eyes wide. "Where? Where is he?" he shouted. When Greg only dropped his head back to the pillow, a string of drool sliding down toward his neck, Gavin jerked his head to the side to stare at Toby. "Where did Benny and Shannon go?"

Toby lifted his shoulders and shook his head.

"Tell me, goddammit or—"

"I don't know, Gavin. They left here in the night and drove back to San Antonio to get an undercover vehicle and bring it back. They were supposed to meet someone at an abandoned store halfway between here and—"

Gavin turned and in two quick strides crossed the room, rounding the end of the bed. Mike got to his feet, hands up in a placating gesture. "Hold on, Gavin—"

"No, I'm done holding on. Greg! Greg, where are they?"

"He doesn't know, Gavin," said Toby. "He's just telling you what he's picking out of their minds. He doesn't know where they are in the real world any more than you do. If they were demons, he would know, but they aren't."

"Christ!" Gavin snapped, already fishing his phone out of his pocket. He found the contact he wanted, turned his back on the room, put the phone to his ear, and covered his eyes with his hand.

Bud MacArthur picked up on the second ring. "Gregory? What's up?"

"Can you get me the last knowns for Marcus Wallace?"

"Might as well. Can't sing, never could dance, and it's way too dry to plant corn. I'll get it all over to you in the next day or two."

"No, Bud. Now." The call hissed through the ether for a moment. "Can you do it now, Bud? Please?"

"Sure," said Bud in a long, drawn-out way. "What's got your house all afire?"

"Can you trust me on this?"

"I s'pose I can at that. Okay. Give me a minute to get this old hunk of lightning booted up and logged in. Got you a fax? I'll send over what we've got."

"How about email?"

"Sure."

"Thanks, Bud. I owe you."

"Naw. It ain't no hill for a stepper. Watch for the email." He killed the connection without waiting for Gavin's reply.

Gavin tuned around and found Mike and Toby staring at him expectantly. "He's going to send over Wallace's address."

"At least the last known," said Mike with a slow nod. "We heard."

His phone beeped, and he smiled.

"Bud's email? He's that quick?"

"Yeah. I'm going over there. Ren is alive, and I can't sit here and wait for that to change."

Mike glanced at Toby. "That could be dangerous for Benny and Shannon."

"I can't help that."

"They know the risks," said Toby. "Besides, they can handle anything this side of Lily."

With a slow nod, Mike glanced at his husband's recumbent form, then lifted his gaze to Toby's again. They stared at one another for a moment, then Toby nodded once. "Better let me drive," Mike said without breaking eye contact with Toby. "You're far too worked up."

Toby nodded again. "That sounds best."

Gavin bristled and narrowed his eyes, but he knew Mike was right. He *was* upset, too eager, too...*desperate*, but he couldn't help it. He tossed Mike the keys. "Let's go."

2

Ranch Road 2818, Odolavesta, TX
Saturday, 2:19 pm CST

"Stop!" Gavin cried, his gaze locked on the emerald-green Cadillac pulled up next to the outbuilding. "That's Westral's car." He pointed at the green monstrosity.

"Are you sure this is the right place?"

Gavin nodded grimly. "Yeah. I mean look around…this has to be the place."

It was true enough. It was the only house on that side of Ranch Road—at least for a mile or two.

Mike nodded toward the adobe and oak arch that guarded the entrance to the drive. "No address, no name."

"I'm telling you, Mike. That's his Caddie."

"I know, Gavin. I'm not doubting that. I'm just saying that maybe the sheriff is a visitor, same as us. Maybe Bud called him and—"

"Nah. Bud wouldn't do that behind our backs. And you heard the esteem he holds the man in." He shook his head. "No, he wouldn't have told Westral."

"Maybe it's something else. Maybe it's—"

"Bud did say the address was three years stale. Last known from a traffic ticket Wallace got in Houston."

"County tax records?"

Gavin waved at the arch over the drive. "Pull in. I'll find the tax assessor's website."

Mike let the G-class roll forward at idle, the big off-road tires chattering through the gravel. Mike smiled a little at the sound—Greg would have loved it.

When they were about halfway down the long, curving drive, Westral came out of the side door and stood on the weathered stoop glaring at them, arms akimbo, a snarl decorating his face.

"He doesn't look happy to see us," said Mike.

"No, I don't suppose he is," murmured Gavin. "Ah. According to the tax assessor, Eldred Westral owns this property."

"Still, there might be—"

"Westral's in on it. I've felt that all along. He's stalled this investigation from the get-go, and knowing Ren, he followed the book to the Ts, so Westral would have known his every move. He's in on it. My gut's screaming that as loud as a ten-piece brass band on New Year's."

Mike said nothing, but at least he didn't argue, at least he didn't scoff and recommend therapy. "I'll pull in behind the Caddie, then. Block him in."

"Yeah. It seems Eldred Westral inherited this property from Jedediah Westral." Suddenly, Westral's sense of entitlement, his rage at having any kind of oversight on his department made sense. "*Sheriff Jedediah Westral.*"

"Nice little fiefdom they've got going here." Mike leaned forward and squinted. "He's not armed," he murmured. "He looks drunk as a skunk, though."

Gavin locked his phone and put it away. "Seems the former sheriff died in a hunting accident. His son mistook him for a stag and shot him."

"You're kidding."

"Nope."

"Now what's he doing?" Mike asked as Westral turned back toward the house. "We can't let this escalate." As if he'd heard them, Westral turned back to face them, a nasty smile on his face. "What's he doing?" he repeated as the brakes squealed and the big SUV rolled to a stop.

Gavin rolled down his window. "We're looking for Marcus Wallace, Sheriff. He listed this as his address."

Westral jerked his chin back, shaking his head. "He don't live here!" he cried. "Get off my property!"

Gavin shook his head. "I don't think so. I think we'll have a look around."

"Not without a warrant!" yelled Westral. He turned his head back toward the house like a puppet on a string, his grimace deepening as they watched.

"Someone's with him," whispered Gavin, trying to hide the fact that he was talking.

"Yeah," said Mike. "Wallace?"

Gavin shook his head, his gaze locked on the sheriff's face. "I don't know." The bantam cock of a man had an expression plastered to his face that seemed out-of-character. His normal arrogance was absent, his "I'm in charge" demeanor was missing, and the expression that seemed to dominate his face was…

Fear.

"Uh… Something's—"

"Who's that in the doorway?" asked Mike.

Gavin leaned left, trying to get an angle that would let him see what Mike was seeing. "All I see is shadow. Are you sure…" He let the words trail away as Red Westral backed to the edge of the stoop, turning his face away from the door, gazing at them wide-eyed and at the same time with a smirk. "I don't like this," Mike and Gavin said at the same time.

Mike laughed. "Two out of two FBI agents agree…"

"Yeah."

Even so, neither of them took their eyes off the door frame, and both men were tense to the point of shaking.

Westral dropped his chin and said something that was carried away by the wind, hopped off the side of the stoop as though afraid to get close to the door, then trotted to his Caddie.

"Watch him!" said Gavin, flicking his fingers toward the green Cadillac.

"What the…" murmured Mike.

A single leg wrapped in baggy fatigue pants and ending in a knee-high combat boot extended from the dark door, emerging from the shadowed interior and into the bright sun as if by some magician's trick, floating in midair, parallel to the ground. The leg hung there as Mike and Gavin stared at it, hung there like a prop from a movie, like a mannequin's leg used in some bizarre art installation.

"A trick?" Mike growled.

Gavin shook his head.

The boot descended toward the worn wooden planks on the stoop like an old red balloon losing its charge of helium. Just before the sole of the boot made contact with the wood, its descent stopped, and the boot hung there motionless.

The shadowed kitchen gave birth to the sole of another boot—this one just as worn as the first—followed by another fatigue-clad leg. But the first foot still hung three inches *above* the porch. It was as if whoever was coming out that door lay on something—a gurney maybe—and was swinging his legs off the gurney to stand.

"What the…" repeated Mike, his voice softer, more hesitant.

Watery orange light flickered from within the kitchen, though the saturation increased by the minute.

Gavin latched onto the other man's forearm with a tight grip.

"Who is that?"

Red's Caddie roared to life, then threw gravel at the house as the sheriff floored it in reverse, slewing the big car around in sloppy circle. He jammed it down into drive with a screech from under the car, then hammered the accelerator again, and more gravel flew, this time off into the fallow field beside the drive. The green car roared away from the house…away from the house and down the only exit—the single lane track that led directly between Mike and Gavin.

"*What are you doin', hoss? We got guests!*" The voice roared and hissed at the same time, a mechanical beast bent on the destruction of the world.

Red Westral never paused, never looked back, just jerked the wheel to the left and rocketed around them through the grass, spitting wide plumes of sandy soil into the air behind him, slewing the car through a massive fishtail sure to scar his own front lawn.

"*Eldred, didn't you hear me, spark? I asked you a question!*"

The Cadillac jounced out onto Ranch Road with shrieking tires and sped north toward town.

"Reverse," Gavin said, his fingers going even tighter on Mike's forearm. "Reverse. Reverse." His voice was soft, feathery. His heart thundered in his ears, but even so, he heard the dry chuckle from the kitchen.

Both combat boots hovered beside one another—three inches up—but the legs above them still angled back into the darkness and ended at the knee. The fatigue pants twitched as if someone were straightening them.

As the fish-belly white face emerged at a snail's pace from the darkness above them, Gavin's mouth dropped open. As the orange tint from the man's glowing eyes gave way to the sunlight, Gavin's other hand flew up to cover his mouth, and though his lips and throat worked and worked and worked, no sound emerged. His gaze was welded to the phantasm straight out of his dreams as it emerged from the kitchen, his nightmare brought to life, the Nightmare Man made real, his hand locked on Mike's arm in a white-knuckled death-grip, his brain on overload, his voice stolen away by terror. The Nightmare Man grinned at him and stepped fully into the light, a night terror made flesh, a smiling, unreal figure straight out of Hell.

"*Who or what in the hell is that?*" Mike yelled.

Gavin's mouth worked, chewing on the word he couldn't give voice to, silently forming the syllable over and over and over, wanting Mike to lift his foot from the brakes and plant it on the accelerator, wanting to scrabble his door open, spring out, and run, *run, RUN*!

The orange-eyed man walked toward the steps leading down into the dooryard, and sunlight danced on the inverted chevrons of a first sergeant, then lingered on the three-lettered name over his right breast pocket, moving on to swoon in the darker olive-drab spots where patches and insignia had once been sewn.

Gavin's gaze danced across the name patch, back and forth, back and forth, reading and rereading the name as if he could erase him from reality if only he could spell the name right. *F-R-Y-Y-R-F-F-R-Y...* his lips moved with each letter, his vocal folds doing their thing, but without air to power his voice.

Fry reached the top step and turned his orangesicle gaze on Gavin and winked. "Ain't we gonna have us some fun, spark? Ain't we just?" His laughter rang against the sky, an insult to creation, an affront to reality, a curse, a damnation.

"Go! Go, *go! Go-go-go-go!*" shrieked Gavin at last, and as though he'd been waiting for permission, Mike jammed his right foot to the floor, holding the steering wheel as though he wanted to choke it, never turning, never checking the mirrors, only staring wide-eyed at the grinning nightmare, at Fry, and running, fleeing, turning tail and hauling ass.

Raucous laughter followed them down the drive, though Fry only stood there on the stoop and held his belly. As the back tires of the Mercedes hit the asphalt, and Mike worked the gear selector to drop the vehicle into drive, they heard it. As if from right behind them, they heard the voice.

As if from the backseat, they heard Fry's voice, low and guttural, intimate and seductive, a prelude to a kiss, foreplay. *"Where you goin', sugar?"* Fry laughed and laughed and laughed, his guffaws melding with something they hadn't heard before—a chirping counterpoint from off in the bleak fields to the east— creating a psychotic symphony; a promise of torment, of torture, of barren wombs and empty minds, demanding their attention; demanding their reverence, their adulation, a divine addiction, a blind affliction; promising cold-hearted retribution, drowning delirium, bloody crucifixion, black and white fear, full color desolation, the Pit, the Lake of Fire, a dwelling place for demons, fallen Babylon made real.

Gavin screamed and the G-class leaped forward, tires screaming, engine shrieking, both men bellowing their terror and neither hearing anything but that damn black orchestra, that damn neon god standing hunched in the gravel drive, hands on knees, belting cancerous laughter, the damn thumping at creation's core.

3

The G-class turned east onto San Antonio Street or rather slid through a turn, adding more tire smoke, more shrieking rubber, to the afternoon's score. Mike's hands danced on the steering wheel, but his right foot planted, never so much as twitching toward the brake pedal. His gaze leaped and danced: sideview, out the windshield, sideview, rearview, the road ahead, rearview, sideview…

But mostly, Mike looked behind them.

Gavin, too, though he wasn't constrained by keeping them alive inside the hurtling three-and-a-half-ton collection of steel and plastic and glass, so he was fully turned around in his seat, sitting on his knees, gripping the seat back with both white-knuckled hands, eyes wide, mouth pressed into a thin white line. His training, his weapons, his phone—all forgotten in the face of his waking nightmare—and what remained was a terrified prepubescent boy.

But nothing followed them.

"He's real…" he muttered. "I mean, flesh and blood real…" He shook his head, his gaze zipping from one potential place of concealment to the next, finding nothing and no one. "More than a nightmare. More than a dream. He's *real.*" The thought scared him far more than the nightmares had, and that had been plenty. "Christ, Mads...he's *real.*"

Whatever Fry was, he seemed content to let them escape. Slowly, as his panic receded, Gavin realized Mike was repeating the same phrases over and over.

"No, no. Not possible. Not possible! We killed him, we *killed* him," Mike repeated, seemingly unaware he was even speaking. He grunted and leaned into the turn north, the rear of the G-class skipping, hopping, and dancing off San Antonio Street's surface and onto the lighter asphalt of Mesa Street.

"Who?" Gavin said, more in control of his fear, but still not willing to turn around and face front. "Who did you see?"

"What?" He snapped his gaze sideways, then glanced at the road before returning his gaze to the rearview.

"No one's following us. I think—" The words caught in his throat, choking and choking him. "I think he's letting us go."

Mike's gaze didn't waver from the rearview, though some of the tension left his back and shoulders. "It's impossible."

"What is? Who did you kill?"

"What?" Mike snapped again, his gaze darting to Gavin once more.

Forcing himself to release his chokehold on the seatback, Gavin took a deep breath. "Fry."

"Fry?"

Gavin nodded and forced his upper body to relax. "Who did you see back there? Who did you kill?"

"What?" Mike said again, his expression one of panic mixed with extreme confusion. "What are you talking about?"

"You keep saying 'Not possible. We killed him.'" Gavin shrugged. "Who? Who did you kill?"

Mike darted another wide-eyed glance his way, tore it away to check the rearview mirror again, then shuddered. "Herlequin. The evil bastard who tormented the others." He twitched the steering wheel, and the vehicle slid onto Lincoln Street, screaming toward the eastern horizon way too fast for a narrow two-lane road inside the city limits.

"And you saw him? Back at Westral's place, I mean?"

Another madman's glance flicked Gavin's way. "What? Herlequin?" Mike shook his head. "No. I mean, yes, but not how he looked back then. He was a gargoyle. A tree. But sometimes he looked like an old man." He shook his head—a little wildly. "I only saw the tree, but the others said... Sometimes, he-he-he—"

Gavin reached across and gripped his shoulder. When Mike glanced his way, his gaze was a little less manic, and when his gaze left Gavin's, it did so at a slower clip and went to the windshield and remained there instead of snapping to the rearview mirror.

With a single curt nod, Mike drew a deep breath into his lungs and let it sigh out between his parted lips. "That..." He shook his head. "That didn't look like Herlequin. Not when I saw him at least, but the feeling..." He shook his head again, and when he resumed speaking, his words came faster, more clipped, more manic. "The feeling back there is like the one I got when we were little kids. When Gray shot at Benny. And before when we were in the park playing paratrooper. Back home. Herlequin was the author of all that, and I haven't felt anything like it since we banished that bitch and her demon spawn."

"Herlequin was a woman?"

"What? No!" Mike took another slow, deep breath and released it. "No. We thought Herlequin was behind it all at first. We thought he was the demon king—or whatever—but he wasn't the worst of them. Not by far. And his daughter... Maybe she wasn't really his daughter, maybe she only pretended that, I don't know, I don't remember, but his daughter was more powerful, and Sally McBride was—she played dumb, meek, submissive, but she was really powerful and a lot higher up the food chain than Chaz, than LaBouche, maybe even more than Brigitta, I don't know, I don't know—"

Gavin bore down with his grip a moment before releasing it, shifting in his seat, coming off his knees, returning his legs to the footwell and facing forward. "All that's in the past, Mike. Right?"

"Right? I don't know. I don't know. That...that-that-that *thing* back there— We must've missed some. We must've messed up the spell somehow. Maybe we got the incantation wrong. Maybe we mispronounced the words, they were Akkadian, after all. Maybe we used the wrong gods or put them in the wrong order." He grunted as he slid the car into the northbound lane of Austin Street, racing the devil toward the edge of town, toward the open country between Odolavesta and Aeonia. "Maybe we used the wrong names for them. They have other names, were worshipped in other civilizations. Maybe Akkadian was the wrong one. Maybe it should have been Enki instead of Ea, or Utu instead of Shamash, or Bel instead of Marduk. Do you think that's it?" He darted a glance at Gavin, one eyebrow quirked. "Could that have allowed some of the *mazzikim* to hang around?"

"Mike, I don't know what you're talking about. I—"

"The *spell,* Toby! The divorce spell we did at Eddie's house. In the pit in his basement! Where we buried the lamp!"

"Mike," Gavin said softly, reaching across the console to grip the man's arm, "I'm not Toby. I'm Gavin."

Mike shot another glance at him and issued a curt nod. "No, I know that." He took a deep breath. "My..." He lifted a hand off the steering wheel and twirled it next to his temple. "My thoughts are racing, *dancing*, you know?"

Gavin gave what he hoped was a reassuring nod. "Yeah. The panic, the adrenaline will do that."

"Right," Mike said in clipped tones.

"I don't think Fry is one of your demons."

"What? The guy back there?"

"Yeah. He wears that fatigue jacket with the name 'FRY' on the patch. That's what the people who...who introduced me to him call him. Fry."

"Fry," Mike breathed. "I don't like that guy."

Gavin chuckled...he couldn't help it. Mike snapped a bunched-brow glare at him, and he held up his hands. "Sorry. Adrenaline."

Mike turned his gaze back to the road. "Well, I don't."

"I don't either," said Gavin. "He scares the shit out of my shit."

"Yeah." Mike sucked in another long, shaky breath. "And what's with the psychotic cricket?"

Gavin closed his eyes. "Another of my nightmares. Glacadairanam."

"That's a stupid name."

"Maybe," said Gavin with a shrug. "I guess it means 'soul stealer' or something like that. He was the thing behind The Smith and many other serial killers if we believe what he claimed." He pumped his shoulders up and down again. "And I guess I do."

"What, possession?" Mike gave him another arch-browed look. "Demons don't do that. Not really. They just kill the person and subsume the victim's identity. They can project guises—like what Shannon does."

As the vehicle crossed over the town line and they left Odolavesta behind, Mike relaxed and released a shaky breath. "Is it him?" he asked in an enervated voice.

"Is what him?"

"The killings. The girls in the desert. Is it this Gladafairanam?"

"Glacadairanam," said Gavin. "Maybe, but they don't bear his signature."

"And psychotic-demon-serial-killers can't change things up?"

"Did any of the demons in Oneka Falls?"

"They switched identities. Guises, I mean. They always acted the same, though, I guess." He frowned at the road ahead. "Except maybe LaBouche. Maybe he *did* change right before his end."

"Glacadairanam marks his victims with the letter gay from Scottish Gaelic."

"G for Glacadairanam? That's original."

Gavin flashed a one-sided grin at him. "Yeah, well, he saved the creative thinking for how and when he killed.

His victims go back a while. He wears people like a disguise—physically wears them, I mean. He's…insubstantial in his own form. Out of phase. He can't act in this world without a human horse."

"And that's what the guy from Westral's kitchen is? A human horse?"

"I…" Gavin frowned down at the dash. "I don't think so. Fry is different. He claims Glacadairanam is one of his sons, though the little chirpy bastard said he was conceived when his mother seduced a priest." He shrugged his shoulders up and down. "I don't know who to believe, but from the stories I was told about Fry, what we saw, that guy back there, that's him, that body is him."

"Things with bodies can be shot," said Mike with a feral, angry gleam in his eye and a grin to match. "They can have their throats ripped out."

"Sure," said Gavin, "but are they affected by it?"

The wattage behind Mike's grin faded a little. "Only one way to find out."

"We need to talk to your friends. Tell them what happened, that Fry's here. I need to get ahold of Kai, to call home, and, and…" He shook his head, and Mike flashed a compassionate glance his way. Gavin sighed, long and slow. "That was…"

"Intense," said Mike in the same tone.

"I think we have to—" Gavin frowned and patted his pockets as his ringtone sounded. He'd been holding his phone when Fry emerged and had no idea what he'd done with it as things progressed. He turned and scanned the back seat without seeing it.

Mike jerked his chin toward the dash. "Up there. You must've tossed it."

Gavin grabbed it and accepted the call. "Hello, Bud," he said.

"Gregory. Did you find that Wallace character? I think that address is a bust. Records search brought back the sheriff as the owner."

Gavin nodded once. "And he was there. Westral, I mean."

"No Wallace?"

"Um… Not that we were able to ascertain."

"Did you search?"

"No, uh, Sheriff Westral basically told us to screw off and get a warrant."

"I know a judge who might—"

"Then he jumped in his car and sped off," said Gavin, a touch too hurriedly.

MacArthur said nothing for few moments, then simply said, "Okay."

"We…that is, Mike and I don't think Wallace was there."

"Don't you mean Rick?"

"Huh?"

"You said, 'Mike and I.' Don't you mean, 'Rick and I?'"

"Oh. Right. Sorry, Rick," Gavin said, rolling his eyes.

"You keep that up and your new partner's liable to think you can't pour piss out of a boot with a hole in the toe and directions writ on the heel."

Gavin chuckled, and it came out sounding forced and false. "Yeah, I need to work on that."

"Work, hell. You need to memorize that man's name, Gregory. So…as you was sayin'?"

"Right. *Rick* and I don't think Wallace was there. It… He… That's what Sheriff Westral said—"

"Something happen over there at Westral's ranch?" asked Bud in a calm but penetrating voice. "A bit of shoe leather across a certain sheriff's mug, for instance?"

"No, uh, nothing like that."

"Okay," said Bud. "Just so you know, no judgments from this side of the river."

"Really, Bud, nothing—"

"Sure, sure," he said, but it came out sounding more like shore, shore. "I'm just saying, if y'all had dirty boots, ain't no one from the Uvalde branch going to say a word."

"Okay. Um, good to know."

"All right, then," said MacArthur, then fell silent.

It was a trick Gavin knew too well—letting the silence build until the interrogee felt the compulsion to fill it—

308   ERIK HENRY VICK

but even knowing that, he felt compelled to speak. Glancing at Mike, who shook his head, Gavin said, "Nothing happened, Bud."

"Yep," said Bud, and no more.

"Think you can come up with any other addresses for Wallace?"

"Nope, that's all she wrote on that subject. But we can talk to a few of the old boys he's known to hang out with, a few of his known accomplices."

"Yeah," said Gavin a little too eagerly, "that sounds more productive than playing the game on Westral's terms. More productive than wasting time with lawyers at any rate."

"That's my take on it," said Bud. "I'll email you."

"Right. We're headed back to the hotel for lunch. We'll head out afterward," said Gavin, and he hung up as they turned west on First Street in Aeonia.

4

Room 1404, Aeonian Motel & RV Park, Aeonia, TX
Saturday, 2:49 pm CST

Mike tapped the door with the knuckle of his index finger and then turned the knob without waiting for an answer and stepped inside. Gavin followed him, pausing only a moment before pushing through the door.

He wanted—*needed*—to talk to Maddie, to tell her about seeing Fry in the flesh, but he felt like he owed his new friends. And they were the ones in Fry's immediate reach.

Inside the room, Greg still lay on the bed, muttering and moving his lips silently. Toby stood by the window, but his gaze rested on Mike and switched to Gavin as he came in. He arched one eyebrow as if to ask, *Trouble?*

Gavin nodded. "Big trouble," he said with a glance at Greg. "Can we…"

"Yeah, we won't interrupt him now unless he's ready to come back," said Mike.

"Tell me," said Toby in a no-nonsense voice.

So, Gavin did, and this time, he held nothing back. He told them everything he knew about Glacadairanam, about Angel Kirk and Debra Esteves, about the antipsychotic zoraperidol they used to ward the wrath child off, about The Smith case in Manhattan, everything he knew about the Program, about Adeline d'Clara, about Kai, about the Bogeyman case in Miami, about his dreams in both cases, about the threats to Maddie's life, about the seizure-visions, all of it. As he wound down, Mike whistled in amazement. "Yeah," said Gavin, "I've had an interesting year."

"I'll say," said Toby. "I take it you're still on the antipsychotic?"

"Everyday. Just in case," said Gavin with a nod.

"Does it work against Fry?"

Gavin shrugged. "It doesn't seem to." He went on to tell Toby about meeting Fry in the flesh at Westral's place. "Mike said it might be Herlequin, that the feeling was the same."

With a sigh, Toby reached blindly behind him to find a chair and sank into it. "Yeah. Your friend Fry sounds like an emotion-eater, but what he doesn't sound like is a *mazzikim*. He…" Toby shook his head. "He doesn't sound *limited* the way they are."

"Lily?" asked Mike in a quiet voice.

Toby closed his eyes and paled a little but shook his head. "No, though he *does* sound like a *seraph*."

"A what?"

"One of Lily's kind. One of the *seraphim*."

"Aren't *seraphim* archangels?"

Toby shrugged. "These are the names they called themselves, their own names for the strata of their hierarchy. They don't care what our mythologies, our religions did with the labels. They don't care that we call them demons, either."

"We're food animals to them," Mike said sourly, his gaze resting on his husband's face. "Why should they care?"

"You know an awful lot about these…whatever they are," said Gavin.

Toby treated him to a solemn nod. "Hard-earned knowledge. Lily was a *seraph*—the highest-ranking demon in our realm—and she was summoned to this realm by some Akkadian priest who wanted to learn magic. Her presence here allowed her to summon others. First her"—Toby's mouth worked without producing sound for a moment—"lover, a demon she'd elevated to the rank of *ifrit*, though I don't know where he began. *Ifrits*—"

"What, she can just do that?"

Toby grimaced and nodded. "She claimed she could do it to me."

Gavin lifted his eyebrows.

"The *ifrits*, as the name suggests, are beings of pure flame, powerful demons. Lily's daughter from her union with Lilu—'Naamah,' they named her, though she went by Brigitta in Oneka Falls—could change the demons beneath her. *Physical* changes, actual changes, not mere illusion. Then there are *djinn*, dedicated servants of the *ifrit* and *seraph*. They are also able to do things the *mazzikim*—the lowest ranking caste—can only dream about."

"Including giving the *mazzikim* real deaths."

"Then Fry could be a *djinn* or an *ifrit*," said Gavin. "According to the stories I was told, he can set stuff on fire with a look, kill with a glance, that kind of thing. And levitate."

Toby raised his hands out to his sides. "Maybe. Or he could be something else entirely. I have no way of knowing. There were things bigger than Lily—as terrifying as that prospect is."

"But you beat her. You sent her packing."

"I…" Toby swallowed hard. "I learned her weakness, just as she learned all of mine. I used it against her in the end. I…" He swallowed again, and his eyes glimmered and danced in the room's overhead light. "I broke her heart."

"The spell—"

"Think back, Mike," said Toby as he turned to look out into the heat-devils jitterbugging across the hot asphalt parking lot. "She stood there and listened to the spell, then invited me to come with her. That's when I—" With a drowning sound, Toby shook his head. "That's when I turned her down, when I threw away my only chance at lasting happiness."

"Toby, no! You—"

Toby chopped his hand through the air. "I know all that, Mike! Do you think I haven't argued this around and around and around in my head for the past five years? Don't you think I've covered everything? I know it was what I had to do. I know it was the *right* thing to do, but none of that matters because what I said before is *also true.*"

"But there are other—"

"Women?" Toby spat with derision. "You saw her, Mike. No mere woman could come close to Lily." He shook his head and turned back to face them. "But none of that matters. My point is, I'm not entirely sure *we banished her.* Yes, she left, she went back"—he squeezed his eyes shut—"home, but I think she *could have* stayed, that she *would have* stayed and probably killed us all, spell or no spell, if she wasn't heart-sick."

"She…" Mike's voice choked off, and he had to swallow before he could go on. "She said she'd be back. That there was always someone willing to pay the price to bring her into this world."

Gavin frowned at Mike, his eyebrows hunching together. "The women? The murders?"

Mike quirked his eyebrow at Toby. "Is that how she's summoned?"

"You think…" Toby spun away from them, turned his back and faced the parking lot, but not before Gavin saw the hope, the yearning in the man's face. When he turned back, his expression had settled into a cold, calm mask. "To answer your question, I don't know, Mike. She never discussed how she was summoned, but human sacrifice isn't outside the realm of possibilities." He squeezed his eyes shut, and his lips trembled a moment. "She told me to go to Eddie's neighborhood and call her, that she would come if I did, but *outside* that circle of land…" He shrugged.

"These women…they were tortured for a time, then butchered," said Gavin in a pensive voice. "What if they are more than sacrifices? What if they are…vessels?"

Toby tilted his head to the side. "The *mazzikim* had physical forms. The way I used to banish them was to exsanguinate them, then destroy the blood and the flesh in isolation from each other. Anything else and they'd come back."

"How did you…" Gavin shook his head.

With a sour grin, Toby said, "Scotty had trouble with that, too." He sobered and then frowned. "Until his wife and daughter were slaughtered." He shook himself and forced a smile. "But to answer your question, I burned the blood and put the flesh into an industrial digester. I also boiled some in lye." He pumped his shoulders up and down. "Anything that left very little trace of their physical form seemed to work."

"That's…"

"Gruesome," said Mike. "And it was, but it was also necessary, Gavin."

Gavin sighed and sank into one of the chairs tucked away with the table. "Yeah, it sounds like it. So why risk this spell you mentioned. Why not bleed Lily out and dissolve her body?"

"Wouldn't work," said Toby. "Lily gave up her body to access the totality of her power—she dissolved it, blood and all, and turned into a…" He shook his head.

"Shadow-monster," said Mike.

"She's not a monster!" snapped Toby.

Mike ticked of his points on his fingers. "Chrome claws the size of samurai swords and twice as sharp. Body made of pure darkness. Shadows. Coherent smoke. Whatever. Eyes—"

"And wind," Toby said in a wistful tone. "Shadows and wind."

"—filled with evil, with evils acts and thoughts best left in the dark." He quirked at grin at Toby. "Did I miss anything?"

Toby frowned down at his feet, and they fell silent for a time.

"I need some water," said Gavin, rising and stepping toward the door.

"We have some," said Mike.

"Yeah, but I need my Hydrolite, anyway." Gavin glanced at Toby. "Still no delivery."

Toby shook his head. "By eight tonight."

"I'll be back," said Gavin as he ducked out the door. Toby didn't seem to notice.

5

Gavin already had the phone warbling as he stepped outside Mike and Greg's room and headed through the curtain of heat to his room. He really did want to get some Hydrolite seeping into his tissues, but the circular argument going on between Toby and Mike held no interest for him. Hearing Maddie's voice, however, did.

"Frank's Plumbing," she said when she answered.

"He's real, Mads. I mean, real as in he has a physical presence. A body, I mean. He's—"

"Wait. Gavin, wait! Who?"

He squeezed his eyes shut, pushing his door open, and walking into his room blind. "Fry."

Maddie gasped.

"Yeah."

When she next spoke, Maddie's voice was calm but low and strained, as though she had laryngitis and speaking took real effort. "Okay. We need a plan for dealing with him in person, then."

"Uh… That's not what I expected you to say." He'd expected her to freak out, to demand he leave, that he come home. The steel in her voice made him proud.

"Should I argue? Tell you to pack your things and— no, scratch that—to *get in your damn car right this second and haul ass*? Do we need to have *that* conversation again?"

"Well, no, but I kind of expected to have it anyway."

"That old argument wouldn't do either of us any good. You need to be there, to fight him. I accept that. I don't like it, but I accept it."

Gavin didn't know what to say, so he settled on: "Thanks, Mads. Have I told you how awesome you are lately?"

"Since you won't do the sensible thing, we need to make a plan to make sure you survive the insane path you are on."

"When you put it that way…"

"Yeah, well, I know an argument won't help, but that doesn't mean I've given up all hope you'll come around." She sighed. "How do I keep you alive, Gavin Gregory? Because I *need* you alive. Here."

"Trust me, I need me alive, too."

"I mean, who's going to change the baby's diapers? Who's going to rub my feet?"

"Well, there's Frank."

Her soft chuckle gave him a buoyant, hopeful feeling.

"Tell me," she said in an unknowing imitation of Toby. "Tell me everything."

"How did I get so lucky?" Gavin breathed into the phone. "I must have really good karma."

Maddie laughed. "Um, yeah. Great karma. Married a writer, but not a romance writer, so we aren't rich. Not one, but two insanely powerful supernatural entities bent on destroying you. Yeah, sounds great. I think you were the guy who beat up the boys who pulled wings off flies for fun in your former life."

"Nah, that guy's a plumber and married to a shopaholic addicted to shoes two sizes too small."

"That's awfully specific. Something you want to tell me?"

"Francis. Frank's wife. They live in Jersey."

"He never said," said Maddie with a throaty laugh. "He drives a long way to service me—our house, I mean."

"You're worth it."

"It's about time you noticed. I guess I can stop cleaning the house now."

"Um, you clean the house?"

"Sure. All the time. I dust, I vacuum. I even do the dishes."

"Not so's you'd notice…"

"If you were here, I'd pop you one in the kisser."

"Promises, promises." They chuckled together for a moment, and the world seemed a better place to Gavin…maybe not a safer place, but a place worth risking his life for.

"Quit distracting me and tell me everything, Gav."

He did so, sparing nothing, holding no punches.

"Jesus…" she whispered. "Just like your dreams, then?"

"Not so much. He didn't turn into the Whore of Babylon, for one thing, and he didn't loom over me like Godzilla."

"And the chirp? Was it really Glacadairanam?"

"Who knows? It could've been, or it might have just been Fry screwing with me, just like that 'Where we going, sugar,' bullshit he's so fond of."

"I'd kind of hoped that part of Adeline's tale was fictional."

"It seems not. I wonder…"

"If Glacadairanam is her child? No, I don't think so."

"Why not?"

"Too easy. Maybe the rumored 'other son.'"

"Heh." Gavin sank onto the bed, then lifted his legs and reclined against the headboard. The room was hot and stale, but he'd already given up fighting that. "Mike and Toby speculated about whether these murders—the women—are some kind of sacrifice."

"Sacrifice to who?"

"The demons they fought in New York were led by a super-demon of some kind. They did a banishing spell to get rid of all the lesser demons, then they convinced her to pack up and head home or banished her, too, depending on which interpretation of events you want to believe. She left them with instructions on how to summon her back—"

"Why in the hell would she think that would work."

Gavin sighed, then sniffed. "She was doing a number on Toby. Mesmerizing him or something. The result is…" He shook his head.

"He loves her?"

"That or he has the worst case of Stockholm Syndrome I've ever seen."

"Then…can you trust him?"

"He did the right thing back then. He says he broke her heart, but it seems more like he broke his own. Either way, he sent her packing, and he turned down her offer to go with her. He participated in the spell they think cut off her access to us."

"Spell…"

"Yeah, I know. It sounds crazy, and it feels crazy to talk about it like it's possible, like magic is real, but…"

"This year's been tough on that logical old man who lives in your head, hasn't it."

"He's not old."

"Ninety-seven at the very least. He wears his pants up to his bottom rib."

"Ouch," said Gavin with a chuckle.

"And the comb-over is to die for."

"Hey! I've got good hair."

"Not so's you'd notice." They both laughed at that, and the tension eased another notch.

"Why…" he started, then closed his mouth and shook his head.

"Why did Fry latch onto you?"

"Yeah. What did I do?"

"You beat Glacadairanam. Fry said as much in your seizure-dreams. You pissed off his son, so Fry latched onto you and is making your life hell. Softening you up for the rematch. *And* you messed with The Bogeyman, and he was one of Fry's disciples."

"Think so?"

"Gavin, this falls into the 'no duh' category."

"Oh."

"Don't worry, I'm still attracted to the comb-over."

"If that's true…if Fry's doing this for revenge, to get even for Glacadairanam, why not just kill me and be done with it. Why not boil my decapitated head and give my skull to the little creep."

"Well, that's a nice image," said Maddie with a sour note in her voice. "Think about it, Gav. If he did that, if he solved the problem for his little brat, it would only reinforce the 'failure,' reinforce Glacadairanam's dependence on Fry."

"Wait a minute. You're saying Fry's trying to be a *good parent*?"

"Too crazy for you? ESPers surrounding you, supernatural serial killers take over your entire universe, but you draw the line at a demon wanting to raise his son to be strong and independent?"

"Another 'no duh' comment is coming, isn't it?"

"Duh," she said, then chuckled. "Sorry, you walked right into it."

"I run toward danger, Mads," he said in his best cliché superhero voice, then chuckled.

Suddenly sober, Maddie said, "I know, Gavin. It's what makes you my hero. Let's get back to how we keep you alive for the medal ceremony."

"I'm open to ideas."

"Good. Here's what I have in mind—"

"Wait, before we get into it, can you do me a favor after you hang up and check on Kai? I haven't heard from him since last night despite trying to, uh, reach him."

"Yeah, I can do that, but right now, I'm trying to figure out how to save you from yourself so you can save the universe and all that."

"Oh, is that all I have to do?" Gavin asked with a chuckle. "Save the entire universe?"

"You might need to pick up milk on your way home, too. Maybe even run the vacuum. Oh, and my feet."

"You want me to vacuum your feet? That's a little weird, Mads."

"Shut up, you."

"Yes, dear," he said with a chuckle. "Might as well outline the master plan for saving everything, then." He waited, but Maddie didn't speak. "Mads?" He glanced at the screen of his phone, which still indicated the call was connected. When he put the phone back to his ear, however, all he heard was a soft fuzz. "What the hell?" he murmured, breaking the connection and hitting redial, but Maddie's phone went right to voicemail. Frowning, he tried a second time and got the same result. As he was about to hit redial for the third time, his phone rang, and he smiled, but the caller ID read "Bud MacArthur" instead of "Madeline Gregory."

He clicked accept and said, "Gregory."

"Check your email, agent. I got you some addresses."

"Thanks, Bud."

"In Texas, we say thanks, then 'Appreciate ya.' You'll need to get in the habit or people will think you're strange."

Gavin switched the phone to speaker and opened his email client and scanned his inbox. "Ah," he said as he tapped the latest email from Bud. "Only five?"

"Well, it's about half the population of Kelly County, so yeah, only five."

"Westral's not on this list."

"Y'all already been there, or did you forget?"

"No," said Gavin quietly. "I didn't forget."

"Besides, Westral might be slicker than a boiled onion—hell, he might even be wilder than an acre of snakes—but he ain't got enough horse sense for criminal mastermindin'."

"Maybe not, but he's involved in this somehow."

"I don't doubt it. His daddy, as it turns out, was sheriff before him—"

"Yeah, we just found that out when we got the property records."

"—and from what my old partner told me a minute ago, was quite a piece of work. Rumor has it, he thumped on his family quite regular. When his wife disappeared, there was a rumor that he beat her to death and buried her out in the desert on the Mexico side of the border. What ain't rumor is that he ran that county like it was his own little kingdom."

"Sounds familiar."

"Yep. My partner went on to say that if you wanted to pull something dark and dirty in southwest Texas, Kelly County was the place to do it. That the elder Sheriff Westral could be convinced to look the other way for the right price, no matter how dark your doings was."

"You think that's what's going on now? That Westral is botching the investigation because someone is paying him to?" Gavin's mind flashed back to the expression on the sheriff's face as he ran for his car and bugged out. Whatever else was going on, Red Westral was scared to death of Fry. "You ever hear of a man named Fry in connection with Kelly County? Maybe Frank Fry? Or Frankie 'Evil Eye?'"

"No, can't say as I have."

"He'd have been a kind of king pin around here, I'd guess. He was once a hitter for the Mob."

"Still don't ring any bells, Gavin. I'll ask Jim, though two calls in one month would surprise him, let alone two in one day."

"It's probably nothing."

"It'll make the old man's day," said Bud. "He ain't got much doin' since his Martha passed."

"Thanks." Gavin chuckled and said, "I appreciate you."

"Naw, now you went and ruint it, Gavin. It's just 'appreciate ya.' Or better yet, just drop the 'a' and that first 'p.'"

"'Preciate ya."

"That's it. I can head back over if you want back up to check out those names—or you and Rick got it covered?"

"We'll handle the initial investigation. I'll call you if we turn anything up."

"Roger," said Bud. "In the meantime, I'll dig up…" Whatever he said next was lost to a wash of static. Gavin looked at his phone, but it was the same as with Maddie's call—connected but dead for all intents and purposes. He spent a moment watching the signal strength display and grimaced as it bounced from four bars to one, then up to three and back down to one.

He tapped Maddie's contact anyway, then watched the signal strength—which dropped to one bar and stayed there until he hung up. "Weird," he muttered and left the room.

6

Room 1404, Aeonian Motel & RV Park, Aeonia, TX
Saturday, 3:28 pm CST

"Come!" Mike shouted when Gavin knocked. He glanced at Gavin. "More addresses?"

"Yep," said Gavin. "Do either one of you have phone service?"

Toby glanced at his phone, frowned, and shook his head.

"You?" Gavin asked Mike.

"SEMPRe phones. Same service," said Mike, but he checked anyway and then shook his head. "Weird."

"Yeah, I had plenty of bandwidth, then the calls just fuzzed out."

"Solar storm, maybe," said Toby, returning his gaze to the heat-hazed parking lot.

"What did MacArthur have to say?"

"Bud got us five more addresses and a little more dirt on the Westral clan." He told them what MacArthur had told him about the old sheriff.

"That fits," said Toby. "He sounds like one of Brigitta's special friends. One of her pet killers. I bet this Fry has some, too."

"I don't know," said Mike. "He seemed genuinely terrified to me."

"Me, too, but Fry definitely recruits pet killers," said Gavin, thinking about Javier Dela Cruz, Dylan Jepson, and Rayson Fergus.

"Whatever," said Mike. "But, I guess he'd terrify me even if we were bosom buddies."

"No doubt about it," said Gavin. He glanced down at his phone and frowned. "Maybe one of these five will know something about—"

"They're back," said Greg in a slurred voice. "They're moving Benny and Shannon. They're... Oh, my God! They're—"

Chapter 7
Twenty
Questions

I

The temple, Southwestern TX
Saturday, 3:35 pm CST

The door swung open so hard it rebounded off the wall with a booming crash. Marcus Wallace stood in the hall and pointed at Shannon. "You. Get a move on." He was dressed in a black robe of a rough weave, and a red cotton sash belted his waist.

"Without Andy?" she said and tittered.

"If I'd wanted both, I'd have called for both of you. Get moving."

I think it's okay, sent Benny. *The words "test" and "questions" are foremost in his mind. Just keep your illusion going.*

Shannon tittered again and got up, glancing at Benny. "See you later, tiger."

Benny turned his gaze on Marcus. "She will, won't she?"

Marcus shook his head and chuckled. "What kind of group do you think we are?"

One that murders pretty women and dumps them in the desert. Benny dropped his gaze and shrugged.

That won't happen, Benny-bear, sent Shannon. *I can take care of myself.*

"She'll be fine, Andy," said Marcus with a friendly grin. "Scout's honor." He glanced at Shannon, and his friendly demeanor slid away like a snake through the grass. "But we are on a schedule, so get a move on."

She dimpled and tittered as she walked into the hall.

Marcus shut the door behind them, and Shannon turned first one way, then the other.

"Where to?" she asked.

"You can drop the act," Marcus as much as snapped. "You ain't half as dumb as you pretend, but at the same time, you ain't half as smart."

"Oh," Shannon said, pretending at chagrin, pretending she'd been caught out. "It's…" She shrugged. "It's just a precaution. Plus, if people think you're a dumb woman, they feel more comfortable telling you the truth."

"It's a mind-game, plain and simple, and around here, we don't cotton to mind-games, Bertie. You'd do well to keep that in mind."

"Oh," she repeated, dropping her gaze to the floor. "I didn't mean to—"

"Save it," Marcus said. He pointed down the hall, motioning her on in front of him. "Go on."

Shannon turned and walked in the direction he'd indicated, keeping the head of her illusory guise pointed at the floor. She scoured the hall with her eyes, wondering if the commotion they'd heard was a fight in earnest or a fiction to elicit a response from them. They'd made it about fifty feet before she found the first pool of congealed blood. *I found something*, she sent to Benny. *Blood.*

I know. I'm with you. Up by the ceiling.

Shannon raised her gaze as if swooning a little and glanced around, smiling at where she imagined Benny hung. "Oh my," she said in a breathy voice. "Is that blood?"

"Mind your business," said Marcus. "And right now, that's doing what I tell you." Second door."

She opened the door on a room the size of a small chapel and stepped inside. The roof was gone—caved in years ago by the look of the exposed timbers—and the hot sun beat down on her mercilessly. The splintered remains of what appeared to be church pews lay at the base of the four walls and showed signs that they'd been scavenged for firewood. A large circular scorch dotted the center of the room, and next to it, the cultists had moved something heavy in and out many times judging by the scrape marks.

Eight black-robed men stood in a knot behind Primo, and nine pairs of linesmen boots emerged into the sunlight from beneath the robes. Each robe was belted by a blood-red cotton fascia. Primo also wore a rough-spun black robe like the others, but his white sash was silk and shined in the sun like a bolt of lightning. The giant man cocked his head to the side and grinned at her. "Hello again, Bertie," he rumbled.

"Hello, Primo." Her gaze danced across the robed figures behind him.

He turned a little and glanced back. "Don't worry. These men are here to assist in the testing."

"Uh, okay," said Shannon, adding just the right waver to her thready voice. "I'm not good with tests."

I can't read the big one, sent Benny. *He's got... I don't know.*

Out of the corner of her eye, she saw Benny float toward the knot of black-robed figures. *Be careful!*

Marcus brushed past her, and as he did so, he murmured, "Didn't we just talk about this act?" He nodded to Primo, then went to stand with the others.

Shannon painted a crimson blaze on the cheeks of her visage, complete with a guilty frown. "Sorry," she mumbled. "Force of habit."

"We all find our own way to deal with the heathens outside these walls, Bertie," said Primo, a hint of reproach coloring his expression. "But inside, we deal squarely with one another. No one manipulates, no one tells tall tales, no one cheats."

I'm getting a sense of the big guy's emotions but nothing else. No thoughts, no images, just raw emotion. Right now, he seems a little amused but mostly bored, impatient.

"I…" She shook her head, then lifted her gaze up, up, up to meet Primo's head-on. "I understand."

He nodded once. "Good. The purpose of the test is to ensure you are a good fit for our group, and likewise, that we are a good fit for you. Andy will also be tested, and if *both* of you are deemed a match, we will accept you as initiates."

"Both of us?"

Primo shrugged. "We wouldn't put you in the position of choosing us over him, nor him over you. Couples who come to us are tested individually *and* as a unit. Do you see?"

She cocked her head to the side. "You said this it ensure we're both right for the other. Does that mean I can ask you questions, too?"

Marcus hissed.

"Yes?" Primo asked, chopping his hand through the air behind him.

Exasperation at Marcus. Mild curiosity directed at you.

"Uh, before you called yourselves the 'Brethren' but there are clearly women in the group. I…I heard one in the hall earlier, and by your own admission, you are considering adding me to your ranks." Shannon made her image blush again and ducked her head. *Keep them coming, Benny-bear. I think I'm going to need all the help I can get.*

Nah, you got this, Shan. You're smarter than the lot of them combined.

Primo half-turned toward his black-robed companions, cocking one eyebrow and grinning. "We do have women in our group, it's true, and I did call these men 'Brethren,' which is more of an honorific among the members. I use it because they do." He treated her to a shrug. "My brother and I are the model for the Brethren, you see."

"Um, I guess?"

"You sound unsure."

"It's just…" She shook her head.

"Go on, Bertie," said Primo in a soft but firm tone. "Ask your questions."

"It just strikes me as strange to be called a 'brother.' Don't you have any sisters?"

Primo nodded as if she'd said something very wise. "Your discomfort will change as you learn and grow. And no, none of my sisters survived their births. Unsuitable, Father always said." He arched one eyebrow and stared down at her. "Now, if you're ready to proceed?"

Go along, Shan. He's losing patience with the questions.

Primo's eyes narrowed as Benny's voice sounded in her head, and he narrowed his eyes and glanced at the air around her, but Benny had moved above and behind the big man.

"I'm sorry," Shannon said, dipping into a curtsey. "My mother always said my curiosity was going to get the better of me."

"Ah, yes. Your mother." Primo tilted his head back and motioned to the Brethren.

"Your mother died when you were seventeen," said one of the men in the pack.

"The coroner called it suicide," said another.

"We don't believe that," said Marcus. "Tell us how she really died."

I told you we needed an in-depth backstory, sent Benny. *Tell them everything we came up with, but don't be too eager.*

You can read him now? Primo, I mean?

No, but the Brethren are much easier to read than he is.

Good, she thought at him. *You can give me the right answers.* To the men arrayed in front of her, she shrugged. "I don't know what you mean."

"Yes, you do," said Primo in a bored tone. "If you can't trust us, you can't join us."

She narrowed the eyes of her visage. "You're asking for a lot of trust and giving none."

Marcus opened his mouth, eyes blazing.

"Fair point," said Primo. "We have abducted an FBI agent. We are holding him captive here in the temple."

Marcus gasped.

Shannon let her gaze go wide. *Identity of the prisoner is confirmed. Tell Greg.*

I'm linked to him.

"There. We've trusted you with a secret that could buy all of us a life sentence." The big man shrugged his cannonball shoulders. "Even death. Is that enough trust for you?"

Careful, said Benny. *He feels irritated.*

Yeah, but at me or at Marcus?

That's why I said be careful. I have no idea.

Shannon nodded to Primo. "Thanks. That makes this easier." She averted her gaze and made her visage swallow hard. "She was… My mom and I never got along like my girlfriends did with their mothers. No trips to the mall, no nail salons. She…" Shannon shook her head. "It was like she hated me from the moment she saw me."

"Jealousy is an ugly mistress," said Primo. "And your relationship deteriorated as you began to develop into a woman."

Shannon nodded, feigning surprise. She reviewed the story they'd decided on one last, hurried time, then said, "Yes. As I started to grow up, she got nastier and nastier. Mean, too. She'd call me a slut if I dressed up. She'd get mad at me if I brought home better report cards than she had at my age. She—"

"That sounds confusing, but nothing some of us haven't experienced, firsthand," said Primo, and behind him, Shannon saw several of the Brethren nodding.

"It… It was."

"And where was your daddy?" asked Marcus.

Shannon scoffed. "What daddy? He fucked my mom and then fucked off."

"Ah, the ways of the world," said Primo in the air of one dropping a pearl of wisdom.

"You killed your mother because she was a jerk?" asked one of the men.

Shannon shook her head and made her cheeks blaze red.

"Go on," said Primo. "There is no shame here."

A single tear tracked down the cheek of the visage she was projecting. "She… She started hitting me when I was eleven. Really hitting me, I mean. She was always heavy-handed, but when I was eleven, she started hitting like she meant it."

"People can be cruel to their children," said Marcus, and for the first time, she thought she heard compassion directed at her.

"That's not all. When I…" She made her blush deepen. "When I started sleeping with my boyfriends, she knew. Somehow, she knew. She did...*things* to me to punish me."

"What an evil bitch," said one of the Brethren.

"She deserved what you gave her," said Marcus. "Didn't she?"

Primo nodded. "Tell us about her murder."

"It was *awful*," Shannon said. "The blood... She—"

"But you loved it," said Primo. His unblinking gaze rattled her.

What does he know? Shannon sent, and again, Primo's gaze flicked to the empty air around her.

Nothing, Shan. He's fishing.

She hung her head. "I'm not going to deny that I felt a certain satisfaction at putting her back on her heels."

"More than that," said Primo, his gaze boring into hers. "More than that."

She tilted her head to side. "Is that so bad?"

"What's bad is trying to hide it from us," hissed Marcus. "Do you think we don't understand? Do you think we suffered less in our time out there with the so-called righteous?"

"I—"

"In these walls," said Primo, "we are free. Totally free. We can say what we please. We can *do* as we please. There are no laws here, no cops"—Primo grinned—"though if you have a ticket you need fixed, we do have members who work in the law enforcement community. Nothing you say or do within these walls will ever come back to haunt you in a courtroom, Bertie."

"But…" Shannon shrugged.

Primo grinned and twirled his fingers in the air. "But you've seen all the documentaries. All the so-called investigations into cults, and there's always that snitch telling tales on camera or to the cops."

"That's…" Shannon glanced at Marcus. "That's right. There's always someone *watching* everyone, someone ready to talk when they get in trouble."

Primo shot a look at his second, then chuckled and threw his arms wide. "When I started…all this, I thought I'd have to start slow, to bring in the so-called regular folks and build up an inner circle, keeping all those 'regulars' at arm's length. But do you know what?"

Shannon shook her head.

With a laugh that filled the room, Primo walked over and lay a hand on Marcus's shoulder. "My father told me it wouldn't be that way. I didn't believe him, but do you know who the first person to come to me was?"

Shannon shook her head again.

Primo lifted his thick paw and patted Marcus. "This guy. Do you think I had to keep *him* at arm's length? That I had to *lie* and *deceive* him?" He shook his head, and Marcus grinned. "Do you think I had to 'warm him up' as they say?"

Shrugging, Shannon cut her gaze back and forth between the two men.

"Well, I'll tell you: I didn't." He gazed into Marcus's face a moment, and his grin widened. "You want to tell it?"

Marcus shrugged. "Why not?"

"Why not, indeed," said Primo, turning back to face Shannon. "Let's test her. Let's see if she can *believe*."

With a grin, Marcus started in. "It was a Saturday night, and I was in a mood…"

2

Last Chance Saloon, Odolavesta, TX,
Saturday, March 18, 2000, 2:09 am CST

Marcus glared at the bartender, not really pissed at her but not willing to go quietly. "Just one more, darlin'. One more and I'll be out of your hair."

"You already used that line, Marcus Wallace," said the woman behind the bar. "You know as well as I do that the state says I got to close at two in the morning."

Marcus looked around. "Ain't no one here but you and me, woman. I won't tell if you don't." He looked at her, then, and let a little bit of mean out.

She folded her arms and gave him that look he hated. That look that made him feel small. "Don't give me no trouble. I used to babysit you, Marcus. I seen you in your damn cartoon pajamas, and you can't give me no evil eye and make it stick. You want to be served next Saturday, you'll get up off my damn barstool and walk out that door under your own steam."

He let his face dissolve into a sneer. "God damn it, Cindy!"

"God damn it yourself, Marcus! I got kids to get home to." She flipped the towel over her shoulder, then turned back to finish counting her receipts. "Go on, now. Git."

He stared at her for a few moments, his emotions simmering, then swept his few remaining loose bills off the counter and stuffed them into his pocket.

"And don't stiff me on the tip, neither."

With an angry frown, he pulled a five-dollar bill out of his pocket and slapped it on the counter. "There! That do ya, or do you want the shirt off my back, too?"

"Nah," said Cindy. "And next week, why not stop to home for a shower and clean clothes before you come by? You stink, Marcus."

"Yeah, well, some of us work for living." He turned and stomped out into the gravel parking lot, feeling a lot meaner than he'd felt when he went inside. Construction wasn't what he'd always expected to do with his life, but it was his fate, it seemed. He heaved a sigh and fished around in his pockets for the keys to his disaster area of a pickup.

"Well, now, lookee here," called a voice. "You lost, boy?"

A low rumble sounded in return.

Marcus peered into the darkness outside the meager, single bulb floodlight Cindy had installed to keep her patrons safe. "Whossat?" he called.

"Mind your business, stranger!"

"That ain't no stranger. That's that Wallace boy. The one who played ball like a pro and threw it all away to drive nails." The second voice was familiar to Marcus, but he couldn't place it.

"Marcus?" asked the first voice. "I'll be damned. C'mere! We gonna have us a bit of fun."

Yes, Marcus, come over here. The voice in his head was low, distinct, but quiet, like a whisper across a crowded room. He stepped down from the stupid wooden walk Cindy had out front of her place, his boot heels crunching in the gravel and desert dust. "What's doing?"

"We caught us a John Coffy motherfucker slinking around out back of Cindy's place," said the first voice.

"Up to the dickens, you can bet," said the second.

"Seems like he's forgotten his place."

Marcus, stop them, and I'll give you what you've been looking for your entire life.

He shook his head. No one knew what drove Marcus to do the things he did…why he chose to turn down all those fancy college recruiters with their snooty good looks and condescending bullshit, why he chose to do manual labor in the heat and sun, why he never found a woman and 'settled down.' He ambled toward the voices, peering into the moonless night.

You'd be surprised what I know, Marcus, what I understand about you.

"Yeah, yeah," he muttered.

"You say something, Marcus?"

"Nah." He hawked and spat. "Let's see this bozo."

You'll take the side of these men who hold you in such dark contempt?

Marcus scuffed his boot across the gravel, sending the scree scuttling into the darkness, slipping and sliding from having put too much behind the kick, and from having put too much beer down his gullet. But as much as he wanted to deny the logic, that voice in his head was right. The last thing he should do is side with the sheep-lovers who might give him the bum's rush next Saturday. The men who did these things were all the same: mean, mad at the world, and ready to blame anyone who didn't play the same game they did, in the same way.

My point.

His eyes adjusted to the unlit portion of the parking lot, and he saw two would-be gunslingers standing on either side of a giant man the color of midnight. They had him pinned up against the tailgate of Marcus's piece-of-shit Chevy, though it seemed to Marcus that the big man could easily sweep up the two loud-mouths, one in either arm, smash their heads together, and leave them in a heap without even breaking a sweat.

He recognized speaker number one as the owner of the feed and tack down the road, Bob Burnaby. His companion Marcus knew all too well—his former coach and mentor, Louis Garcia. They'd had hard words when Marcus had turned down all the scouts and hadn't had much to say to one another since then, though he stood there grinning like they was old pals. The two men wore what could be called the local Saturday-night uniform: fancy snip-toed stockman boots decorated with fancy stitching, skintight Lee denim that might have been starched in place across their thighs, a tooled leather belt complete with a ginormous rodeo buckle that flashed and gleamed in the starlight though neither man had ever rode in a rodeo, button-down western shirts, and wide-brimmed cowboy hats with suede bands. To Marcus's mind, both men were sheep, rather than elders who deserved his respect.

To my mind, you couldn't be more right.

Marcus narrowed his eyes and raised his gaze to find the giant looking at him, a faint smile on his lips. The man gave him a single, slow nod, as though they were old friends. "You picked the wrong parking lot to burglar in."

The man cocked his head to the side. "I'm not doing anything but walking from point A to point B. And I'm not a stranger, not anymore. I bought the old church out on Bonnie Street."

"You a reverend, are ya?" asked Burnaby. "What kind?"

The man never so much as twitched his gaze away from Marcus's. "I am," he said, "though of a non-traditional sect."

"One of them hippie kinds?" asked Garcia. "Down this-a-ways, we don't much care for hippie-shit."

A faint, secret grin surfaced on giant's lips, but only briefly, and maybe only for Marcus's benefit. "No, no 'hippie-shit,' though I do preach equal respect for everyone."

"Sounds like hippie-shit to me," said Burnaby. "We *ain't* all equal, no matter what you hippies want the world to believe."

"'Thou shalt love they neighbor as thyself,'" quoted the big man. "If that is a hippie sentiment, then I guess you'd be correct."

"Seems to me, the man's callin' you a hypocrite, Bob," said Marcus. He quirked his head to side. "*Are* you a hypocrite?"

Burnaby gave him a dirty look. "You takin' his side?"

Marcus folded his arms and swayed a little until his drunk brain caught up to his body. "I ain't sidin' with nobody. Yet."

Louis Garcia sneered at him, shaking his head. "I taught you better, Marcus Wallace."

"Did you, Coach? Or did you teach me *exactly* this? All that about standing up to bullies? That ring a bell?"

Gracia frowned. "How'd you get it so wrong? That was about protecting our *own*, protecting the *town*, our *neighbors* from outsiders who—"

Through it all, every time Marcus glanced at the big man, he found his grin a little wider. "What's this man, this *minister*, done to anyone? Who's he a threat to?"

"He was *skulkin'* around out here like a horse thief—"

"I was *walking*. I took a *shortcut* through the parking lot."

"He steal anything? He touch one of these trucks?" Marcus swept his hands around the parking lot.

Garcia's hands curled into fists. "You was always mouthy, Wallace."

Without warning, and with a grace that belied his size and bulk, the black man danced forward, fists already slicing through the air in wide arcs. He slammed into Garcia like a great white going after a seal, left fist the size of a boulder slamming into the side of the football coach's head, followed immediately by the right on the other side, and Garcia staggered back a few steps, dazed and confused.

"Get him, Marcus!" shouted Bob Burnaby as he charged forward, one hand cocked back, back, back over his shoulder, primed for a hill-billy haymaker.

Marcus had time to glance at the big man, and despite facing Louis Garcia, he found the man's gaze and his broad smile on him.

Choose, Marcus Wallace. Choose me and everything you've ever wanted, or stand with these men and what they represent.

You don't know what I want, thought Marcus. A dark part of him, the part he tried to keep buried—or at least hidden—from everyone else, cried out in denial.

Burnaby yelled, and Marcus made his choice.

3

The temple, Southwestern TX
Saturday, 3:43 pm CST

"And that was it," said Marcus.

"Hardly," said Primo with a wide grin. "We beat those racist motherfuckers into the dirt and left them for dead. Burnaby still walks with a limp—if you can call the hobbling crabwalk thing he does walking—and drools. Garcia never came out of his coma." He turned and lifted an eyebrow at Marcus. "Did I lie to you that night?"

"You mean…" Shannon feigned awe. "You mean that voice in his head wasn't his imagination? It really was you? Your words?"

"You didn't lie," said Marcus in a voice filled with quiet reverence. "And yes, it was his voice in my head, it was *him* in my head."

Something's not right, Shannon. Marcus is gloating. And someone's unlocking the door to our cell.

Her pulse quickened as Benny spoke in her head and fear blossomed in her guts, but it was already too late.

"So…now I told you something you can use to get out of trouble," said Marcus.

"From the police, at least," added Primo with a chuckle. "Do go on, though. You were about to tell us how you enjoyed murdering your mother."

"I…" Shannon shook her head, fighting not to step back under the force of their stares.

"Go on. Tell us, *Shannon*," said Primo.

HE KNOWS!

Smiling, Marcus took a step forward, a step *toward her*. He withdrew a pair of chrome handcuffs from beneath his robe and looked at Primo.

BENNY!

Primo nodded to his second, though he never took his galvanic stare off her. Marcus stepped closer, his grin turning mean, a glint entering his eyes.

THEY KNOW!

4

The temple, Southwestern TX
Saturday, 3:48 pm CST

HE KNOWS!

Shannon's mental voice thundered through Benny, the fear, the anguish, the *panic* woven into it shaking him to his core. But the door to their room was unlocked and opening, and he zipped back to his body.

BENNY!

He flung himself to his feet, already sprinting toward the door, already steeling himself for an impact—with the door or the person opening the door, he didn't know which. A distant wail reached his ears, sounding as if it came from far out in the desert, and at first, he thought it was her, thought it was *Shannon*.

THEY KNOW!

Shannon's thought rumbled and growled to the very depths of him, boomed and bellowed in the hallways of his mind like a madcap brass band, shrieked and squalled like a million million newborns roasting in the Pit, shaking his soul, rending it, tearing it. Panic soared beside the echoes, and adrenaline filled his frenzied charge toward the door.

But through it all, eerie string voices added themselves to the desert wailing, music like he'd never heard, a barbarous, brutish threnody, a lament, a requiem of lost souls, of stolen lives and ruined hopes. Colors flashed in his mind, terrible colors, burnt oranges, dark reds, tan—desert colors, desert anguish—and his steps faltered. For the first time, as the music wormed into his brain, he understood what Toby had tried to tell him about his time with Lilitu.

GREG! he screamed with all the mental force he could summon.

The door banged open, slammed back against the wall as it had when Marcus came for Shannon, and Benny lurched away. The tempo of the elegy soared, pounding and pounding and pounding into his brain, sonic blows of obscene power, flinging his thoughts left and right, knocking his consciousness back and back and back, leaving his mind reeling, and he collapsed.

GREG, THEY KNOW!

He expected Marcus. He expected Primo. He expected Shannon, trussed up or dead, but instead, a woman walked into the room, her scathing glare cutting him down like chaff. Behind her, came a man with a guitar slung over his shoulder, and the terrible, awful, mesmerizing music came from him, came from his fingers, came from his infernal power.

GREG, RUN!

The woman grimaced, then stepped forward to squat over him and slammed her fist into Benny's face, again and again, rattling the thoughts from his head, again and again, battering at him, flinging his blood to the walls on every backswing, bludgeoning his consciousness, splattering his blood to the floor with every impact, hammering his will, crushing any hope he once had. He tried to lift his hands, to defend himself, to fend her off, to strike back, but the music…the music rode him like a loa, controlled his body utterly, drove him to stillness, commanded his obedience.

"Ease up, Cece," said the man with the guitar. "Primo said to keep him alive for tonight, and I got him. I got him, Cece!"

Greg… Greg…

His once-soaring mental voice whispered like a ghost in the wind, dripped down his chin, mumbled like a brook in the fall, splattered across the front of his shirt, and he despaired. Helpless and alone, Benny sobbed.

help us… greg… greg…

The music changed, grew insistent, the rhythmic wailing matching his racing pulse, *became* his racing pulse, and his mind turned sluggish, somnambulant, hysterical, but at the same time apathetic. The tempo of the fists pounding into his face married the gruesome melody, twisting and clashing at first, then mixing and melding, eurythmic, horrible, savage.

greg... greg... greg...

He reached out with his mind, the way he had during that horrible battle when they'd lost Scott, when Shannon had been hurt. He reached out with his mind and tried to swat the music, tried to crush the guitar, tried to set the man playing it aflame, but the music...

greg... the music... greg...

the music... the music...

greg, watch...out...for the music...

He tried to shout it, tried to project his thoughts to the very ends of the universe, but in the end, could barely summon the will for a phantasmic whisper, for a chimerical wail.

One more blow slammed into his face, and his head lolled back, his eyelids slid open—as much as they could, anyway, swollen as they were—and Cece's hard face grew closer to his, her oppressive gaze pinning him, stabbing him.

"There, you shifty bastard. That's what you get, you crooked motherfucker." Her gaze left him then, fell to her swelling, bruised knuckles, and she frowned. She turned and left him lying there, then, but the music…the transcendental music didn't.

5

Westral Ranch, Ranch Road 2818, Odolavesta, TX
Saturday, 3:55 pm CST

Red sat outside his own damn house, huddled down in the front seat of his magnificent Cadillac, too scared to go inside, too terrified of Shay, of what he'd seen him do, of what he knew he *might do* to Red for turning tail and…

A triumphant shout rattled his kitchen window, and a monstrous, deformed leopard lizard fell from the blue palo verde that gave what shade it had to the stone walk that curved around the house. The thing's fifteen-inch body smoked and spattered as though sprinkled with boiling oil or hot acid, and it hissed, a pain-filled counterpoint to the victorious cry that still echoed and echoed and echoed—chasing his thoughts in vicious circles—in Red's mind.

The door slammed open, and Shay stood there, a horrible, truculent half-smile twisting his bloodless face, dark kohl bands ringing his fiery, whirly-gig eyes, drawing his already almond eyes to even sharper points. His hoodie was thrown back, and his bleached papyrus skin hung from his skull, loose, poxed, gangrenous. His smile spoke of long basement corridors, of manacles on the ends of rusty metal chains held by spikes driven into living stone, of torturers and cannibals, of pain, of anguish, of despair.

Moving at a deliberate pace, Shay lifted his hand and pointed at the Caddie's passenger seat. Thinking he was asking for a ride, Red nodded vigorously, trying to smile, trying to look anything but how he felt—terrified of the man…of the *thing* on his porch.

Shay grinned, and the sight of it made Red want to scream and gouge out his own eyes, and pointed at the passenger seat with more force. Something chirped, something that sounded as maniacally happy as Shay seemed, something that sounded like it would be happy to eat a small child alive.

Red wanted to open the door and run, to throw the car in drive and mash the accelerator while pointing the green dinosaur at the monster on his stoop, to do anything but *look* at the thing he could now feel beside him, the thing that caused a terrible cold to steal away the desert's heat. Ignoring all that, ignoring what he wanted, what he commanded his muscles to do, Red turned his head.

A mass of black shadows swirled inches from his face, drawing substance from the world, from Red. Translucent wings way too small for the beast to have mass flapped lazily in the air. The thing solidified, long ears flopping back from his nightmare head, hatred blazing in its crimson gaze.

Red threw himself back, hands scrabbling for the door handle, managed to jerk-jerk-jerk it up, to push the heavy steel door open and fall onto the gravel drive. The thing in the car bayed and thrashed and, proving it had mass after all, made the car rock on its springs. Its keening cry hurt to hear, and when Shay roared from the porch, Red sprang up and ran in mindless dread.

He ran, but he got no farther from the car, from the thing inside it…

Because Shay wasn't on the porch. Shay stood beside him, holding him, arms wrapped around him, horrible fetid breath in his nostrils, down his throat. "Where you goin', sugar?" he breathed in Red's ear.

Then the thing in the car sprang at him, and for the first time, he saw the monster's barbed tongue, saw its clawed three-finger hands, saw its beastly bifurcated tail. But it was too late.

Too late to regret.

Too late to escape.

After a moment, Glacadairanam smiled. "I've got him, now, Father," he said.

Laughing, Shay gave him a hug, then released him. "Have fun with your new toy. His father was a loyal servant, but he leaves something to be desired. Just don't burn him up too soon, we may need good old Sheriff Westral before all this is over and our foothold in this realm is secured." Looking on as Glacadairanam began making the man dance, learning which neural pathways twitched which muscle groups, Shay flashed the smile of a self-satisfied, indulgent father. "Take him to the temple." He swept his hand to the east, turning his head to look back at Ranch Road and the scrub marking the other side.

He narrowed his eyes, baleful orange light flashing like heat lightning and grimaced at the empty air. "Another one? *Another one?*" Then, quick as a hammer blow, he darted forward, arms outstretched, dreadful mouth of grisly fangs gaping wide, a gruesome kiss with a deadly consummation.

Behind him, Red Westral chirped, then let go of a bedlam laugh that raced into the desolate wilderness, echoing back and back and back, a thousand demented whoops before the desert fell silent in their wake.

Chapter 8
Poisonous Shadows

I

"NO!" Greg screamed, still lost in his trance, thrashing against it, fighting the bedclothes, fighting Mike, shoving him, kicking at him. "NO!"

"Greg! Stop fighting me!" cried Mike.

"*NO!*" Greg fought harder, slashing the air with hands and feet and elbows and knees. He whimpered, abject terror dancing in the air. He jerked his head back and forth, great, sweeping arcs as though trying to keep his head away from something horrible.

His head snapped to a halt like a giant had reached down and pinned him to the bed, and the bedframe creaked beneath him as if a great weight had settled on his chest. Mike looked around at Gavin and Toby, his eyes wide with disquiet, with despair. Greg arched his back, a horrible squeak escaping his lips, sounding as though someone had him in a strangle grip, and his larynx bobbled in his throat. He shook his head back and forth, back and forth, back and forth, mouth agape, tongue lashing his teeth.

"Greg!" cried Mike. "Greg! What's happening?"

Greg's back arched, bowing and bowing, while his head and neck seemed to dig deeper into the pillow and mattress, digging in, imprinting the foam with his outline. His mouth formed unvoiced syllables, his tongue thrashing, his voice box bouncing and bouncing.

"My God! My God!" Mike dove at the air above his husband, arms wide like a linebacker going in for a sack. He sailed across the bed and slammed to the ground on the opposite side. "Help him!"

Gavin lurched forward, not knowing what to do, but that instinct of charging into danger to protect others too strong to ignore. He leaped onto the bed, knees to either side of Greg's chest, chopping his fists through the air above the man's face, hitting nothing.

"That won't work," said Toby in a listless voice. "Herlequin's got him, now."

"*Herlequin's dead!*" Mike shouted. "We *burned* him!"

Greg bowed and bowed upward against Gavin's weight, almost bucking him off, almost dislodging him and sweeping him aside. His mouth worked and worked, and his eyes snapped open, finding Gavin's, beckoning him.

"No, he's in the woods, now," continued Toby, sounding broken, sounding ruined.

"Shut up!" shouted Mike. "*You shut up, Toby!*"

Gavin leaned in close, turning his head to place his ears against Greg's lips. "*Quiet!*" he roared, pouring as much command voice into the word as he could muster.

Greg lunged forward as if fighting something holding his head to the bed. His lips parted, and he sucked in a massive, tornado breath. Then searing cold blasted into Gavin, and he was flying—away from Greg, away from the bed. He had time to wince before he slammed into the wall with enough force to disintegrate the old drywall, then he slumped to the ground, the black, bottomless pit of unconsciousness yawning, yearning, beckoning, a twisting morass of dark abyssal colors— midnight and grave and horrible, horrible alleyways filled with stink and death and human remains. His vision narrowed to tunnels, blood-tinged blackness closing in on him, squeezing him, forcing him down, down, down…

2

Alley near Third and 36th, Manhattan, NY
Saturday, 4:59 pm EST

Gavin stood at the mouth of the alley, hands shoved into the pockets of his pants, feet sweating inside the rough-and-tumble hiking boots he wore. His breath came in ugly rasps, and with every inhalation, something in his side ground and shrieked and hurt like the motherfucking end of time. He stared into the dark alley, captivated, captured, mesmerized by the swirling quagmire of deadlights, of death dreams, of caliginous torments, of deep, dark colors bent on destroying him, the world, everything.

Somewhere deep inside him, a voice screamed and screamed, but the rattling despair drowned that small, still voice to dust. He'd been standing there for an eternity, just staring, just fearing, listening, peering into the black, waiting for…waiting for…

Waiting for what? he asked himself.

"Say hey, sugar," a monstrous basso voice said, echoes descending below human hearing, rattling the dumpsters, the garbage can, the skulls, the rotting remains that littered the alley like the promise of massive volcanic eruptions to come. "Took you a bit, but you found your way. Let's you and me palaver a spell."

Gavin screamed and jumped, and an offshore breeze caressed him. He breathed it in, sucking the dark scents of murder and desecration and despair into his throat, gagging on them, trying to sick them up, failing, drowning, coughing. He shook his head, feeling strangled by the odoriferous wind.

Above, the night sky twirled, a massive machine turning, tumbling, malignant tenebrous mandibles that masticated the universe in never-ending silence, running *ever on and on and on. Gavin stared into the stretching stillness, slipping his gaze from spot to spot in the Stygian starless sky, spinning his head from side to side, looking for solace, for shelter, for escape, but there was no sunshine to be had, only endless, eternal nights, eternal wailing, and the gnashing of brutal teeth.*

Then, that horrible voice that had whispered in his ear laughed—a lunatic's lullaby, the screams of the tortured interspersed with guttural guffaws, the nocuous cachinnation of a thousand serial killers plotting and planning and dreaming in the secret darkness of their bleak hearts—and Gavin had the sense of something huge looming over him, casting him in the shadow of a demented predator.

He ran, then, charged into the bitter black void that enwombed him. He ran with anger, with purpose, with vengeance in his heart, slashing and tearing, biting and kicking, punching, punching, and punching at the dark as if it were alive, as if it were his tormentor, his dream, his nightmare.

"How much goddamn pain do you need to feel, old hoss? How many goddamn times do I have to make allowances for your doggedness, for your mulishness? You ain't worth much more hassle." The voice boomed and roiled and thundered around him, penetrated him, pounded and pounded and pounded him, smiting him like lightning, striking him dumb, dumb, dumb. "I'll tell you one thing, hoss. There ain't no sunshine in your future,

just endless, endless nights, and there ain't nobody there, ain't nobody who cares when you cry."

Gavin lay gasping, and an immense face hovered above, orange-red eyes shining down on him, coating him in the baleful radiation of the damned—the baleful face of a man given wholly to mischief, to mayhem and murder, to menace, to malignancy. Death and destruction filled those hateful fiery orbs, hidden by the darkness, but the author of it, the maker, the creator of it. Grinning a death's-head grin, Fry's gaze burned Gavin, gobbled him up and spat him out, beat and punished him, all in terrible, total silence. A cold, animal-pen wind wafted at him as though the terrible demon had opened his mouth and exhaled, and a lone sheet of newspaper cavorted in its eddies, spinning, lurching, kicking in an eternal dance. There was no poetry in the eternal, senseless night— nothing but Fry and Fry and Fry and Fry.

"Is it my face you see?" he crooned. "Do I haunt you in your sleep?"

Gavin shook his head, pressed his hands to his eyes.

"Naw, boy. None of that. You listen here, Gavin Gregory of the F-B-I, and I'm going to tell you how it is. You're going to say, 'Yessir' and 'How high, boss?' and I'm going to smile and rain down my blessings upon you. Otherwise,"—his expression darkened, branding Gavin's soul with terror—"I'm going to rain down my displeasure, my pique, my anger, my wrath. Capiche? You get it, old hoss?" *The dulcet tones of Gjallarhorn, the rolling blast of*

the seventh trumpet, rang in Fry's voice, forever denying light, love, truth, freedom, grace.

Gavin quaked in horror, frozen, tharn in Fry's magnificent malicious predator's gaze. As if from a great distance, a memory whispered. A memory of Kingdom Cross Psychiatric Hospital, of a treatment room on its top floor, of a horrible amnesiac, of Joe Doe, Tom Madsen, praying. "Saint Michael the Archangel, defend me in battle," he rasped. "Be my protection against the wickedness and snares of the devil; may God rebuke him, I humbly pray. And do thou, O Prince of the Heavenly Host, by the power of God, thrust into hell Satan and all evil spirits who wander through the world for the ruin of souls!" His voice built and built as he spoke, until, at the end of it, he was shouting, spitting the words into Fry's face. His mind ached with the effort of it, and as the echo of the last syllable faded, Gavin flopped back, cringed back, dreading what was to come, dreading the foul doom Fry would no doubt deal out.

Fry's dead eyes bulged, and the muscles in his throat knotted and released, knotted and released as though he were about to vomit bile in Gavin's face. His lips quivered, his eyelids twitched, and Gavin knew the end was nigh.

But it didn't come. Instead, Fry exploded with laughter, great booming guffaws of belly-aching laughter. A single crystalline tear formed, and he shook his head, flinging it away, flinging it into the night where it glowed, where it *became a star, a galaxy, a pocket universe of its own. "Oh, my Good God, boy, you do make me laugh sometimes," he snorted between gales. "But ol' Mike ain't comin'. Nawp. Mike's done, boy. I served him up for Sunday supper to my boys."*

Gavin drew back in the face of Fry's mirth, somehow as terrible as his fury, and he huddled in on himself, curling around his belly as if that—or anything—could protect him from Fry's wrath.

"Heh," murmured Fry. "On your hands and knees when you crawl through your nightmares, boy. When there ain't no more grace"—he burst into song, his voice harsh, and a dark music thundered from out of nowhere to accompany him—"and your heartbeat starts to race, crawlin' everywhere in these dark, poisonous shadows." Fry cocked his head to the side and spoke, "That ain't exactly right, but you get my meaning, don't you, boy?"

Gavin said nothing, only huddled tighter.

"Listen here, spark... The point is: how many sins you got to hide? How many secrets you keepin'? In here, in the haunted mess of your mind, we done blackened the sun, and you'll pay for everything you done to my boy. One by one, spark ol' spark. One by one. It's my face you're gonna see. I'll mock you in your dreams, in your nightmares, right here, in these poisonous shadows. Capiche, ol' Gav ol' spark?" He sucked his fangs, the sound like the uncorking of a giant bottle of champagne, then thundered,

368   ERIK HENRY VICK

"*Quit that!* Quit it, *I say! Quit the muling and hiding. I ain't going to hurt you, boy, because you're going to make the right choice. You're going to pick the right team…My team. Let them others alone. I've got the powerful ones, anyway. There ain't no help for you there.*"

Kai*! Kai, help me! Gavin shouted the words in his mind, putting as much behind them as he could, hoping to attract the man's attention once more, worried he didn't have the ability, the power, the focus.*

Fry threw back his massive head and laughed, great trumpeting blasts of amusement, almost more felt than heard, then leered down at him. "*Ah, naw, boy. If ol' Mike can't help you none, you think this reject from Adeline's bloodline can?*" *He chuckled a bit more.* "*Nawp. I got him 'round here somewhere. I'm planning my next Sunday dinner, you see? He'll make a fine first course for my mate-to-be.*"

Gavin shook his head and squeezed his eyes shut. In the distance, a chorus of deep, booming voices began to chant: Perditus sum, omnia pereunt*!*

Fry cocked his head, then chuckled. "*You see that there, hoss? That's one of them things that makes me laugh so. Your mind is like…is like…*" *His massive brows furrowed.* "*Who's that funny man? That one with the hammer and the fruit?*" *He shook his great head.* "*Well, it don't matter none. 'I am lost, all is lost,' ha! I love it, son!*" *He snapped his head to the side.* "*Dratnabit! Don't do that, you*

trumped up sonuvabitch! Leave him be!" Thunder
rumbled across the swirling miasma behind Fry's head
and with it, purple-white lightning flashed, almost
forming letters, almost spelling out...

3

Room 1404, Aeonian Motel & RV Park, Aeonia, TX
Saturday, 4:13 pm CST

"That did it," said Toby, but his voice came from far, far away. "He's coming back, now."

"Great! Wonderful! What about Greg? Do you have time to help *my husband* now?"

Toby sighed. "I told you, Mike. I have no idea what's caused his unconsciousness, but I don't think Greg's in any danger. Gavin, on the—"

"Wrong," grated Gavin. "We're all in danger. Mortal, soul-draining danger." He tried to push himself up, but hands held him fast.

"No, just lie there, Gavin," said Toby. "I resuscitated you, but you're not out of danger. You—"

"Ha!" shouted Gavin. "Out of danger? Are you mad?" He pried his eyelids open, wincing at the muted light flooding in through the draperies, too used to utter darkness, to the black grave, the desert of the afterlife. "Fry's *here*. He's not like your demon king. He's *powerful*. For fuck's sake, he just knocked me into a nightmare!"

Toby shook his head. "No. He knocked you, all right, but that wasn't a nightmare—at least not in the traditional sense. You were very close to death, Gavin, not asleep. In medical terms, you suffered a massive ischemic attack and shouldn't be conscious, let alone talking and moving."

"Death?" Gavin said in a small voice. "What do you mean, close to death?"

"Death as in no pulse, no breathing. No pupillary response, no response to stimulus, no eye movement, nothing. Flatlined on every measurable scale."

"Then how did…"

"I *treated* you. I *am* a doctor. I carry emergency medicine everywhere I go."

"Medicine?"

"I gave you an IV injection of tissue plasminogen activator—"

"Give some to Greg!" cried Mike. "It worked for Gavin—"

"But it wouldn't work for Greg, Mike. He's not showing signs of a stroke. He's in a coma, but—"

"You looked at him for *ten seconds*, Toby!"

"Stroke?" Gavin murmured.

Toby grimaced and gave Gavin a stern look. "You, don't move." He stood and walked over to the bed, leaning down to peel open one of Greg's eyes and peer into it. He rubbed Greg's breastbone with his knuckles. "Greg, wake up!" he said in a sharp voice. "We need you to wake up, Greg!" He grasped the man's hand. "Squeeze my fingers if you can understand me." He raised his gaze to meet Mike's. "Nothing, Mike. He's in a coma, a…vegetative state."

"No, Fry has him," said Gavin. "Somehow, Fry has his mind…whatever makes him him."

"What does that mean?" demanded Mike. "Fry has him?"

"I wish I could tell you," said Gavin in a forlorn voice. "He seems to be able to draw me into one of my nightmares. Usually, only when I'm asleep, but at the end of my last case—The Bogeyman case—I had a series of seizures related to dehydration. We always wondered if Fry had something to do with that. I guess he did." He pushed himself against the wall and levered himself into a sitting position.

"Nuh-uh!" said Toby. "You stay right where you are!"

"Relax, Doc," said Gavin in an enervated voice. "I'm just getting comfortable. But we're going to have to move soon enough, anyway."

"No, we're not moving an inch from here," said Toby. "Neither you nor Greg—"

"They know where we are," said Gavin in a quiet voice that nevertheless cut through Toby's speech. "They know where we are, and they'll be coming. Especially"—he nodded at Toby—"since you pulled me out before Fry got his answers."

"Answers?" asked Mike.

Gavin's grin was sour, exhausted, hopeless. "He wants me to join the family firm."

"You mean kill people like Glacadairanam wanted you to do."

"That would be the least of it, I think."

Mike sniffed, and his gaze cut to Greg's supine form. "Unless he's safe…"

"I know the feeling," said Gavin. "Trust me. We can get the HRT out here in a—"

"No," said Mike, "we can't. According to the FBI, my name isn't Mike Richards, and Greg isn't my husband. I'm Rick Michaels, remember? Bachelor, blue-flamer with no time for love or life outside of the Bureau."

Gavin grimaced. "I can tell Pete. He'll understand. He already knows part of this—my part of it."

Mike shrugged and shook his head.

Gavin looked at Toby, who sat on the bed looking down at Greg. "You, Toby, need to pull your head out of your ass and get the G-class packed. You and Greg in the back seat, Mike can drive, and I'm shotgun. We've got to run, and we've got to start ten minutes ago."

"No, you're in the back seat, Gavin, and Greg goes in back. Toby can take shotgun."

"You want us to run away?" asked Toby. "But Shannon and Benny are—"

"If you don't want to join them, do as I say," said Gavin in a cold voice. "We can't help them if we're all captured. We need time—time for me get Pete up to speed, to get the FBI's resources into the area, to—"

"No," said Mike. "We've got a team staged in Presidio County."

"Team?" Gavin arched an eyebrow at him. "We?"

"SEMPRe," said Toby. "We have…security assets."

"No," said Gavin shaking his head. "Security isn't going to cut it. We—"

"Security assets trained like Force Recon teams," said Mike. "They're capable of what two or three SEAL teams could provide, from firepower to tactics and training. Our security force is paramilitary."

"Scott got them started, trained the initial crew," said Toby. "Before…everything happened. But it's no good. The team will just get slaughtered."

"What's wrong with you?" Gavin demanded, staring at Toby. "Why are you so…so…"

"So hopeless?" asked Mike.

"I…" Toby dropped his gaze. "My whole life has been dedicated to eradicating the demons that treated me and the people I love. This"—he closed his eyes, shaking his head—"just proves that it was a pipe dream. I gave her up for nothing."

They fell silent then, Mike and Gavin frowning, concerned, Toby frowning, filled with enervated despair.

Finally, Gavin cleared his throat. "It's not a pipe dream. Maybe the fight isn't over yet, but it's not a pipe dream."

"You don't understand," said Toby with a sigh. "You don't—"

"I *do*," said Gavin. "I've been face to face with evil—with *Fry*, with his goddamn son—and I found ways of beating them, of surviving, of keeping my family safe."

Toby scoffed. "You didn't beat them, Gavin. You've existed beneath their notice, is all. Now that they're aware of you, now that they *want you* for something, your life is over. You'll either spend what time you have left on the run or in servitude."

Another silence stretched, but this time, Mike broke it. "Jesus, dude, when did you get so pessimistic?"

Toby lifted his gaze and sniffed. "You know when."

"She mesmerized you."

"I know that, Mike," said Toby with an air of infinite patience as if he were arguing with a child. "Do you think it matters? That knowledge? Because it doesn't. I know she mesmerized me with that damn singing of hers. I know she took away my choice about how I feel about her, but what you don't know—because I've never told anyone—is that I was already falling in love with her. If she'd not been so impatient…" He shook his head and sighed.

"You're wrong," said Gavin. "I did beat them, both of them, Glacadairanam and Fry. And we can beat them now."

"No, we can't," said Toby. "All of this…is stupid. We can't fight these creatures. They are too powerful. Too…"

"We can fight them," said Gavin, "because I know something they don't think I know."

"Yeah?" asked Toby without looking up.

"Yeah. I know *where they will be* tonight at midnight. We just have to survive long enough, to meet up with this team of yours and spring a trap of *our* making."

Toby sighed and shook his head. "How do you know that? Did Benny—"

Gavin snapped his attention to Mike. "Load us up."

Mike turned his gaze from Toby to Gavin and then to his husband. "Greg—"

"Dammit! You're not helping him by sitting there. You won't be hurting him by *not* sitting there, but if you continue to sit there and argue trivialities with Toby, you *will be hurting him*. And Shannon. And Benny." Gavin frowned and shuffled his gaze back and forth between them. "Don't you see? He's taken the most powerful members of your team, and he's done it all right under your noses. He's learned far more about us than we have about him. He's *won* this round, and if we don't get out of here, he'll win the game without any serious resistance from us at all."

Mike glanced at Toby and lifted his eyebrow.

"Goddammit, Mike! *Go!*" Gavin shouted. He fished the key fob out of his front pocket and tossed it at Mike. "Get moving!"

Eyeing the fob, Mike nodded, then bent to retrieve the chunk of plastic. "Call in our security forces, Toby, or say goodbye to Benny and Shannon," he said as if saying nothing more than, "Please pass the salt."

Toby nodded but didn't move. Mike stood and went to his friend's side, staring down at his husband's serene face. "Come on, Toby," he said gently. "I need you. Greg, Shannon, and Benny need you. So do Eddie, Amanda, Sean, and Kristie—along with everyone else on this damn planet. We all need you, and we need you present."

Toby heaved a sigh and nodded once more. "Go on," he said softly. "Get the car ready, then throw some clothes in a bag or something. Make sure you pack my medical bag."

"Right," said Mike with a curt nod. "Get Gavin ready to move after you make the call."

Toby sighed again, and then, as if by force of will alone, smiled in a forlorn, desperate sort of way. "We can do this."

"Damn right," said Gavin, though deep down, in that place he didn't even let Maddie see, he wondered if he were lying, even to himself. With a sad sigh, he let his eyes close.

Chapter 9
These Deadly
Sins of Mine

I

The temple, Southwestern TX
Saturday, 4:15 pm CST

"Benny," Shannon whispered in his ear, tears filling her voice, fear filling her thoughts, fear for him, fear for herself, fear for everyone. "Benny, wake up. I need you Benny-bear."

His pulse pounded in his temples, pounded in the sides of his neck, and his head ached and ached and ached, especially around his right eye. Blood and some other viscous fluid had dried on his cheeks and lips and now hung there like offal, biological waste, like forgotten memories of deadly sins, of dark deeds done in the desolate wilderness of men's hearts. He moaned.

Shannon's hands butterfly-kissed his cheeks, fluttered across his neck and chest, touched his ears, her fingers cold, cold, ice-cold. He moaned, again.

"Shh, Benny-bear, shh. I don't want them to hear you. I don't want that foul bitch to come back and-and-and-and—"

"She'll be back," said a craggy voice, a voice that warbled to and fro as if staggering down its drunken path. "She always comes back. She always comes back and…and… She always punches or hits or kicks. There's no escape."

"Benny, Benny, did you tell Greg? Did you—"

"Tell whoever you want," said the voice after a haggard sigh. "It doesn't matter who you tell…who you call on the phone…who you're talking to when she finds you…"

"Shut up," Shannon hissed.

Benny could only moan. He tried to lift his hand to his face, but even that small movement made his head spin like a top. Bile surged from his belly like the inevitable storm surge of a class five hurricane, and he moaned through it, gritting his teeth. Emesis filled his mouth—foul, bitter sick—and he choked on it, would have choked, but Shannon was there, turning him, rolling his head to the side, and he let the steaming ick go, his cheek resting in the evidence he'd been sick before.

"Oh, my Benny-bear," Shannon sobbed. "Oh, Benny, what are we going to do? They know, they *always* knew. Primo… Primo can *hear* us. He saw through my—"

"And the guy with the guitar…with that bizarre, freak-show music…he always comes along…he tells her to go easy, to stop, but that only makes her hit more, hit harder."

Benny breathed hard, letting the cool air stream in through his nostrils, but laden as it was with the scent of his puke, it sickened him. "Roll me back," he croaked. "Puke stinks."

"Oh! Sorry, I'm sorry, Benny-bear," said Shannon, and her oh-so-cold hands danced across the back of his head, slid down his neck, and turned him, carefully turned him, rolling him back, cradling his head.

"Herlequin…was…worse," he forced out through gritted teeth. He'd spent enough time around Toby to know the woman had beaten him into a concussion, that his right orbital socket was likely fractured, but that, as horrible as he felt at that moment, he would live, he would recover, and everything would… He stopped that thought. Nothing would be okay, not unless he could reach Greg, not unless the others could find them, not unless he could lead Greg to their dungeon like some ESP beacon.

Though his head hurt, though it felt like it was killing him, Benny thrust his thoughts out into the world: *Greg*? He felt nothing—no reply, no sense of communion, of communication, not even the sense that Greg was even still *there*. *Greg*? he sent again.

He opened his eyes and gazed up into Shannon's face, saw the fear in her gaze, saw the fear in the lines sprinkled at the corner of her eyes, the corners of her mouth. "I can't reach him," he said softly.

"No, you can never reach him when you need to," said the other man. "Can't ever reach anyone, not when it counts, not when there are five guys and a psychotic woman who thinks she's the reincarnation of Joe Louis. Sure, here's his cell number. Run your ideas by him, sure, sure, but call him when you're in trouble? Nah. Never do that."

"*Shut up!*" she hissed with more venom. "No one's talking to you!"

Benny focused on his wife's eyes as tears welled there. He lifted his hand and dropped it on her forearm, intending it as a pat but losing the thread, losing the strength to keep his hand airborne. He forced his numb lips to form the words cleanly, to make his tongue dance in only the right ways. "I can't find Greg," he said, and a single tear streaked down her cheek and plopped into her lap. "I…"

"You're hurt," she said. "She beat you so bad, and you were already all beat up when they dragged you in here. That man…he just played that guitar…it was…" The light left her eyes for a moment, then she shook her head as if trying to clear away the detritus of a heavy slumber. "Why did he play that horrible song? Why didn't he stop her? Why did—"

"That song! That damn dirge!" The man's voice cracked on the last word. "It…it-it-it-it…" He shook his head, hard enough to make his teeth clack together like a broken ventriloquist's dummy. "It does something to your head," he whispered.

Shannon threw a startled glance to the side, and Benny followed her gaze. A man lay slumped against the minefield of splinters that served as the room's opposite wall. He wore shiny blue tracksuit pants and a heather T-shirt that bore some emblem in dark navy. He had no shoes, no socks, and his feet were dusky, spattered with dark blood and terracotta streaks of desert clay. His heels were abraded, the top part of his foot bruised. His face was an inflamed mess that had more in common with a catcher's mitt than a human face, both eyes blackened, lips torn and mashed, nose crumpled to the side with repeated breaks. He opened his eyes wide, and his irises rolled and rolled like a fire-panicked horse's, one pupil dilated, one constricted into a tinny black dot, no more than a speck.

"Shannon…" Benny whispered. "Hide. Hide yourself…and-and escape."

"I can't, Benny," she said with a soft cry. "I tried, but Primo just points at me no matter where I go, no matter what skin I wear. He—"

"He…was…looking…at…you. Hide, *now*, when no one's looking. Go to the side of the door, think about being invisible. When they come for me, you can—"

"No! No, Benny! I won't do it!"

"Yes, Shan," he said, more weariness than any one person should ever feel in his voice. "You will. You *have to.* You get away, then…then it doesn't matter what they do to me if I know—"

"Shut up, you idiot," she said, tears dropping like rain. "Shut up, you brave, loveable idiot."

"Shan—"

"No, Benny. Where you go, I go."

"No, Shan," he mumbled, but the air seemed thin, the room darker, and his hold on reality more tenuous. "Shan, you have to…" His eyes closed, but he forced them open. "*Hide!*"

"I—"

"Shh!" said the other man. "Someone's coming!"

2

The temple, Southwestern TX
Saturday, 4:25 pm CST

Cece whistled tunelessly as she walked, swinging her hips, and swinging the chain that held the keys to the cells. For once, Jon wasn't drifting behind her, strumming that damn guitar, learning the damn magic that should've been hers by rights. She glanced at him.

He walked at her side, his head down, his guitar wizard hands held behind his back as though he were some olden-time schoolteacher pacing back and forth in front of his students. His gaze was on the ground before them, on the ground their strides consumed with each passing second. He seemed…distracted, focused on something other than the task at hand.

"Get your mind off that gosh-darn music, Jon!" she snapped.

He glanced at her sidelong, his expression inscrutable, but for a moment—just a moment, mind—Cece would have sworn his irises were spinning like ice-blue tops, glittering with gold-flecked bits embedded in the paint. For a moment—just a moment, mind—her belly did fear flip-flops like on that tilt-a-whirl at the Bexar County Fair Jon had sweet-talked her onto the previous spring. He always could sweet-talk her into any-damn-thing he pleased. But then she looked into his eyes again, and he was just a man, a man who loved her, not some kind of guitar wizard, not some kind of warlock with a demon-stringed fiddle like in that Charlie Daniels song.

"Sorry, Cece," he said, "but I wasn't thinking about the music. I was thinking about what Primo said. About tonight."

Cecelia compressed her lips into a thin line lest they go all a-twitter again like they had in the assembly. They'd been trying the summoning ritual for *months*, and it might have been that she was starting to doubt they'd ever succeed, starting to be okay with never succeeding, but they'd never tried what Primo said they had to try later that night. The "black sabbath to end all black sabbaths" he'd called it. Not one sacrifice, not two, but *a whole pack of 'em*—most of 'em just nobodies from up to Dallas brought in for the pain and desecration of human flesh, one for spite, one to teach the FBI a damn lesson, and one to punish that gol-dang beauty who'd fooled her, the trickster, the illusionist.

She didn't want to think about how close the two spies had come to getting in—not that Primo would *admit* they'd gotten close. No, he said he'd known all along, but if that were true, why'd he let them get to the temple at all? *Why not lead them out into the desert and leave them? Get them all turned around and sneak away? Or shoot out their tires out there in the wastes where there was no one and nothing to raise an eyebrow at the gun shot? Heckfire, why not just shoot* them?

Hell, why let them come at all? The voice in her head didn't sound like her own, but she had to admit the thought *was*. She wrinkled her nose at the doubts, at the *heresy* swirling around in her brain.

That's why Jon can do the magic, dummy, she sneered at herself. *You think* he *has doubts?* She shook her head. Not with the way he could suddenly play that dang guitar, he didn't. No sir.

She peeked at him and found him grinning at her. "What?" she asked.

"You," he said. "Still as beautiful as the day we met."

"I was fifteen, Jon Clark, and I ain't looked that good since."

"That's a lie, Cece Clark. You've gotten more beautiful every day since."

She smiled a little and reached across the gulf yawning between them to take his hand.

3

In the desert near Odolavesta, TX
Saturday, 4:27 pm CST

Marcus whistled tunelessly as he walked, swinging the ax in one hand and the machete in the other. For once, Roger wasn't blathering on and on and on at his side, dreaming his too-big dreams or expounding on the nature of the universe. He glanced over at his long-time associate.

Martinez walked by his side, his head down, his useless hands held behind his back like some citified banker with a jumped-up opinion of himself, playing the big man for the initiates, strutting while sitting down, all gurgle and no guts. His gaze was on the shifting sand beneath them, on the scree, on the occasional bit of igneous rock the sun and wind and washout had unburied, on the yards and yards their strides consumed with each passing second. He seemed scared, lost in thoughts, his fears, focused on weak shit instead of the task at hand.

"Get your mind on the goddamn play, Roger," he snarled, "or so help me, I'll brain you with this ax and be done with you."

Martinez started and shot a terrified glance his way, his expression guilty and ashamed and as easy to read as a second-grade primer, and for a moment—just a moment, mind—Marcus thought he might snatch a shovel or pick from one of the initiates and swing for the fences. For a moment—just a moment, mind—his loins tightened the way they had that night in the parking lot when he'd helped Primo beat those two rednecks near to death, and he almost danced with excitement, with longing. Violence always had made him go all a-flutter. That's why he'd played ball in high school—not to win some damn scholarship, but for the chance to hit a kid so hard they'd have to trundle that old ambulance out onto the field and cart his broken ass away. His jaw clenched, and his eyes burned as he stared into Roger's jelly-fish face, giving him the hard look he was half-famous for, and if the man had been thinking of a cheap shot, of taking his chance, he gave that shit up in a hurry, and he was back to being a sheeple, to being a rabbit to Marcus's wolf, of being the same sycophantic asshole he'd always been.

"Sorry, Marcus," he mumbled. "What Primo said…" He jerked his chin down, drawing his gaze away from Marcus's narrowed eyes. "About tonight, that is…"

"Jumpin' Jesus Christ, Martinez, you ever been anything but a yellow dog?"

Roger frowned, squeezing his teeth together as if that could withdraw the words, if that could turn back time and suck the air from his lungs instead of letting the weakness dribble out like an old man's piss.

Marcus compressed his own lips, knowing it made him look one bubble off plumb, making him look like he had too many cobwebs in his attic, but at the same time, knowing it made him look as tough as a nickel steak and twice as mean as a mama wasp. They'd been attempting the ritual for months without a win. Sure, they'd eaten well, and Marcus had felt the power that brought them, but they hadn't summoned so much as a fart at a church picnic, and he knew that left some of the weaker-willed among the flock with doubts, with fears, and secret heresies in their hearts, but he couldn't be bothered about those boxes of rocks, those barrels of horsehair. Primo could worry about that if it was important. He was the one with the long-eye, the deep-sight, after all. Even so, what Primo had in mind—all those sacrifices, all those extra prisoners bought up in Dallas to take care of, all of them bitches who'd get all riled up after they started in on the first set, women who would kick and squall and fight. The blackest of black sabbaths he'd called it, and most like, he was right.

Marcus grinned at the thought of what they were going to do to them spies. To the one who thought he could poke around in Primo's mind without getting his ass kicked, to that damn nosy FBI-man from the Resta, but most of all, to that tall drink of water who looked like she'd stepped right out of one of those swimsuit magazines he'd loved so much as a teenager. He knew his grin and his dilating pupils were scaring the shit out of Roger, and that made him grin all the wider.

The man never did have any sense. It wasn't like Marcus would pound his ass with all that manual labor in front of them. Sure, he could make the initiates tagging along behind them pick up the slack, but there was a time limit, and Primo had been explicit about that.

And he'd promised special guests would attended. That weasel Red Westral for one. Marcus didn't think much of the sheriff, but Primo'd said he was to be treated like the dark lord hisself, and what Primo wanted, he got. He must've needed something covered up, some politickin' done. No one better than a weasel to sic on them other weasels.

Plus, *He* was coming.

The thought sent a shiver of excitement down his spine.

His mother had always said Marcus didn't have the sense not to dance with rattlesnakes during a tornado.

Maybe Roger might could have an accident given his recent performances.

The voice in his head sounded a little like Primo, and his mouth stretched into a wider, toothier grin. Seeing this, Roger gulped, suddenly finding something very interesting on the ground in the widening gulf between them.

4

Westral Ranch, Ranch Road 2818, Odolavesta, TX
Saturday, 5:10 pm CST

Fry grimaced toward the north, eyes narrowed to slits. He was beginning to see Glacadairanam's point of view about the troublesome Gavin Gregory. He dithered on the cusp of sending his boys to settle his score rather than bring Gregory to heel. The man had caused him no end of frustrations, but on the other hand, recruiting a man like Special Agent Gavin Gregory would be quite a feat.

And then there was the man's future whelp…

He shook his head, a sigh of frustration leaking between his lips like the hiss of a deadly, poisonous snake. The sound soothed him, filled him with anticipation, and for the umpteenth time, he checked the position of the sun and wished it were closer to the horizon.

My son, he thought toward the east, *go forth and secure the assets in Aeonia. Go yourself and take your brother. Ensure Gregory does not escape.*

And the others?

Fry grimaced. Primo's reply was faint and filled with a buzz that hurt his head—his mother's influence, that and his mortal weaknesses. *Alive. Especially, the one named Greg. Their screams must buttress our ritual tonight.*

A buzz filled his mind like a thousand mistuned radio calls overlapping, feeding back, sustaining one another, and Fry pinched the bridge of his nose and sighed. *I didn't catch that, but don't try again, and don't waste the time by coming over. Do as I say.*

He turned his mind away from Primo, shutting himself off from any further bursts of brain-splitting static. *The ritual* must *succeed,* he thought. *I've waited long enough for a suitable son.*

Chapter 10
The Simple Plans of Demons and Men

I

A hand on his shoulder roused Gavin from a dreamless void, from a restful slumber, and he groaned with the waking. His head hurt, his ribs hurt, *everything* hurt.

"Wake up, Gavin. It's time to go."

With a sigh of resignation, he opened his eyes and looked up into Toby's face. "Is the—"

"The G-class is loaded up. We stole all the water from the rooms, and I made sure we got your Hydrolite." He frowned down at Gavin for a heartbeat. "I suggest you take a couple of doses back-to-back. You don't look that great."

"That's your medical opinion, that after being attacked by some frickin' demon and knocked almost-dead, that I 'don't look that great?'"

"Yes," said Toby with a little grin. "I went to school for like ten years to acquire those awesome bedside and diagnostic skills."

"Might want to ask for a refund of your tuition," Gavin grumbled as he accepted Toby's proffered hand

and let the man pull him up. Upright, the world spun a little at the edges, and wooziness threatened. It seemed better with his eyes closed, so he left them that way.

"Steady," said Toby. "That's more of my platinum-level medical advice."

"Yeah," said Gavin, just standing still and breathing. "See my earlier comment, Doctor." He forced his eyes open and glanced at the bed. "Greg?"

"In the car," said Toby. "We made a little nest for him in the back and snugged him in. You're next."

Gavin nodded and the world seemed to lurch one way while he went the other. "Uff," he said as Toby guided him for the door. Outside, Mike laid on the horn.

"Better speed up," said Gavin.

"Can you?"

"Can I not? I'll be okay as long as you keep me on my feet. The whole"—he twisted his hand in the air—"thing is spinning."

Outside, feet pounded toward the door. "We have to go!" shouted Mike. "Now!" He shouldered the door open and rushed to Gavin's side, looping one of Gavin's arms over his shoulders and snaking his own around Gavin's waist. "There's a whole string of cars headed this way from 385!"

"Go!" grunted Gavin. "Drag me if you have to."

They stumble-ran to the car, Gavin doing his best but holding them back, nonetheless. Mike opened the passenger backdoor, and Toby gave him a shove. "I've got him! Get this bastard started!"

Mike gave a curt nod and raced around the big vehicle. He jumped inside and cranked the engine.

Gavin's gaze slipped toward First Street and saw the sun dance across five windshields—one of which belonged to Red Westral's emerald-green Cadillac. "Gotta move…" he murmured.

"You think?" asked Toby. "Duck your head." He half-guided, half-shoved Gavin through the door, then shoved a water bottle already gunked up with the swirling foul browns of Hydrolite into his hands. "Drink that, then make yourself another. Doctor's orders."

Gavin slid into the backseat and pulled his legs in so Toby could close the rear door. "Yeah, about that," he said as Toby threw himself into the passenger seat. "I don't much listen to my own doctor, and I've been seeing him since forever."

"You'll do what I say or I'll sic Mike on you."

Mike grunted, his gaze riveted to the rearview mirror. When Toby's door thunked, he shouted, "Hold on!" then hammered the accelerator.

The earthshaking offroad tires on the big Mercedes scrabbled for traction, the engine screaming as Mike held the go-pedal to the mat. The back end slewed on the hot blacktop, then the vehicle lunged forward, shrieking like a banshee, tires squalling, Toby and Gavin holding on for dear life.

Mike's glance kept darting to the rearview mirror, and as the edge of the parking lot neared, he didn't lift his foot, didn't twitch the wheel to the left or right, didn't do *anything* to acknowledge the short drop off separating the paved lot and the scree and yuccas and prickly pear. The G-class thundered over the ridge, tires seeming to thump the edge with disdain, then they sailed momentarily through thin air, only to slam down on the gravel, wailing and shouting like a beast in rut, spinning the massive 33-inch tires in the loose gravel, the sound crunching beneath them accompanied by a clatter of sharp stones to the undercarriage.

Gavin threw his arm over the seatback and hoisted himself against the gees to stare out the back window. Westral's Caddie was roaring straight after them, seemingly without any concern about launching the heavy sled off the same cliff the G-class had just flown over—despite the lack of the suspension and body lifts, despite being on street tires. Behind them was the same old beat-up Chevy he'd seen on the road from San Antonio—Jon and Cece Clark's vehicle—a newer pickup, an old Nissan Pathfinder, and a small passenger car that sensibly slid into one of the empty parking spaces rather than destroy itself trying to follow them. The passenger car's occupants jumped out and ran toward their rooms, not bothering with keys, just lifting booted feet and kicking the doors in.

The Pathfinder drew Gavin's attention—it was close to the right vintage of the one Adeline d'Clara had professed to buy and drive on her "rescue" of Kai Washington from the Program back in the late 90s. A huge man hunched behind the wheel, his gaze locked on Gavin's, a feral grin stretching his lips wide. He had the darkest skin Gavin had ever seen—not chocolate or blue-black or any of the other cliches; his skin appeared to be the same color as coal, the true black of soot.

Westral roared up to the drop off without lifting his right foot, not looking at anything but the Mercedes, and he never hesitated before sending the car flying through the air to slam onto the desert floor, two of its hub caps spinning and dancing off into the dirt and gravel. Sparks flew from its undercarriage as two and a half tons of Detroit iron met the West Texas desert up close and personal.

"They're coming right after us!" Gavin shouted over the screaming engine, the scrabbling tires, the desert plants scraping against the metallic olive-green paint.

"I see them!"

"I didn't think Westral would follow us," Gavin said.

"Of course, he would," said Toby.

"But he seems to love that car."

"I bet he likes living even more."

Gavin glanced forward, and Toby met his gaze with a slow smile and nod. "Yeah," he muttered, looking out the front window. "Speaking of which...since they're following us anyway, wouldn't it be better to cut around to the road?"

"Nah, they won't be able to keep up with us for long. Not with this animal on our side." Toby slapped the console and grinned like a lunatic, his strange melancholy left behind, left back at the motel.

"Off road driving's risky at these speeds, it's hell on the cars," said Gavin, "not to mention rough on the passengers."

"What, did you think it was going to be easy fighting evil?" Toby asked.

Gavin turned his gaze back out the window. "I should call in the HRT."

"No, it's fine," said Toby. "We have support inbound, three separate teams, and like you said, we know where they have to be later tonight. They can't say the same."

"No, I guess not."

They raced onward, racing the sun toward the western horizon, Mike flinging the vehicle left and right, dodging through the desert willows, the crucifixion thorn bushes, the stubby elephant trees, the king-sized boulders. The G-class danced through the desert as if born to it, charging up the short hillocks and then leaping down the other side, skipping across dry washes, across exposed rock, scrub bushes, and scree.

Westral's Cadillac was the first victim to fall by the wayside, an immense plume of white steam billowing from under its front bumper, its front fenders crumpled skyward from one too many full-speed jumps over desert ruts, emerald-green paint chipping and scratched. The sheriff flung himself out of the driver's seat before the car even stopped, sprinting after them with abandon, a look of intense hatred dominating his features, his gaze seemingly locked on Gavin's. The Clark's pickup plowed doggedly behind them, belching gray-black smoke like any chemical plant up north. The giant of man—a man who could only be Primo—jerked his Pathfinder wide, slewing the backend out in his haste and passed them on the right, not sparing the Clarks a glance but skidding to halt next to Red Westral and blipping the horn.

The newer pickup screamed around both of them and barreled forward, racing after the G-class like a cat after a bird. Gavin had never seen the man before, but his intense gaze left no doubt that their pursuers knew who and what they were and had orders to stop them—and maybe worse.

Mike hurled the Mercedes over the arid landscape, spinning the steering wheel to control the spinning wheels, his feet dancing on the accelerator and brake pedals, using all his training, all his skill and experience—not to mention all his luck—to keep the vehicle balanced on the razor's edge separating wildly out of control and fast. Somehow, the Pathfinder caught up to the chase, though the Clarks had fallen back substantially, and working with the unknown man in the pickup, they tried to flank, each taking one side and trying to herd Mike in the direction they preferred. When Mike didn't comply, the pickup lurched toward them as if to ram, and Mike twisted the wheel, gunning the accelerator but then spun back to his original course north when he outpaced the truck.

"Might need support soon," said Mike, not sparing a glance at the rearview to meet Gavin's gaze, but everyone in the car knew who he was talking to and what he wanted.

Shaking his head, Gavin said, "I don't know how you ran things in Oneka Falls, but that kind of Hollywood bullshit doesn't work in the Bureau, Mike."

Toby shook his head once. "In Oneka Falls, we did what we had to, Hollywood bullshit or not."

"And if they box us in, what then?" asked Mike, a touch of fury in his voice. "Are you going to stand by while they take Greg away from us? Is that what you'd do if *your* spouse was in the back?"

"Of course not, but—"

The G-class lurched to the side and skidded in the loose sand, a metal-on-metal shriek grating from the driver's side rear. Gavin lifted his head and peered between the headrests, seeing the pickup swerving away in a cloud of dust. "Did they just try to PIT us?"

Mike growled and shook his head. "He wasn't checking his make up." He snapped his gaze to the review, angry-eyed gaze seeking Gavin's. "So, what now, Mr. By-the-book? You up for some Hollywood bullshit, or should I just stop and let them take us?"

"I'm not shooting at one moving vehicle from another one!"

"In the city, I'd understand," said Toby. "But out here?" He waved a hand at the windshield. "Who's it going to hurt?"

"Whoever the damn bullet hits."

"You don't want to shoot? Fine," said Mike. "But we'd better come up with *something* or they'll have us."

Gavin slid fully upright and put the unopened bottle of Hydrolite obscenity in the cupholder. He pulled out his Glock and checked the chamber. "Call out which side you want me on, and I'll do what I can." His vision still swam a bit, and he hoped their pursuers would be scared by the prospect of getting shot because he doubted he could hit a fixed object from a stationary shooting position at that point, let alone an off-road vehicle racing through the wild desert from yet another one...even if he suddenly became willing to engage in such folly.

"I can help," said Toby. "Where'd you put the shotguns?"

"All the way in the back," said Mike with a grimace.

"Let me handle it," said Gavin. "I have the authority to defend us if it comes to that. You may not."

Toby chuckled. "I think you forgot this is Texas." Even so, he didn't move from the front seat, and behind him, Gavin nodded.

"Coming up on the left, again!"

"Affirmative," said Gavin in a voice that almost sounded bored. He slid across the wide bench seat and wound the window down, letting in the heat, letting in the flinty desert scent, letting the gun out. He drew a bead on the pickup, and the driver veered away before he had to pull the trigger.

"Pathfinder!"

Gavin slid back to the passenger side and opened the window, but Primo only narrowed his eyes at the sight of the pistol, tightened his grip on the steering wheel, and accelerated. With a grimace, Gavin steadied the pistol against the rear pillar of the door. "I may have to fire!"

Red Westral sat in the passenger seat, and by the expression on his face, he would've liked to see Gavin burned at the stake. Gavin glanced at him, and their gazes met and locked. The sheriff slumped to the side, and Gavin heard the last thing he ever wanted to hear again—the mocking chirp that haunted his nightmares.

Glacadairanam appeared on the dash, a shadow where no shadow should've been possible, a translucent gray-black shape drawing substance from the air. Tiny wings beat the air in a slow, almost languorous tempo. His long tongue still hung from his gaping maw, still curled around the back of Red Westral's neck.

"Shit," Gavin breathed. "Change of plans, Mike. Haul as much ass as this thing can. Don't slow down for anything."

"What's up?" demanded Toby.

"Glacadairanam is in that Pathfinder."

"Your little gargoyle?"

"Bingo, and if he possesses you, he'll wreck you. I've got my zoraperidol, so he can't get into me, but you two"—he glanced in back—"not to mention Greg…"

"Shit!"

When Gavin returned his gaze to the window, Glacadairanam stood on the hood of Primo's SUV like a grotesque hood ornament, one arm outstretched, an evil grin stretching his face, his red eyes glowing and gleaming. His tiny wings beat faster and faster, like he was winding up to…

"He's trying to *fly*!" Gavin cried. "Go faster, Mike!"

"Unless you think sliding around on the roof of this car is faster, this is the best I can do!"

"Going loud!" Gavin snapped off two rounds. One starred the windshield two inches to the left of Primo, but the other went zinging off the Pathfinder's roof. Even so, Primo's eyes widened, and he jammed on the brakes. As the SUV fell back, Gavin heard a metallic chirp in the dead-center of his brain, loud enough to make his eyes water, and Glacadairanam's eyes glowed like a volcano about to erupt.

"That did it," said Mike, sounding a little relieved.

"Good," said Gavin. "Don't let them get close, Mike. Don't ever let them get close or it's all over."

"Keep your Glock handy, then!"

In the back, Greg moaned as they rocketed over a brush-studded mogul, and Mike's gaze snapped to the rearview. Gavin swung around and glanced in the back as Greg rolled on his side, grabbing his head.

"He's coming out of it," said Gavin. "Get back there, Toby."

"That's going to be fun."

"What, did you think it was going to be easy fighting evil?" said Gavin.

"Smartass."

"You don't know the half of it."

Toby grinned, then climbed over the console, over the back of the rear seat. The G-class thumped over a ridge, and Toby sailed into the cargo space in the back. "Easy!" he called.

Mike only grunted.

Gavin stole a glance at their pursuers—the Pathfinder and the late model pickup drove side-by-side in their wake, and Primo seemed to be yelling into the passenger window. Falling farther and farther behind, the Clark's old wreck had started to smoke. "Looks like the old one's out of it," he said.

"Yeah," said Mike, "but I don't like what the other two are doing."

"Greg? Can you hear me?" Toby asked.

Greg groaned.

"Give me that Hyrdolite."

Gavin grabbed the bottle and passed it over the seat.

"Drink this, Greg." Toby held the bottle to the man's lips, but Greg shook his head, pulling away from the bottle as if the smell revolted him. "Drink it," Toby insisted, pushing the bottle against his lips again. He tilted it up, dispensing a small swallow of the brown liquid—most of which raced down to Greg's shirt. "Dammit, Greg! *Drink*!"

Greg opened his eyes, and his gaze tracked from Toby's face to the rear side windows and the desert sky beyond. "What the…" he muttered. "I was just in… Well, I don't know. Was it all a dream? A nightmare?"

"I don't know," said Toby.

"Yes," said Gavin at the same time, "but still real."

"Hang on!" snapped Mike, and beneath them, metal shrieked, then went quiet as the wagon leaped into the air. They slammed down on the other side of the four-foot cliff with a jarring thud, then the shocks rebounded, and the vehicle lurched to the side, tires slewing on the scree, threatening to spin in the sandy dry wash beyond, body rolling hard to the side, engine shrieking as Mike fought for control while trying to maintain his speed. "Be ready!"

Gavin spun one hundred and eighty degrees and steadied the Glock against the doorframe again. He aimed at the lip of rock they'd jumped off, but neither vehicle made the jump. The wind and roar of their own drivetrain drowned out any sound of pursuit. "Did we lose them?"

"Don't I wish," muttered Mike. He wrenched the wheel toward the west and put the hammer down, racing along in the relative smoothness of the wash. "They are paralleling our course on the ridge."

Gavin slid to the driver's side and peered up at the ridge. From the passenger seat of the Pathfinder, Red Westral glared at him with blind hatred, his eyes seeming to burn. He opened his mouth as if to speak, and deep in the center of his brain, Gavin heard a horrible chirp.

"We've got to…" slurred Greg. "They've got…"

"Yeah, we know," said Toby. "They've got Shannon, Benny, and Gavin's agent friend. We know where they're holding the ritual tonight. Relax, it's under control."

"No," said Greg, then moaned as he shook his head.

"Drink more of this," said Toby, holding the bottle to his lips again.

Greg shoved his hand away. "Listen! Listen to me!"

"We're listening, Greg," said Mike, his gaze snapping to the rearview at the tone of his husband's voice.

"Tell us," whispered Gavin, his gaze locked on Red's malignant stare.

"That… Where I was… Whoever…"

"Relax and talk, Greg," said Toby, putting a hand on Greg's shoulder.

Greg swallowed and beckoned for the water. He took a massive swallow, then nodded. "That…that…*thing* that captured me, he… It… He…" He shook his head and took a deep breath, then locked his gaze on Gavin's profile. "He has your friend."

Toby nodded. "Yeah, we know he has Agent—"

"*Not him*!" Greg thundered. "The psychic!"

Gavin snapped his gaze away from Westral, and again, deep in the dark parts of his brain, he heard a barbaric chirp that threatened to split his skull. "What did you say?"

"He has him. The demon…the…" He shook his head and flopped back to the floor.

"Fry? You mean Fry has Kai Washington?"

Looking miserable, Greg nodded. "The same way he had me, but I had the sense that your friend was lost in…" He flopped his hand on the cargo mat. "In wherever."

"In Hell," murmured Gavin. "I think it's Hell." He turned and looked out the window, watching Primo's Pathfinder, wondering if Glacadairanam was in possession of Westral's body or sneaking up on him.

Toby shook his head and turned his gaze on Gavin. "I don't think Hell exists—at least not the Hell you can read about in our holy books. I think it's— Mike! *Look out!*"

2

In the desert near Odolavesta, TX
Saturday, 5:37 pm CST

Marcus sat in the lee of a smoketree and squinted at the western horizon, trying to judge how much time they had before sunset. Not that it mattered all that much, they had a task, set for them by Primo, and via his authority, by the dark lord himself, and they were going to finish it whether it killed Roger Martinez and every one of the initiates or not. "Hurry it up! We're losing the sun."

Roger gave him a sour look, then turned and yelled at the initiates. "You heard him! *Move faster!*"

The initial excitement of the initiates had waned with each second's hard labor in the desert sun, and by Marcus's judgment, they needed a little goose. He climbed to his feet, dusting off the seat of his pants, then walked around their work, paying attention to the lines cut into the desert's sandy skin. He hummed in the back of his throat—barely audible, more of a buzz, really—and stared into their faces, narrowing his eyes if he sensed a belligerence, a rebellion, then moving on to the next.

Roger fidgeted, picking at the rubber coating on the handle of his shovel as Marcus approached him.

"You, too," growled Marcus.

Martinez pulled his chin back and furrowed his brows at Marcus. "What do you—"

Like a striking rattlesnake, Marcus uncoiled, snatching the shovel out of Roger's grasp, reversing it, bringing it back down with all the strength he could muster, and burying the shovel blade in the man's skull with a sickening crunch and a spray of blood. He let go, leaving the shovel hanging in midair until Roger Martinez fell backward and the impact of the ground knocked it free.

Marcus turned back to the initiates—seven men and two women, ranging between late teens and early seventies—and glowered at them. He stabbed his finger at Roger's cooling corpse, and as he opened his mouth to speak, the buzzing died. "*He* has been with us for twenty years. *He* was one of the Twelve, and Primo knows his name. Look at him now." One by one, the men and one of the women looked over at Martinez, faces blanched of color, grimaces painted on their lips. The last, a woman in her mid-twenties, cast her gaze on the sand, instead.

With a guttural roar, Marcus sprang at her, the buzzing hum erupting in his throat like a scarab lodged deep inside. "*I said look!*" he cried, but this time when he spoke, the buzzing hum didn't stop. "*You think there's room in this church for weak hearts? You think it's okay to ignore what you're told to do?*" The last he screamed in her face, his flashing teeth fractions of an inch from her lips.

She cringed but cast a quick glance at the body.

"No. No, woman, you *look at him!*" Marcus hissed.

"I…I saw him. I don't…I don't want to see more."

"Primo wanted him dead, and he wanted you to see it! *Primo!*" he screamed in her face. "So you better motherfucking look, sister, or I'll fetch me that shovel and then you won't have to look at nothin' never again."

She sobbed, but she turned her head toward Martinez.

After thirty seconds, Marcus turned away. "Keep your damn eyes open," he said. "That goes for the rest of you, too." He glared from face to face, until he'd stared each of them in the eye. "We've been given a task, people. We've been given a task by Primo, and by the auspices of his birth, by the dark lord. You want to explain to Primo why you failed?" He stomped back and forth in front of them like a drill sergeant dressing down a bunch of recruits. "Because I will promise you this: I don't! I *won't*." He stopped, and he stopped the humming. "And neither will you, because I'll kill every last one of you to get this site done up right. I'll split your noggins like I did his, and I'll leave you here for the fuckin' vultures like I'm gonna leave him here." He stared at each one of them again, eyelids mere slits. "Does anyone have a doubt? Anyone believe I don't mean it?" The desert fell absolutely silent as though it waited for their answer, too. Marcus waited, though it almost hurt to let the silence have its way. His anger mounted with each passing second.

When he could stand it no longer, he opened his mouth to speak, but before he could, the oldest of the crew, a seventy-four-year-old woman, bent and snatched up the bloody shovel. She straightened with a groan, then moved to stand in her place by the work site. Looking him right in the eye, she said, "Any of these bitches slacks off, you just say the word. I'll smack 'em down with God's own wrath."

Slowly, Marcus smiled.

3

Fry stood, too impatient to take his rest, too impatient to take shelter from the setting sun, despite the angry red color marking half his face. Both his sons were out there, racing north in the desert, being shot at, jouncing through the brush and scree and hills. Glacadairanam couldn't be hurt by the likes of all that, but Primo…

Primo *could*.

And with Glacadairanam's single-minded fury and focus on Gavin Gregory, he wouldn't stop to consider his younger brother's safety. Fry turned and paced across the gravel between the kitchen and the barn where Red used to park his Cadillac.

He shouldn't worry. His worry had led to that last one's escape, that *Greg*. Even as he thought the name, his lips twisted with disgust at his own lack of focus. Primo's blood was weak, watery, but he was still Fry's son. He told himself that the boy's loss wouldn't affect him or his plans very much, but the worry was a distraction. Glacadairanam could take someone and play the role of cult leader, take them and perform the tricks necessary to convince people to follow him—if he could be convinced of the role's importance.

If he could control his temper and not take foolish risks.

He spun on his heel and strode back toward the house. *I should head on up there*, he thought, raising his gaze to take in the north, but then he shook his head. *No matter how much I wish it might be different, I can't go a-scamperin' up there to rescue my weak-blooded son.* The night's festivities would require his full power, his full attention, and he needed to conserve his energy. Keeping Adeline's other descendant contained was tiresome, draining. He shook his head. *No, I can't go rushing out there. I have to rely on my sons...my worshippers.* He turned, climbed the stairs, and strode across the porch, Primo already forgotten. He'd laid in a little snack to tide him over, and he felt a bit peckish.

4

"We're too slow," Cece cried in a mournful voice. "This heap of shit's worthless!" She pounded on the steering wheel with her closed fist.

"It's okay," said Jon in a dreamy voice. "Primo's Pathfinder can keep up."

"It's not okay!" she cried. "Oh, sure, *for you*, it doesn't matter if we miss the most important operation in the past decade—you're the secret wizard! I'm not, Jon!" She shot a burning, scathing look at her husband. "Don't you understand? I'm just one step away from being Roger! From being the one everyone jokes about! Heckfire, if not for him, I *would be* the butt of the jokes! The only one who can't manifest even the teensiest bit of power."

"It's not like that—"

"*Yes, it is,*" Cece hissed. "You know it is."

"No, you're looking at it all wrong, sweetie. Yes, I can play…the *music*…" Even saying the world made his eyes go dreamy and his voice soften. "Marcus can do what he does, the buzzy thing, and the others have little tricks, little powers to rely on, but only you, Cece, are truly irreplaceable.

She snapped her head to the side, a bit of poison on her lips, sure he was making fun, but he only looked at her with solemn eyes and an earnest set to his face. "What are you talking about?"

"You don't see it, but Primo does. He dotes on you and so will…the one we seek."

"Sees what?"

Jon smiled at her. "Your devotion. Your faith. It's like Primo always says: that's far more important than magic tricks."

Her doubts from an hour and a half earlier came rushing back, and the color rushed to her cheeks. "You're wrong," she said in a lifeless voice as she turned her gaze back to the front. "You don't—"

"No, Cece," said Jon in a tone that brooked no disagreement. "We all see it. When you grow into whatever power you are destined for, it will be marvelous. A fitting reward for your dedication and devotion."

Cece shook her head and dislodged a single glittering tear, but even as she did, her heart grew lighter, and a smile twitched her lips.

5

In the desert near Odolavesta, TX
Saturday, 5:55 pm CST

Gavin spun his head toward the front, feeling old and slow and stupid. The hair on the back of his neck stood straight up, and his skin prickled like it had the time ball lightning had burned a hole in the screen door and waltzed right into the middle of the cabin his dad had rented for their summer vacation one year. His pistol felt like it weighed a million pounds in his lap—not that he could use it against one of Glacadairanam's victims…not unless it was life or death.

"Mike!" screeched Greg.

"Oh, shit," murmured Toby. "*What in the blue fuck is that?*"

Gavin's gaze caught up to Toby's as the last syllables faded from the air, and at the same moment, Mike jammed on the brakes, twitching and jerking as if mid-seizure.

As if possessed, Gavin thought, his eyes resting on the insubstantial bifurcated tail wrapped around both Mike's neck and the headrest, then skipping to the long floppy ears, the three-fingered hand clamped to the top of Mike's head, the long, long tongue…

"*What the hell is it?*" Toby cried.

"Toby, meet Glacadairanam," he muttered as the G-class slewed first left, then right, throwing them all around like bags of cotton batting—all of them except Mike, who still wore his seatbelt. "Say goodbye to the world, because we're *fucked.*"

A resounding chirp, a sound of celebration, of victory, of snide self-congratulation filled the G-class as the vehicle slid sideways, and the meaty tires caught on a lip of stone and then the vehicle was in the air, rolling, spinning, then bouncing and rolling again, spinning again, slamming down, a swell of raucous metallic sounds, the sharp shattering of broken safety glass, Toby's cry of surprise, the crunch of gravel, of folding metal, of safety glass exploding from window frames, the psychotic, chirping laughter of Glacadairanam, the soul stealer.

The G-class tumbled across the desert, and in his Pathfinder, Primo followed.

Chapter 11
A Tornado of Souls

I

Gavin regained consciousness in stages. First, hearing the constant murmuring, the constant shifting of too many booted feet, the constant rasp of rough-spun cloth, the ticking-ticking-ticking of a clock…all of which he found annoying. Next, feeling the pain in his head, the warm stickiness coating the side of his head, the chill in the night desert air caressing the back of his neck like a lover, the rough scratch of the ropes that bound him…all of which made him long for unconsciousness. Third, the metallic taste of blood in his mouth, the scent of an unwashed multitude, of sulfur, of fire, of brimstone and sharpened knives and rocks and death—all of which scared the shit out of him.

"Oh, quit playing possum, old hoss," Fry grated in his ear. "You'll miss all the fun."

Finally, Gavin's eyes snapped open, and he saw a great bonfire linking the desert and the expanse of black sky above it. He took in the crowd of black-robed figures—a crowd big enough that it encompassed the entire population of several of the small towns in Kelly

County—some of which wore red fascia like the bishops had in his youth, then became aware of the others, his new friends from SEMPRe, bound and gagged, stripped naked—all except for Mike, who stood behind them, his gaze burning and burning and burning into Gavin's. Then, as he turned his head, he became aware of Fry's face, a fraction of an inch from his own, his orange, unblinking madman's gaze locked on his own, the irises spinning and spinning and spinning like the hands on an insane clock running down at the end of…well, *everything*…all of which stoked the fire of his panicked brain, and he knew horror and despair and wretched desperation.

"Say hey, fella," said the Beast. "Smile, it's prettier."

Gavin's muscles lurched into action, jerking and tugging and pulling and trying to get the ropes off, to thrust himself up and away, a mindless animal of terror, rubbing his skin raw, abrading his flesh, injuring himself like a fox trying to chew his own leg off to get away from the trap that held him fast.

"Oh, relax, spark ol' spark. There ain't no more fight between us. I decided for you. You're here and you're mine, and if you straighten up, if you repent your stubborn, hardheaded ways, I'll let your woman and child live. If you do the work I put to you, I might even let you visit 'em from time to time, though if you'll take a bit of advice from an old friend, women ain't worth a shit in the long run. They let you down."

"Is that…" he croaked. He worked at dredging spit into his mouth and tried again. "Is that what happened between you and Adeline? Did she let you down?"

Fry threw back his head and laughed, and every living thing in the desert froze, listening, hearts lurching, hoping the terrible sound would end, that Fry would pass them over. "Adeline? Shit, boy, you do make me laugh. She tweren't nothin' to me. A dalliance." From across the fire, Gavin felt Primo's gaze on them like a weighted blanket. "Nawp, hoss, I was talking about a woman like your Maddie, a *mate*, *capiche*?" He rested an ice-cold hand on Gavin's shoulder, and Gavin's heart raced and his mind roiled. "Stick by me, spark. I'll get your thinker back to the right side of crazy." He cocked his head to the side. "Well, maybe after my honeymoon and all."

"I thought you just said—"

Fry chuckled, and even that chilled Gavin's blood, while a blast of heat poured off the demon that made his eyes tear up and sting. "Boy, what I said was meant *for you*. For *your kind*. My mate"—he exhaled with a contentment and shook his head once—"well, you're going to see in a few minutes, but my mate ain't *one of your kind*. *Capiche*?"

Gavin felt sick, woozy, and he squeezed his eyes shut.

"No, no," said Fry. "Don't you start that carryin' on and that hootin' and hollerin'. I won't have it. Nawsir, I won't stand for it."

"I feel sick, is all."

"Ah. Well, that'll pass, hoss. That'll pass as your noggin gets right and you get used to the idea that you're mine and your world is mine and *mine* and *MINE*."

Opening his eyes a crack, Gavin gazed across the circle. Glacadairanam was using Mike's eyes to look at someone off to the side that Gavin couldn't see, and a small, vicious smile decorated Mike's face. Greg sat at his feet, looking like the world had ended, like he had no reason to live. *You can save him,* he thought at the man. *A little antipsychotic and Glacadairanam is out of there. Do it soon enough and his mind won't even be damaged.*

Fry leaned down and gazed into his eyes. "You playin' possum on me, spark? Thinking those wrong-headed thoughts?" He tsked. "What would poor Maddie think? Should I go ask her? I could be there by morning, sparky-spark. *In person.* Would you like that? Would you like to *watch*?" The Beast's breath was fetid, humid despite the arid locale, hot and muddy—exactly as Gavin imagined an alligator's breath would smell. Fry's gaze drifted to the side, to where Glacadairanam stared, and he chuckled. "My, my, how time does fly. It's time to start the party, Gav ol' Gav. Ain't that just fine? Ain't that just exciting?" The ice-cold hand left his shoulder, and the straight-backed chair he was tied to went all tilty as Fry dragged him around a quarter turn. When he came to a rest, he could see the entire forlorn oval of torment Fry and his followers had devised.

To the side of the roaring fire, a square of earth had been cleared and flattened. Field stones had been laid as a floor, though they were set dry, and the raw desert peeked from around them. A wide altar carved from ironwood stood in the center of the field stones, its surface stained brown and rust and red in places. The top of the altar bore tool marks that hadn't been caused by its making—they'd been inflicted in the time since, by sharp blades and cruel hatchets and savage cleavers.

Five horrible constructions stood around the altar. Around one of them, coals had been banked using more field stones, and they glowed bright despite the cavorting light from the bonfire. Over the coals, a brazen bull stood, its brass belly glowing an evil orange that matched Fry's eyes. The crude door in the bull's side stood wide, and the interior was still empty except for the awful hellish heat. An immense ironwood wheel equipped with iron spikes stood next to the bull, mounted on an A-frame of two-by-fours that bore metal wheels. Gavin could guess its use—one of his friends would be tied to the wheel then moved into place over the coals. A strange device stood opposite the wheel, almost like a sawhorse but for the scale of it, a thick wooden beam suspended between four legs. Pulleys had been attached to the foot of each leg, with ropes already strung through them, one end secured to a staple on the underside of the beam itself, the other lying loose atop it. To the side of the wooden horse was a bizarre, hinged hoop of iron set vertically in a bed of concrete. The top hoop had an attachment that could pull the two parts of the hoop together using long screws and would no doubt crush whoever was inside if those screws were turned tight enough. The last device turned Gavin's stomach. It was a giant iron sarcophagus with a front that split down the middle into two doors. Wicked iron spikes extended from the interior of the device and from the inside of the twin doors, including two spikes set at eye level.

Cece and Jon Clark stood at the edge of the square of stones, a hooded man slumped between them. The man's head lolled as the couple stood waiting, and he started to mutter, but Cece turned and kneed him in the stomach hard enough to double him over and drive the strength from his legs.

Beside Gavin, Fry chuckled. "Ain't she a pear?" He lifted one fish-belly white hand and beckoned. "Bring him, Cece, then come over here by me and meet my friend, Gavin Gregory."

Jon Clark turned to his wife and smiled, mouthing something that looked like "Told you so" to Gavin's eyes.

"Where would you like us to put him, Lord?" Cece asked.

"You pick," said Fry. He leaned close to Gavin and whispered in his ear. "Three gets you five she picks the Scavenger's Daughter. She seems to have taken a special interest in your boy, there, and it's lucky he's survived this long."

Gavin's heart raced, and he leaned forward as far as the ropes would allow, peering across the distance, his gaze crawling over the stooped figure Cece and Jon dragged toward the altar. It was Reynold Hall, and he was just this side of death's door. He squeezed his eyes shut as Cece pointed to the iron hoop thing and Fry chuckled.

"Sucker's bet," said the demon. "I knew she'd pick that 'un. Wait 'til you see it, sparky. It was dreamed up by an old friend of mine back in Britannia. Skevington, his name was." Fry's gaze grew wistful and far away. "I do miss that boy." He shook himself and smiled. "Great choice, Cece. Get him set up, then come on over. Bring that man of yours, too."

The Clarks set about shoving Ren into the device, forcing him down into a crouch, then positioning the two parts of the hoop across his back. Hall seemed not to know where he was or what was being done to him.

"Come on, Ren," murmured Gavin. "Fight them!"

Fry glanced down at him. "Now, I'm makin' allowances, old hoss, due to you gettin' your bell rung and all, but let's not have any more of that. This here's a party, boy! This is a celebration!"

"Of what?" Gavin asked before he could stop himself.

"Of the arrival of our guest of honor, of course. My future mate. We just need to make everything perfect to make the transition as easy as possible. Relax. Just sit there and enjoy the show."

The Clarks secured the hoop over Reynold's back and attached the screws to the plate. Hall sagged against the sides of apparatus, his belly and sides hitching like he had to throw up. Cece spun a crank and the ends of the two half-hoops drew closer together, forcing Reynold down even more.

"Take his hood off, Cece," yelled Fry. "Let's see how he likes ol' Skevington's baby girl." He laughed, and several of the people wearing red sashes laughed with him. "Let's get this show on the road!" Fry shouted, and the cultists whooped and hollered to raise all hell.

"Let him go," whispered Gavin. "Let him go, and let my friends go."

"Now, why in the hell would I go and do a dumb thing like that?" asked Fry.

"I'll stay. I'll do whatever you want."

Fry winked at him, and the sight of it made Gavin want to vomit. It was the expression of a man who knew he'd already won. "You'll do that anyway, spark, or I'll bring Maddie down here and we'll put her in one of yon toys." A lecherous smile split Fry's face. "Or maybe you'd rather see her ride the Pear of Anguish? Would that make your rod stiff?" He shrugged. "I doubt she'd be much good afterward, but you could have her—you know, that one last time while her body cooled."

"*Shut your fucking mouth!*" Gavin growled.

Fry squatted and lunged closer. "There he is! There he is, by the snake!" He leaned closer, eyes wide, pupils dilated, nostrils flaring. "I thought we lost you. Or more like, I thought *you* lost you, spark. Or lost your *spark*. Welcome back, hoss. Welcome back." He grabbed one of Gavin's shoulders in each hand. "This is the Gavin Gregory I want, boy. I got sycophants for days, for *centuries*, you hear? I don't want that. I want someone to push me, to challenge me, to make life *interestin'* for me and my mate." He leaned back, and some of the fire left his gaze but only a touch. "To help us educate our child."

"Just leave Maddie alone."

Fry held up his hands, palms toward Gavin. "Like I said, Gav ol' spark. You'll do what I want. There was never no question about it."

"Glacadairanam thought that, too. Look what it got him."

Fry chuckled. "There's your mistake, boy. In case you haven't noticed, *I ain't Glacadairanam.*"

As Reynold Hall started to scream, Gavin squeezed his eyes shut and despaired.

2

The three of them sat huddled together as the echoes of the horrible shriek of laughter faded—Greg didn't huddle, he sat apart, at his husband's feet, morose and ignoring all attempts to communicate with him. Toby sat on one side, and Benny sat on the other, offering what protection they had to Shannon.

A horde of cultists—an *unwashed* horde by the odor—ringed around behind them, encircling them, the massive bonfire, an altar, and what looked like an outdoor torture chamber to Benny. Gavin Gregory was tied to a straight-back chair across the bonfire from them, though *he* still had his clothing. Benny caught Toby's eye, then jerked his chin toward Gavin. *What's up with that?*

The chair, you mean? No idea. Maybe they—

Not that! He's still clothed, and we're naked.

Toby shrugged, and his gaze zipped over the crowd of murmuring black-robed figures. *What's up with the sashes some of them have?*

You're worried about fashion? Now?

Hey, you're the one worried about clothes.

Boys, cut it out. Shannon's mental voice carried a note of exasperation mixed with gentle reproach. *We're in trouble if you hadn't noticed. You can resume the banter after we're out of it.*

Sorry, sent Benny.

Relax, both of you.

Relax? Relax?

Yeah, that's what I said. Toby's face and eyes danced with secret knowledge. *We'll be okay.*

Benny frowned for a moment, then his expression cleared. *SEMPRe.* He looked at Shannon and grinned. *They knew about all this. Greg must've gotten a message out before that creep got him.*

Not until later, sent Toby. *Gavin had a…* He stopped as three figures approached the torture area surrounding the altar.

That's the bitch that beat Benny up! A wash of anger came across with Shannon's thought and swept over them like an out-of-control forest fire.

The man and the woman paused at the edge of the field stones that marked the torture area, and they talked to the freakshow near Gavin.

Toby watched a moment, then he turned his attention back to Shannon and Benny. *Gavin had a nightmare that presented as a stroke, and during it, someone slipped him the information. I assumed that someone was you.* He turned his gaze on Benny and arched one eyebrow.

Not me. I tried to warn Greg. Both men turned their heads so their gazes touched first on Greg, then slid upward to Mike. *He's...not Mike.*

No. It was a...hell, I don't know what it was. Gavin described him as a ghost-like gargoyle the size of a monkey but...

But that's not what you saw.

Toby shook his head.

Well? Are you going to tell us?

It looked like... He dropped his gaze to the ground in front of them. *What do you see when you look at the freak across the fire?*

Shannon glanced at the white-skinned man near Gavin.

What I see is different, sent Benny. *Or at least, parts of it are. He has long claws the color of ancient bone. His eyes are dead-white—what I always imagined when that guy talked about "deadlights" in that long book Shannon loves. He's dressed in a black robe, like the others, like the big black guy, but his fascia is brilliant orange, and it looks like it's on fire.*

Visages, said Toby.

Then they're like...

Toby shook his head. *No. Not like what we saw in Oneka Falls. These two are...* He shook his head again, shrugging his shoulders. *They are something different.*

Describe them, sent Shannon.

Toby pointed at Mike with his chin. *I can both see Mike and something else, something out-of-focus that has more in common with a snake or a crocodile than a gargoyle. It's the size of a small monkey, though. Gavin described smoky wings, but I don't see anything like that.* He turned his face to the pair across the bonfire. *He, on the other hand, looks like—*

A terrible scream rang into the night, and all three of them snapped their heads up to stare at the man being crushed inside a contraption of iron hoops.

Good God! Shannon thought.

No, I don't think he has anything to do with that device.

3

The ritual site near Odolavesta, TX
Saturday, 11:29 pm CST

Greg sat at his husband's feet…only the man wasn't his husband anymore. It was Mike's body, but Greg couldn't touch the parts of Mike that made him who he was. He couldn't hear Mike's thoughts, couldn't sense his personality, couldn't feel his love, and the lack of those things made the world a horrible, desolate place.

The others were, and had been, trying to gain his attention, and while Greg sensed their efforts, knew they needed him, his power, he couldn't find the will to care. Mike was *gone*, and nothing else mattered.

Not even the horrific screams pulled him out of the abyss of his grief.

4

The ritual site near Odolavesta, TX
Saturday, 11:29 pm CST

Fry beamed down at Gavin. "That boy's got a set of lungs, don't he?"

Gavin could only grimace and close his eyes, but neither thing helped Reynold, neither thing set him free, neither thing could mute his terrible screams. "Stop it," he murmured. "Make them stop. I'll do anything…"

"That, again? We already discussed that, hoss. No sense revisiting a dead horse."

"Then put me in that thing instead. Let *him* go, torture *me*." He bit back the rest of what he wanted to say, the names he wanted to call Fry, his goddamn sons, and his followers.

"Ah, now, is that any way to be?" asked Fry. "I done told you what your future is, spark. Ain't no sense railing against me. Things is how they is, old hoss. Happiness can only exist in acceptance."

Gavin scoffed and shook his head.

"Well, now. I can see you're all twisted out of shape about your friend over there. Maybe it's time to advance the card? Should we move on to the next act, spark?"

"What does that mean?"

Get ready, whispered a voice in his mind. *They're almost here.*

Fry's brows drew together, and his eyes blazed like the Sun itself. "Whossat? Who you got in there with you, spark?" His jaw worked and worked like he was chewing on the souls of the damned, muscles bunching beneath his death-pale skin, arctic cold coming off him in wave after wave despite the bonfire, his anger a palpable thing, a living thing.

Gavin shook his head. "I don't know what you mean."

"*Oh, for fuck's sake!*" Fry snapped, and his hand flashed out, his ice-cold fingers clamping on Gavin's jaw like a hydraulic press, jerking Gavin's head back, tilting his face toward those malignant, creamsicle eyes. "Why do all of you meatbags think you can lie to me? Why do you think you can *cheat on me*?"

Projecting a calm he didn't feel, Gavin shrugged and stared up into Fry's glare. "You're wrong."

"The hell I am, spark!" snapped Fry. "*The hell I am!*" His head pivoted at a speed that would've broken a human neck, and his gaze fastened on first Benny, then Greg. "Which one…" he murmured.

He still held Gavin by the jaw, but Fry seemed to have forgotten him for the moment. Gavin's gaze rolled toward the Scavenger's Daughter, toward Ren's tortured body, then snapped toward the darkness outside the bonfire's circle.

"Is it Adeline's kin?" Fry murmured. "That boy from Arizona? Nawp, nawp. I done got him locked up, buried away, entombed." Fry snapped his gaze back to Gavin's face. "Better answer me, spark. I ain't exactly known for my patience and even temper." He said the words in an utterly flat voice, a voice devoid of humanity. "I'll have my answer one way or another. Surely, you know that by now, spark ol' Gav."

"I don't—"

"Nawp!" snapped Fry. "No more of that nonsense. I want to know who it is that thinks he can send you secrets right under *my goddamn nose!*" As he spoke, Fry's voice wound up and up and up to a demon's shriek seeming to shake the foundation of the world. "*I want to know, spark, and I don't cotton to your LIES! You want me to withdraw my BLESSINGS from your HOUSE? Is that it? IS THAT WHAT YOU WANT?*"

The threat vibrated in the space between them, enraging Gavin, but at the same time, draining away everything but his fear for Maddie. "I don't know who it is. That's what I was going to say."

Fry's eyelids narrowed until the bright orange light of his fevered gaze seemed to focus into blinding beams of coherent light. His lips twisted, bunched, then twisted again, and through it all the rest of him remained as still as sculpture cut from glacier ice. "You better not be lying to me to curry favor, old hoss. I don't cotton to that, either. I'll pound her, spark. Your Maddie, your baby. I'll grind 'em beneath my boot heels. I'll hammer them from this world with my fists, my magic, my hate. You want that? You want that for them?" Despite the threats, Fry's voice was calm, quiet. His gaze, however, was loud and warlike.

Gavin shook his head, meeting Fry's awful gaze with as much steadiness as he could muster.

"Then you start talking, spark, and you start right goddamn now."

"I can't answer your question. I don't recognize whoever it was that spoke in my mind. I don't even know if it was my imagination or—"

"Yes, you do. Yes, you do, spark. You believe. You *do*."

Gavin shrugged. "Okay, I do *believe* what I heard, but I don't recognize the voice."

Fry leaned closer, his face fractions of an inch from Gavin's, and he peered into Gavin's eyes for nearly a minute. In the face of Fry's rage, the crowd of revelers had fallen dumb, the night had gone quiet, and only Reynold Hall dared break the dark silence. And Fry didn't seem to hear Hall's screams, or if he did, he didn't care. Not in the least. "Tell me what secrets your mysterious benefactor passed on to you," he crooned. "Tell me. Tell me. Tell me, tell me. *Tell me, tell me, TELL ME, TELL ME, TELL ME, TELL ME!*" His voice rose and rose and rose, ending at an ear-shattering, brain-melting volume, his words called out so fast Gavin had no chance, no moment in time, in which to answer. Fry ended his tirade with his nose touching Gavin's forehead above his left eye, his teeth flashing against his cheek. He froze there, waiting, not even breathing, his blast-furnace lips at odds with the algid, post-rant silence. After a thirty-second respite, Fry said, "You better fucking tell me, spark, and it better be right fucking now." Across the bonfire, Mike gloated, his eyes sparkling.

Gavin swallowed, and his throat clicked. He swallowed again, consciously summoning saliva. "He said, 'Get ready. They're almost here.'"

"And whossat, hoss? Who's 'they?'"

He opened his mouth, but before Gavin could speak, Fry waved a bone-white finger in front of him. "And no more dissembling, hoss. You do that again, and your Maddie…" He snapped his fingers in Gavin's face.

Swallowing again, Gavin tried to nod, and he bumped Fry's face with his forehead. "Sorry," he murmured.

"*Who*?" the demon said in a jet-engine shriek.

"SEMPRe. Some of their security forces."

Fry laughed, spinning on his heel to pin Benny, Shannon, and Toby with a glare that might've turned diamonds to dust. "Oh, *them*." He lifted his gaze to Mike's face. "Where'd you leave your other toy, son?"

Mike pointed at Primo. "In his truck." His voice grated and squeaked as though Glacadairanam were having trouble making it work…or as if Mike were fighting him.

Primo stepped forward, snapped his fingers at the crowd of worshippers, and waved them apart. Marcus came then, holding Eldred Westral by the arm with a white-knuckled grip. He shoved the sheriff forward, and the man staggered, his eyes wild and drunk and insane.

"Eldred, I need you," said Fry, and at the sound of his voice, Red Westral whimpered and shook. "Now, now, boy. None of that. Get on the horn, spark. Call up the reserves. Tell them an illegal militia is making moves tonight. Tell them to block the roads, to stop all traffic." He glanced up at the night sky. "And tell them to be quick. It's almost time."

Gavin's heart sank as Marcus Wallace produced a phone, scrolled through the sheriff's contacts, dialed a number, then held the phone to Red's ear. He jabbed the man in the ribs and hissed, "Do as you're told, Red."

Westral mumbled something, and Marcus jabbed him in the ribs again. "This is…um…"

"Sheriff Westral," hissed Wallace.

"Right. This is Sheriff Westral out in Westral County. I need— What? Oh, no. I meant, uh…" He looked at Marcus.

"*Kelly* County, you half-wit!" Marcus's face crumpled into a grimace of annoyance.

Again, Red nodded and opened his mouth to speak, but as he did so, he happened to look up at the ridge a football field away and gasped. "Who're they?" he asked.

Fry whirled around, his eyes blazed even brighter, and then the night exploded with lights and noise and gunfire, and through it all, Reynold Hall screamed and screamed and screamed.

5

The ritual site near Odolavesta, TX
Saturday, 11:36 pm CST

Pandemonium erupted out in the desert, shouted commands, orders to charge, the stamp of booted feet, the roar of at least three all-terrain personnel carriers. Shannon's gaze, however, stayed locked on the demon with the dead white skin. He was the key. He was the wildcard that she needed to control, to sideline, to minimize. She marshaled her not inconsiderable power and brought everything she had to bear on the demon running the show. *You see nothing out in the desert. You hear nothing. Your followers have lost their minds, seeing things that aren't there. You should stop them. You should make them stop everything they're doing: fighting, yelling, guarding, breathing.*

Fry hesitated, spun his head back and forth as though confused, then frowned at the bonfire.

That's right, big fella. You should tell them to stop. Everything is fine, and you don't need us anymore. You don't need Gavin. Your kid needs to get out of Mike.

Fry glanced at Mike and his jaw dropped open, but instead of speaking, instead of ordering Glacadairanam out, *he laughed*. He laughed and seared Shannon with his sunlike gaze.

In the desert, the SEMPRe troops made a calm, orderly advance, weapons drawn but pointed in safe directions, moving in small units, but moving with precision like a well-oiled machine. Around the altar, Fry's worshippers went crazy, producing weapons of all kinds: guns, knives, blunt melee weapons, motorcycle chains, even a huge headsman ax forged from Damascus steel—that one carried by a giant man with blacksmith's shoulders. They ran to meet the SEMPRe teams without organization, without thought of strategy or tactics, only rushing forward to attack, screaming and shaking their weapons as if possessed.

Shannon fell over backward in the face of the power in Fry's glare, his rage, his amusement. She flopped to her back, muscles contracting, twitching, dancing beneath her skin, her eyes rolling up in her head, her tongue lolling.

Who are you to command me? Fry's voice blasted down the pathways in her brain, laying waste, a band of marauding berserks, chasing down her thoughts and offering them only violent, bloody deaths. Images of terror, Benny mutilated by hundreds…thousands of sharp blades, Mike burning with empty eyes and a mouth hanging slack and drooling, Toby dismembered, butchered, and consumed by black-robed figures, Greg raving under the desert sun. *This is your reward for your impudence. This is my* mercy. The last word was like the sneer of a psychopath. *I am a god, woman, and you fuckin' offend me!*

6

The ritual site near Odolavesta, TX
Saturday, 11:41 pm CST

As Shannon fell onto her back, Gavin started to struggle, his gaze frozen, locked on her as she started to convulse. He fought the ropes as Reynold screamed on, fought the chair, and succeeded only in tipping himself sideways into the dirt. His muscles bunched and strained, and though the thick rope and the chair he was tied to both creaked, neither gave way. He flopped in the desert sand, throwing himself against his bonds, against the wooden chair back, his gaze riveted to Shannon's writhing form, flicking to Benny as the man lunged up, naked and alone, and ready to attack Fry.

"Benny! No!" he shouted, but Benny didn't even hesitate.

7

The ritual site near Odolavesta, TX
Saturday, 11:43 pm CST

Benny lunged to his feet, lashing out with his mind, going for fire, for pressure, for anything and everything that might distract the demon from killing his beloved. *Greg*! he shouted. *Greg,* help me! But from Greg, there was only bleak, black silence.

He flung all his mental energy at Fry, all his pent-up emotions, just as he had during their battle with Brigitta, but unlike that day, his will wasn't enough.

Fry glanced at him, and Benny Cartwright's universe exploded in a shower of orange light.

8

The ritual site near Odolavesta, TX
Saturday, 11:43 pm CST

Cece watched the fight start, watched the outsiders emerge from their cloaking darkness, watched the Brethren mobilize and attack, watched her husband, Jon, run to fetch his guitar, and she drew her knife. She looked down at it, admiring how the orange firelight danced along its mottled blade, loving the pattern of dark and light—a metaphor for so many things in her life. Good and bad, healthy and sick, the dark lord and every-fucking-other thing under the Sun.

She lifted her gaze and saw the dark lord glance at Andy—no, *Benny*—saw the explosion of power that erupted between them as a gout of miraculous orangesicle light, saw Benny's pretty wife enjoying her just deserts, and smiled. She glanced down at the FBI agent she'd been tasked with for the last few days, then raised her face once more and found the dark lord's gaze on her face.

You will know when, the dark lord said inside her mind, and with his voice came an eternal exultation, a wave of orgasmic pleasure that nearly carried her away.

But when her wits returned, it had only been a split-second, and the dark lord's gaze still rested on hers, waiting, and she nodded.

9

The ritual site near Odolavesta, TX
Saturday, 11:43 pm CST

Watching the battle unfold, unsure and anxious, Toby sat frozen. His instincts were to run, to fight, to kill any demon motherfuckers who stood before him, but ever since the talk back at the motel, ever since he'd learned that there were more true demons in the world than those he'd helped defeat in Oneka Falls, he felt…lost. Alone. Directionless.

So, he dithered and watched his friends rise up and attack, watched them get swatted like insignificant bugs, watched…and didn't lift a finger.

His gaze switched to Greg, who also sat frozen, doing nothing, and understood his friend completely.

What's the point? he asked himself. *We can't win. We can't beat this thing. I gave her up for nothing.*

For nothing!

10

The ritual site near Odolavesta, TX
Saturday, 11:43 pm CST

Dark, grim thoughts formed a miasma inside Greg's mind. He thought of death, longed for it. Mike…Mike was *gone*, and Greg couldn't find a way to bring him back. There was nothing, no strand to pull, no avenue of attacking the thing that possessed his body, no chance, no hope, only bleak desperation and horrible suffering.

Without Mike, there's nothing left for me! The thought wailed through the avenues of his mind, shrieking, wailing, gnashing its teeth.

Nothing!

11

Nowhere
No time

Benny flew backward through a black void. He fell through a timeless, shapeless black hole, skin burning, eyelids singed, eyes melted, eardrums gone, hair burnt off, bones crushed to dust.

Everything and everything hurt. Thick, ropey remorse and desperate despair lashed him. As much as he hurt, he hadn't managed to distract the fiend hurting Shan. His suffering was nothing in the face of hers, and he'd gladly have suffered for eternity if only she didn't have to.

Hey, stop it.

But he'd failed. Failed so utterly that he'd ended up causing her MORE pain. He was worthless—he always had been. She'd been stupid to hook her wagon to his, to tie herself to a loser like Benny Cartwright, the insane kid from Oneka Falls.

Listen, you've got to stop—

He'd always thought the void of deep space would be sort of comforting—like floating in a pool of body-temperature water, invisible support—kind of nice, but it wasn't…it was dreadful, horrendous, dis—

Hey! You've got to stop all this self-pity and *help* me!

Benny frowned. He was alone, useless and alone, just like he'd always been before he'd met Shan, and just like he'd be when Fry was finished, and she lay dead. Help you? *he thought derisively.* You don't want help from a loser like me? You're fucking insane, pal.

12

Greg! shouted a voice in the back of his mind, but he wanted to ignore it, like the voices of his friends, and he turned his mind away.

His life was over. Finished.

Mike is gone and—

For fuck's sake! Listen to me! There's a chance, but only one, and I need help because my body's in Ohio and Fry has me—

Greg sighed and blocked the voice out.

13

Closing his eyes, Toby shut out the great failure unfolding before him and focused on his greatest regret. She'd raised her hands to encompass the entire world and told him he'd been right, back there in that other desert, when he'd told her she was to blame for the rocky endings of her love affairs—at least in part. She'd seemed so sad, so…heartbroken.

Hey! Stop all this nonsense! Don't you see what's happening? You and your friends are in real trouble, and you're all—

Shut up! Toby snapped, filled with an irrational, unending rage. *Just shut up! Get out of my head!*

Toby hung his head and sank into the abyss of his despair.

14

The ritual site near Odolavesta, TX
Saturday, 11:45 pm CST

Gavin ripped at the knots securing him with his fingernails and tugged at the ropes and pulled his arms apart until his fingers were raw, his wrists bled, and his elbows felt dismembered, and still, nothing happened. He watched the tableau of defeat across the bonfire: Toby sitting morosely, Shannon convulsing in the dirt, Greg staring up at Mike, and Benny lying face down, not moving, maybe not even breathing, maybe dead and gone already, and a wave of his own uselessness washed over him, drowning him in a bleak hopelessness. He wanted to cry, to close his eyes and let unconsciousness wash him away, let Glacadairanam take him over so he could retreat into unconsciousness.

What the hell is the matter with you all? Kai cried in the back of his head. *Your new friends are… They're giving up, dammit.*

Yeah? asked Gavin, barely able to summon the will to care. *Where the hell have you been, Kai*? *We can't win this. Fry's—*

Fry captured me. He sensed me tapping into the sheriff's thoughts, and he caught me. But there's no time to swap stories. We've got to get you out of there!

The others—

Yeah. They're out… What the hell is the matter with you, Gavin? *Your thoughts are… Hold on a minute.*

Don't… The colors of the rainbow seemed to dance through Gavin's mind, along with the sound of waves on the beach, the lap of cool water against the pilings of a dock on a lake on a becalmed day, Maddie humming in the other room. He opened his eyes wide against a sudden stinging, a sudden dryness. Memories exploded in his mind's eye, playing at ten times normal speed, images of holidays as a kid, of meeting Maddie at that stupid little sports bar, of their first date, of their wedding…and more. And more. And more until Gavin again felt like he was drowning, but this time in love and warmth and bonhomie and joy and hope. *Jesus...what was all that?*

Clearing out the foreign influences. Fry and his tricks. I'll explain it later. Right now, you have to listen—there isn't much time. I didn't see it until right now, but your friends are trapped in Fry's power, and I don't have time to free them all. They can't help you anymore, so you need to leave them behind. I'm about done, but I can summon one last burst of TK to get you free. You need—

"No," Gavin whispered, his gaze darting toward Reynold Hall, crumpled up on himself in the Scavenger's Daughter. *No, free Ren.*

Gavin, that's very noble, but—

Free him, Kai! He's being tortured...and there's worse coming for him.

For you, too, you idiot! I'm going to cut those knots, and you're going to get up and run! Do you—

No. Gavin's mental voice rang with authority, sang with determination. *You set Ren free.*

Don't you think they'll torture you, too? No, my plan—

They won't touch me, Gavin said, suddenly devoid of energy. *Fry said as much. He wants me around. I'm* safe, *Kai. Reynold isn't.*

Kai didn't reply, but Gavin felt a peculiar sensation, a tingling in his head, deep in his brain. After a moment, Kai sent, *Fine. But I'm sending him to untie you. He won't make it very far without help anyway.*

Help one of the others—all of the others. They can help Ren.

I can't. It's like they want to wallow in it. I can't rouse them. I don't have enough power left...keeping my power hidden from Fry, tricking him into thinking I was out of energy...it's taken a lot out of me. I've got to move, got to do it now, Gavin. Sorry I let you down. Tell Maddie I said so. Tell her I said goodbye.

Goodbye? This isn't goodbye, Kai. We'll find a way.

Gavin waited but there was no response.

Kai?

With a metallic clang, the Scavenger's Daughter fell open, and Reynold stumbled forward, and as he did so, his gaze locked on Gavin's.

15

The ritual site near Odolavesta, TX
Saturday, 11:47 pm CST

Her eyes danced back and forth from the battle in the darkness outside the ring of light cast by the bonfire and the group of spies writhing on the ground. Behind her, Jon played his beautiful, hypnotic threnody, his guitar making sounds she'd never heard another guitar make, soaring into the midnight sky, thundering across the desert sand, jangling the rocks, the lizards, the Brethren like shattered glass bells. The tempo rose and rose and rose, and she swayed with it, her feet moved to it, she spun and twirled to it, but always, always her gaze swatted the maggots who'd tried to trick them or caressed the Brethren fighting the invaders. Energy coursed through her in ecstatic waves, making her skin thrum to the secret frequencies of the universe's underlayment, making her pores open and shout hallelujahs, making her nerves dance and sing.

And all because of approval and notice of the Dark Lord. That, and the music her husband had learned to play.

She still held her knife in her fist, still flicked it toward the bonfire to see the orange glow dance along its length. She threw back her head and loosed a long ululation, her voice filled with mourning, with longing, and Jon trilled his melody to follow her.

She spun and spun and spun, seeing the suffering of fools, the righteous battling the infidels, the suffering of fools, the righteous smiting the heathen, Agent Hall stumbling forward, the suffering of the spies, the battle, Agent Hall fixing his gaze on the other FBI-man, suffering fools, fighting, Agent Hall stumbling…

Cece's brain caught up to the images, and she planted her feet, a little dizzy but her gaze focused on Reynold

Hall's stumbling run. A wide smile cracked the insane mask her face wore, and she sprinted after him, knife blade held high, a long, thin ululation streaming from her mouth as she ran.

16

The ritual site near Odolavesta, TX
Saturday, 11:47 pm CST

Gavin watched Ren lunge to his feet, the man's face a rictus of pain, and he wanted to shout, to dance with happiness. The woman, Cece, was spinning in circles, not paying attention to Ren, and her husband was bent over his guitar, playing a jangling kind of dirge, low mournful chords interspersed with jarring runs up and down the neck. The music beckoned him, called to him, but he kept his gaze locked on Ren's face, willing the man to see him, to understand Gavin was channeling encouragement, strength, everything he had through his gaze.

Reynold ran with his arms wrapped around his middle, and every other step, he gasped in pain. Kai was right—there was no way Ren would make it back to a vehicle, let alone out of town, on his own.

Gavin shot a glance around the ritual site—Fry was focused on torturing Shannon, a sick smile on his fish-belly face, and Mike stared at Red Westral as the man shouted into the phone Marcus carried. Gavin snapped his gaze back to Ren, a soft smile of triumph on his face.

He locked gazes with the man, and then she was there, her face a caricature of a madwoman's, eyes open wide, mouth agape, one eyelid twitching, twitching, twitching, her Damascus Bowie held high, high, high over her head. As the wide blade started to fall, Gavin shouted, "*Ren, look out!*" and began his struggle with the ropes anew.

17

The ritual site near Odolavesta, TX
Saturday, 11:47 pm CST

Cece shrieked with joy as she brought the blade down, an orangesicle streak in the midnight air, a fiery victory dance, an orange lightning bolt consecrated to Reynold Hall's doom. The wide blade split his flesh easily, coating her face in a spray of warm blood. She raised the knife and plunged it into Hall's back again, laughing, swallowing the blood that landed on her tongue, her lips, then jerked the blade free. She raised it high, slammed it down, raised it up, stabbed Hall, raised it, slammed it home, over and over, she stabbed and stabbed and stabbed him, hunching down as he fell, keeping him within reach, always keeping him within reach of her orange blade, stabbing, stabbing, stabbing.

From behind her, Jon's freaky music played on and on and on, filling the night, filling her.

Her arm grew heavy, and still she rammed her blade into Hall's flesh. Her throat rasped with thirst, and still she pierced Hall's flesh. Her back sang and her eyes dimmed, and still she killed and killed and killed him. She kept on until her arm refused to rise, until she staggered with exhaustion, until Jon's song celebrated her victory, until Hall's blood covered every inch of her.

When she straightened, her entire arm was numb, and she could no longer feel the Bowie in her palm, but it was there, it was always there, it would always be there. She swayed with exhaustion, but she kept her feet. Her gaze zipped around, saw Jon's exultant pride, saw that the invaders were in full retreat, saw that the spies were still suffering—and that kindled her bloodlust—saw the dark lord watching her, grinning at her, lust dancing in his eyes.

18

Gavin lay still, paralyzed with disbelief, with crushed hope, with agony, with a terrible, mournful wailing filling his mind. "No," he muttered. "No." He couldn't take his eyes off Reynold Hall's face, his open-eyed death stare, his face and eyes flecked and mottled with his own blood.

"No," he almost whined. "No, no, no."

The murderous bitch stood over Ren's bloody corpse, breathing hard, swaying even, covered in his blood, the Bowie she'd stabbed him to death with—*beyond* death—clutched in her fist. She looked...

She looked *happy.* Ecstatic.

Rage boiled within him, but he had no outlet, no way to run over there and knock her down, to beat her down, to drive her into the sand and bloody dust and kick her and kick her and kick her. He could barely think for the want of it, could barely do anything but imagine his vengeance.

He was so focused on his revenge fantasies that he never even saw Fry approach. He was just there, grinning into Gavin's face, orange eyes gleaming. "Say hey, sugar,"

Fry murmured. "I like the way you think, but I have to say, Cece is one of my favorites—like you are—and I can't let you have her." He straightened and glanced toward the woman. "Maybe if she fucks up, but until then, you play nice." He returned his glowing eyes to Gavin. "You want one of them others? Pick any of 'em with a red sash, and I'll see her brought over."

Gavin screwed his eyes shut, trying to block out Fry's voice, trying to forget where he was, what was happening. But there was no use. Fry wouldn't allow him to drift away.

"Now, now. No reason to play it that-a-way, hoss. It was good plan, these security people, but..." Fry shrugged. "My people are *devoted*, Gav. That's where you all messed up. My people will die for me, and it don't matter how much you pay a man, he ain't going to die for you for pay. You need something more, a promise, a contract for the here-after." He lifted his gaze to Cece Clark once more. "You got to excite them, spark ol' spark. *Inspire* them." He returned his gaze to Gavin. "You got some of that by nature. I'll give you that. But, sparky-spark, you got to develop that talent. You've got to work at it. Ain't nothing in life comes for free."

Gavin could do nothing but lie there, his face on the still-warm desert sand, his head cocked downward, his right arm and leg going all pins-and-needles from lying on them, his hands purpling from the tightness of the damn ropes. He couldn't think of anything to do, couldn't make a plan, couldn't even dredge up the image of Maddie's face—he didn't even want a memory of her in that horrible place, on that horrible plain in the Texas desert.

"I get it, hoss. You had your hopes up. I don't blame you none. But"—he raised a boney index finger, his long age-yellowed nail broken and cracked—"you got to get your mind right, hoss. You can't keep this up. My patience isn't boundless, you know. You get me riled, there ain't no telling what I might do. *Capiche*?"

"Sure," Gavin said listlessly—anything to get on with it, to get Fry to focus his attention on someone else. *Kai? Kai, are you there?*

"Oh, he's here, spark. I got him back under control, thanks to your heads up about him being out." Fry grinned. "Did you think your thoughts were hidden from me? Really?"

Gavin closed his eyes and heard Fry straighten, then turn away.

"Bring out the undercard!" Fry bellowed. Gavin sagged against his bindings as the demon lifted him, chair and all, one handed and carried him toward the alter. "Cece! Bring them others over here so they can have front row seats." The woman sprinted toward the bonfire. "And, Cece?" She skidded to a halt and turned, her boots scraping in the loose scree of gravel and stones. "You done good, girl!"

Gavin opened his eyes in time to see her flush at the praise, and his rage-beast awakened again.

19

The ritual site near Odolavesta, TX ### *Saturday, 11:49 pm CST*

Toby could hardly be bothered to care when the blood-soaked bitch grabbed him by the arm and pulled him to his feet. His enervated gaze tracked across the ground, sliding over Benny's unmoving form, skittering across Shannon's slack face. He didn't care when she shoved him down next to Greg, slamming their heads together as she did so.

It seemed Greg couldn't be bothered to care, either.

Rolling his head back, Toby stared up into Gavin's sad eyes, almost without recognition. Beyond the FBI agent, the creep with the creamsicle eyes watched him, a smile crooking his lips.

20

Shannon came back to herself as she slammed into the ground, jostling someone as she came to rest on her side. Everything hurt—inside and out. It felt like she'd taken the world's greatest ass-kicking—one that extended far past the physical, far into the mental, even the spiritual.

She felt used up, wrung out. She felt sick, hot, and broken.

Beside her, Benny groaned.

21

Benny groaned but didn't dare move. Every inch of him felt sand-blasted, burnt-up, dead. Even his thoughts hurt him as they moved sluggishly around his brain.

All his thoughts were variations of the same thought, anyway.

Shannon is gone. Shannon is dead. Shannon is no more.

He didn't react to the thoughts as he once had, didn't cringe away, didn't break inside. He felt numb. Numb and dead.

"Benny?"

He realized someone had called his name several times. A woman. Wearily, he forced his eyelids to part, to retract.

Shannon leaned over him, concern for him etched in her face, and he squeezed his eyes shut, tears squirting out from the corners.

"Benny?"

It sounded like Shan, looked like her, but it had to be a trick. The cruelest trick.

Benny-bear? *What's wrong*? *What can I do*?

He opened his mouth to speak, but a woman screamed nearby, and his eyes flew open.

22

After Toby looked at him bleakly, without recognition, Gavin let his own head hang. He didn't know what to do, where to turn for help. Random noises sounded from all around him: the burble of the crowd of black-robed figures, a raving laughter from somewhere to his left, Fry's incessant babble as he spoke to his sons. There was no respite, no possible respite from Fry.

It would be better to be dead.

23

"Cece! Get them dames in here. Get 'em stripped off and set up. It's almost time!" Fry shouted.

She staggered through the crowd, exhaustion making her ears ring—or maybe the sound was only in her head—shoving people out of her way if they didn't move quick enough. Jon was…somewhere. Playing his guitar, no doubt.

She went to the blacked-out van, the one they'd bought from that strip club up in Dallas and pulled out two of the whores in their burlap bridesmaid dresses and shoved them toward the altar and their special fate. This time around, the crowd drew back as if scared to touch the women for fear their fates might be catching.

She shoved the first bitch, a short Mexican woman, into the Iron Maiden, and as the woman shrieked, she bumped one of the doors shut with her hip, then kicked the other closed and flipped the latch. The woman began to scream in earnest, and somehow, her cries augmented Jon's music.

The other one—a blonde bimbo with fake breasts—began to pull away, but Cece only had to show her the bloody knife to cow her. She pointed at the Scavenger's Daughter with her Bowie and shoved the bitch toward it. After she secured the device across the woman's back, Cece turned and went back to the van for the next two.

24

As the two women started screaming in earnest, as Cece Clark walked back toward the van with a smirk on her lips, Gavin lost it. Snarling, he struggled against the ropes that bound him, a continuous stream of cursing dribbling from his lips, interrupted only when he needed to draw breath. He glanced down at Toby Burton. "*Do something, God dammit!*" he shrieked.

Toby only shrugged and shook his head.

An ice-cold hand dropped onto Gavin's shoulder—Fry's hand—but he didn't stop struggling. In fact, Fry's grip made him struggle harder—at least until those yellow nails dug into his skin with the power of a rattlesnake's fangs. "Cut that shit out, old hoss," Fry hissed in his ear. "The ritual's well under way, and I'll not have you *fuck it all up*!" With each of the last four words, he jerked Gavin savagely back into the chair's back, and each jerk felt like being rear-ended by an out-of-control big rig.

"Under way? You're just starting…" mumbled Gavin.

Fry chuckled. "No. The deaths of your rescuers were the hors-d'oeuvres. Poor Agent Hall was the amuse-bouche. These women are the appetizers."

"*Appetizers*?" Gavin snarled.

"Yeah, hoss. Appetizers." Fry chuckled. "After we're done makin' them scream, we'll offer them up, and if none of them suit, we'll partake of their flesh. Then, I'll prime the pump with Kai Washinton's soul—his body's out of reach, but you got to take what you can get." His gaze crawled toward Shannon. "I think that pretty one over there will win the prize, but who knows? Could be the husband, or this one." He jerked his chin toward Toby.

"The prize…" Gavin repeated dumbly.

Fry laughed, another brain-burning special, and every one present, and every animal or insect or bird out on the plain froze. "*Me*, spark! I'm the prize!" His laugh wound down. "Sort of. This… *All this*"—he stretched his arms wide—"is to bring my mate across."

"Bring her across?" Toby muttered. "You're trying to summon another demon?"

Fry pulled his chin back, frowning. "I'd hardly say that! You think I'm a *mere demon*, boy?" Toby didn't answer, and after a short eternity of Fry staring at the man, Fry shrugged. "But, yes, of course I have to summon my mate to this realm. Ain't you been paying attention? That's what all this is *for*!"

"Isn't the world evil enough for you?" demanded Gavin. "Aren't you enough? Isn't one devil enough?"

Fry threw back his head and laughed. "Oh, spark. Oh, you can be so funny! There's always been evil in the world, hoss. Always will be. All it takes to bring someone like me across is someone willing to pay the price. To bring more, all—"

"Someone willing to the pay the price!" yelled Toby, his voice rising over even the screams of the women being tortured.

Fry shot him an irritated look. "That's what I just say, boy. You hit your head in that car wreck or something? You ain't right *en la cabeza*." He turned his attention back to Gavin. "Like I was saying, there's always been evil. Always will be. Always been people like Westral and his daddy. Always will be. It's *easy* for my kind to come here, spark. Easy. Someone's always callin' out to us."

"Then you're just a…" murmured Toby, shaking his head. "You're a *mazzikim*? An *ifrit*? A *djinn*? What?"

Fry chuckled. "Me? Boy, you done lost your mind. Me and mine, we been here a long, long time. Way before all that Arabic nonsense. All them Mesopotamian religions are based on rumors of my kind, but they don't have no truth behind them." He glanced up at the sky, then turned and shouted, "Primo! Get the chant going, boy! What the hell's wrong with you?" He glared at the

Brethren assembled around them. "Well?" he thundered. "Didn't you hear me?"

Primo came jogging up, his eyes a little wide, then he turned to his flock and raised both hands.

25

The ritual site near Odolavesta, TX
Sunday, 12:01 am CST

Someone willing to pay the price. Someone willing to pay the price. Someone willing to pay the price. The phrase kept repeating in Toby's mind, an insane, internal chorus. *Someone willing to pay the price.*

As the big black man with the white satin sash came running up and started his flock chanting, Toby closed his eyes, riding his memories back, looking for the moment…

Lily turned and stared into his eyes. "I will go then. But I will come back one day. There is always someone willing to pay my price in exchange for my favors. Someone will call to me across the void. Someone will offer me a place here." She dropped her gaze and stood with her arms hanging at her sides. *"If…"*

Toby shook his head. Fry didn't know about Lily…about the *seraph*. He thought the *mazzikim*, the *djinn*, the *ifrit* were *creatures of myth*. He didn't know those myths were *real*. Creatures of power, different from Fry, but creatures of power, nonetheless.

The air thickened as the chant progressed, as the women's pain and terror mounted.

Toby's gaze snapped to Shannon, then to Benny, then up to Fry. "Hey!" He had to shout to be heard over the chanting, but eventually, the demon looked at him and cocked an eyebrow. "Why English?"

Fry chuckled. "The language don't matter, boy. It's the intent! How else do you think we hear your kind? Ain't a one of us come here speaking that monkey-talk!"

Toby nodded, returning his gaze to his lap, to his memories.

Lily dropped her gaze and stood with her arms hanging at her sides. "If…" She swallowed hard. "If you change your mind, there's a place you can go, Tobes. It's in New York, near Genosgwa. You needn't find it with precision, just being in the right area will suffice. It is near your friend's house." She gestured at Eddie and Amanda as she faded to translucence, her eyes growing wild. "Enter the circle and call to me, motek. *Ask me to come, and I will."*

He'd used that offer to find the place to break Lily's link to the world, to rescind her invitation—in essence, to offer a divorce between the *seraph* and humanity.

Doesn't that mean she can't *come back, even if she wants to?*

Ask me to come, and I will. Ask me to come, and I will.

Toby turned and found Benny leaning against Shannon, his head on her shoulder.

Benny quirked and eyebrow and asked, "What?"

"The circle, back in New York. Near Eddie's old house."

Benny's eyebrows bunched. *But we don't know who summoned this bastard. Or even when.*

"And we don't really have the time to ask on the SEMPRe app," Shannon said. "We can't pull the same trick—the spells, the lamp."

Toby shook his head. "Since we broke the bowl and all, is that circle still in play? Is it still important?"

Benny cocked his head. *I have no idea. Why?*

But Toby only shook his head and turned his face away.

Ask me to come, and I will. Ask me to come, and I will. Ask me to come, and I will. Ask me to come, and I will. Ask me to come, and I will.

26

The air seemed as laden with power, with hate and hard feelings, as it was with the shrieks of the women in the torture devices and the chants of the idiots who worshipped Fry and his sons. Gavin longed to plug his ears, to block out the chanting.

"*Great one! Hear us!*" Primo thundered, his voice rolling out across the desert as if amplified by a public address system turned all the way up.

"*COME!*" screamed the Brethren.

A toothy grin split Fry's face, and orange-white lightning split the sky.

"*Great one! Drink this blood we prepare in your honor! Eat this flesh we place on your altar!*" He waved at Cece, and she jerked the doors of the Iron Maiden open, spilling the Mexican woman to the sand, bleeding from twenty-seven puncture wounds, eyeless, sightless, screaming. Cece jerked the woman up by both arms and lifted her in a fireman's carry, only to throw her on the altar.

"*COME AND FEAST!*"

Primo grinned at Fry, then shouted, "*Great One! Consume the pain of these paltry women, partake in their suffering!*"

"*COME AND FEAST!*"

Beneath them the ground trembled and roiled like a stew pot of water at full boil, and fear ran Gavin down like a stampeding herd of buffalo. Clouds rolled in from every horizon, obscuring skies that were clear a heartbeat before. A hazy fog, like something off the Nile, rolled in, clinging low to the brush and dunes, coating the land like frosting on a cake.

Fry watched Primo, an expression of pride and limitless enjoyment decorating his face. He snapped his fingers at Cece, and she slit the Mexican's throat, then went to remove the blonde from the Scavenger's Daughter.

27

The ritual site near Odolavesta, TX
Sunday, 12:03 am CST

Toby watched Primo closely, not wanting to miss any secret, any phrase, or word of power, but the ritual was…almost pedestrian. He shook his head and glanced at Fry as the second woman was sacrificed, as the air thickened with her death-scream and the fine spray of blood flew from the Damascus Bowie the bloody woman in the black robe held in her fist.

Someone willing to pay the price. Ask me to come, and I will.

The sentences hammered at his mind. He screamed at the memories in his mind. *What is the price? Will you still come? Even now? Can you still come?*

But there were no answers.

"*Great One!*" shrieked Primo. "*We seek you out, Storm Darkness. We call upon your holy name, O Snake of the Desert! We invoke the ancient rites, the old covenant, Sea Dweller! Walk among us! Lend us your power! Come, Walker on the Wind!*"

"*COME, SHADOW!*" screamed the idiot cultists.

"Christ!" Gavin screamed into the sudden silence, and somewhere, in the back of the crowd, a man tittered like a drunk schoolgirl.

"*Come, Darkest Night! Come, Bringer of Chaos!*"

Toby's nostril's flared, and his eyes widened. *Someone willing to pay the price. Ask me to come, and I will. Someone willing to pay the price. Ask me to come, and I will.*

"*COME!*" thundered the Brethren.

The woman with the knife looked to Fry, and when he nodded, she went to the horse and began to untie the

478   ERIK HENRY VICK

woman's hands and feet, evoking yet more screams from the poor victim.

"Stop! *Stop it*!" cried Gavin as he frantically tried to extricate himself from the ropes, and Fry narrowed his eyes at the agent. The woman with the knife put another victim on the altar and slit her throat.

I've got to do something, Toby thought.

"*Veni, tenebris noctis! Veni, lator chaos! Veni, tempestatum lator! Age, amator noctis! Veni, ambulator cum vento! Age, serpens magne de eremo!*" cried Primo, and Fry grimaced at him.

Someone willing to pay the price. Someone willing to pay the price. Someone willing to pay the price. Ask me to come, and I will.

"Latin?" Fry sneered. "I done told you, son, the *language don't matter*. Anyway, I never learned it."

Ask me to come, and I will. Someone willing to pay the price. Someone willing to pay the price. Someone willing to pay the price.

Primo nodded once, a glimmer of rebellion in his eyes for a split second, but then he repeated the chant in English: "Come, Dark Night! Come, Bearer of Chaos! Come, Bearer of Storms! Come, Lover of the Night! Come, Walker on the Wind! Come, you great Serpent from the Desert!"

Ask me to come, and I will. Someone willing to pay the price.

Lightning danced around them, bolts of it racing from the horizon toward them, then veering off at the last second. Orange bolts, pale blue, purple-white, orange again.

Someone willing to pay the price. Ask me to come, and I will.

"Come, Dark night! Come, Bearer of Chaos!" screamed Primo.

Ask me to come, and I will. Someone willing to pay the price. Ask me to come, and I will. Someone willing to pay the price. Toby made his decision. "I'm willing," he murmured.

Fry's gaze snapped around toward him, his eyes narrowed, but Toby didn't care.

The blood-soaked priestess dropped another victim on the altar and raised her knife.

"No!" called Fry. "Use this one!" He pointed at Shannon.

Beside him, Benny gasped and turned to him in horror. "No!" he cried. "You can't!"

"I'm willing!" Toby shouted, pushing himself to his feet.

The priestess hurled the woman, broken on the horse, to the sand and stomped toward Shannon.

In the distance, Toby heard the dissonant song of the desert on the rising wind. The song Lily had hummed in his ear. "*Come, Daughter of Night! Come, Sister to Wind and Storm! I'm willing!*" he cried, his voice rising to rival Primo's.

"*NO!*" Fry thundered. "*You'll ruin everything!*"

"*COME, SEDUCTION! COME, DESOLATION!*" Toby didn't know where the words were coming from, he only knew they sounded right. *Felt* right.

"*God-monkey-shittin-dammit, you nutcake! I said to STOP!*" Fry took a step toward Toby, but Gavin flung himself, chair and all, into Fry's legs, knocking them both ass-over-teakettle, and the demon roared like all the devil himself, while Toby ducked away.

Primo frowned down at Fry and Gavin, then cut his eyes toward Toby, then back. He stepped toward Fry and grabbed Gavin's chair with one hand, flinging him up and over Toby's head, toward the ring of worshippers. "Kill him!"

"Do *not* kill him! I want that boy alive!" Fry yelled as Gavin came crashing to the ground, the chair shattering beneath him at last.

He untangled the ropes and sprang to his feet.

"*COME, MOTHER CHAOS! COME, HARVESTER OF SORROW! COME, LILITU! I'LL PAY, LILY! I'M ASKING!*" screamed Toby.

"*NOOOOOO!*" thundered Fry, whirling to face the altar. "*COME, APEP! COME, NOW! DAMMIT COME TO ME!*"

The air above the altar shuddered, turned smoky, and the smoke roiled and bubbled. Fry pushed himself up and ran to the altar, staring at the smoke. Above him, the air turned in a vicious circle, spinning, spinning, and in the circle surrounding them all, people started to drop, dead before they hit the ground, their souls sucked upward, sucked into the conflagration about the altar, streaks of white and black and every color in between.

"Something's gone screwy!" Fry whirled, his eyes so bright it was death to look upon them. "*WHERE IS HE?*" he thundered, and many of Primo's flock turned to flee. Cece Clark didn't though. She came to Fry's side and raised her hand to point at Toby. Fry's deadly gaze fastened on him, and he lifted his foot…

But before he could take even a single step, someone grabbed Toby from behind and spun him around. Mike leaned close, Glacadairanam staring out of his eyes, and he grabbed Toby by the throat. "*You will stop now!*" he hissed.

Gavin ran forward and hammered on Mike's arm, and Glacadairanam narrowed his eyes, then slammed Mike's fist into his temple backhand, and Gavin went sprawling.

But Toby only smiled, looking over Mike's shoulder. Behind him, a thing of velvet darkness stood, and his smile widened. The thing had blacker than black eyes and long chrome claws and was made of black smoke and shadows and unseen, unfelt wind, a thing of chaotic form, constantly shifting, constantly changing. "Hello, Tobes," she said.

Glacadairanam squeezed his throat, twisting Mike's head around to look upon Lilitu, daughter of sky, sister to night and wind, and everything ground to a halt.

28

Another desert
Sunday, 12:03 am CST

"*Ay, que chulo,*" she breathed in his ear, and it was as if someone had dropped a live wire in the pleasure centers of his brain.

Toby cried out in ecstasy, singing her name at the top of his lungs, "*LILITU!*"

"Just Lily, Tobes. I like it when you call me that."

He spun around to drink her in, her cherry-red hair, her elfin face, beautiful red lips, then his gaze dropped lower, to her perfect breasts, across the pale expanse of her belly, then down to her sex, and he gasped.

"Oh, Toby Burton, you say the *sweetest* things," she breathed in a voice that was like pure, liquid sex dribbled into his soul.

From far off in the distance, something started to screech and scream. Lily glanced in the direction of the scream, then shrugged.

"You came!"

"I told you I would, didn't I?"

"But we—"

"We needn't speak of it ever again, *cazador*." The scream mounted, shifting up the registers, sounding like a hunting cat's squall.

Toby shivered. "What *is* that."

"Pay him no mind, Toby. He can't hurt you. Not with me by your side."

"I didn't know if you could hear me. I didn't know if you *would* hear me, and even if you did, if you would…" He hung his head, gulping back sudden tears.

"Forgive you, Tobycakes? If it were anyone else, I wouldn't, but I told you before: you are special."

"So are you, Lily," he sobbed. "I've been so…" He shivered as a particularly long, a particularly rage-filled screech broke the night.

"Lonely? Heartbroken? Me, too, *motek*. Me, too." She pulled him closer and wrapped him in a hug, kissing him hard. When it was over, he could barely stand, and she wore a cat-that-ate-the-canary grin. "You still like me," she said looking at his groin.

"Oh, Lily… I… I…" His gaze darted toward the thing shrieking in the darkness.

484   ERIK HENRY VICK

Lily chopped her hand through the air, and the thing's screech cut off with a squeal. "You what, *kisa*?"

"I love you, Lily. I do. I know you mesmerized me back then, but it's been years, and I've had time to think about…about…*everything*, and I was already in love with you when you did it, when you sang in my ear, it was already too late, I just hadn't admitted it."

She patted his cheek and ran her nails down his cheek. She dropped her chin so that her cherry-licorice colored hair hung in front of her face, but he knew she was smiling. "I love you, too, Tobycakes. We're going to walk through time together, your king to my queen, and all will fall to their knees. Let me take you home, let me elevate you to the *seraphim*, let me—"

"Yes, yes, and more yes, but first…"

She nodded, a knowing grin on her face. "But first you have a little demon problem. The one riding your friend and trying to squeeze your head off."

"Him? Yeah, but there's a bigger one, a stronger one. He goes by the name—"

"I saw him, *neshama*. He's not one of my kind, but you already sussed that out."

Toby nodded. "Can you…"

"Can I kick his ass? You bet I can, *habibi*." She turned and walked toward the moon for a few steps. "But, first…" she said in a tone that mimicked his from a moment before. Her smile seemed to light the entire universe from within.

"There's a price," said Toby in a voice that shook.

"Yes," she crooned, "but you're willing to pay."

Toby swallowed hard but nodded. "I am, but there's one thing we have to agree on…"

29

The ritual site near Odolavesta, TX
Sunday, 12:03 am CST

Glacadairanam squeezed, though it looked like it took considerable effort to get Mike's body to squeeze Toby's throat. Behind him, a thing of black smoke and shadows swirled, dancing on an unseen, unfelt wind, long chrome claws clicking and clicking together as her rage built, orange whirly-gig eyes spinning and spinning. "Look away, Tobes," she rasped, and he did, but not before he saw them dim to black, not before he saw the images, the worst humanity had to offer spinning there, the rape, the murder, the war, the lies, torture like what Cece Clark's victims had experienced before their turn on the altar. He shuddered, suddenly very, very cold, suddenly afraid of the creature of shadow.

"Get your hand off him," she rasped. "One chance, half-breed."

Mike's lips twisted in a sneer, and at the same moment, Primo took a step forward. He only made it one step. Lily raised her eyes, and there was a flash and a pop, smoke curling from the space where Primo's eyes had been a moment before, and his huge, matte black form crumpled to the ground.

A wail of fury came from behind Toby, and with the sound of a freight train crashing into a bumper block, Fry bolted to Primo's fallen form. Blue fire crackled in the air, dancing from his nose, the tips of his ears, his lips, his chin. He stared down at Primo, fists clenched. "*WHAT HAVE YOU DONE?*" he thundered.

"Not impressed," crooned Lily. "Is someone trying to make up for a grievous lack below the belt buckle?"

Mike's tendons creaked, and Toby choked, gasping for air, and Lily's voice lost its mocking edge. "I *warned* you," she said in a voice that rang flat in the night air.

"Don't you *dare*!" Fry shouted.

Lily shrugged and sucked Glacadairanam's soul out of Mike with a slurping pop. Mike gasped and dropped his hand away from Toby's throat as if his skin were scalding hot, staggering back a step.

Behind him, the tornado of souls spun on, growing larger, sucking the life out of more and more of Primo's followers, even as they turned and sprinted for the open desert.

Greg leaped up and shouted, "Yes!"

"*NO!*" screamed Fry at the same moment. Behind him, Cece took two running steps, but Lily's gaze snapped to hers, and Cece froze, mid-step. Fry threw his head back and screamed at the heavens, pure rage thundering into the infinite void. "*Who the fuck are you, you malignant bitch?* I want your name before you die!"

Lily chuckled and quirked her smoky face into a semblance of a half-smile. "I am Lilitu," she said, "daughter of sky, sister to night and wind. The Akkadians called me the Hand of Inanna, others, the Irritant of Asherah. I am the Spirit in the Tree, the Anzû bird, queen of disease and pestilence. I am the bane of betrayers, I am Ardat Lili. I am seduction personified, desolation deified, disease canonized, and chaos comes when I call." She tilted her head to the side. "Who the fuck are you, *montro?*"

"What? *What? Who am I?*" Fry sputtered, tongue dancing in his mouth, spittle flying. "I am…I am…*I am Fry!*" he shouted exultantly. "I am the Whore of Babylon; I am the Beast! I am…Shaytan! I am…Furfur, Earl of Hell! I am…" His brow furrowed. "I've never been good with names, dammit! I am Frankie Evil Eye! I am *Nun'Yunu'Wi!* I am—"

"*BA-PEF*!" a voice rumbled from the very air itself, a voice so low, it was more felt than heard. "Ba-Pef, why have you brought me to this place? Who are these…*creatures*? Why am I not greeted with a feast?"

Though Toby didn't think it was possible for Fry to get any paler, he did. "Apep…Apep…I—"

"Who is this that stands before me with the dregs of your half-breed son on her lips?"

"Oh Jesus…not again," Lily said with a smile and a secret wink at Toby. "Can you two just exchange notes? I'm tired of saying it."

"Why is there no vessel ready, Ba-Pef? What sorry state have you left me in? Why have you left the ritual incomplete? Why have you only half-summoned me? What do you wish to gain from this treachery?"

"It ain't treachery!" Fry shouted, tongue dancing as fast as he could make it go. "These pains-in-the-ass interrupted the ritual! They run off most of my worshippers!" He raised his hand and pointed at Lily. "This one ate *both* my sons! I had planned an array of forms for you to choose from—"

"*THEN PROVIDE THEM, AND I WILL MAKE MY CHOICE*!" A ghastly image formed in the funnel cloud swirling over the altar, an image of an immense golden serpent, winged like Quetzalcoatl, seeming to stretch for eternity. Behind that image, a colossal ebony crocodile loomed.

Fry winced. "Apep, they have ruined everything!"

"Then I go." The images in the tornado of souls began to fade.

"No! No, don't do that!" cried Fry. He lurched into motion, grabbing Shannon by the wrist and jerking her to her feet, pushing her forward a step. "Take this one!"

"Interesting," said Apep, king-sized glowing eyes flashing. "She is…interesting."

"Take her! Or one of these naked men!"

"Perhaps I will take her." The translucent golden snake was back, and its huge feather wings beat twice, sending it slicing through the air, more sliding than flying.

"Lily!" Toby cried.

"Don't worry, *chico mio*," she said.

"But our deal—"

"Yes, I recall it. *Don't worry.*" Lily moved to stand next to Shannon. "These humans are mine," she said. She cocked her head at Fry and quirked her eyebrow. "Do you dispute my claim?"

"I saw 'em first!"

Lily chuckled deep in her throat. "No, you didn't. My claim goes back to 1979."

Fry sneered. "So what? They're mine *now*."

Apep slid forward, golden-hued snake eyes fixed on Lily's black form. "We shouldn't fight. I sense a…*similarity* between us."

"I sense that you will bow before me."

Apep laughed, a monstrous sound that spoke of death and ruin and entire civilizations laid waste. "I don't think so."

Lily shrugged and lifted a languid hand, beckoning toward the bonfire. Two beings stepped from the conflagration, one composed of crimson fire, the other of golden flame.

"Toby…" said Benny.

"Relax. We made a deal."

"Uh…a deal?" he whispered.

"Hello, Naamah dear," Lily said to the crimson *ifrit*. When the golden one bowed to her, she said, "Hello, Abyzou. Say hello to Apep and Ba-Pef. They're assholes, and we hate them."

"Oh, shit…" murmured Shannon.

"A mistake," said Apep. "Why would you choose these mortals over your own kind."

Lily shook her head. "There's your mistake. You're not my kind."

Toby started backing away. "Get Gavin," he said to Shannon. "Greg? Mike? Are you alright to run?"

"Uh…" Mike shook his head. "I… What happened? How did we get here?"

"I'll explain later," said Toby.

Shannon pulled Gavin up, his head lolling to the side, and ducked under his arm. "Help me, Benny." She darted a at glance at the demons. "All hell's about to break loose."

"You don't know the half of it," said Cece Clark as she stepped out of the darkness, Bowie gleaming, and swiped the blade at Shannon.

Benny cried out, snapping out with his mind and knocking the blade up and away.

For a moment, Cece stood frozen, watching the knife spin through the air.

"Apep! Not her!" cried Fry, and then the golden snake lunged out of the darkness and disappeared into Cece's back. Her body gave a titanic clonic jerk, bending forward at the waist, hands thrown forward, one knee coming up. Her eyes rolled back in her head, and she fell, going tonic when she hit the sand, arching her back hard enough that her vertebrae crackled the length of her spine. "Dadgummit! She was one of my best!"

Gavin, Toby, Shannon, Benny, Greg, and Mike backed away from the woman as she slipped back and forth between clonic and tonic states as though being possessed by Apep might be catching.

Abyzou appeared beside them, the blazing heat of her body stunning in the cool of the desert night. "*Run, you fools!*" she snapped, and then they were, sprinting into the darkness in a blind panic, dodging what Brethren remained, looking for a vehicle or a place to hide.

A shrill wind blew past them toward the altar, seeming to suck all the air out of the world.

"There!" Mike said, pointing at an SUV with all the doors open. "Look for keys!"

"We should help," said Benny.

"Easy for you say. We don't have guns. No darts. No shotguns. It would be you and Greg, trying to cover us all, and Shannon trying to make us all invisible."

"We'd be destroyed," said Toby in a reasonable voice. He lunged into the driver's seat and flipped down the visors, grimacing when no keys fell into the seats.

"But if we leave, Lilitu and Brigitta and Aby will—"

"I made a deal with Lily. It'll be fine."

"Toby—"

"We don't have *time* for this, Benny! Now, help me find the goddamn keys!"

30

The ritual site near Odolavesta, TX
Sunday, 12:12 am CST

Naamah shrieked and clawed at Ba-Pef's eyes, and he reeled away from her, swiping back at her with his long, cracked fingernails, hitting only air as she disappeared with a pop. "Settle down! Just settle down and let's palaver!" he cried. He spun in a circle, looking for the glowing vermillion thing, but Lily stood behind him, flickering like a strobe in a bad horror movie, her eyes glowing black and black and black. She slashed at his throat, her chrome claws doubling in length as the blow came, and Fry barely snapped his head far enough out of the way to avoid being decapitated.

Not far enough, however, to avoid having his throat opened to the night sky. His midnight-blood sprayed into the blue-black sky, and he couldn't even scream or howl in rage.

Not without a larynx.

31

The ritual site near Odolavesta, TX
Sunday, 12:12 am CST

Abyzou slapped Apep, clawing her cheek as an afterthought. Apep opened her eyes wide as Abyzou backed away, circling to the left. Her gaze caught on Apep's, and the sudden urge to curl up and go to sleep struck her. She staggered a step, and the other demon laughed.

Wind roared around them, and lightning struck between them. Hail stones the size of grapefruit hurled down from the sky, but none of them struck Apep—they seemed aimed at Abyzou, and she reeled away, seeking shelter from the storm.

Apep jeered and made to follow her into the darkness but hadn't made it five steps when she heard a pop and scalding crimson arms encircled her chest. Abyzou streaked back, golden flames scalding Apep's vision, and she roared so loud the earth shook beneath their feet.

32

Parking at the ritual site near Odolavesta, TX
Sunday, 12:12 am CST

A storm appeared out of nowhere, massive hailstones rattling off the SUV's roof, and they all crowded into the car, Toby in the driver's seat, Benny riding shotgun, Mike behind him, Gavin behind Toby, Shannon in the middle, and Greg in the back. "Keys!" shouted Toby. "We need the damn keys!"

Back toward the bonfire, figures leaped and danced, disappeared, reappeared somewhere else. A resounding roar shook the ground, rattling junk around inside the SUV.

"Holy shit," said Benny as he rooted through the glove box.

"Can they win?" Mike asked. "Toby, can she win?"

"I…" Toby shook his head. "She says she can. I hope so."

In the back seat, Shannon gave Mike a look.

"You all fucked everything up," said a flat, atonal voice from the darkness. "We were almost there…" A man with a guitar hanging at his side stepped closer, and a jagged bolt of blue-green lightning lit up his face.

"Idiot," snapped Mike. "They were going to eat you. It's what they—"

"Liar!" The man shouted the words so loud his voice broke. He glanced down at the guitar and flung it away. "*I can't hear it anymore*! Cece is—"

"She's gone," said Benny in a quiet voice. "Your wife. I'm…I'm sorry. Apep…" He shook his head. "She didn't suffer. There was no time."

Jon Clark's shoulders slumped, and he stood sobbing in the rain for a moment, appearing broken, crushed by his loss, but then he lifted his gaze and met Toby's, and his face was filled with rage. "*You did this!*" he shouted.

33

In the desert near Odolavesta, TX
Sunday, 12:14 am CST

Fry ran, both hands pressing into the gaping maw where his throat had once lived. As he ran, he summoned azure flame behind him. *Not that it'll hurt one of those goddamn-monkey-shittin'* ifrits, he thought sourly. He didn't dare glance behind him, if he did, he couldn't keep his wound closed, and though Ba-Pef was immortal, his body *wasn't*, and he didn't have a spare lined up.

34

The ritual site near Odolavesta, TX
Sunday, 12:14 am CST

Lily let Ba-Pef run off, chuckling to herself. *One down*, she thought, then she turned, saw her daughter and her maid fighting Apep, and joined them in a pop of desert air.

Naamah and Abyzou adjusted their stances, dividing the wary circle they'd made around Apep into three instead of two. When Apep hugged the darkness to herself, seeming to call it out of the night itself, Lily laughed and summoned her own dark shadows to hide in.

Naamah darted forward, a crimson arc in the dark illuminating the desert for yards around. As Apep turned Naamah's attack, Abyzou lunged forward and raked claws made of sunlit flame down her back. Apep shrieked, turning inside out as she did so, then did it again, this time facing Abyzou, and she lashed out with midnight-purple power that scoured the golden *ifrit* and knocked her asprawl. "You think *you* can flay me with golden flames when Ra himself could not? I shall teach you, waif, what—"

Lily danced forward, aiming her long chrome claws at the neck but misjudging and raking the flesh away from Apep's upper shoulders. She shrieked in anger and spun away to avoid another outpouring of primordial magic from Apep.

35

"*You did this*!" Jon Clark shouted and raised the pistol he'd kept hidden by his side. He pulled the trigger three times, the report booming in time with the thunderstorm's outbursts. Two of the rounds flew wide—one struck the A-pillar, the other missed altogether, flying high.

Gavin charged from the SUV, thinking they got lucky, that the rounds had missed, then leaping on Clark and knocking the pistol into the stormy night. He swept the man's legs and fell on top of him, weaving his arms through Clark's and wrenching them back.

He darted a look over his shoulder and saw the blood. "Shit! How bad?"

36

The ritual site near Odolavesta, TX
Sunday, 12:16 am CST

Raisin-colored light flashed at Lily's eyes, and she ducked away, weaving and bobbing like a master boxer. She slashed with her claws, then teleported behind Apep and kneed her in the back, driving her toward Naamah, who channeled a great gout of cerise fire. Abyzou raced in from the side, preferring physical contact to magical combat, as always.

Apep thundered at them, shaking the ground in her fury, showering dark magic on their heads, and calling to the storm above.

37

Parking at the ritual site near Odolavesta, TX
Sunday, 12:16 am CST

"How bad?" Gavin asked.

"Toby?" asked Mike. "Are you…"

"He's hit," said Benny. "There's blood all over me!"

Mike sprang from the rear passenger seat and raced around to the driver's side, while Gavin ripped off his belt and cinched it tight around Clark's wrists. The man was sobbing in earnest now and muttering his wife's name, but Gavin felt no pity for him—though a tiny part of him understood the man's impulse.

By the time he got to the vehicle, Mike had Toby lying back in the driver's seat and had his hand pressed to Toby's chest. "Christ," he muttered. "Find those goddamn keys, Benny!"

Shannon was jammed forward between the seats, one arm supporting Toby's head, the other holding herself up. She held her ear to Toby's lips, then shook her head, tears racing down her cheeks. "No. I'm not going to tell them that!"

"What?" asked Gavin, but Shannon only shook her head and cried harder.

Benny slumped in the passenger seat. "He said it's too late for the keys."

"No, it isn't!" Shannon snapped. "No, it isn't!"

Mike closed his eyes.

"He wants me to call *her*."

"Don't you do it, Benny Cartwright!" Shannon's face had turned ugly in her grief, tears and mucus mixing on her cheeks.

"I already did," said Greg in a numb voice.

38

Lily drove Apep backward, drove her down, and landed atop her, driving her claws into the woman's neck and chest. Apep shrieked as her body's blood spurted out around Lily's claws, but she kept struggling, kept raining chaos down on them from the night sky, but Lily needed no shield from chaos, and she grinned into Apep's stolen face.

Naamah was capable of deflecting it away from Abyzou and herself, and the pair huddled close by, waiting for the *coup de grâce.* Lily ground her claws into the mortal body of the other demon, twisting, tearing, ripping at everything in their path. Apep called down lightning, and Lily smiled. Apep hurled hatred and midnight-colored chaos at her, and still, Lily smiled and put all her strength behind her claws.

But then, she sat up and frowned.

A bolt of pure fear raced across the face of Lilitu, daughter of sky, sister to night and wind, and she cried out, startling both Naamah and Abyzou. Without a second thought, she yelled, "With me!" and disappeared.

Naamah glanced at Abyzou, and then they both disappeared.

Apep groaned, and as the blood drained away from the chosen vessel, she abandoned it and swam through the air toward the altar as insubstantial as a ghost.

39

Parking at the ritual site near Odolavesta, TX
Sunday, 12:18 am CST

"Stand aside!" Lily commanded.

"You stay away!" shouted Shannon. "You've done enough to him!"

Lily's guttural growl was her only answer, and though she raised her hand, she glanced at the vehicle, then lowered it again.

"Destroy this bitch, Mother."

"No," said Lily softly. "I made a bargain."

"Then let me!"

Lily shook her head again. "No, I made a bargain."

"Shannon," called Benny softly. "Toby says it's what he wants. He says…" He choked up. "He says he wants her by his side when—" His voice died in a squeak of grief.

"But…" Shannon threw up her hands. "She *mesmerized* him in that desert!"

"We know that, Shannon," said Mike in a horrible, flat voice.

"He's knows that, too," said Gavin. "He said as much at the motel."

"You shut up!" snapped Shannon.

"Shan," said Benny with a hint of reproach in his voice, and Shannon hung her head and sobbed.

"It's okay," said Gavin.

"I can help," said Lily in a slow, careful tone as if the words might hurt her. "I can…"

"She could go around you, Shannon," said Greg. "Or *through* you. You know that. But she isn't."

"I made a bargain," Lily murmured with a shrug.

Shannon shook her head, and more tears fell.

"Let me go to him, Shannon. Puh-please," said Mother Chaos, and behind her, her daughter and maid exchanged a glance. "I luh… Toby is special to me. I can help him."

"Shannon, Toby says…" Benny's jaw worked, and he swallowed hard. "He says he's dying, Shan, and he wants to be in Lilitu's—*Lily's*—arms when he does. He said he loved her before she sang to him in the desert. He…" Benny shook his head and dashed the tears from his cheeks. "He asked me to say 'please.'"

"Can you *save* him?" Shannon demanded of Mother Chaos.

Slowly, Lily raised one of her black-smoke shoulders and let it drop. "I can."

"And leave him human?"

Lily looked her in the eye. "I can try."

With a fresh spate of loud sobbing, Shannon stood aside.

As Lily approached the car, parts of her shadowy, wind-swept body solidified, shrank, and paled and paled and paled. In other places, black smoke became black leather and candy-red hair and lips. Her eyes warmed, turned orange, and began to spin like whirly-gigs. She smiled at Mike and gently guided him away. She looked at Toby, and a single chrome tear formed in the corner of her eye.

Then she glanced at Benny. "Get out, please" she said. She turned her gaze back on Toby's face and her lips parted just enough to allow air to pass between them, to allow a jangly, wrong-sounding melody to slip into the night like a viper. The night darkened, the air grew thick and warm and wet like fresh blood, then blazed as hot as the deepest desert ergs where sand devils thrived and no mere man dared move to the music of the wind, lest Lilitu pay him a call and find him wanting.

He hesitated for a fraction of a second, then slid out and came around to stand with the rest, putting his arm around his wife's shoulder, crying softly into her hair while she hugged him tight. Mike and Greg stood beside them holding hands, staring at the beautiful woman seeing to their friend.

Chapter 12
A Tangled Web

I

For a moment, Gavin stood between Benny, Shannon, Greg, and Mike, and two women built entirely from colored flame, listening to the soft, eerie threnody coming from the SUV. Lily paused every now and again to speak in soft, hushed tones, her words just past the edges of his hearing, but the tone was one he'd expect—and, in fact, had heard a week earlier—from Maddie if she were caring for him in a hospital bed. He turned away when he realized the woman would save Toby or he was beyond saving.

Three steps took him to the side of the golden *ifrit*, and he stopped there, gazing back at the ritual site, his gaze jumping from shadow to shadow, his shoulders twitching with each new sound. "Is it over?" he asked in a soft voice.

The *ifrit* turned her head a little and quirked an eyebrow made of golden flame. "Define over."

Gavin glanced at her tone, annoyance dancing on his features. "Fry dead. Apep dead. Humanity safe."

Scoffing, Abyzou turned her head away. "Where's Eddie?" she asked no one. "Where's Amanda?"

Naamah raised a scarlet arm and pointed at Benny. "I don't know, but I recognize that one. Perhaps there will be time to take my revenge before first light"

"Naamah, Abyzou!" snapped Lily from the vehicle. "No more! I made a bargain, and if you can't abide by it, you will *depart*."

Naamah rolled her eyes, but Abyzou sighed and turned to Gavin. "*Ba-Pef*, I can't speak to. Mother Chaos dispatched Apep's vessel, and the serpent returned to its vortex. Humanity will never be safe, not from us, not from yourselves." She cocked an eyebrow in challenge. "Does that satisfy your curiosity?"

Gavin frowned and turned back toward the vehicle. "Is Fry—*Ba-Pef*—dead?" he asked again.

Naamah shrugged. "Mother dealt with him."

Frown deepening, Gavin strode toward the vehicle. He stopped next to Mike. "Is he…"

Mike shook his head and shrugged. "Your guess is as good as mine."

"I need to ask her a question."

"Leave her be," muttered Shannon.

"Fry said…" Gavin squeezed his eyes shut. "He threatened Maddie. He said he could be there by morning. I… I have to know if he's still out there."

Mike pinched the bridge of his nose and sighed. "Will it never end?" he muttered, and Greg squeezed his hand. "Lily? Is Fry dead?"

"I'm busy here," she said over her shoulder using the same soft voice she'd been using with Toby.

"It's important," Gavin said.

She turned a cross gaze on him, but he didn't look away. "Possibly. Probably his vessel succumbed."

Gavin squeezed his eyes shut.

"Relax," she said. "You are safe among us."

"It's not that," said Benny. "Fry threatened his wife. We need to know if—"

"Abyzou! Take him to his wife."

"Why, I'd be *delighted*."

Lily turned and leaned out of the car to pin the golden *ifrit* with a stare. "Recall my words. You are to do *nothing*, to take no sustenance, until we've had a chance to discuss the new rules. Break my promise and risk your tenure here."

The crimson *ifrit* stomped her foot. "Mother! What did you commit us to?"

"Naamah…" Lily said with a sigh and turned back to Toby. "I need peace."

Cocking her scarlet head, Naamah said, "I doubt you'll get it." She nodded to the east. "Sirens."

Gavin's anxious gaze found Mike's. "I can't deal with Bud. I've got to get home."

"Go," Mike said. "We'll handle it." He nodded his head toward Shannon. "Aby, take them to the house on Lake Erie where we…fought you."

For a moment, Abyzou's eyes blazed so bright that Gavin was worried, but then she glanced his way and snapped her fingers and—

2

1289 Welcrest Drive, Minnieville, VA
Sunday, 1:29 am EST

They arrived in the kitchen with the soft pop of displaced air. Gavin looked at Abyzou and started. The fiery body of the *ifrit* was gone, replaced by a raven-haired, dusky-skinned woman wearing a black leather dress and no shoes. Her eyes were arresting—bright blue, and like Lily's, they seemed to spin, to cast sparks. She smiled at his inspection and ran a finger down her cheek.

"You like?"

Gavin frowned at her. "Is he here?"

"Who?"

"You know who!" he snapped.

Abyzou shrugged, then shook her head. "Just a woman in that hall." She raised a perfect finger tipped with a perfectly lacquered black nail and pointed at the hall that led to the bedroom he shared with Maddie.

"Gavin?" A shotgun slide punctuated the question.

"Yes, Maddie. It's me, and we have a guest."

Maddie sniffed. "A guest you invited?"

"Yes."

Maddie padded into the kitchen, thumbing the safety on the Mossberg 500. She stopped and did a double take when she saw the *ifrit*. "Uh…"

"Hi," said Abyzou. "I'm Aby."

"Maddie." She leaned the shotgun in the corner of the cabinets and gave Gavin a quizzical look.

"Long story," he said. "Maddie, I need you to listen and not interrupt."

"Yes, sir!" she said, throwing a mocking salute at him.

"It's important, and there's no time. I need you to get dressed and to pack what you need for a little while. Also, anything you can't stand to lose."

"Uh…"

"This is the part where you don't interrupt, where you don't argue."

She frowned at him but didn't say anything.

"Fry is still out there. He's made certain threats." He glanced around the kitchen and sighed. "We can't stay here. Not anymore."

"Gav, if you think—"

"Dammit, Mads! He might be on his way right now!"

She took half a step back, her gaze zipping toward Abyzou, then back. "Uh…"

Gavin took a deep breath, forcing serenity into his brain, into his veins. "Fry said if I didn't do what he wanted—"

"I'm going to guess that you didn't do that."

"Categorically not," said Gavin. "Though I didn't have much to do with it."

"Ah," she said, then turned and walked toward the bedroom. "How long?" she called.

"A few days or a week. Maybe more. We'll be able to come back…at least to move out."

"Uh, okay. Pete and Gloria?"

"Know nothing yet."

"Can you at least let me know where we'll be staying?"

"Up near Lake Erie. With friends."

"Um. Sure, okay."

Abyzou turned a thousand-watt grin on him. "You're in a shitload of trouble, 'Gav.'"

Gavin heaved a sigh. "As long as she's alive, I don't care."

Aby's snarky grin lost a few watts. "Go help her. I don't have all night."

3

*Parking at the ritual site near Odolavesta, TX
Sunday, 12:42 am CST*

Mike and Greg stood shoulder to shoulder, each wrapped in silvery thermal blanket, each holding a cup of horrible coffee. Bud MacArthur stood facing them, his gaze flicking back and forth between them, and though Greg was naked under his thermal blanket, the ranger didn't see that—in fact, he didn't see Greg at all, he saw Gavin Gregory, as did everyone else except for Benny, Shannon, and the demon that stood with them wearing the guise of a blonde supermodel in a fifteen-thousand-dollar dress.

Lily had insisted on wearing the visage of probably the sexiest paramedic the world had ever seen, and the old SUV they were in had become an ambulance. Neither Bud nor any of the other first responders seemed to notice that an ambulance had beaten them all to the scene.

Bud MacArthur shook his head, his gaze shifting back and forth between the two men. "There's something you're not telling me, Michaels."

Raising his cup of coffee as if in surrender, Mike shook his head. "No there isn't, Bud." He pointed at the ritual site with his cup. "I was out here because I followed Marcus Wallace. He had Dr. Withers in the back of his car—"

"And we're to take him at his word, is that it?" Bud sniffed and narrowed his eyes.

Mike widened his eyes. "Should we disbelieve him? He's one of the victims."

"I guess," said Bud, dropping his gaze to the sand beneath his feet. "There are a lot of bodies out here, Agent Michaels."

"Yes, there are. Most of them, though, are dirtbag cultists who tortured those women—not to mention murdering Agent Hall in cold blood—"

"Yeah, about that."

Mike lifted an eyebrow.

"We haven't found any giant Bowies, fancied up or plain jane. You sure y'all got that part right?" He cocked his head to the side and squinted at Mike, then turned his gaze on Greg.

"Yes. It was the murdered woman who's covered in blood, the one with the red sash. She... I don't know what her malfunction was. Her husband is the one who shot Dr. Withers," said Greg.

"So y'all both have said." The ranger scratched something on his pad, but to Mike's practiced eye, it looked like the kind of chicken-scratch he, himself, might have made to mess with a suspect's mind a little.

"Look, Bud, I know it's…" He shook his head and sighed. "It's far-fetched, is what it is. There's no getting around it. It's also what happened."

Bud sighed and nodded, then looked up at Mike. "Tell me again about all them dead cultists."

"It must have been some kind of suicide cult," said Mike. "That's all I can figure."

"And they had them a big ol' ritual to carry 'em over to the other side?"

Mike shrugged again, shaking his head. "Yeah, you got me on that part, Bud. All I know is we followed Wallace to this parking area, saw him pull Dr. Withers out of the back of his car, all tied up like a Christmas turkey, and haul him through the crowd toward that altar. The women were already in those…those torture machines, and the Clark woman was riding herd on them."

"Uh-huh."

"We identified ourselves to Wallace, ordered him to stop, to hit the dirt, and tried to get Dr. Withers out of there. That's when the people started keeling over."

"Including that big black fella."

"Right."

"And Red Westral?"

Mike grimaced. "We didn't see him until after he delivered the threats against both Dr. Withers and Agent Gregory's family."

Bud heaved a sigh. "His story is…"

"Demons, Bud? I think it's plain he's lost the plot."

"If he ever had it," Bud said and grinned.

That was when Mike knew everything was going to work out.

"But you know, the name of the town…" Bud sucked his teeth and shook his head.

"Odolavesta?"

"That's right, that's what it is. *Now.*"

"Now?"

"The story goes, it used to be called, *Ojo de la Bestia.*"

Greg shrugged and shook his head.

Bud nodded. "It means 'Eye of the Beast.'"

Greg and Mike exchanged a glance.

"Interesting, ain't it?" asked Bud. "Somewhere along the way, things got confused, and it turned into Odolavesta."

Greg shook his head. "That's—"

"—quite a coincidence," said Mike.

"Sure is." Bud switched his gaze back and forth between them again. "There's something…"

A look of intense concentration flicked across Greg's face.

"What, Bud?" asked Mike.

MacArthur shook his head and turned to Greg. "Let us cart you over to Alpine. They got a municipal that'll handle one of your Bureau jets."

"No need," said Greg. "I'm all set." Bud frowned a little, and again, Greg's eyebrows spasmed with concentration. "But I'll make myself available to your investigation as soon as I get my family safe."

Bud nodded, then turned and gazed out at the ritual site, which was now being lit by the headlights of game wardens, fire trucks, and vehicles belonging to the Texas Rangers. "What a fuckin' mess, boys." He shook his head and spit into the dust. "And you say there were a lot of townsfolk out here?"

"Yeah. One of them shot Dr. Withers. He was screaming that Withers ruined everything." Mike cocked his head to the side. "And that bladesmith was in the crowd. I'd say there were nearly a thousand out here."

"Masterton? That low down so-and-so." He cocked his head and looked at Greg from the corner of his eye. "Think you can identify them?"

Greg shrugged. "I'll do my best, but *after*—"

"Oh, sure. Go take care of 'em, Gregory. We'll be here when they're safe."

4

Maddie and Gavin sat on the deck, gazing out at Lake Erie. "It's nice here, right?" asked Gavin.

"Sure," said Maddie. "Nice enough." She glanced around, then leaned over to whisper. "They're demons? The supermodels, I mean."

Gavin nodded. "Two are *ifrits*, fire demons. The one with the punk-rock hair is—"

Maddie chuckled. "Punk-rock, Mr. Gregory? Really?"

"What?"

"A woman can have any hair color she wants, Gavin."

"Yeah, and that goes triple for that woman. Truth to tell, she doesn't have any hair at all."

"Well, she can do that, too." After another glance, she whispered, "And you're sure this is safe?"

"Benny says so. It seems Toby extracted a promise from Lily—she's the boss, I guess. She's the *seraph*, whatever that means. She's the one Toby summoned to mess up Fry's whole deal."

"And what's the promise?"

"They, uh, won't dine on anyone unless that person meets a certain criterion as defined by us."

"And we trust them to keep that promise?"

"Again, Benny says we do." Gavin grinned at her. "I guess there's some kind of magical contract."

Maddie nodded and sipped her coffee. "And Fry?" she asked, feigning nonchalance.

Gavin grimaced. "SEMPRe is 'on it' according to Benny. At least Glacadairanam is out of the picture."

"Thanks to her."

"Yeah," said Gavin. "Thanks to Lily."

They said nothing for a while, content to enjoy each other's company. Then Maddie looked at him and said, "What do we do if they find him?"

With a deepening frown, Gavin said, "Kill him. Send him back. Whatever it is they do."

"Ah," she said, sipping her coffee again. "And what do we do if they don't find him?"

Toby's words from the Aeonian Hotel & RV Park came swimming back in his memory: *You didn't beat them, Gavin. You've existed beneath their notice, is all. Now that they're aware of you, now that they want you for something, your life is over. You'll either spend what time you have left on the run or in servitude.* He smiled at her and reached for her hand. "They'll find him, Mads."

"But what if they don't?"

"They will."

She turned her head to the side and treated him to a special Maddie-stare.

"Okay, okay," he said with a forced chuckle. "If SEMPRe can't find him, if our special guests in there can't find him, then…well…I'll just have to find him."

"I was scared you'd say that." She sipped coffee and looked out at the lake. "And Kai? What did Pete say?"

"They found him this morning." He glanced at her. "They're calling it a coma."

She frowned down at her cup. "Fry's got a lot to answer for."

"Yes."

She looked out across the lake. "And what did Pete say about you?"

"Officially, I'm on loan to the CIA."

"Unofficially?"

"He'll feed me the 'special' cases, and Mike and I will investigate them—with help from SEMPRe."

"And our new lady friends?"

This time it was Gavin who looked out on the lake. "I don't know. Maybe." He looked down at his feet on the weather-grayed deck and prayed the day would never come when he'd have to answer that question.

"And…" Maddie frowned into her coffee cup.

"He's alive," said Gavin with a grimace.

"And the other thing? Do you think…"

"I don't know, Mads. By all accounts, she said she could 'elevate' him, which is evidently code for turning him into the same kind of demon she is."

"And…did she?"

"I don't know. I can't exactly just ask him."

"Gav…"

"What should I say? Hey, Toby, are you a demon now?"

"I suppose not. And Benny can't…"

Gavin shook his head. "He says he can't be sure he'd know."

"Oh." She drained the last of her coffee. "Then I guess we hope for the best."

"Yeah," said Gavin, his lips drawn down into a flat line. "And watch and wait."

"Watch and wait," Maddie repeated with a grim nod.

I hope you've enjoyed *Demons Dance* and would like to know what comes next my personal journey. To be among the first to know what I'm up to and when the newest book I write goes live, please join my Readers' Group by visiting https://ehv4.us/join. Or follow me on BookBub by visiting my profile page there: https://ehv4.us/bbub. Or, if you prefer to stick to Amazon, you may follow my author page: https://ehv4.us/amausa.

If you haven't already read *The Bloodletter Chronicles*, you can view all three books on Amazon (please note that if your local Amazon marketplace supports series pages for Kindle ebooks, all three links point to it): Book 1, Demon King: https://ehv4.us/4demonking, Book 2, The Hag: https://ehv4.us/4thehag, and Book 3, Our Lady Chaos: https://ehv4.us/4ourladychaos. For my complete bibliography, please visit: https://ehv4.us/bib.

Books these days succeed or fail based on the strength of their reviews. I hope you will consider leaving a review—as an independent author, I could use your help. It's easy (I promise). You can leave your review by clicking on this link: https://ehv4.us/2revdd

AUTHOR'S NOTE

When I reach the end of a series such as the one you've just finished, one that has consumed my creative energies for more than a year and a half, I often spend a day or so consumed by introspection. Did the series do what I wanted it to do? Have I met your (and my) expectations? Did I do right by my readers, my characters, and, of course, Mr. Story? What do I do now?

And so on.

This past year, 2021, was difficult for my family and me (as it was for many people). First, there was the exhaustion—both mental and physical—brought about by the pandemic, Petunia, an unexpected move across the country, several trips, getting a house ready to sell and another ready to live in, a new diagnosis (a new friend for Petunia) along with its unique set of medications to try and develop side effects from, all while trying to finish a publishing schedule that fought me. I didn't publish as many books in 2021 as in 2020 (though the word count of those two sets of books is within spitting distance), but I did *write* as much. You see, I've been working on a super-secret project—a new series—on the sly. It's a bit different, but I'm having a ton of fun with it. Stay tuned for more information by following my

Facebook page at https://ehv4.us/fb and joining my Readers' Group found here: https://ehv4.us/fbog. Both Supergirl and I would love to see you over there.

I can't tell you what *exactly* will happen this year, but I'm excited by the possibilities. We ran a massive contest on Facebook accompanied by twenty-million polls about reader experiences and are analyzing all that data and putting it to good use. 2022 is going to be an interesting—and *fun*—year. I hope you'll ride along.

Thank you, my friend, for reading my novels and reading this Author's Note. I don't say that enough, and I don't say enough that, without you, this journey would be useless. I'm fortunate to have found readers like you—readers from all walks of life, including a whole whack of you who underscore that I'm not alone in this struggle against my own body. As always, I'd love to hear from you—whether your thoughts about my books or just to say hello—via email at berserkerik@erikhenryvick.com or via the Facebook group mentioned above.

I'll leave you with the heartfelt sentiment that I don't express enough: *Thank you*!

ABOUT THE AUTHOR

Erik Henry Vick is an author of dark speculative fiction who writes despite a disability caused by his Personal Monster™ (also known as an autoimmune disease.) He writes to hang on to the few remaining shreds of his sanity.

He lives in Western New York with his wife, Supergirl; their son; a Rottweiler named after a god of thunder; and two extremely psychotic cats. He fights his Personal Monster™ daily with humor, pain medicine, and funny T-shirts.

Erik has a B.A. in Psychology, an M.S.C.S., and a Ph.D. in Artificial Intelligence. He has worked as a criminal investigator for a state agency, a college professor, a C.T.O. for an international software company, and a video game developer.

He'd love to hear from you on social media:

Blog:
Twitter: https://twitter.com/BerserkErik
Facebook: https://fb.me/erikhenryvick
Amazon author pages:
   USA: https://ehv4.us/amausa
   UK: https://ehv4.us/amauk
Goodreads Author Page: https://ehv4.us/gr
BookBub Author Profile: http://ehv4.us/bbub

Printed in Great Britain
by Amazon

39045148R00303